Forewo

In a world of tumult I wrote the preq
At that time I didn't want to be just a
voice. In the words of John Maxwell Coetzee:

*"...I wanted to find a way of speaking to fellow human beings that
will be cool rather than heated, philosophical rather than polemical,
that will bring enlightenment rather than seeking to divide us into
the righteous and the sinners, the saved and the damned...."*

I wanted to entertain and educate; pass on the information I 'own'
about the things we don't readily see or choose to gloss over, so that
people, enlightened, can decide.
That book carried the caveat: *Warning; The Soul Cages might well
change your life...*
I haven't issued a health warning in that vein with *Free Radical;*
although....

In the intervening year or so the world has become even more
turbulent and maybe as a result of this, or perhaps as a consequence
of my searching for ways to calm the furies which plague me I have
become an ardent believer that we human animals owe a duty to all
the other creatures with whom we share this amazing planet.
For animals *are* abused; needlessly, sometimes openly, all too often
invisibly. I know that this is slowly altering, and yet I don't have
forever, and I shall take every opportunity to accelerate this
vegetable-tempo mindset change.

Rewardingly, I have received much correspondence from 'ordinary'
people whose lives *have* been altered, I think for the better. Job
done.....or not?
Not.
Subtle persuasion and the sharing of critical information are lifelong
commitments. If I achieve these in any small measure, then this
labour of love shall have been worth every hour of painstaking
thought, research and tears.

As with *The Soul Cages*, if you choose to read this mostly fictional crime thriller then you are also accepting your responsibility to think about the underlying message. That's all I ask of you; to think. If you then choose to do nothing differently I will accept that of course, for we live in a relatively free world. But I would also be surprised.

Dedicated to the tireless supporters of Cruelty Free International (formerly British Union for the Abolition of Vivisection (BUAV) and of the Dr Hadwen Trust for animal-free research.

My deepest thanks, as always to **Mr Alan Walker** for the cover photos and his infinite patience.

Free Radical

Geoffrey Stanger

ISBN-13: 978-1530769667

ISBN-10: 1530769663

Free Radical

Prologue

The air is damp and still, with that suspicion of mould that inhabits such places, and there's another odour, one that she should recognise, yet can't put her finger on.

The dingy cellar is one cavernous room running almost the entire length of the hulking, isolated farmhouse, sandwiched at either end by two smaller chambers and has been subdivided with temporary bare plaster-board walls into several discrete areas.

With the now sleeping baby resting in her arms she slowly walks the length of the stud-work passageway linking these internal compartments and sees within each dingy area a similar, yet uniquely different set-up. Each contains a wireless webcam on a tripod, a simple audio system and a restraint mechanism of one kind or another. The latter provides the point of difference; each restraining method is subtly dissimilar to its neighbours.
All but one are occupied.

Jenny looks around aghast. This is freakishly familiar; slightly more humane than the hideous little cages where she and the others had been imprisoned by the freak, and yet at the same time somehow more macabre. The bleak enclosures seem to have been individualised; made personal.

Her voice, when she finally speaks, quavers:
'Whatever are you doing here Colin?'
In the gloom he twitches, unseen, then coughs lightly and clears his throat.
'Ah! My latest project; my Coup de Grace! The final experiment – for the time being, at least. Come here.'
He leads her to one of the small cellar rooms on the end of the main chamber.
The contrast is immediate; it's brighter here, comfortable almost, with lights and colourful cushions. Sophisticated modern computer

equipment sits on the solid old pine table with several wide flat-screens mounted on the walls.

'Behold, the polling booth of the future!' The hand holding the pistol does a 180^0 sweep of the walls before them.

'It's an online system where the public gets to vote. By the click of a button in the comfort of their own home the nation shall decide who is to live and who to die….'

Part One

1

Δ *My grandma's mink coat so soft and dead "Come, pet it!" she coos* Δ
Jillouise Breslauer

In his cell he's finishing the punishing exercise regime. It's not easy to maintain peak fitness in a room designed to hold a person in the most basic of circumstances, although he's fortunate to have it to himself. Owing to decades of neglect and under-resourcing of the UK prison system the other cells – even in this extreme risk environment – are mostly doubled up. But the nature of his crimes and his mental fragility pose far too high a risk to any potential cell-mates. He'd been stuck in with another guy on his first night but the sound of that creep grunting his way to interminable self-gratification in the dark had finally driven Colin to creep silently across the small space between them and, groping in the dark for a fistful of hair he'd rained a series of rapid, savage blows to the nose, eyes and mouth to ruin the guy's fun.

Word quickly gets round about the new boy on the block and the other inmates will now go to extraordinary lengths to avoid cell sharing with him. Now he is guaranteed a place to himself, and that's just the way he likes it.

He's completed two hundred press-ups, in repetitions of fifty; the same number and reps of crunches, ten minutes of squat-thrusts alternating with burpee star-jumps and finishes now with a five minute plank which sees his entire body shaking with the effort of completion. For him it's as much about the mental strength required to complete the sets, and he'll do the same punishing regime in three hours' time, and then again three hours later and he won't be stopped by the lights going out. It helps to take his mind off the situation he's in and he sleeps better for it.

He's always been extremely fit and his leg does that involuntary twitching thing in the dim light of the single, protected 20W bulb, as he emits an animal-like growl deep from within his chest cavity; half snarl, half howl.

They can take away his freedom but not his constant craving for justice and revenge; he won't allow anyone to change that.

Maybe they are right; maybe insanity is his friend. It's all a matter of perspective.

Now, despite the limiting space he's running through his twenty four Taekwondo patterns, starting with Chon-Ji, and working through to the controversial Tong-Il. As an ex-member of the International Taekwondo Federation he has practised the patterns – essential elements of the martial art – four times each day for as long as he can remember, starting at four years old as a white belt with the simplest movements and progressing in complexity and duration through the grades until he became a senior master. At that time he had withdrawn from the public training and competing in tournaments due to his increasing discomfort at the social demands it placed on him, happy to practise in private and use the skills he'd learned to finely hone his mind and body.

Each of the twenty four patterns has a meaning, with the first, Chon-Ji representing the heaven and the earth, and the last, Tong-Il denoting the resolution of the unification of Korea.

On completion he's sweating heavily and he stretches his left leg muscles out on the floor in the corner, looking around the tiny cream-painted space while recovering his breathing.

And thinking....

He's been doing that a lot lately, since being banged up and awaiting trial for multiple kidnaps and the violent and brutal triple murders of a Muslim preacher, a Serbian pig farmer and a kinky collector of animal skins. His cell is in a world-renowned high security mental hospital in southern England, where he is supposedly undergoing psychiatric tests for pre-trial reports; a process which, he understands, is expected to take up to eighteen months. He's buggered if he's going to sit and scratch his arse whilst outside the abuses continue unabated, unacknowledged and mostly unnoticed.

He *needs* to be doing something, not lying here vegetating and slowly wasting away. Outside he was *somebody*, he *did* stuff, and challenged the moronic retarded mind-set of humanity. He has funds and capability; out there he *made it better* for those who have no voice.

Here in this hell hole he is slowly dying. He needs to plan, to apply that intelligence and use those resources to engineer an escape and get back to doing what Colin Furness does best; retribution.

His leg jiggles a little as it is prone to when he becomes agitated. He claps his hands together, almost silently; repeatedly. All signs that he's not quite in possession of the full spectrum of the essential elements of human self-control.

2

Boner is what most people would call a dosser, a scrounger, a lazy tyke. He is a scallywag.

But Boner isn't *actually* lazy at all, far from it, he just doesn't see the point in exerting a lot of effort for the benefit of others. He is usually very busy running his little scams. Indeed everything he does seems to have an element of scam to it. Boner is unemployed (and arguably unemployable), has a criminal record as long as a judge's wig and is on nodding terms with most of the local small-time gang leaders. He is also a hunter; he hunts anything he can sell. Rabbits, pigeons, ducks and pheasants fall to his guns and/or ferrets, dogs and traps. He catches hares at night with his mates in an old SUV kitted out with powerful spotlights. Lamping, they call this activity and he likes to take his mate's dogs too; they enjoy tracking and retrieving and it makes the whole experience somehow feel more *real*.

He is happiest when tracking elusive little beasts and slotting them with his shotgun then cashing in on their corpses. That isn't work, he couldn't do a proper job; fuck that, life is way too much fun; hunting and scams are the way to do it.

Even his daily coffee break in the supermarket has become a ritual scam.
Boner walks through the brightly lit aisles in the huge store full of the hardworking, innocent people of society and grabs a copy of his preferred trashy tabloid as he heads for the escalator to the first floor where the café is housed. On the way through the stationary department he grabs a pen from the clip-strip display and rips off the flimsy clear-plastic packaging with his teeth, spitting it out as he walks. He emanates disregard.

He realises he has left his wallet at home and only has two quid on him, too little for the large Skinny Latte he wants. He nips back downstairs to the main supermarket aisles and looks for an unattended trolley. There are a few oldies in store at this time of day, they're always easy targets.

The device is simply the metal piece which is normally attached to the end of a short chain on most supermarket trolleys which releases the captive pound coin needed to take a trolley from the holding areas. He'd bolt-cropped it off one night in a moment of inspiration and has been helping himself to quid coins on a regular basis since. Easy money! He spots an old bag scrutinising the contents of a carton of eggs and deftly sticks the key into her trolley slot, pocketing her pound coin and whistling on his way. She can afford it. Back up the moving walkway to the café.

'Large Skinny Latte darlin' please; extra shot.'
He pockets the change from the three pounds with smug satisfaction; things always taste so much better when a discount is applied.
He takes the coffee, borrowed newspaper and stolen pen to a sofa corner, brushes some crumbs from the black faux leather, sweeps a couple of till receipts off the table onto the floor and settles down into one of the comfy seats for the next half-hour to ogle the contentious Page 3 tart, read some of the crap in the tabloid and then do the Sudoku puzzle. This is a routine he follows most days, it means he gets a free newspaper with his coffee. Technically, he tells himself, it isn't stealing, as he never removes anything from the premises.

This is also his 'office'; the place where many of his arrangements are made, and he can often be seen on the 'phone whilst the aging security guard takes his leisurely strolls around the upper floor.
'Morning, Boner.'
'Hiya Eric, how was the pheasant?'
'Bloody delicious! Any chance of another next weekend? The missus has a couple of friends coming round and she wants to dazzle em with her culinaries!'
'I'll see what I can do Sir, might be expensive though to make an extra trip out into the country just for you.'
'Well, how about I ignore the damage you've done to that newspaper with that *borrowed* pen and we agree to have an arrangement!'
The guard winks slowly and moves on.
'Haha, OK, OK; I'll drop one in mate.' Boner calls to his retreating back.
The older man raises a hand and waves without turning.

Detective Inspector Neil Dyson of the Sussex Police is relaxing on an endless golden sandy beach on the Spanish island of Gran Canaria, listening to the yawping gulls and the mesmeric churn of the waves endlessly rolling upon each other. His contented sigh is interrupted by his mobile telephone vibrating beneath the soft beach towel.

It's Samantha Milsom, one of his team.

'Samantha?'

'Sorry to bother you Guv, but there's something I need to run past you.'

The bliss retreats and he's yanked into reality.

'Don't tell me, you can't bear my absence any longer and are missing the authoritative sound of my voice?'

'Something like that Sir. Actually, we've had a request from our veggie murderer friend to speak with you urgently.'

'Jeez, it's only been a few days; tell him to piss off, we're on holiday – supposed to be recovering from some of the shit he put us through!'

'Tried that Sir, he's saying it's imperative and is being pretty insistent. Sorry – what do you want me to do?'

'What's his problem then?'

'He won't say, just that it's vital he talks with you.'

'Tell him to write to me.'

'Tried that too Guv, but you know how dyslexic he is! Anyway, says he needs to talk before the end of the day.'

'Oh for goodness sake. OK, seriously Samantha – tell him to write it down and send me a scan of it. I aint speaking with that psycho for the next two weeks or my relationship with Jenny is dead. She will forgive me most things, but not *that*.'

'Will do Guv – and sorry to intrude. Hope you guys are OK.'

'Yeah, very OK thanks Samantha, found out that Jenny's nearly four months pregnant. Speak soon.'

He cuts the line.

Samantha isn't quite certain she heard his parting comment correctly, but she's damned if she's going to interrupt his holiday in the sun again to ask him.

Δ *The world is a dangerous place, not because of those who do evil,*
but because of those who look on and do nothing Δ
Albert Einstein

Despite the best efforts of the guards, for any prisoner with
resources, getting their hands on desirables such as drugs, alcohol,
porn and mobile 'phones is a piece of cake. Colin Furness has access
to considerable wealth, the like of which no normal person could
possibly spend in a lifetime of gluttony and excess. He could have
chosen any model Smartphone from the latest gadgets available on
earth and his contacts inside would have got it for him within a day
or two. Such is the reality in under-resourced British penal
institutions.

Colin knows which side his bread is buttered and gains high respect
through his generosity and support of the wing seniors. Wing seniors
are those characters who rule the roost; the Alpha males and females.
Gain their trust and obstacles disappear; opportunities present
themselves.
Colin is using the 'phone now, a simple Blackberry 9720 that had
cost him £1000 and came with unlimited credit. Probably cloned
from another '*clean*' device. He is talking quietly to David
Abrahams, his loose-moraled accountant who has squirreled away
tens of millions of pounds into off-shore accounts which are pretty
much invisible to the UK tax authorities and instantly accessible to
Colin Furness from anywhere in the world – including the
supposedly high security psychiatric prison unit.

'I need one other thing, Mr Abrahams.'
Colin finds any conversation with the nasal-voiced stuttering
accountancy nerd tedious in the extreme, but he's exceptionally good
at underhand money operations and beggars can't be choosers.
'Er yes, but I er, well, *we* need to limit transactional activities in the
funds because some sophisticated monitoring systems will, er will
detect excessive or reiterative transactions of certain magnitudes and
could begin to unravel the multiple convolutions I have built into the
process and we, that is to say I don't want a knock on my front door

in the middle of the night from the big-booted HMRC boys Mr, er Mr Furness.'

Colin hates the way the man over-complicates his sentences with silly jargon and just wants to shout down the telephone; *fucking hell Abrahams, just speak normally for goodness sake.* But he resists the temptation and bites his lip some more.

'Just one teeny weeny final transaction Mr Abrahams, and then you will be free of me forever. And an awful lot richer, might I add!'

'Yes, er well that's certainly the truth. What's the final transaction?'

'I need you to buy me a house. Then I need you to arrange a few deliveries there for me and to set up accounts with the utilities companies, internet connections etc. – all the things a person might need to live a normal life. I will send you the details immediately after this call. Buy it under the name of Sam Dyson and text me the word '*done'* when it's successfully completed. I *must have* this house, Mr Abrahams, and won't accept failure. Am I clear?'

'Er, crystal Mr Furness. I shall, er I shall do my best.'

'Good man. If the seller says it's already been sold, then double the money; get that house. There will be a *significant* benefit making its way into your account upon completion. Goodbye Mr Abrahams.'

'Good, er goodbye Mr...'

The connection has already been cut.

Happy with the outcome of the conversation Colin turns off the device and conceals the 'phone behind the sink unit in the kitchen where he is mixing his next batch of vegan food. He is encouraged to experiment with recipes as part of his assessment and Joel, the guard tasked with his one-to-one care this afternoon is more than happy to be otherwise occupied for the duration of the call.

Joel Button is not a particularly corrupt prison warder, but nor is he immune to the allure of wealth. The implied offer from one of the lunatics for a dazzling sum of money for simply turning a blind eye to a couple of telephone conversations is too much to resist.

Initially cautious, a down-payment of ten grand convinced him that Furness would deliver on his promise and Joel turns a blind eye on three occasions within two days, earning considerably more during those seven minutes than he would in a year from his salary.

14

Joel watches the prisoner talking rapidly into his 'phone and thinks of the heinous crimes he has committed. He feels a momentary pang of guilt, after all, he has no clue what the telephone conversation is about, he might even be organising an escape, but that would be next to impossible. There had been huge media coverage of the murders and the way he had kept his kidnapped victims imprisoned like battery hens before killing some of them. And the murders had been the most gory he'd ever read about. One, a foreign pig farmer had been rigged up like a human hog roast in the centre of a town; an Arab guy had had his throat slit in some ritual sacrifice and a woman was skinned alive for Christ's sake. He was clearly one of the more serious cases of raving insanity in the whole prison hospital, and that was some claim!

Joel had read about the police investigation, how they had stayed one step behind the guy and how he'd really made a mockery of the detectives until one of them had spotted clever clues hidden by one of the captives in messages sent to the media. That had nailed him. Bloody good job too, fucking basket case.

Colin finishes the call and Joel swiftly reverts to business mode, re-fastening the cuffs and ushering the prisoner towards the cell area, whispering that he expects the remaining money to be transferred into his account before midnight.

Colin's reply is quiet but holds a convincing undertone of sickening menace.

'Don't you *dare* try to lay down demands with me you wanky little *nothing!* The dosh is already in your bank.'

Joel says nothing and tries unsuccessfully to hide his fear and his euphoria. He'll check online at his next break. Meanwhile he just wants to get away from the magnetic influence of this sicko.

'Very good, if you need any more favours you know I deliver on promises; some of the others will grass you up.'

He gently nudges Colin into his cell, removes the cuffs and leaves, locking the door and checking through the sliding steel vision panel that all is in order. He's trembling with a mixture of emotions as he heads off for his break and to see how rich he has just become and swears that he'll use the money to get a job away from these freaks.

Neil Dyson's 'phone pings to indicate a message. As expected it's from Samantha and she's simply written:
"Sir; as discussed. And, er did I hear you right?".
He smiles as he opens the email attachment; a scanned sheet of police notepaper.

Deer Mr Dyson.
I hope yor injuries are heeling OK. I am still quite sore!
I rite to you as the person most likely to treet the information I have sensitively.
I have been thinking about sum of the things that I learnd in the weeks up to my arrest and they now make more sense.
If you go to the sellers of the <u>old</u> *farm building you will find some big solid doors underneath the old Killing Lines. There is a keypad and I beleev the combination will be 150000.*
Something is in that seller that my father tried to keep secret.
As you no, when I was young my mother disappeared one night. My father claimed she had run away and abandoned me, but I beleev he may have murdered her and hidden her body in there somewhere.

PS what has happened to my horse Vengeance? I hope he is being looked after; he needs food and water and regular exercise and grooming. I am happy to pay for everything he needs.

Dyson grunts and calls Samantha straight back.
'Hey boss, you're supposed to be taking it easy in the sun not calling in to work!'
'Listen, get forensics over to the Furness place can you? You've read the note so tell them to take the place apart carefully, looking for any human remains or any sign that the mother might have been held there at some time. It's the old part of the farm we're interested in, some big cellar doors with a keypad. If the code 150000 doesn't work take the doors out any way you can.'
'Already onto it Guv; for god's sake get back to your *presumed pregnant* wife and the beach; I will email you a summary of findings but you've got to focus on your recovery – and Jenny's!

And you are actually meant to be forgetting the whole damned Colin Furness affair –remember? Over and very definitely out.'
'Wait Samantha – check to see what happened to his horse too would you?'
'Yep. Sure thing. I assume it was kept at the farm?'
'No idea – ask him.'

Samantha rides in the squad car with two forensics officers. They are following an unmarked car carrying Dave 'Sicknote' Harrison, Brian Liddel and Steph Walters; three members of the team which had tracked down the killer some weeks earlier. The final member of the team, DC Carol Saunders needed to take a couple of hours out to pick up her sick daughter from school and arrange emergency child care. The police are more flexible on such issues recently, finally understanding that the hiatus of personnel due to workload and poor working conditions is crippling the force.

The detectives are silent as the cars slowly negotiate the potholes on the track down towards the old farm buildings, lost in their own private worlds. The horrors they'd recently uncovered here have affected them all. Indeed, speaking afterwards to the media, DCI Sharon Moody who had led the final stages of the investigation described the scenes that greeted them when they broke into the huge barn as the most horrific she'd seen anywhere in all her policing years. The kidnapped victims of the monster Colin Furness had been imprisoned for weeks in rows of small wire mesh cages, barely large enough to accommodate them with no access to any kind of basic sanitation. The stink had been overwhelming, with even hardened emergency services personnel unable to retain the contents of their stomachs. The lunatic had claimed that he was merely trying to convert humans to vegetarianism by showing them what industrial farming did to animals.

Interestingly, Steph has since abandoned meat from her diet. Maybe there was method in the murderer's madness.

DS Samantha Milsom is quickly out of the car when they arrive in the farm yard.

'OK, we learned the hard way that it's a complex layout here, so we need to be methodical. Sicknote, these are the only drawings we have from the planning archives; I want us to be certain that we cover the place in a logical manner, leaving nothing to chance. We will start with this zone.'

She indicates a yellow shaded area on the drawing with the words *Chicken slaughter* hand-written in the centre of the rectangle. If Sicknote has any issue with being commanded by a woman of equal rank he shows rare common sense in hiding it.

'I think this was known as the *Killing Lines*, and we should find a cellar running the full length of the structure. I want to remind you all of two things; we are here to facilitate forensic analysis, not to fuck it up and secondly, perhaps more importantly, we know what this freak is capable of, and by all accounts his father was as bad, just be prepared for something unpleasant.'

There are subdued murmurs but eye contact with each of the team confirms to her that they are up for the job.

'OK, let's wait a few minutes for the rest of the paper suit brigade to get here.'

'I expect they had to have a coffee or three on the way Sarge!'
'Yeah, quite possibly Brian. Meanwhile we can make our way to the cellars which should be...'

She turns ninety degrees to her right and looks up at the farmhouse building, tracing a path on the drawings with a long dark finger.

'...over here. We need the rest of the forensics guys here so touch nothing unless I give the go-ahead.'

Together they pick their way across the yard trying to avoid the mass of puddles and protruding stones.

'OK, this looks promising. Focus now please people.'

They are faced with a set of two-metre wide concrete steps descending to large grey metal double doors set in the basement of the building. On the wall is an electronic keypad.

Samantha's 'phone rings.

'DS Milsom.'

She listens for a moment.

'OK when you get into the yard head for the gap in the north-east corner; you'll see some old wheelie bins, turn left there and you'll see us at the bottom of the steps. I'm just going to try the keypad, we may strike lucky.'

She terminates the call.

'OK the other forensics guys are here, let's try the code number.'

She glances at the paper to be absolutely certain she hits the right code the nutter has given them and punches 150000 into the system. Immediately there is a series of high-pitched bleeps and a click. She grabs the handle of the right hand door and twists clockwise. It turns easily and she pulls the heavy door towards her.

'OK, touch nothing; Sicknote, got the torch?'

A powerful beam cuts into the darkness as a waft of stale air hits them like a train.

Brian claps his hand to his mouth and his usual thin Geordie voice is even weaker as he squeaks.

'Oh my god, something's definitely died in here!'

All four hold their hands to their noses in a vain attempt to block out the odour.

Somewhere inside an electrical circuit is made and a fan motor kicks into life.

They find themselves in a large hallway with four doors leading off, one to the front, one left and two to the right.

'Find a light switch Dave, we might still have power.'

The torch beam traces the frame of the entrance door they'd used and picks out a bank of six switches arranged in two rows of three.

Steph hits each switch rapidly in turn and the place is flooded with bright light.

All four doors appear to be made from the same solid grey-painted metal with industrial looking black metal handles. The one immediately in front of the group has another keypad to its left.

'In for a penny…' Samantha approaches the door and enters the same code; 150000.

The same bleeping sounds accompanied by a click. She grabs the door and pulls…

6

Boner is back in the supermarket café. Today, alongside his usual Latte and free newspaper he is busy writing a birthday card to a friend. He had plucked the most expensive card he could find from the display downstairs and unwrapped the plastic foil as he made his way up the escalator. He'd stuffed the plastic wrapper down the back of the black sofa he was sitting on, amongst the old crumbs and pieces of chewed gum.

Placing a row of kisses he stuffs the card clumsily into the big red envelope, writes a name and address and from a small bunch of sticky stuff in his pocket finds a postage stamp.

Good of the supermarket to donate a £4.99 birthday card. He knows that even if the security guy knew what he was up to nobody else would challenge a regular customer who had a stamped, addressed envelope in their bag – if challenged he could simply state that he'd clearly bought it elsewhere! He smiles again, undetectable crime was just beautiful.

With a smug grin still fixed to his face he waltzes through the till and into town where he has to meet the local organic butcher to discuss the unfortunate rise in the price of his poached pheasant and pigeon. Life, as always, is good! With a flourish, he drops the card into a post-box.

Detective Constable Carol Saunders has sorted her emergency childcare issue. *"That's what grandmothers are for!"*, her mum tells her as she drops her feverish nine year old daughter around. The tall, blonde 33 year old detective enters the police station canteen just as the constantly running TV info-screen flicks from the standard police recruitment clip it's been showing to a BBC newsflash.

'More now on the earlier announcement from the Home office. The Government has just stated that the UK is to be placed on the highest terror alert level – *critical* – which indicates that an attack is expected imminently. This escalation from the previous *severe* level comes following specific, credible threats. In the last few minutes a Home Office spokesperson issued this short statement:

"Whilst specific details cannot be released presently, owing to a fear of jeopardising the unfolding security operation, government agencies are working round the clock to keep the country safe. In the light of these new, specific threats it is absolutely critical that everyone raises their personal level of vigilance. Anyone who has suspicions regarding an imminent threat should call 999 or ring the Anti-Terrorist Hotline on 0800 789321 without delay".

More details have not been made public at this stage, although a further announcement is expected shortly.'

The grey metal door is extremely heavy and two inches thick. There is a short rush of air into their faces as some difference in atmospheric pressures equalises. The brightly-lit inner room they now enter seems fresher and clean; the stale smell hardly noticeable. They are stood at the entrance to some kind of domestic kitchen with a small table and two chairs, worktops and cupboards and a microwave oven. In the far corner is a single sink and along the right hand wall a washing machine, tumble dryer, fridge/freezer and an oven with electric hotplates. Not modern, but certainly serviceable and clean. The cream-coloured painted walls and light-brown tiled floor are spotless and there are hand-made, coloured paper ornaments dotted here and there.

Straight ahead is another door leading to a further inner room. This is well illuminated and they can see, at a table, pen in hand, a petite and frightened-looking old lady. Her grey hair heaped in a huge pile on top of her head and her mouth wide open, as if she has been caught mid-yawn and frozen in that position.

'Bless my soul! Who are you?'
Her voice is cracked and dry, as if from little-used vocal chords.

'My name is Samantha. Detective Sergeant Samantha Milsom from Sussex police. Can we assume you are Mrs Furness?'
Flashing her warrant card seems hardly appropriate and it stays in her pocket.

Shakily, the old woman slowly rises from the chair, knocking it backwards behind her and stumbles around the table. Her cracking voice angry now.
'Tell me this is not another trick of the brain…tell me this is real this time…please…please tell me that…'
Samantha and Brian rush to her side.
'It's no trick Mrs Furness, we are real and we are as surprised as you are; we thought we had come here to find …well, something else!'
'Oh my dear god, it's really true? You have come to rescue me? After all these years...oh my my…'

The little lady is lost for words and simply breaks down in a flood of sobbing tears.

Samantha takes her carefully into her arms and hugs her gently for a few moments while she issues instructions to the team.

'Steph – ambulance pronto. Brian, go meet the rest of the forensics guys and tell them to hang fire until we are clear and then they can have the floor.'

Dave 'Sicknote' Harrison appears with a glass of water.

'Here, drink some of this Mrs F, soothe your throat, I reckon you've got a lot of talking to catch up on!'

The old woman pauses from her crying and smiles at him through her tears.

'Thank you young man, are you a policeman too?'

Sicknote eyes a mole on her chin which is sprouting a commendable crop of dark hairs.

'Yep, we are all the boys and girls in blue, rescuing little ladies from cellars is our speciality! How long have you been..'

'*DAVE*!' Samantha cuts him off abruptly but quietly. 'That can wait – let's concentrate on the positives until we can get her stabilised. Come on Mrs Furness; let's get you to the fresh air.'

'Oh gosh, you mean outside? Oh my, what does the world look like these days?'

'I expect it's changed a little since you last saw it my dear.'

The small party makes its way slowly through the kitchen and out into the entrance part of the cellar complex. The smell remains but is barely noticed now. The old lady is quite agile on her feet but Samantha and Sicknote flank her in case she becomes overwhelmed. The steps are more of a challenge. Taking them one at a time and pausing every two or three for a short breather they finally reach ground level where the old lady just stands gaping around her, the tears flowing freely, belying the huge beaming look of wonder on her wrinkled face.

Samantha too has a tear in her eye, and as they stand there, allowing her to savour the first moments of freedom in decades the sun breaks through the clouds.

'Sir, it's Samantha.'

'Hi Samantha, what's new?'

'We got to the farm and the key code number was right – 150000. It also opened an inner door, and guess what we found there?'

'Sam, I'm on holiday and not gonna play guessing games – I dunno, a hundred dead bodies, all crammed into tiny wire cages like the first time?'

Samantha lets the abbreviation of her name go unchecked.

'His mother!'

Dyson swallows.

'Yeah, well we kinda knew that…'

'No Guv; she's alive!'

'*What*? Are you *serious*?' Dyson, upright and all ears now. 'He kept her banged up in a cellar for how many years? And then he tried to blame the old man? The sick, warped bastard!'

'No it's worse than that, Colin knew nothing about her being alive, she verified that – the mother I mean, she told us the whole gory story and the statements make grim reading. I'll debrief you when you're back in the real world – not that anything feels very real right now.'

'No. tell me now, give me the short potted version.'

'OK, well, incredibly, at the very moment we discovered her she was in the act of writing her goodbye note to her son Colin. She had also written a farewell letter to his father, her husband Graham – you know, the one who died in a machinery accident. It was definitely *him* who imprisoned her. She said they argued all the time about how to bring up the boy and how to run the chicken farm. She was anti cruelty and he was a pig, eventually one night it blew up out of the usual proportions, he lost control and dragged her down to the cellar. She said he must have secretly prepared it for years because it was fitted out like a proper apartment, kitchen, shower etc. No TV – she wished there had been a TV. She said he even brought her a microwave after about three years' confinement but she had never used it because she didn't trust the thing, thought it was some kind of radiation source.'

'My god! How long had she been down there?'

'Doesn't know for sure, maybe twenty years!'

'*Fucking hell*! All that time living under our noses – unbelievable!'

'Yeah, and right under the nose of the son. Apparently the father used to deliver her food and essentials once a month. Then a few months ago he just stopped coming and she assumed he'd had some kind of accident and that she'd never be found. Hence the letters she was writing.'

'And then the son Colin gave us the key code and told us where he thought her body would be…why did *he* never look there?'

'Not sure, you saw the letter he wrote you. He just didn't put two and two together in time I guess.'

'Hmmmn, well, she's free now. Incredible. I bet the media are having a field day. Have you told Colin?'

'Not yet, going to the prison hospital this afternoon to see him. The press know nothing yet, going to tell the son first.'

'OK – just text me afterwards to say how it went, OK?'

'Sure thing Guv. Enjoy the sunshine!'

'Furness; visitor.'

The normally curt screw standing at the cell door is particularly abrupt today. Colin doesn't know why, but assumes he is annoyed or even jealous that a psychopath might have someone who would want to talk to him. Colin assumes it will be another one of those fucking tedious Jesus freaks that seem to somehow circumvent the system and get face time with the lags. Fine! He always quite enjoys shooting down all their ridiculous arguments, and today he's in a very belligerent mood and will take extra pleasure in sending them off with their holier-than-thou tails between their genuflecting legs.

He decides to adopt a '*well, if you can believe in an insane and prehistoric ideal that there's an all-powerful deity, then I can believe in pixies*' stance as he makes his way slowly to the visiting rooms. He'll milk it for every possible minute; being banged up for sometimes 23 hours at a time can be pretty soul destroying and if he can drag this out a few hours more he will. His favourite argumentative stance is the pixies one, where he challenges the idiots to shoot that down. Or, watching them squirm when he asks which god they would believe in if they were born elsewhere. He knows that statistically you believe in a god based purely upon geographical birthplace; born in Western Europe? Chances are you'll be Christian; from Mid-East? You'll be Muslim; Indian? Hindu etc. What a laughable and convenient coincidence!

When he is seated, smiling in front of the thick reinforced glass panel the screw has a final dig. He leans forward and speaks quietly but with petty venom:

'Enjoy the view Furness, she's pretty, horny and black and loves men in uniform. I might date her tonight while all you will be able to do is wank in your shitty little cell pit!'

Colin doesn't rise to the bait; but the look in his eyes is such that the guard instantly regrets the taunt. He has no sex drive in any case and can think of nothing more vulgar than "*wanking in his shitty little cell pit*".

The woman who enters five minutes later is immediately recognisable as the black detective to whom he'd urgently relayed his suspicions about the cellars. She must have an update.
'Detective Sergeant Milsom I believe; to what do I owe the pleasure?'
Samantha looks into the eyes of the multiple killer and shivers. Those eyes – they really are set a long way apart. She'd learned that he suffered from an extremely rare condition known as 1q21.1 duplication syndrome, a chromosome defect which causes physical and mental abnormalities. In his case the physical manifestation is hypertelorism, a condition which causes the eyes to be sited further apart than is usual. The effects in Colin Furness' case manifest as a form of autism. He also suffers unusual spontaneous leg twitches and is prone to random grinning and hand clapping when excited or agitated.
Out of sight of the visiting detective right now Colin's left leg is beating a tattoo.

'Mr Furness. How are you?'
'Colin, please! I am as well as anyone in this hell hole can be expected to feel thank you. I was expecting a missive from God, but this is a pleasant surprise. I assume you have come to tell me what you found in the cellar? Did the code work?'
The God reference puzzles Samantha, but she brushes it aside.
'Yes, the number was right. How did you work it out?'
'My monster father used to bang on about it being *the magic number*. If his disgusting chicken murdering operation processed – lovely descriptive word that, don't you think *processed* – 150000 animals a day he would make a healthy profit. The number was ingrained into my memory. Just didn't realise its significance until it was too late. I assume he murdered my mother and concealed her body there for twenty odd years; and I was so close to her and yet so very far away.'
'Well, you are partially right yes. Your mother *was* there...'
'What, he moved her at some point? Typical of the bastard to worry that I would go searching for her. I hope he is rotting in hell. I killed him, you know. It was no accident. Well, it was and it wasn't. I rigged it all up and he walked right into it like I knew he would. No harm telling you now, might as well be hung for a sheep as for a

lamb – another hideous expression, don't you agree? We do tend to use nasty animal abuse statements to get across silly points.'

Samantha holds her breath a moment.
'Are you telling me you murdered your father?'
'Yes, well, I rigged the machine fault and he did the rest. I videoed it too if you want to be cheered up any time. Used to help me when I was feeling low on confidence or miserable about my mother, just pop the DVD into the player and watch the old bastard get chewed up. I like to think that the souls of a billion tortured chickens are looking down from some better place and enjoying the show with me.'
'Oh gosh, well, we will have to take a statement later. Let's deal with this other matter first and then we will worry about your further crimes.'
'No forget it, what I just told you was all made up – not going to say any more on the matter. You sort it out.'
'Well, we shall have to see, I will take some advice. Anyway, I've brought you a couple of letters to read. Your mother wrote them.'

Colin sits up in surprise. He had only recently found a letter she had written to him all those years ago and secreted in one of her old poetry anthologies. It had almost broken his heart when he'd discovered it, yet the relief in learning that she hadn't forsaken him, that she hadn't simply run off and abandoned him, had been unquantifiable.

'You'll have to read them to me, my dyslexia…well, it's difficult.'
Samantha knows this to be true; his reading and writing difficulties had indirectly been a factor in his being caught for three murders when he'd relied on one of his kidnap victims, Jenny – DI Neil Dyson's fiancé – to write messages for the media. She had hidden clues in the texts and he had not spotted them.
'Sure. OK, well one is addressed to your father, the other to you. Where shall we start?'
'Start with the old man's letter. No, mine first please.'
'OK.'
Samantha shuffles the pages round. This letter is folded around a very faded and worn photograph, taken outside the Royal Ballet in

London and showing a smiling young woman and very young Colin eating ice creams. Samantha shows him the picture and he remembers that day as if it were yesterday. It had been one of his life-shaping experiences, a trip to watch the ballet '*Still Life*' *at the Penguin Café.*

The policewoman clears her throat and reads aloud:

My darling boy. My life.
You didn't come for me, but then, I guess you never knew I was here. Your monster father probably told you some story about me having deserted you. It's the kind of thing he would do. I don't know if you ever found the letter I left for you in my old poetry book? I can't remember which one now; it's been so many years. How many? I have lost count, prisoner down here for an eternity. I suppose it has been twenty years. Twenty summers come and gone; winters, with those frosts that you used to marvel at, when the grass turned white and the cow-trough froze. How many Christmases have I missed the delight on my little boy's face as he unwrapped that precious thing he had so wanted…and me here, not even knowing what those things might have been, and you, maybe not even thinking of me anymore. Those thoughts broke my heart a million times.
All I had to keep your memory alive was this old photograph. I wonder if you can remember where we were? No, but why would you; how could you, that was a lifetime ago, and besides, I suppose that for you my memory is dead.

If you ever read this letter that means I have ended it all; unable to bear the loneliness and torture for any more days, weeks, eternities…
Be safe my precious boy and always stay true to your heart.

Mummy x

Colin sits in stunned silence. A puzzled frown playing across his face.
'Wait a minute. What does she mean? Was she alive down there for…I mean, how long had she survived? Was I living a few yards away and never knew? She says twenty years…Oh god why did I

29

never think, why did I let my fear of that disgusting place prevent me from exploring? Why didn't...'

Samantha interrupts.

'Colin. You couldn't have known. Listen, I have something to tell you, but let me read the other letter first, OK?'

A now tearful Colin silently nods.

Samantha coughs to hide the emotion in her voice and continues.

Graham

You never came for me; you abandoned me in one final act of treachery. Now I am so weak that even holding the pen is an effort I can hardly bear.

You never explained or tried to justify the terrible things you have done to me. Locking me up here is something I will never understand, and I hoped against hope that each time you came you would have softened, realised the horror of what you were doing and set me free.

I have tried to stay strong, and for much of the time I am able to cope by inventing scenarios here in my terrible, terrible loneliness. I realise I am insane for much of the time, and that's a blessing, I could never have survived this long without the comfort of losing my mind.

I could have taken my life at any time, but the dream that you might change and let me out to see the sun, feel the grass beneath my feet and the wind on my face...and of course, let me see my darling, special little boy again made me cling to life. I know for certain now how those poor, poor animals will have felt as they spent their entire lives like me, cooped up away from their families, the rest of the world and their natural environments, all for the sick pleasure of a monster like you, and the other monsters upon whose greed you feed. I suppose I am lucky; at least I can move around and wash and ...well, no point dwelling on it now.

But I am too weak to continue, and the loneliness and despair have overcome me. I shall end it now, on my terms. In my way. At my own hand.

I have written a letter to my little boy —well, he won't be little now, I wonder, did he grow big and strong? Did you protect him from the vicious world that hates anyone who is different? That is the thought that tortures me most, not even that I can't see him, hold him,

30

nurture him, no, it's the fear that you might have abandoned him, as you abandoned all the things that you should have protected. My very worst nightmare is that you might have imprisoned him somewhere too. Like me, alone in a dark and dreadful hell. If you have I beg you to let him free. If you haven't, I beg you to pass the letter that I have written for him. He deserves at least that much.

I am not going to turn this into an assassination of your character; you don't have one, and I don't have the strength.
Just know this.
As I sit here now in this god-forsaken place, I hate you more than it is possible to say. I hope that the reason you abandoned me and fail to bring me food these past weeks and months (can it really be that long?) is actually because something terrible has happened to you. I hope too that it was slow, painful and very permanent.
But wait, I hear…

Colin is openly weeping. 'So he returned and murdered her when he read those words I assume? Oh the evil, sick bastard. Why didn't I kill him sooner?'
'Er, actually no. Colin, he didn't kill her; your mother survived. It was us she heard when she was writing those words, she assumed it was him but it was the police. You giving me that code led to her rescue. She's alive Colin, weak and in hospital, but alive. And you saved her.'

Despite all she has seen from this man she is also crying now, tears of sadness and joy; confused, mingling emotions. She should hate this killing monster, but isn't he really just a victim of a brutal father and an obscene culture that allows us to murder animals as if they didn't matter? Clearly he sees the world differently. Had his heinous deeds only been his way of trying to redress the balance, speak out for the voiceless?
She shuts off these thoughts deliberately; that way lies only doubt and uncertainty. She needs a clear head for the next few minutes.

He sits with a stunned expression. His mouth working but no sounds emerging. His bizarre eyes blinking ten to the dozen.

When he finally manages to speak, his voice is a squeak.
'Are you telling the truth, or is this some sick prison game designed to break me down? If it is, I swear to you I will...'
'It's the truth Colin. I would never do such an awful thing. She is in St Richard's hospital in Chichester undergoing tests and being beefed up on a special diet. She hasn't eaten properly for, well, at best weeks, maybe months. She has a lot of repairing to do to her mind and body. She will need specialist counselling for a long time to get through the mental trauma she has suffered. I think you will too.'
'When can I see her?'
'Well, it's not that simple. Due to the nature of your crimes you are on the highest level security and leaving the hospital here for anything other than life-saving emergencies is not allowed. Not in *any* circumstances. I need to seek advice and see if there is anything that can be done for such a special case, but I really don't hold out much hope. I think the best we can wish for is that she gets well enough to visit you here.'
'She knows I am here, she knows I am alive?'
'No, she knows nothing yet, not until we work out the best way to debrief her with the psychiatrists. We might do more harm than good if she takes on board too much in one hit.'

Colin jumps up and begins to shout, banging the glass between them.
'I want to see her, I demand to see her, don't you fucking well *dare* to think you can keep me from her you fucking shit bitch.'

Samantha stands too and holds up her hands in a peace gesture.
'Reacting that way will not help your case one iota. You need to demonstrate that you are in control of your emotions, or the only place you will be going is the padded cells. Think about it.'
With that she turns and quickly leaves the room, leaving a red-faced and fuming Colin Furness dancing agitatedly alone.

Remembering suddenly his horse, Vengeance, he shouts a question at the already closed door but nobody hears.

Boner struts along the high street as if he owns it. Indeed, in his mind he may well do, after all, life is good. He has plenty of money coming in and loads of scams lined up. He'll pop into the butcher's, give him the good news then nip in for a pint and do some business in the Dog and Duck.

But first he'd better collect his giro. The fortnightly benefit money pays for his extras – nice ciggies, quality old single malt whisky and sexy girls. He has developed a taste for a young Polish tart who he spotted one night after a good Lamping session and she hadn't seemed to mind the smell of Mother Nature on his skin, nor the spots of blood. He thought she'd been a little aroused by it, probably assumed he'd been fighting. Most girls liked a hard nut. He didn't know the Polish for hare or rabbit and she spoke next to fuck all English. He let the mystery hang between them for the two hours he'd bought with her. Except he'd been unable to get a rock on, kind of shameful for one with the nickname 'Boner'. She had been sweet though, let him play around with her and didn't make a fuss when he did odd stuff. That got him going and in the end he'd got it up and rogered her pretty roughly. The marks on her neck would fade – if not, she'd have to wear a choker of some kind for a while. She got paid and he got his twisted kicks, he believed that was known as a win:win.

'And have you been actively seeking employment since our last meeting Mr Bones?'

'Yeah course. I reads the papers every day an' I checks the computers downstairs.'

Boner omits more consonants than he includes and the *Job Centre Plus* employee inwardly shrieks when he uses the third person present when talking about his own actions. She wants to correct him and tell him it's no bloody wonder he isn't being offered jobs. She decides to take a harder line, he is a well-known skiver in any case.

'Specifically then, which roles have you applied for?'

'Wot ya mean, pacifically? All of em. No bastard wants me, cos of me tattoos an piercins. They's all prejudice, that's wot.'

'Well, your luck's in today because I have a little more time than usual so we can go through each of your applications and I'll call the employers for any that we think might have a change of heart, and we'll get some feedback so we know what we need to work on.'
'You shittin me or wot lady? I gotta get places, fings ta do, missus.'
'Mr Bones, your language is really unacceptable and it's my job to help you. You, on the other hand receive regular and generous payments from the government on the understanding that you are available, and actively seeking work. Having *places to go and things to do*" will not be allowed to interfere with your job searches, are we quite clear on that?'

This is not going well; Boner has never been spoken to like this in here and for the first time is a little nervous that one of his staple freebies might be in jeopardy.
'Yeah course, I only meant once we sorted out the stuff we have to do here like, you know, get me giro an stuff.'
'Well. Let's first see what it is, *specifically* that you have done to earn this week's benefit payment, shall we. OK where are the applications you've submitted?'
Boner swallows. He doesn't need this and he has no way to show he's done so much as lift a finger to find a job.
'Ya know wot missus? You wanna treat me like some skivin wanker, you can ram your few poxy pence where the sun don't shine. I don't need your friggin charity!'
He springs from the seat, sending it sprawling over backwards and is gone.

Colin is back in his cell, pacing and punching the air; elated to have learned that she is still alive after all these years and yet fuming at the situation which is denying him the chance to do the only thing he desperately wants to do in the world; see his beautiful mother again. He wonders what all those years of loneliness and torment will have done to her mind. How will she look? Will she still seem the same, or has she become insane from the dreadful isolation and knowing that he was so close to her and yet so completely unaware.

He falls into a daydream as he often does when faced with problems of a psychological nature, problems he can do nothing to solve.

The daydream takes him back to school; he is in the school library, with its dark old oak-panelled walls and high, decorative pale-green ceiling with the occasional crack and gap where, over centuries a piece of ornate coving has lost the battle with gravity. Two grand brass and crystal chandeliers hang at either end of the room, one slightly off-centre, as if the fitter had mis-measured the fixing point and not bothered to check afterwards. It pleased Colin, he remembers, that imperfections could be found in this, the most correct of places, with its thousands of examples of third person omniscient, plus quam perfectum and accurately conjugated verbs. He loved, and loathed this place.

He adored the rows upon rows of dusty old books, some well-worn others almost pristine, and clearly rarely taken down. He would seek out these, the crisper, abandoned tomes, and bury his head throughout the long Saturday and Sunday afternoons, when the other children were at sports fixtures. Being clumsy and poorly coordinated Colin was rarely required at these events. He would struggle with his poor reading skills and search for little gems of wisdom or wit in the unread pages, jotting down short passages in a little notebook he kept in his blazer pocket.

He hated the room because alongside all this wisdom and genius it housed the school's ridiculous menagerie of small animals. Nobody paid them any heed, and they led an existence limited to being fed, watered and cleaned when necessary. Colin was the only one who ever spent time comforting the hamster or guinea pig. Trying desperately to relieve some of the frustration and boredom they must have felt. The lizard or dragon, whatever it was, scared him; he saw it as a monster, sprawling over the slab of rock beneath its heat lamp, waiting for the next live cricket to be fed into its torture-chamber glass enclosure.

The crickets were in a clear plastic tub with a small container of water, which was actually the cut-down bottom third of a small yoghurt pot. This cricket enclosure caused Colin so many sleepless nights. He would watch the fat crickets leaping against the side of the tub, trying to understand why they couldn't escape this see-through barrier which imprisoned them, and all the while able to watch the monstrous green lizard as it lay basking and licking its lips less than a foot away. They'd be forced to watch as a huge human hand roughly grabbed one of their number in a daily lottery and suspended it over the lizard's lair, dropping the poor animal into the enclosure at the mercy of the giant beast. Colin imagined this to be a living hell for the poor little creatures and he hated the lizard and he hated the English-teaching librarian who held dominion over this gruesome house of horrors.

One Sunday he had just finished a particularly moving short story by Hemmingway called *On the Quai at Smyrna,* which was confusing to his young mind but seemed to be about Greeks who, whilst evacuating Smyrna in 1922 were seen breaking the legs of their pack donkeys and pushing them into the sea to drown, rather than let them be taken and used by Turks. Such brutality set him on edge for the rest of the day and when he then caught sight of the helplessly trapped crickets, he saw red and in a moment of indignation stormed to Miss Butterfield's office to demand that the crickets be freed.

Fighting his nerves he rapped firmly on the big oak door to the English teacher's study and waited. He knew she was inside, as he could hear voices from the radio she had in there.

When there was no answer he knocked again, longer, harder, insistent.

The heavy door was slowly opened by a bemused looking Miss Butterfield, half-moon spectacles perched on the end of her nose.

Colin wondered why she wore her specs that way, it made her look so much older than she was – she can only have been in her thirties. The teacher furrowed her brow questioningly.

'Furness! Whatever is the matter?'

Lyrical Highland accent at odds with the horror show she presided over.

Colin had never seen the inside of this room properly, there were two huge bay windows framed by heavy dark green drapes, a polished wooden floor, half of which was covered by a large rug with some Chinese motifs and an old desk the size of ten of their school desks.

The air was stuffy and warm and smelled of something like Brussels sprouts.

'Please Miss Butterfield, it's the crickets, we have to let them go.'

'Let them go? And what shall the bearded dragon consume then…2nd year boys perhaps?'

'We can let that go too Miss Butterfield. It must be driving all the animals insane, shut up in tiny enclosures for us to look at, except nobody ever does.'

'Furness, those animals are an integral part of the school's social development programme; pupils learn to care for them, to feed, clean and nurture them.'

Colin interrupted..

'Nurture them Miss? We are torturing them, and I can't stand to watch the little crickets so desperate to escape, and that big lizard looking at them all day and the waiting and the nightmares…I am going to have to set them free.'

The normally placid teacher raised herself up on her toes and took a lungful of air that seemed to take minutes – inhaling through her nose until the boy thought she might explode.

When she spoke her soft accent was gone; the tone now harsh, loud and controlling, a complete contrast to her normal demeanour.

'You'll do no such thing boy! In fact you can stand over there by the window until I have decided what to do about this rebellious behaviour.'

Cowed, Colin shuffled across the worn rug to the window and looked out through the old, dirty glass onto a bleak garden.

A cold draught was whistling in through unseen gaps around the window frame, and this was countered by warm air rising up from the old-fashioned steam radiator which was so hot that when Colin's knee accidently touched it he recoiled from the sudden burn. The shock seemed to spur him into action and he span around and dashed through the still-open door.

Back in the library he rushed to the lizard tank and scooped up the plastic tub containing the desperate crickets. Within ten strides he was at the exit door and heading outside.

Once in the fresh air Colin sprinted towards the games fields where most of the school were chasing balls, opponents or reputations. Colin's race was a very different one, for him this was a fundamental life-or-death affair for the trapped insects, and in that moment he didn't care a damn for the consequences. His mother always told him to follow his heart and he wouldn't go far wrong. Well his heart said the crickets hated their prison and that he should free them.

At the boundary of the sports fields ran a small brook and Colin thought the crickets would be safe there among the tall vegetation. The area was over-hung with willows and sycamores, their fallen leaves lying in a thin slimy carpet and he skidded to a halt, his shoes slipping in the wet foliage that bordered the stream. He expected the insects to leap to their freedom as soon as he removed the lid of the tub, but in fact they lolloped laboriously as if uninterested in what he was offering. Undeterred, Colin began to fish the fat little creatures out in little handfuls, gently casting them into the greenery with comforting words to send them on their way to safety.

Once they felt the grass they came to life. These had probably been bred in a pet shop for the sole purpose of feeding bigger creatures and had almost certainly never seen grass before, yet they took to their new environment like ducks to water. As he watched the last of them laboriously lollop away to freedom Colin became aware of heavy breaths behind him and twisted his head to see the apoplectic face of Miss Butterfield bearing down upon him.

'You stupid, stupid boy! They will all probably die now, it's too cold for them and they have never experienced the world outdoors.'

'Well, Miss; they *may* die out here, but they would *certainly* have died in there.' He pointed back towards the school building.

'At least now they have a fighting chance.'

She grabbed him by the left elbow and steered him back towards the old buildings.

Her voice in his ear was a sinister hiss; he could feel the heat in her breath and her spittle peppering his skin.

'You'll be in front of the Headmaster just as soon as he has finished with the rugby. I wouldn't be surprised if he doesn't send you away, you are a disgrace to the school and a disappointment to all pupils and staff!'

His head was hung low, not in shame, but the better to watch the little creatures bounding high in their new-found freedom.

Colin smiled to himself and tingled with the wave of victory that coursed through him. Let the headmaster do his worst, Colin had followed his heart, and it felt good.

He is wrenched back to the present by an urgent thought of his horse, Vengeance. He shouts for a guard.

Samantha Milsom dials Dyson's mobile from the hands-free set in her unmarked car and gets his voicemail.
'Sir, it's Samantha. Just got a call from the admin team looking after Furness. Seems in all the excitement his horse got completely forgotten. I'm heading down there now. I've asked for a police approved equine vet to meet me at the farm; I'll let you know.'

She cuts the call and takes the scenic route for the eight mile drive to the old Furness farm house. Not that there's really an alternative; it lies in an isolated spot in the middle of the South Downs north of Chichester and the nearest neighbour – as she knows from the previous investigation – is exactly two miles distant. She takes it steady because the vet won't be there for at least forty-five minutes, and although she's not squeamish she doesn't really want to discover a dying horse all on her own, she wouldn't know what to do.

Killing time, she pulls into a garage on the outskirts of the town to grab a snack. The rows of white-bread sandwiches look mundane and unappetising and she searches for something without meat. It's not a conscious action, nor one that she has given any prior thought to, but since the Furness investigation she hasn't been able to stomach the thought of eating an animal. She supposes that, in time, this will change, but right now she wants to avoid meat. There's nothing on offer and that's disappointing; she decides to ask the rotund gentleman behind the counter.
'Excuse me; do you have anything without meat?'
'Sorry love, we only get a couple of cheese and pickle a day and they go pretty early doors.'
She's tempted to pursue this, and ask him why they don't order a couple more then, but realises the futility; it's not going to help her today, and she probably won't be coming here again in a hurry. The fat man doesn't seem in the slightest concerned that he's lost a potential customer. She leaves the shop and continues her journey slightly more irked than is probably reasonable.

She's not particularly hungry, so the lack of a sandwich doesn't really matter, but it's annoying; somehow unfair. She wonders if this is a regular experience for vegetarians, and supposes it must be. She feels sorry for vegans; their options must be practically zero. She wonders how long she could live like that, eternally up against '*food prejudice*' before she ripped some idiot's head off.

The mini dilemma is forgotten as she turns off the B road and heads down the long bumpy track to the farm. She's been back here a few times now since the discovery of the kidnap victims and the horrors of the world that Colin Furness had created, and still she feels her skin crawl approaching the first yard.

Surprisingly there's already another vehicle, a van with the logo of the approved veterinary service and she pulls up beside it.

There's nobody around as far as she can see.

'Hello, anyone here?' She feels a little silly; clearly the van didn't drive itself.

A head pops over the wall behind the parked van and a waving arm appears.

'Hi, over here.'

She marches swiftly over to the wall.

'Hi! DS Samantha Milsom.' She hasn't bothered to remove her warrant card.

'Hi! James Bellows. Nice to meet you.' A thirty-something, blond-haired and ruddy-faced man reaches over the low wall with his arm outstretched. Samantha leans forward, trying to avoid the growth of nettles and they shake hands awkwardly.

'Any sign of the horse?'

'Erm, yes. Afraid it's not good news though. Poor thing must have been shut in the paddock for anything up to a couple of weeks or longer – hard to tell. Been drinking from the gutter downpipe by the looks of things, but food's been almost non-existent. He's wasted away to practically nothing. Might need to put him out of his misery. Who's the owner? Is there an animal neglect prosecution going on?'

'Er, not specifically no. To be honest, we were told about him, but, well, with one thing and another he slipped through the net. Is there anything you can do?'

'I could put him on a drip and get some rapid build-up into him, but no promises. And it's not cheap – who's footing the bill?'

'The owner has made it clear that he'll finance whatever's needed, so please just do it; I'll square it with him later.'

41

'Where is the owner then?'

'He's not at liberty to care for the animal.'

'Oh! I see, he's inside then, is he?'

'Yep, and likely to be for a very long time.'

'Ah, OK. Well in that case let me get my stuff and we'll see what we can do in a hurry. Don't really want to move the poor thing so if money's really no object I'll treat him here and have someone care for him around the clock until he's strong enough to be moved...assuming he makes a recovery. If not, then I will call *Humane Solutions* – they're a firm that will take care of the details if he doesn't look like he's going to pull through.'

Humane Solutions sounded like they were probably anything but.

'OK; please do whatever you can James. Thanks. I'll let the owner know the status here.'

She retires a short distance to make a few calls.

When she's finished she walks back to where the vet is beginning to treat Vengeance.

'Here's my card; call me at any time if there's a development? Thanks.'

'Sure, OK. He's clearly been well looked after up until recently so he ought to have a good chance to pull through, but you never know. I'll call you later with an update.'

Samantha heads back to the station, cursing herself for having let the animal's welfare pass her by.

Still smarting from the incident at the job centre, Boner needs a pint before negotiating a price rise with his customer base. He dives into *the Dog and Duck* and takes a pint of mass-produced lager with a large Laphroaig. He doesn't much enjoy beer of any kind, but wants to feel the volume of liquid in his throat. The whisky is different, and this is one of his favourites. He swirls it around inside his mouth, breathing through his lips and savouring the smoky flavours as the spirit explodes at the back of his tongue and grabs the attention of all his senses.

He very quickly finishes the drink and decides he needs another, which makes him feel much better and two soon become six. Before he knows what has happened he is heavily under the influence and ready to take on the bully boy butchers.
Boner literally falls into the butcher's shop, dragging a tray of best home-made whole-grain sausages to the floor as he clutches around desperately for a hand-hold on his way to meet the old black and white checked floor tiles.
'Fuck me, arve drunk a bit too much, sorry, sorry…'

Smithwell, family butcher since 1869 (according to the sign) looks through his spectacles along the ridge of his hawk-nose at the heap of common trash on his otherwise immaculately clean floor.
'Mr Bones, please try not to wreck the bloody shop, I would prefer to expose the customer to the product than sling it all in the pig bin!'
'Sorry, sorry – bit pissed, sorry…'
Boner fights the need to vomit and rushes through the door to the back of the shop where he knows he'll find the toilet. He retches as he reaches it just in time.

After cleaning himself up a little Boner makes his unsteady way back into the shop area and sees old Smithwell talking with two uniformed men. His inebriated brain tells him they have come to arrest him and he goes into his apologising routine afresh.

'Sorry, sorry, didn't mean to get so drunk, I will give you all free rabbits and hares and donkeys tomorrow morning, sorry, sorry.'

He laughs as he falls back into the wall and pulls a pile of charity leaflets advertising a car boot sale for the local hospice down with him.

Smithwell rolls his eyes at the two security guards who are regular customers on their trips to the local prison.
'This is one of my organic produce suppliers, gentlemen; Mr Martyn Bones. He's normally very sober, but clearly had a skinful today – celebrating were we, Boner?'
'Sorry, sorry Mr Smithwell, got tricked into a few whiskies, won't affect my harvesting skills tonight!'
He leans close towards the two security guards, breathing stale alcohol into their faces.
'Have my business card gentlemen, call me any time you want high quality fresh produce straight from the field.' He fumbles for a while in his back pocket and hands each a grubby card. Smithwell turns to the guards and explains that tonight Boner was meant to be hunting hare and rabbits, but by the look of things might be sleeping off a hangover instead.
'That's a shame.' One of the guards interjects. 'I'm quite partial to rabbit. Does he go often?'

'Never fear, Mr Policeman!'
Comes the retort, as Boner thrusts his rosy face a few millimetres away from the taller of the guards.
'Hey, you look like that football bloke, you know, thingy Charlton. I shall be out in my truck and rabbiting as per usual, have no fear of that! It'd take more than a few tots of scotch to scupper my hunting plans!'
Smithwell is a little more philosophical.
'Let's wait and see, shall we Boner? Tell you what gents, give me a contact number and I'll give you a tinkle if he manages to drag himself out into the fields!'

The taller guard does as suggested, leaving a mobile number with the old butcher.

15

Dyson and his new wife Jenny are lying beside the pool.

'It's amazing to think of you being pregnant when you were going through all those horrors with that bloody monster. The cages, the depravity, the food – or lack of it – the abuse, the last nightmare on the Downs, the fight on the boat, escape... Christ, it's nothing short of a miracle that you survived, let alone the baby.'

'Stop talking about it darling; what's done is done, he's locked away for good and there's no way he will *ever* be looking at release. There'd be a riot.'

'You're right honey; he'll die in prison. But I'm still glad we fitted that tracker device to your car; the thought of you ever being out of my reach again would drive me insane.'

'You and your silly tracking device! I'm sure it will never come to that!'

Dyson's mobile 'phone pings and he opens the message.

Furness horse on the mend, responding well to food and liquids and on a string of anti-biotics. Vet says he'll be fine. S x.

Neil Dyson sighs inwardly and relaxes a little more. He'd been feeling very guilty about the horse and had been dreading bad news.

'That was Samantha; the horse I told you about is on the mend. Fancy a celebratory mineral water?'

His mischievous smile is wiped from his face in an instant.

'No, get me a beer please!'

'What? You *serious*?'

'Very, I'm in the second trimester, thirsty and hot and I want a beer. Go fetch.'

Grinning, he goes and fetches.

16

Δ No one in the world needs a mink coat, but a mink Δ
Murray Banks

Charlie *'Charcoal'* White is an arsonist undergoing assessment and serving three life sentences for setting fire to his previous employer's premises, killing him and his heavily pregnant wife.

Charlie is very open to suggestions and opportunities to make his considerable future time in jail as comfortable as he can. So when Colin approaches him at recreation and hints that, in return for Charlie inflicting some superficial wounds he would be rewarded with twenty Grand, the fire specialist agrees in a trice.

Charlie doesn't give a damn about Colin's reasons for wanting to be burnt, all he wants is the dosh, and upon receipt of the 5K down-payment arranges to do the deed. The remainder will be handed over upon completion of the job. There is honour among some criminals, and mutual trust to deliver on promises.

For an additional 2K Charlie procures the services of the local 'Fixer'. Every prison has one; often there's one in every cell block. The two Grand gets Colin a Stanley Knife with retractable blade. Stanley's are popular amongst inmates owing to their robust design, notoriously sharp blade and concealability. The plastic-cased versions are rarely detected by the cumbersome prison metal detectors as the proportion of blade to casing is tiny. The knives are small enough to hide in personal body cavities if needed and as a last resort the blade can be removed and the outer casing discarded. In that case, although fiddly to use, the blade remains a very lethal weapon – a particular favourite for settling internal prison disputes. Colin is happy to pay over the odds for the weapon, if it means he can decide where the collection point will be. He opts for the common drugs drop in the prison; the toilet cistern in one of the canteen loos.

The toilet is unique in the establishment as the only room to have its own '*Minder*'. The Minder's role is to ensure that for an agreed period sole access is available to the individual paying the '*rent*'. Colin is paying two hundred notes for the pleasure of storing his knife in the drop for less than an hour, but critically, he will have immediate access to the cubicle when he needs it. The high demand and secrecy surrounding toilet 15H in room 236 make it probably among the most expensive 2.2 square metres of real estate in the world.

At the agreed time Charcoal White strolls across the dining room floor and collects the small aerosol can which has been secreted behind a large foam fire extinguisher. He walks purposely towards the table where Colin sits, slightly nervously awaiting the pain that is about to come his way but keen to set his plan into motion.

The arsonist sits opposite Colin and a muscular accomplice materialises from out of nowhere. Before Colin has time to react the accomplice has his arms pinned down onto the dining table. Colin could probably move, he is incredibly strong, but he plays along for the sake of authenticity; if needed he wants the witnesses to bear testament that he'd been attacked and forcefully burned. Almost simultaneously Charlie White raises the aerosol tin, depresses the button on top of the can and strikes a flame from a disposable lighter. The propane propellant gas in the pressurised tin ignites and Charlie aims the flame at Colin's left wrist. In spite of his preparation, Colin whimpers as the flames scorch the skin around his wrist. The smell of burning hair and skin is nauseating. Sweat that is not caused by the heat erupts on Colin's brow.

When the sadistically leering White repeats the action on his right wrist Colin's nerve gives way and he screams an animal roar as he tries desperately, against all his instincts and martial arts training to resist the temptation to retaliate.
Charcoal White's eyes are impassive.

Within five seconds the deed is done and he jumps clear of the small crowd and rushes to douse his arms under the cold tap in the washrooms.

The effects of even such a short exposure to direct flame are interesting. The skin from Colin's thumb knuckle half way to his elbows is livid, black and blistering. Some has already flaked off, leaving exposed welts which are starting to ooze yellow puss. The pain really is quite acute, but it is bearable and the injuries suit his needs perfectly. An hour earlier Colin had guzzled four tablets each of Ibuprofen and Paracetamol to numb the pain he knew would be heading his way and he makes his way now to the first aid room where he is checked over and has the wounds dry-dressed. A ream of paperwork is instigated.

'We'll need statements from you and everyone at the table.'
The orderly informs him, not believing for one moment that anyone would come forward. Still, protocols must be followed for audit purposes and to keep the prison inspectors quiet.

'I need a specialist burns doctor. The pain is excruciating.' Colin complains.
'I'll see what we can do.'

Colin sits in a caged waiting area for more than an hour before he is offered any pain relief. He pretends to swallow the tablets; he doesn't want any more drugs to be working in harmony with what he's already taken and numbing his senses; he wants to keep his wits about him. The medication he had taken earlier is keeping the edge off the pain, but what remains is useful in keeping his attention focussed.

He is told they are waiting for a high security escort to take him to a Southampton burns unit. Until then he'll have to sit tight. The male nurse has more to tell him.
'Meanwhile, interesting that you should need medical help, got a message for you about your Mum. Seems she's back in hospital, unclear what's wrong exactly but she's in the medical assessment ward at St Richards, Chichester. Maybe you'll need to put in a visiting request; good luck with that!'
He laughs as he walks out of the holding area, locking the caged door behind him.

When the two-man high security escort team arrives they waste no time in searching Colin from head to toe and all the hidey holes in between.

One of the guards looks like a young Bobby Charlton, and the other not unlike an older Diego Maradona. Colin is not the least interested in football, but even he can't miss the similarities.

The search shows him to be clean.

On the way to the secure ambulance he develops a sudden desperate need for the toilet.

'I gotta go to the loo, sorry but it's desperate!'

'OK, shock reaction I expect, happens to people who are not used to pain or violence.'

Clearly the escort has no idea of Colin's history; a couple of burned wrists didn't even register as violence in his book. But the rationale suits him perfectly.

Colin mutters through clenched teeth. 'Yeah I guess you're right- give me a minute.'

'OK, but I'm coming in with you!'

'Sure, good luck with that!' says a sheepish looking Colin.

He nips into the gents with the security guard in tow and is relieved to see Harry the Minder just coming out. Without acknowledging each other Colin grabs a squirt of soap and darts into cubicle 15H alone, sliding the bolt across.

He makes a great pretence of noisily emptying his bowels, albeit hardly dropping his trousers, it is all bluff. Meanwhile, trying not to let the liquid soap drip from his fingers he silently removes the top of the toilet cistern and extracts the 5" Stanley knife. Now he drops his underpants and squats. Biting his bottom lip to the point of piercing the skin, he rubs the liquid soap over one end of the knife casing and pushes the thing into his anus as quickly as he dares, terrified that he'll accidentally catch the blade-release slider and rip himself apart in the process. With hindsight, he should have requested the thing be wrapped in tape to keep it in a safe state. The experience seems almost as bad as the wrist burning event but is quickly accomplished without mishap.

Colin's slightly awkward gait as they continue towards the ambulance is synonymous with someone who's just had a sudden and violent bowel movement. As they reach the final security door the guards stop and complete more paperwork.
'We gotta cuff you now son.' Announces Maradona.
Colin has anticipated this and that's why he's had his wrists burnt.
'You have to be joking. Look at my wrists, cuffs will strip the skin to shreds and I'll be in agony.'

Bobby Charlton strokes his chin.
'Hmmn, good point, we'll have to cuff you above the elbows then, with your arms to the front please.'

Colin had hoped he'd be excused hand-cuffs, clearly that wasn't going to happen. But above the elbows would allow him a pretty wide range of hand movement. All in all not a bad result, and worth the pain of the burns. As they prepare to leave the building, Bobby Charlton's 'phone rings. He answers it and speaks in hushed tones. The conversation catches Colin's attention, thinking the call might relate to his transfer he leans in close to overhear what snippets he can.

The discussion though is all about some rabbits. Apparently it's a local hunter who specialises in tender baby rabbit meat.
'Yes Mr Bones, thank you; I have your mobile number and will definitely call you.'
Bobby Charlton is smiling and holding up a business card as he speaks.

Colin files this info away for future use. Nothing is worse in his book than someone taking an animal's life. Except perhaps someone taking a *young* animal's life. He wonders how many the caller has killed and promises himself, and the souls of those dead creatures, that he'll try to put a stop to this particular murderer.

The guard explains that he has to deliver a patient to Southampton right now but he'll call very soon and arrange to collect the young animals from the butcher's shop where they met.
The guard then relays part of the conversation to Diego Maradona.

'That was the drunk guy we saw in the butchers – he wants to apologise for being so wasted and said he will give us some supremely delicious young rabbit whenever we want. Do you want his number?'

'Sounds good! No thanks, I have it right here.'

He too takes out a tatty business card and waves it in the air as if to prove he hasn't mislaid the number.

They ready themselves to leave.

Colin is ushered through the exit door metal detection. It bleeps to register the handcuffs but nothing else and then, duly secured with another set of cuffs linking Colin to Maradona, they leave the secure prison hospital and head for the transport to the Southampton burns unit.

The vehicle is a modified ambulance, specially adapted to carry high-risk prisoners. The escorts separate; one in the back with the prisoner the other up front with the driver in the cab, which is partitioned off from the prisoner section by a lockable sliding sheet of solid metal. There is an internal intercom system between the two. Maradona takes a key from his right-hand trouser pocket and frees the cuffs that had linked the two men.

This is great news!

During the sixty minute drive from Chichester to Southampton Colin concentrates on easing the knife from his rectum, happy now that it wasn't taped up for safety, he'll need to act fast and removing wrappings of sticky tape would have been difficult under these conditions. He raises his backside very slightly from the bench seat and tenses his stomach and bowel muscles. After a few attempts he feels the first movement and squeezes harder, trying to mask his pain by complaining about his earlier emergency evacuation. He has to rise a little higher to achieve his goal and then sits down, sweating a little as the thing bursts clear. Now he has to ensure it doesn't fall down his trouser leg before he's ready.

The windows are tiny, high set and in any case completely blacked out so he has no visibility of the outside world and tries to guess where they are; he will need to time his attempt to perfection in order to give himself the best chance of getting away and, importantly, evading recapture.

'We must be nearly there, right? I am busting for another shit.'

'Not far now.' Mutters Maradona. 'As far I am concerned you can sit on the can all day once we have handed you over. Until then no more toilet breaks.'

Colin squirms a little.

'How far exactly is *"not far now"* in real terms?'

'About ten minutes I think; we are just coming off the motorway now.'

Colin pulls up the mental image he has of the local road layout. He has to get the knife from its current resting place in his prison-issue pants under his backside and into his left or right hand; whichever doesn't really matter. He wriggles forward on the bench seat, again grateful that due to ergonomic limitations they'd had to cuff his elbows in front rather than behind his back.

He knows there will be speed bumps coming into the hospital grounds, there always are, and with luck they'll be regularly spaced. That's when he'll create a minor distraction, drop the knife to the floor and either cover it with his foot or, better still, scoop it up. He lowers his elbow onto the seatbelt fastener and coughing hard to cover any noise depresses the release button. Nothing happens. He tries the move again, digging the point of his elbow as deep as he can into the mechanism and this time is rewarded with a soft click. The belt clip, free of its constraint pops up a little faster than he'd anticipated, but he manages to stop it with his arm so that it still looks to be fixed in position. With that constraint removed he'll have some wiggle room when the time comes to move.

After a number of left and right turns they slow to a walking pace and Colin guesses that they must be coming onto the hospital grounds. He readies himself for the inevitable speed humps and is rewarded a few seconds later when he feels the front of the vehicle lurch skywards. Even at the slow speed the movement is enough to cause Maradona to grab for a support and Colin starts to count seconds until the next bump.

He gets to seventeen when the truck lurches again. He starts to count again…fifteen, sixteen, as the front rises over the next bump he neatly drops the knife down the leg of his trousers and plucks it up before the guard has even noticed him moving. Gingerly he reverses it so that the aperture where the blade will appear is bottom-most and he slips it up inside his right sleeve, holding it in place by slightly cocking his right wrist.

The warm plastic casing feels reassuring, nestling against his skin.

Ideally he wants to make his move before he gets anywhere near the inside of the hospital buildings. These places are so complicated and he could run around for precious minutes trying to find the exit. That would be way too risky. Much better to make an early surprise break. He knows he'll probably have one chance only and needs to be ruthless and exact.

For some reason they pull up and sit, engine idling for a few minutes.

Maradona picks up the intercom unit and asks Bobby Charlton what's going on.

'Air ambulance flying in.' Comes the tired reply. 'We have to give way; won't be long.'

Colin sees this as a great opportunity and readies the knife, allowing the plastic casing to slip down into his hand and with his thumb, sliding the blade out via the spring loaded clip on the top.

He looks towards Maradona and mumbles something unintelligible.

'Sorry? What did you say?' Leaning slightly towards Colin.

'I said…'

He mumbles a little more and the guard leans further, offering his ear. In a lightning fast movement Colin pulls forward, throwing his straight arms out in a double-fisted strike at the guy's head. Using his forehead to force the head back and expose his soft throat, Colin awkwardly drags the one inch razor sharp blade across the skin, opening a huge gushing gash with that one quick movement. Any gurgling sounds disappear as Colin hugs the guard's face tight into his chest to muffle the sounds. The guy's feet are beating a tattoo for ten seconds and blood pumps all over Colin's face, arms and upper body, but at this rate he knows he'll be dead within a minute, he has scored a direct arterial hit. Very messy; very effective.

He'll need to think quickly now to pull this one off. A guy dressed in prison-wear in hospital grounds at peak visiting times is one thing; a blood-drenched guy in prison clothes is something quite different.

First things first. As soon as Maradona slumps into unconsciousness Colin lays him down and takes the hand cuff keys from his right-hand pocket. He can't believe their standard operating procedures allow the keys to be carried in the rear of the ambulance, but their loss is definitely his gain. It's an awkward manoeuvre but within a few seconds he's out of the cuffs. He realises that they were not so dependent on the handcuffs for security because the back doors have no internal handles; the only way out is if they are opened from the outside.

Fuck, fuck, fuck, fuck, fuck! How could he miss such a basic but critical point? He really is making too many mistakes lately. Sharpen up or fail.

But Colin knows that modern safety design is such that most things are built with emergency situations in mind and sure enough, the roof contains a small emergency escape panel with a red release lever under a protective cover. Colin assumes that removing the cover will activate an alarm in the driver's cab, but fuck it. He is tall and fit and it's really no challenge to reach up, remove the red cover over the activation lever, operate the lever and open the panel.

He will need funds, so fishes out the guy's wallet and helps himself to the fifty quid in notes and a couple of credit cards. There's also a mobile 'phone which might come in handy. Just before he attempts his escape he remembers something else and quickly whips Boner's business card from the top pocket of the guard's jacket.

Expecting to hear a warning buzzer at least, he isn't going to hang around to see the effects. A few seconds later he is perched gingerly on the roof of the truck, quickly reconnoitring the scene for the best escape route. There's an old couple, arm-in-arm negotiating a pedestrian crossing some fifty yards behind them, but they are concentrating hard on not falling over. No audible alarm has sounded, but that means nothing, they may have a flashing beacon or similar in the cab.

A short distance behind them and to their left is a long, low building. Government organisations love their signs and the NHS is no different. A big blue and white sign identifies it as the hospital laundry and Colin almost whoops with joy. Still no evidence that he's triggered an alarm…couldn't have panned out better if he'd planned it!

He drops down the back of the ambulance to avoid being spotted by the driver or Bobby Charlton in the wing mirrors and, keeping himself in their blind spot walks quickly backwards, away from the vehicle until he feels he has gained enough distance to make the short dash into the laundry. Once inside the automatic swing doors he stops for a second to get his bearings. He wants to check to see if he's been spotted by either guard or driver but he'll find out soon enough in any case.

To his right is a long corridor and to his left a changing room of some kind. He goes left and immediately strikes gold. The room has shelves piled high with clean hospital attire, from orderlies' uniforms to patients' gowns and surgeons' scrubs. He grabs an armful of each and darts into a toilet cubicle. There he uses the tiny sink to quickly wash the worst of the blood from his face and arms, the water running bright red for a long time. Still dripping wet, he changes into one of the orderly's uniforms. It isn't a great fit but he only plans on wearing it for a short time, just long enough to get the hell out of here.

17

Still inside the laundry complex Colin spots a pile of linen bags of various sizes and on a whim grabs a smallish one with a shoulder strap and stuffs another set of orderly's clothes inside. He has a vague plan to get to the hospital in Chichester where his mother is being treated and thinks a set of hospital clothes could be useful to disguise the visit of a soon-to-be very wanted man.

He is highly conscious that he doesn't have a strict plan from this point. In truth he hadn't really expected to succeed with his getaway so easily, and now that he is almost free he needs to work out the next steps. Colin is a man who needs to work to a plan, risks arise when plans fail.

The most urgent thing is to get away from this immediate area and find somewhere to hide out until he's had time to think things through. Every minute he spends hanging around the hospital will bring more and more resources to bear down upon him. He knows that the only thing to do, now that he is clean and has a disguise of sorts, is to get the hell out of the hospital.

He leaves the building via a fire escape on the opposite side of the laundry to the door through which he'd entered and follows signs for the main hospital vehicular entrance, constantly scanning for signs that his escape has been flagged. Things outside seem remarkably calm – could it be that they haven't realised yet? Surely not, it had already been six or seven minutes.

Colin feels very naked, he has only the stolen money and an unfamiliar 'phone but he is a survivor and he'll get through this as if it were a tactical game. Build resources slowly and steadily, minimising risk and leaving as little sign as possible of his ever having been there.
Once outside the hospital grounds he feels a little conspicuous in his orderly's clothing, but people will be used to seeing hospital employees going in and out at all hours so it's no big deal right now. The further away he gets, the more bizarre and memorable he will appear so he has to come up with a better disguise.

After walking through a maze of small residential roads he comes to a large wooded area. He knows from the maps he'd studied during his planning stage that this is either Lord's Wood or Dymer's wood. Either is fine, and he knows that if he heads east he's going to hit the golf course and north of that the M27 motorway.

If he can make it to the golf club he can hide out somewhere there overnight and organise himself some transport for the morning, plenty of early morning golfers would be leaving car keys in inappropriate places – changing rooms or similar – eager to shoot a few birdies or whatever stupid names they give the shots. He walks through the wooded pathways for half an hour, highly alert and diverting off the track on the two occasions when he hears other people. He comes to a small housing development that wasn't on the map and lurks just inside the woods, watching the residential roads and houses and thinking; always thinking.

As he watches from a tree-shielded hillock overlooking the settlement a tall guy carrying a laundry basket walks from his garage into the small square of green that passes for a garden. He starts to hang a load of washing onto a rotary line and interestingly Colin sees him peg out a large pair of dark green overalls. Now, they would be a good fit, and a great neutral disguise! With overalls like that he could blend in just about anywhere. Even on the golf course he'd become invisible to the punters, they would ignore him, assuming he was a groundsman or similar. He wants those overalls and he's prepared to wait for the opportunity, although he doesn't want to sit here all day while the cops get the sniffer dogs out on his trail.

The woods are deserted and, sat on a piece of dry ground with his back against a tree Colin plays with the mobile telephone to see if there are passwords or any other obstacles to its use. Thankfully it lets him straight in. He turns it off in case they try to trace it and sits back, letting his mind drift for a while. It's a warm day and birds are singing; the sound of the cars on the motorway is surprisingly clear, even though that road must be over a mile from where he sits. He can also hear some school kids playing at break. He begins to daydream as he often does when he has time on his hands, and his mind wonders back to sometime at school when he remembers being just as scared as he is now; alone in an environment a little alien to him, vulnerable and, back then, at the mercy of bigger, stronger, emotionally retarded people.

He is back in the playground of the little independent school, must be a year or so before the incident with the crickets. The school is old-fashioned in its ideals and ineffective in its teachings. The elderly Masters and mistresses – even those titles indicate ownership and superiority – hold archaic values and reinforce these with inadequate teaching following strictly no-nonsense methods. Bullying is rife and Colin is a natural target. He suffers with his rare chromosome defect and even at this age it's clear that his eyes are positioned much further apart than is usual; *normal*. Being different in just about every possible way – his odd appearance, dyslexia, ungainliness and natural loner tendencies – Colin is easy prey and often the favourite playground entertainment.

Bullies usually follow an invisible pecking order, and top of this particular tree – and therefore first to get stuck in – is Swedish slob Anders Lindegaard.
Lindegaard is the son of a Swedish Colonel on secondment to the British military and a mother who seems to spend more time in the school office than the headmaster. Lindegaard is two years Colin's senior and takes the utmost delight in showing his peers his prowess with fists, feet or twisted, hurtful words. His English is good but not perfect, and somehow the insults seem to cut deeper when delivered in a slightly foreign accent; almost as if to say *I have learned some of your language just so that I am better able to insult you in your own tongue – imagine what I could do in Swedish!*
Of similar age and running a close second to Lindegaard is Melissa Goodrich; a thin and waspish girl with sharp features and lank mousey hair. She isn't up to any kind of physical antagonism, but takes great pleasure from dishing out psychological abuse and even at that age seems to delight in tormenting Colin about his sexual naivety.

His reminiscences get no further as he's wrenched back to the present by movement ahead of him. Colin clocks the boiler-suit guy leaving his house. Excellent, give it a few minutes to make sure he isn't coming straight back and then a quick nip over the fence and all change in the woods.

He watches the guy walk round to the front of the house and loses sight of him there. There's only one road out and there's a gap in the tall wooden fence about twenty metres ahead so whether he drives or walks Colin should catch sight of him there. Sure enough, a few moments later he spots him walking briskly past the gap and on down the road. Colin slowly stands, stretching his cramped muscles and is reminded of his burn injuries as he accidentally brushes his bandaged right wrist against the rough bark. He picks his way slowly towards the back of the guy's garden. It's a small plot, typical of modern housing estates and overlooked by two neighbours. Colin can't see any obvious signs of life, and in any case, he'll be over the fence and out again in a jiffy.

Taking a deep breath he jumps, hooks his arms over the top of the wood and almost screams out as the bandage on his left wrist catches on a nail and the blistered skin is exposed to the rough wood. He falls back to the ground, nursing his wound and cursing silently as the bandage blossoms with fresh red colouring. He has already made too much noise and needs to do this and get out of the area in case he is spotted. If a neighbour reports an intruder and gives a description the cops will be swarming all over the place within minutes and he'll be properly buggered.

Screwing his face up against the anticipated pain and looking for any more rogue nails he jumps again. His feet scrabble a little in thin air as he struggles to pull himself up over the top without causing any more damage to his arms but he quickly hooks his left leg over the top and is dropping silently down to the other side. He sprints the 4 metres to the washing line and yanks the overalls straight off the line without touching the pegs. He needs to leave as few clues as possible; fingerprints or DNA left at the scene would only work against him even if nobody clocks him in the act.

In the corner of the small garden is a child's faded yellow plastic play table and he nudges it up against the fence with his foot. Using it as a step he's back on the safe side within moments and jogging off towards the woods some thirty metres away. When he reaches the cover of the trees he keeps running for a bit and takes a right fork when he spots a deer or badger track heading that way. After 5 minutes he stops and, checking first for any sign of life, strips off the hospital clothes and jumps into the boiler-suit.

The hospital gear goes down an old badger sett and he fills that in with dead leaves, twigs and other greenery. A good sniffer dog would guide the police straight to the spot, but no point making things easy for any chance observers. Dressed in his new disguise he begins a brisk walk north-east towards where he guesses the golf club should lie.

18

Things at work have been manic and Samantha Milsom is *retaxing –* her word for relaxing in the bath whilst working her brain on the Times crossword. There is an almost obligatory glass of white at her side and the bath bubbles lap her chin as she ponders the stresses of the job. Her boss, Neil Dyson had suffered badly after the Colin Furness affair and is on a couple of weeks' paternity leave right now with his young family. She envies them.

But this is her special time and she drags her mind back to 15 across:

Planning floater with sound cladding? 8 letters.
She has the third letter already – that's an *'a'.*
Planning...hmmn, plotting, organising, designing..none of them have the letter a in the right place.
OK – let's think about it Samantha...Sound cladding probably means another word for *sound* wrapped around (cladding) a word for *floater* and the whole thing would mean *planning.*
Ah ha! Drafting! *raft* is the floater, with *ding-* the word for a ringing sound wrapped around it, the whole thing meaning to *draft* or *plan.*

OK, 17 down; *Buried under lump of turf is a drink; (4 letters).*
Lump of turf is a sod, bury the letter *a* under it - Soda...easy!

Just this pesky 11 across to get; *Sounds as if this spanner is an also-ran, beginning to rotate, accessing both nuts in kitchen appliance (5 & 6 letters).* Spanner...Wrench? Tool? Adjustable? Maybe not a tool at all, maybe someone or thing which spans something, like a bridge.

Hmmn.
OK. Famous bridges; Tower, London, Brooklyn, Golden Gate, Forth – that's it! Sounds like also ran – a horse that doesn't finish in the top three is an *also-ran. Forth* sounds like *fourth* Forth Bridge.
As often happens, she has the answer and now has to work out why. Like a suspect in a case where you know they did it but have to find the evidence.

Sounds as if this spanner is an also-ran, beginning to rotate, accessing both nuts in kitchen appliance.

OK, she has the first bit – *Sounds as if this spanner is an also-ran.*
That's Forth Bridge; now why?
Beginning to rotate-that means the beginning letter of the word
rotate – R.
*Accessing both nuts…*hmmn, accessing – that must mean put the *R*
into the word *both* mixed up (or *nuts,* as in *crazy*), so that's the *b, o,
t, h and r.* Now all of that inside a kitchen appliance – which is
clearly a *fridge.*
Forth Bridge; excellent – finished within time as usual.

In the bedroom her mobile rings.
Samantha has a golden rule, retaxation is king; nothing disturbs it.
However, with all the crazy developments lately, and with her boss
Neil Dyson on paternity leave for a couple of weeks she makes an
exception. Springing lithely from the water, grabbing a big white
bath sheet and wrapping it loosely around her black body she just
grabs the 'phone before it goes to voicemail.

It's Sicknote on the duty desk.
'Samantha, hi. Sorry to disturb but there's been an incident.'
'What's happened Dave?'
'We have a report of an absconded high risk prisoner who you need
to be aware of.'
'Who – oh god, not Furness?'
'The very same yeah. Where are you?'
'In the bath – or rather I was.'
'Hehe wanna switch to webcam!'
'Fuck off Dave. Tell me, what's happened?'
'Seems he had an accident in the nick and was being transported to
Southampton general for burns treatment and did a runner. Topped
one of the escorts, messy apparently. He won't get far; he is dressed
in prison garb and must be covered head to toe in blood.'
'We both know that's bollocks Dave, he's a resourceful bastard.
When did this happen?'
'About two hours ago – there was a reporting delay, he wasn't
clocked as missing for anything up to twenty minutes. The so-called
secure transport was held up waiting for an air ambulance landing
that fucked up and he got out sometime during that delay. No

witnesses and no clues about where he is. But like I said, the world and its mother is looking out for him so it's only a matter of time.' Samantha picks up on a word Sicknote had said.

'Dave, he'll be heading for St. Richard's in Chichester – his mum's there.'

'Yeah, yeah, already got it covered, Steph and Brian are gonna be in situ there, they both know him by sight and will be taking turns at her bedside and patrolling with some uniforms. Got photos being run off as we speak. It's nailed down girl, chill! Just wanted to let you know in case, well, in case he has any vengeful intentions.'

'Sure, thanks, I appreciate that, but I don't share your confidence. I'll get dressed and head in.'

'Sure – don't overdo the getting dressed bit, we could do with some eye candy!'

'Fuck you Sicknote!' She laughs, despite being peeved at his never ending childish, sexist and everything-else-ist quips.

19

Dyson is being pulled through a swimming pool of thick black soup. Something is screaming and he can't find his warrant card to shut the noise down. He knows he needs to open his wallet and wave the card inside its plastic window towards the disturbance and the world will return to normality; like some magic wand the banshee will be sent scurrying back into its hovel.

'Your turn detective.'

Jenny's voice, fat with sleep close to his ear.

What is she doing here, he has to get her out before whatever is making that racket gets hold of them both.

He feels his shoulder gripped by the beast and lashes out with his elbow, striking something soft.

'Ow! What are you doing Neil?'

The noise, magnified a few decibels through the monitor becomes a baby's cry as full consciousness takes hold and realisation dawns.

'Oh god Jenny, I am so sorry, bad dream...'

He is already out of bed, feeling the reality of the rough carpet on his bare soles, its comfort juxtaposed against the dilemma of their tiny daughter's tears.

'Daddy's coming sweetheart, don't worry.'

Neil Dyson is on paternity leave as Jenny had given birth to Samantha six weeks earlier. The little one had yet to grasp the principle that nights were for sleeping sweetly and days for playing, eating and making soft gurgling sounds. She sleeps in the adjacent room – against Jenny's wishes – but Neil and the host of post-natal experts (including Jenny's mother) had insisted that babies sharing parents' rooms were on a slippery slope to spoil-dom. They would make a rod for their own back and so, reluctantly, after three weeks of sharing a room Jenny had agreed to the move.

She is glad of that now, as it means that whilst Neil is feeding the expressed natural milk, changing the wet (and probably worse) nappy and burping little Samantha, Jenny can drift back into that semi-dozing state that seems to pass for sleep these days. Any port in a storm, and she guiltily stretches out her arms and legs as if trying to reach all four corners of the 2m x 2.2m bed and then curls up into a small ball right in the middle. She is almost instantly gone.

In the nursery father and baby are doing some early morning bonding. Crooked in his arm, Samantha is suckling away strongly on the small bottle as if she hasn't eaten for a week. Neil is amazed at the contrast between her tiny delicate form and the power in her lips. The midwife had warned that they'd need to enlarge the hole in the rubber teat before too long as she is demanding more milk in shorter time and was in danger of taking in too much air in her desperation for sustenance.

Like most fathers, Neil is head over heels in love with this amazing little creature and as he often does, finds himself whispering that he will protect her from anything that ever tries to harm her, in whatever shape it might come, until his dying breath. Trauma has been only too real in their lives recently and he is determined that this tiny person is not going to go through any of the horrors he has known.

A sudden change in the sound coming from the bottle snaps him out of his reverie and he realises that Samantha has been gulping down mouthfuls of air. Gently he removes the bottle from her cloying mouth and puts it down on the changing table. As he raises her up to lay her over his left shoulder she begins to wail.

'Shhhh little one, we need to get the trapped air out. If you are still hungry then I will give mummy the good news.'
He smiles in the semi-darkness to think how Jenny might react to being woken again so soon with a request for milk that only she could supply. Neil thanks his lucky stars that bio-medicine has yet to solve that little issue. A sudden loud belch explodes about an inch from his left ear, and he laughs as the shock of the noise stuns Samantha into silence.
'There's a good girl Sammi.'
He allows himself this secret nickname when he is alone with the baby. Jenny would chastise him if she ever heard him use the diminutive term. They'd named the girl after Dyson's police partner Samantha Milsom, a good, confident and beautiful woman who had

been through some of the toughest assignments with Neil as his understudy and professional partner. Most recently it had been Samantha Milsom's intuitive detective work and uncanny puzzle-solving skills that had almost certainly saved Jenny's life, when she had been kidnapped by the psychopathic animal rights lunatic Colin Furness.

Jenny had left clues hidden in the media messages he had forced her to prepare and Samantha had spotted and deciphered them and been instrumental in leading Dyson and the team to the killer. For that, Neil and Jenny owed her an irrecoverable debt of gratitude; naming their daughter after the brilliant friend and partner had seemed the most natural thing to do.

The senior Samantha had a pet hate; the shortening of her name. She was held in great respect and as a result was always referred to as Samantha. Jenny had decreed that the same would be the case for her little namesake, and Neil takes a guilty pleasure in breaking that rule; after all, fathers and daughters have to have some secrets!

The soft, regular breathing tells him his little angel has fallen asleep, so with infinite care, he lays her on her back in the little cot. With equal care he tiptoes from the room, avoiding the spot near the door where the old floorboards complain whenever the slightest weight is applied. Not until he has pushed the door closed and slowly released the handle does he realise he's been holding his breath, and he exhales now and takes a huge but almost silent lungful of air.

By sheer coincidence at exactly that moment Samantha Milsom is dialling Dyson's number.
His mobile is set to vibrate so the baby isn't disturbed, but Neil is cross at the intrusion. He steps further from the bedrooms and whispers into the 'phone.
'Yeah, what's up Samantha?'
'Sorry Guv, a development you need to be involved in.' Samantha realises that the baby must be asleep and is also whispering.
'Seriously? I'm on paternity leave!'
He realises she wouldn't be calling him for trivia.
'Go on then, what's burning?'

66

'There's been an escape from the high security mental unit.'

'And?' As he says the word he already knows the significance. 'Oh shit – not Furness?'

'Afraid so; sorry to always be the bearer of bad news.'

'Oh jeez, that's serious shit. How the hell did he manage that?'

'Not quite clear yet Sir, but they have at least one high profile escapee a year, so it's hardly Alcatraz.'

'Hmmmn, OK, what's done is done. Who's on it?'

'No decision yet Sir, but my guess is that we'll be involved.'

'Yeah, that's a given. OK, thanks Samantha, keep me in the loop OK?'

'Sure thing. Wanted you to know in case...well, you know. Night.'

With luck the other Samantha – Sammi – will sleep through now until the normal morning routine needs to start. Neil gently slips beneath the duvet and wraps himself around his sleeping wife, intoxicated by her smell and warmth and despite the shocking news and the conflicting emotions arising from the close proximity of his wife's warmth; he drifts into a deep and untroubled sleep.

20

He's abandoned all plans of hanging around near the golf club – it's far too close to the escape scene. Instead Colin stops in the grounds of the club long enough to swipe a pair of sunglasses and a baseball cap from a golfing cart that has been temporarily abandoned while its transitory owners play with their balls in the sandpits. Round the back of the clubhouse he spots a nice bicycle, conveniently propped against the wall and unsecured – the owner probably works in the kitchens and has blind faith in his workmates and the clientele. He quickly learns that the gears need adjusting, as it doesn't want to go into fifth, but Colin can live with that for the few hours he needs to put some distance between himself and the Southampton area. Progress is slow, he has to keep a low profile and avoids any major settlements on his ride, but he's covered probably forty miles by the time it gets dark and has done well to get so far away without the police getting even a sniff of him. Finally, on the outskirts of Petersfield he ditches the bike in a deep pond and makes his way on foot over the hills to the old house that he'd purchased – via his amoral accountant – whilst he was inside the nick.

Although there'll be nothing to link him to the place, other than the obsequious accountant, he exercises extreme caution on his approach, checking that he hasn't been set up or compromised in any way. All seems dead still and he finds the key where he'd instructed Abrahams to leave it. He enters the grand Victorian farmhouse in darkness, preferring to get a feel for the place on his own terms; being forced to explore a new environment without the benefit of sight etches certain key features into the mind, and he wants to become intimately familiar with every nuance of the place.

There's a heap of mail on the floor inside the front door which he silently nudges aside with his foot, concentrating on the permanent physical features and filing away all the little creaks, clicks and echoes. He's like a blind man feeling his way through a maze as he makes his way from room to room pulling the heavy curtains across the windows as he goes so that when he does come to switch on the lights he can't be observed by anyone – not that there's much risk of that; the property lies some distance from the road and the nearest neighbour is probably a mile away. Clocking the subtle changes of atmosphere and smell he explores the old place; this room clearly used to house a smoker, probably a small lounge or a gentleman's study; in the next chamber the fireplace has been more frequently used in the past, the lingering rich tang of soot permeates the wallpaper. Beyond the huge kitchen the scullery feels damp – probably just because it's cooler in here by design. Upstairs the odours are softer and rounder somehow, with suggestions of long-forgotten perfumes. A girl's room then; too light-feeling and fresh for an older lady.

Finally satisfied that he is alone and safe he starts to familiarise himself with the layout with the aid of lights. It's a substantial building which retains its timeworn feel, despite extensive modernisation and he's glad that the heating system is big and robust as the radiators start to take the chill out of the air. Piled on the massive kitchen table are three brown cardboard boxes. Abrahams has done well and these will contain the computers and other devices he needs to get cracking in his new life. He carries them through to the cigarette-tainted study and unpacks his new laptop.

He is no technical genius and due to dyslexia is a very slow reader so it takes him a while to work out where everything has to go. He finally realises that the array of cables and leads are largely superfluous; he only has to plug the thing into the mains to get power, because everything is wireless and he doesn't yet need any of the little boxes of tricks he has bought. Even the laser jet printer is wireless. Once the machine is booted up everything kicks into action automatically, all Colin has to do is insert discs when prompted and watch as progress bars move across screens declaring that such and such a programme was now 93% complete and that there are so-and-so seconds to go. Before too long he is able to connect to the internet and is downloading the Tor network browser connections.
He learned all about Tor in prison from experienced drugs and arms dealers as well as suppliers of just about anything illegal. It's a network which facilitates anonymous contact, via the so-called *dark web,* to such people as he would be needing over the coming days. He has been told that his computer IP number will remain hidden from anyone who might be alerted to trigger words, such as *bomb,*

drugs, *missile* or *Islam*. Once ready with Tor he gets himself an encrypted email address through the *Hushmail* set up he was told about and he is in business.

Colin needs a new ID and the associated paperwork, such as passport, driving licence, birth certificate and National Insurance number. He also needs a CCTV system of the highest quality, assorted security paraphernalia and weapons – particularly a sniper's rifle, night-vision goggles and ammunition. All of these things are readily available through Tor and it doesn't take much digging to find them using mostly links he's been passed inside and by 2am he has set the wheels in motion to obtain everything he had planned to get, plus a few optional extras.

Wherever he is heading, he intends to stay out of the way as much as he possibly can and adds a few items to a hand-written shopping list, including a small tent and a comprehensive range of good quality camping equipment, dark glasses and a cap of some kind. He will very quickly be amongst Britain's most wanted criminals now and he needs to think about frequent disguise changes. He has already started to grow a short, stubbly beard, and that will develop quickly, but most critically, he has to hide his eyes, which are a certain giveaway to anyone who knows about his hypertelorism.

A few further calls in the morning on one of his new pay-as-you-go mobiles to his accountant David Abrahams ensures that significant funds will be available at very little notice in accounts under his new name, Sam Dyson. He's chosen the name as a little dig at the police, they were the first and last names of the two detectives most prominent in his arrest, Samantha Milsom and Neil Dyson. He smiles at the thought and his legs do a little jig of joy.

On a whim he decides to reward Abrahams beyond his already generous fee; the guy has done exceptionally well and he's the only really weak link in the chain of secrecy; Colin needs to guarantee his ongoing silence and the weasely man will do anything for money. The alternative is to ensure his silence in a more definite manner, but Colin has enough on his plate and assassinations are a complication he can live without right now.

Neil Dyson and Samantha Milsom don't often argue, but they are
close to it now.

It's not yet seven in the morning and with all non-essential staff
seconded to the emergency anti-terror operation the police station is
otherwise deserted, just the two of them and the skeleton night shift
team.

Samantha is standing looking out of the window, without actually
seeing; arms folded trying to control her emotions.

'You damned well *did* have a choice; you are entitled to the time off
and you both *need* that time together for Christ's sake. It's not so
long ago that, well, you know, and what you two went through
was....'

'Don't tell me what we went through Samantha; you think I don't
fucking know what we went through? I also know that if this sick
psycho is at large I am not gonna be lazing around changing nappies
and wondering who he is fucking well skinning alive as I scratch my
arse singing yet another verse of the sun has got his fucking *hat* on!'

'Sorry Guv, I'm just trying to give you a bit of balance because I
know how stubborn you can be and let's be honest; you *can* let work
rule your life. Jenny needs support and I am worried that you won't
see that.'

He comes round the desk to stand next to her at the window; their
shoulders touch and his voice is calmer.

'Jenny is a lot stronger than you think, than any of us think, and she
is holding up just fine. We spoke about it at length; I didn't just leap
for my car keys when I heard he'd escaped. We discussed it and she
agreed that neither of us would be able to relax now that we know
he's busted out. The best place for me – for both of us right now – is
here. Trust me.'

'I do trust you, mostly, but you have other responsibilities now and I
am not going to let you forget that.'

'Cool, I'll call you Jiminy from now on then.'

She turns towards him with a puzzled frown.

'As in Pinocchio's conscience; Jiminy Cricket; you can be my
conscience.'

They both laugh and the tension that was so tangible moments before disperses.

'Well I guess the team will be surprised to see me back, what have you been up to so far?'

'They won't be at all surprised; they were surprised you stayed away so long! We only started yesterday afternoon. We've procured the small ops room and got just the basic facts up on display, we were all thrown a bit by the terror alert and to be honest we're dead lucky we kept the whole team – including Brian and Steph.'

'Yeah tell me about it, I was watching the news and saw the state at the airports; apparently it took three hours to move fifteen feet at Heathrow passport control, the suppliers of rubber gloves must be licking their lips, bet nobody's seen so many body searches since 9/11. OK – let's get into the ops room and have a strategy worked out before they all come charging in and riddle me with guilt trips.'

In the daylight it becomes clear that the place is id
long access route, visible over its entire length fro
from much of the woods that surround the house.
needs for a safe house. Plenty of outbuildings – so useful ior ....
devices, full cellar and numerous other features, attractive to
someone who wants to keep himself to himself and know when he
might have been compromised.

Abrahams had wanted too much anonymity and so the contract in
the end had been signed by a 'ghost' – prison slang for a middleman
who would do a job and then disappear. Become invisible and
untraceable. That suits Colin just fine and by mid-morning the first
of the equipment he'd only ordered last night begins to arrive; the
wonders of the modern supply chain!

Colin knows that time is not a luxury he possesses and cracks on
with his security installations immediately. His stretch in jail has
been very productive; he's learned a lot about personal security from
people who really know their stuff, and he gained contacts in several
very dark areas. The things he needed had cost him dearly, but
money really was no object, and Colin would willingly have forked
out ten times as much for the level of security he was buying into.

He has always been a practical type, enjoying the challenges of
fabricating and following schematic drawings for assembling kits
and systems, so putting together the CCTV assemblage when it's
delivered is actually quite fun. He spends as much time as he can
spare siting the cameras; deciding where best to place those with
infra-red capability and where he could make do without, concealing
pressure plates and light beams. It feels like he is building a fortress
– which, in a way he is – and protecting his project through planning
and preparation. One of the guys he had become friendly with during

t spell inside had been ex-military and had told him the
m he lived by in the field.

"Remember your seven 'P's mate". He had told Colin on a few
occasions as they had cleaned the communal areas. *"Prior
preparation and planning prevents piss poor performance"*.

Colin had agreed that this was a good mantra to adopt, and one that
echoed his own way of thinking. He quotes it to himself over and
over now, as he sets up the wireless camera relays back to the main
server in the loft of the house. He needs line-of-sight between
devices for cameras to be able to feed back to the hub, but where that
is not achievable he can set up tiny relay modules which will divert
the signal. It is really quite simple but gives Colin uninterrupted
coverage of the house, the approach routes and much of the
surrounding area – certainly any open ground that unwelcome
interlopers would have to cover. The other possible approach routes
through the woods are covered by the pressure plates and light
beams.

Colin feels very secure in the knowledge that anyone trying to pay a
secret visit would telegraph their approach just as clearly as if they
walked up and rang the front door bell. He takes his security very
seriously, having seen first-hand how switched on the police can be,
and wants as much notice as possible of any visitors whilst he's at
home. He also wants to know in advance if anyone comes calling
when he *isn't* around – he doesn't want to be walking into any nasty
traps, and his system will notify him wherever he is if somebody
does pay him an unwelcome visit.

Dusk is fast approaching and with the installation finished he moves
into testing mode. He's opted for light beams at waist height; this
will eliminate approximately 90% of false alarms where the sensors
might otherwise be triggered by foxes, badgers, squirrels and any
number of smaller animals. Only deer would be tall enough now to

74

trip the alarms, and possibly the odd freak bird activation; he can live with that as it will keep him alert and show the system is working. Similarly he's chosen pressure plates that need upwards of fifty kilogrammes activation weight. A human transfers their entire body weight onto each leg as they walk – more if they are running, whereas few four-legged animals in this country will trigger such a device.

Back inside the house he climbs the pull-down aluminium ladder into the loft space, turns on the system and activates the equipment with the password. He's opted for a musical hint for the password, relying on his sense of pitch to prompt the tune. His memory for digits has always been a little sketchy, but melodies are different. Apparently, he has a highly developed tonal memory, or aural recall as it was sometimes referred to by the music therapist in the prison hospital. The chap had even gone so far as to involve Colin in a series of tests to demonstrate the extent of his perfect pitch, declaring afterwards, somewhat theatrically, that it was *"Absolute"*! With some basic training he was able to state which notes were being played without reference to an external source; something that only a tiny percentage of the population are able to do.

He knows that any computerised system is potentially vulnerable to hacking and the lengthy number sequence he chooses is *343213432161134111143221311*. This complex and un-guessable code sequence makes him chuckle; it's the digital representation of the musical intervals from a song he'd once heard by a band called the Police. The song was called something like *'Every breath you take I'll be watching you'*. Ironically appropriate on a number of levels, he muses, as he punches in the digits.

The first of the bank of four monitor screens flickers and then awakens displaying an alternating dull, grey/green series of images of the world outside the front door. Each of the other screens then follows suit after this, the master screen, has come to full life. Aside from the alternating images from all installed cameras, the master screen shows a number of pictograms or icons which indicate the mode and functionality of the system at any given time. The other three screens are sub-divided into four quadrants and each quadrant represents an area of the yard, surrounding woods or driveway.

He can't help thinking that he's going to all this effort for very little gain, but he's enjoying himself, it's taking his mind off other things – such as his mother – and, well, there are those seven Ps to consider!

Colin plays with the master control joystick, zooming individual cameras and sweeping across the range of images to see if they are all acceptable. Despite the failing light the pictures really aren't bad, and he quickly masters the controls and can isolate different screens at will. He is quite pleased with the quality; he's opted for state-of-the-art cameras, which use VLE (Visible Light Enhanced) technology as well as electromagnetic and thermo-graphic imaging (infra-red). This means that they amplify every tiny amount of light that's available, and – via computer wizardry – combine the results with infra-red imaging. The result is far superior to equipment that just uses one or the other of these technologies and it's almost like looking at a daylight scene.

Panning across the range of cameras, Colin picks up an animal scurrying in the hedgerow alongside the long driveway. It looks like a weasel or a stoat – he can't remember the difference – but it is a clear, sharp image in the near darkness and gives him the perfect opportunity to test the recording facility. On the touch-sensitive master screen he pokes the on-screen *record* icon in the top right corner and it flashes red. He lets it run for a few seconds and then touches the icon again. The flashing image becomes static and white, indicating neutral mode. He hits the playback icon and watches again as the weasel/stoat creeps across the monitor as smoothly as it had, in reality, moments earlier.

Colin touches the erase icon and resets the system to *movement sensor* mode. It would now record any camera which is activated by movement or linked to one of the remote light beam or pressure mat sensors. Instantly a text message will be sent to his mobile 'phone telling him which camera has been triggered, and what has triggered it. He will leave the system set at this default level and decide later if he needs to adjust the frequency of the alerts or the sensitivity settings. It's worth investing this time and effort in security because he intends to be using this place for a considerable time, and for some really quite interesting activities.

Feeling safe and relatively secure Colin descends the ladder, sliding the loft hatch closed behind him and goes to make himself some food. It will be a long, busy night, so he needs to get a good meal inside him. Tonight Colin Furness is going visiting...

23

It's almost 9pm and Colin has spent an age preparing himself for the most important meeting of his life.

He has recently been busy online ordering all manner of hair and beauty products and researching makeup tips and watching blogs and video clips. Now is the time to apply them.

He feels bizarrely excited as, after several practise sessions he sits at the dressing table to commence the transformation for the main event.

Applying foundation and colour to make his normally pale face ruddier and somewhat darker, shaping his eyebrows and shading his cheekbones, using simple tricks that girls learn in their teens to enhance some features and hide others. His nose is even looking smaller through clever application of colour and the blond wig caps a masterpiece of manipulation.

He wishes there was more he could do about his eyes; set so far apart and a dead give-away to anyone who is looking for him. He tries each of the four sets of thick-framed, neutral lensed spectacles, trying to find the pair that will conceal enough of his face to disguise the hypertelorism.

He tries them in varying positions, high on the nose, low-slung and central; with and without baseball caps and hats. He finally settles on the third pair he tried, a deep blue, chunky pair which are plain enough not to draw attention to that part of his face.

He changes into the hospital garb he has purchased from various sources, careful not to dislodge any of his meticulously-applied embellishments and looks in the full length mirror with some satisfaction. He winks at himself, raising his two thumbs in acknowledgement of the successful changes.

Taking the clipboard, stethoscope and fake photo ID badge he makes his way out to the van that he'd taken delivery of today and takes a final moment to compose himself and to go over the plan once more. The ID badge wouldn't pass close scrutiny, but it's good enough as a general prop.

Satisfied that he has done everything possible he starts the engine and heads down the long driveway, checking the two concealed security devices on the way for any signs of unwanted attention. Colin Furness is on his way to see someone who he had for many years thought was long gone from his life.

He's trembling with excitement and fear. Not of being caught necessarily; he's confident that his disguise will fool any casual observer, and he knows they are run off their feet in hospitals these days so nobody will have time for idle curiosity. No, his fear is more centred on how she will react when she sees him; will she recognise her own son? After all, the last time she saw him he was a small boy. Now at over 6 foot tall he is very different. What will she say, how will she react? He needs her to stay calm and not give him away by any overdose of emotion, but at the same time, well, he wants to feel her love.

As he parks the van in the quietest corner he can find in the main car park of St Richard's hospital, Colin thinks one final time through the plan. Maybe he would have been better with the hospital porter idea, after all, they get to push beds around all over the place and he could just locate her, stroll in, wheel her out somewhere quiet and *then* let her see the whole picture. *Oh well; too late now. Let's do this.*
He sticks an extortionately-priced parking ticket inside the windscreen and locks up the van, wondering whether he ought to have worn gloves whilst inserting the coins for the ticket machine – nah; even if his presence is somehow suspected they wouldn't have the resources to finger-print every coin in every parking machine.

Remembering the layout from the online plans he heads straight for the medical assessment ward and, bowing his head slightly to shield as much of his face as he can from cameras and potential witnesses, enters the corridor. The smell reminds him of his brief time recently in the laundry of the Southampton hospital and sets him a little more on edge. He applies some of his breathing techniques to calm his nerves and does that thing where he thinks about something abstract to divert his mind as he was taught to do by the therapists. Diversion therapy, they had called it. His mind is blank.

Think, think, think – that hospital smell, reminds him of Southampton –why do people always pronounce it as if there were two letter '*h*'s in the city name. South *H*ampton is so wrong. South *A*mpton is right. He guesses it would be a tough argument to win, the existence of a West or East Ampton would swing it; he'll research that when he gets home, he likes to be sure of things.

He realises he has managed to divert his mind after all, but the very act of realisation only serves to drag him back to the tense reality of the moment.

Sign.

Medical Assessment Ward.

Here we go.

Very nervous now; no, more like excited.

Without hesitation he walks straight up to the big white plastic doors and pushes the one on the left.

Heavier than he had anticipated.

Heart hammering.

Large square room; beds on all sides surrounded by green plastic curtains.

Most curtains closed.

Impossible to see occupants.

No medical personnel in evidence – relief!

He sees in the bays where the curtains are open that each bed has a small square white board attached to the foot end. The names of the patients are scribbled in red pen on the boards. *Red, blood.*

He can feel his heart racing and hammering in his chest. *Is he going to have a heart attack? Got to calm down.*

He quickly scans all the names on the beds that are exposed but none starts with an F.

Someone can come in at any time. What will he say if challenged? He's forgotten his plan.

OK, time to take a chance.

He quickly heads down the left hand side of the room, brushing the curtains briefly aside at each bed to read the name. Why the fuck don't they have the names *outside* the curtains? Must be a constant series of mistaken fucking identities going on and people getting woken up in error.

Calm down, control your breathing.

Think.
Oh gosh. Third bay, Mrs Furness ...

Without allowing himself time to think, and thus possibly hesitate, Colin tugs the curtain gently aside and enters the small bay, pulling the curtain back into place behind him, quickly checking for any gaps.

The old woman who lies sleeping there looks to be at peace. Her impossibly pale and thin arms lying outside the blankets – *gosh, they still use blankets* – and her hands folded across each other in a position of perfect repose.
She is more beautiful than he remembers.
Age and her hideous years of lonely incarceration have been kind to her. Maybe denying her face exposure to the damage that the sun can do over decades has preserved her skin.
Conscious that he can be interrupted at any moment, Colin nevertheless allows time to stand still and the moment to drift on as he absorbs her image.
He catches himself smiling broadly.
There before him is the very face that he wept for on all those lonely nights while growing from child to youth and then to man. Those countless, immeasurable times he yearned for her touch, her voice, her wisdom and her love.
He leans a little closer, and an unnoticed tear slips from his face and causes a tiny splash on her cheek.
Her eyes open slowly and stare directly into his.

A slight furrowing of her brow as her sleepy brain tries to make sense of what she is seeing. No recognition yet.
Colin slowly removes the spectacles and her eyes become wide, her mouth opens in a silent gasp and her hand leaps to cover it.
'Colin? Colin – oh my goodness, it is you isn't it?'
He's weeping openly now, fluidly; his head nodding rapidly.
Her face splits into the widest smile and she raises her arms to envelop him.
'My precious little boy!'
In the space of a heartbeat the years and all the torments recede and Colin feels like he has found his way home.

24

Δ *The question is not, Can they reason? Nor, Can they talk? But,
Can they suffer* Δ
Jeremy Bentham, 1789

The young cow doesn't have a name, just a plastic tag with the
number D0227.
She is the only female in a shed full of otherwise male calves.
Bullocks – young male cattle – are mostly useless to the dairy
industry and so usually become veal. Occasionally a farmer will
decide that he has enough girl cows for his milk quotas and will also
put females to veal.
D0227 doesn't know this, nor that she has an ear tag, nor that it
identifies her with an invisible electronic microchip giving her
country of origin, herd number and her own unique number within
the herd. The last digits – her internal herd number – are reproduced
in the thick black writing on the yellow plastic tag.

D0227 doesn't know very much at all. Taken from her mother at just
22 hours old she is fed solely on iron-depleted powdered milk
compounds from China. Whilst the anaemia induced by the mineral
deficiency allows many diseases to proliferate, it certainly produces
a highly desirable pale meat for the gourmet restaurants. She knows
nothing of that, nor that the milk intended for her is extracted from
her mother every day and sent to humans instead; the only species on
the planet to harvest the milk of another animal.
All she knows, in fact, is a world of cool semi-darkness where she is
confined to the small area, just a tiny bit longer and wider than her
own body. She'll grow into it. She doesn't yet know just how
familiar she will become with the metal bars that confine her.

She does still have vague memories of her mother; after all, cattle
mums bond with their babies within five minutes – amongst the
fastest of all sentient beings – much quicker than the weeks it takes
for humans to form that critical link. She will certainly have heard,
in those first hours and days of separation, her mother's desperate
bellows as she tried in vain to raise the alarm. *Something's wrong.*

She might have been calling; *My baby has been stolen, <u>again</u>, and I don't understand.*

Her cries were echoed and drowned out by dozens of others who had suffered the same distress in the hours and days before.
And since.
Their shouts will continue for weeks to come, but will eventually fade, along with their memories of the little creatures they had borne for around 274 days, only for that mysterious bundle to be whisked away by the men with the sharp tools and angry boots. Then they'll be artificially impregnated again, and so the cycle of abuse will continue.

Neither the cows nor the calves can possibly know that veal crates have been outlawed in the UK since 1990. That fact seems to sit lightly with the land-owner, Tommy Graves; for *veal crates* is the only appropriate term to describe the tiny enclosures that house the forty bullocks and one cow in the large metal-clad barn on his remote farm in rural Buckinghamshire.

Graves chooses to ignore the international agreements which had been speedily implemented in the UK (if debating a problem for decades can ever be defined as *speedy*). The rest of Europe had dragged their feet for seventeen further years, seemingly unmoved by the trauma suffered by millions of creatures whilst they debated and dallied and dithered. The Americans, being the land of the free, have only so far implemented the ban in two states. Compassionate democracy at its snail-paced best.

These delays put British veal farmers at a distinct disadvantage from Tommy Graves' perspective. Why should he pay more to produce inferior meat? Makes no sense and he is buggered if he is going to tolerate the French farmers in their profiteering, whilst the hard working English guys go down the pan.

No, D0227 knows none of this stuff; only the confines of the crate, the barn, the insipid feed and the harshness of the green or white clad humans.

25

'Mother, don't make a noise, I mustn't be found here. Too much to explain, but let me wheel your bed out of here and find somewhere quiet.'

He realises he hasn't thought through beyond this point, his entire focus was set on finding her and fantasising over the drama of the reunion, as a result he has no idea where he can take her and mentally kicks himself for the failure. *...piss poor performance...*

He tries to move the bed but it won't budge and upon investigation he sees a brake mechanism locking the wheels in place. He struggles to find the release mechanism and when he does the pedal won't shift. He shakes the bed in frustration, half expecting one of the medical team to enter at any moment.

'Leave the bed dear, I can walk fine. Help me up.'

He takes her proffered hand and she leans against him as she slips her tiny thin feet into a pair of hospital issue white paper slippers. She seems to have sensed the urgency and they quickly make their way to the double doors.

'This way; there's a little cafe area where we can sit without anyone interrupting.'

She squeezes his hand with surprising strength.

'Oh Colin, I wondered when you would come. They wouldn't let me come to see you and I can't believe you are here. This is the most wonderful surprise.'

'Don't talk mother, wait until we can relax, save your energy and save your voice, we have a lot to talk about.'

She chuckles.

'Oh I have bags of energy, don't you worry about that, and if I lose my voice we will have to manage with sign language.'

Her voice is older, dryer and frailer sounding but he can feel that old inner strength cutting through. They pass a couple of visitors and an orderly pushing a meal trolley.

'Turn left here. There we are, let's sit over here out of the way.'

The area is more like a wide corridor than a room, semi open-plan but, importantly, deserted.

There are drinks and snacks machines and a wall festooned with posters about diseases and domestic abuse. Other notices inform about research programmes, some requesting volunteers, although the dates imply many must have been long concluded.

Colin doesn't know how to open the discussion; what does she know? What have the police said? The issue is solved with her first statement.
'I understand from the police that my little boy has been a very bad little chap!'
Her twinkling eye and mischievous look relegate the gravity of the situation to the level of a playground spat.
'Ah, yes, well I can explain; or probably not actually...'
'No explaining to do my sweet, but do tell me all about it. How long before you have to disappear?'
'Not really sure, is there no police guard looking out for me?'
'Oh there were a couple of coppers lurking, taking it in turns to watch over me and protect me supposedly, but they told me they had been pulled in to investigate something. They did make it perfectly clear to me how dangerous you are and that if you were to appear I should sound the alarm immediately.' The twinkle is back.
Colin wonders at the strength of the woman. She has lost none of her character and fire; simply amazing after what she has been through.

'Well, let me start at the beginning then mother and we'll see how far we get.'

26

The TV in the police canteen is running a seemingly constant loop on BBC news with a reporter standing before the gates of Downing Street explaining the grounds for the terror threat level escalation. *"...said that so-called Islamic State extremists had obtained the weapons system through disenfranchised elements in Iran and confirmed that if they possess the knowledge to use it we should expect casualties in the tens of thousands. The Pentagon spokesman went on to say that ...."*

'Like we should really be worried – as if those ragheads would know where the fucking on-button is!' Sicknote is predictably disparaging and Samantha feels compelled to put him straight.
'Dave you are so blissfully bloody ignorant sometimes. It's not a nuke, it's a biological agent delivery system and the *on button* you are referring to is a bloody computer programme – they just tell it what to do, no thinking involved. I don't know about you but I am terrified, these guys are seriously dangerous and they don't give a shit about consequences, as long as they get to rule the world with their disgusting prehistoric ideology!'

Colin has been speaking almost non-stop for close to three hours with only occasional interjections and questions from his mother and his own voice is now beginning to crack.

They have covered his childhood, her captivity, his father's death – she was genuinely pleased to learn that the '*accident*' was in fact anything *but* that. They have spoken about horses, chickens, murder, justice and love. They both understand what it is to be wronged by individuals and systems and what it means to overcome those constraints.

Now she is tired and he is increasingly nervous that she'll be missed in the ward, despite them having passed on a message via a friendly porter that she had a visitor and was fine. They are blissfully unaware that the poor health service communications system, so detrimental to public safety is the only thing preventing their discovery.

Colin takes her by the hand and they walk back along the corridors to the ward.

'I am going to be away from the area for a while, so I won't be able to see you. But I will be back in a couple of weeks or so and will be certain to find you then.'

He gives her a small piece of folded paper.

'It's a contact number. The police don't know it's mine, and I will only turn the device on once a week, Sunday at 12.00 UK time – to pick up any messages. After fifteen minutes I'll switch it off again; that will keep the number safe and the police in the dark. If you want to get hold of me in a hurry call the number and leave a message or 'phone at around12.00 on a Sunday and I will answer.'

'Gosh, how modern technology has moved on in the years I was in that dreadful cellar. A kind man was visiting his sister on the ward yesterday and showed me a computer – absolutely amazing! But I'm sure it's all very boring for you youngsters. You will have to show me how it all works when you come back.'

'OK, deal! Until then mother...'

They embrace and he kisses her cheek, then turns and quickly leaves through the same stubborn doors without looking back.

Alone now, the old lady finds herself reliving the last few hours and trying to make sense of her emotions. What does she feel about the man her son has become? How would she feel if she was a neutral, unrelated. The atrocities he has allegedly committed – although he certainly isn't denying anything – are clearly out of kilter with society's expectations. But who's to say what is right and wrong? When he is recaptured (for she has no doubt that he will be sooner or later) the very judiciary who'll be passing judgement would statistically almost certainly be carnivores; maybe supporters of hunting, animal captivity and other abuses; what right would they have to condemn him. Speciesism; the very idea that being homo sapiens is a good enough reason for human animals to have greater moral rights than non-human animals. Hypocrisy. One day, certainly not in her lifetime, things will be different; just like slavery is now largely eliminated. One day animals too will be given the status that they truly deserve.
She remembers the rats who had kept her company for so long underground. At first terrified of them, they had become her companions; her friends. They had individual characters and emotions. Although she knows they are survivors and will be fine as things are, she makes a mental note to make sure they are not forgotten in the turmoil that is her immediate life; they deserve so much more than that. She'll certainly visit them often as soon as she's able to leave this place.

28

He isn't really sure how he feels now about the coming together after all those years. His mum had been frail, sure, but he'd seen enough glimpses of that old strength and depth behind the fragile veneer to feel confident that she'd be able to deal with the psychological shock of release from that cellar dungeon. He's certainly carrying the scars of his own failure to fully investigate the buildings, had he had the strength to explore the area that was always his father's domain he would almost certainly have found her long ago. But the very name given to that part of the farm had been enough to strike fear into him. Ever since childhood *the killing lines*, the area where unimaginable numbers of chickens had met their gruesome demise had given him nightmares. In truth, they still did, only now there was the added torment that his own mother had endured decades of isolation in that very same place; like the chickens, unseen and unheard.

If he's learned anything from all the psychologists he's seen in his life, it's that ruminating over past failures is unhelpful. She is free now, that's what counts, and he had felt a measure of understanding in her words, pride even. Her little boy had grown into a man and followed his heart just the way she had pressed him to do as a small child.

But he is about to desert her again. During his months in prison he had made plans to carry his crusade beyond the shores of England and he is driven to fulfilling those dreams; there are so many wrongs that need to be addressed. He knows he will return to her, and he's pretty sure she understands what drives him, and he will leave safe in the knowledge that she will be with him in spirit.

Now that he's processed those emotions he feels better placed to plan his next moves. He logs on to the *deep web*, seeking and learning.
The data stored on the internet is growing every second of course, but much of this is only accessible on what's known as the surface web. The surface web contains an ever-growing index of something like 100 billion pages.

Colin is searching at a completely different level. The deep web is not generally accessible to standard search engines, due to the way files are indexed, and where he is browsing it is said that the internet holds something like 1.5 Zettabytes – or 1.5 trillion gigabytes. In one of those useless facts that nerds like to calculate he has learned that if all that data was stored in fully-loaded iPad devices, this would equate to a stack reaching 400 miles into the sky.

He is in a sub-section of the deep web known as the dark web, using the Tor Directory search facility. He'd used the Tor Directory to lead him to places where he bought all the useful things he needed, but the deeper he looks now the more he uncovers of that secret, hidden world.

He quickly discovers criminal gangs working through their own versions of media pages, drug traffickers on an immeasurable scale, paedophile rings, openly chatting about what they like to do, and Islamic religious extremist groups, discussing some of the ways that they disagree with Western ideologies.

He learns about *Torchat,* an instant messaging system where a randomly generated sixteen digit ID allows you to chat with other dark web users with absolute anonymity.

He sets up his own Torchat ID and, with a simple process that takes minutes, gains access to a couple of the specialist chat rooms he finds. He spends some time chatting with people on an animal rights activism page. They seem to talk a lot but not really have much substance and his dyslexia makes it slow going; he soon loses interest. In any case, this is not why he came to this murky cyber-world.

Out of interest he creates a log-on and password for group calling themselves Underground Jihad. It's clearly a Muslim group and the chat room is full of talk about direct action against something they keep referring to as *the system*. From the stuff they are writing Colin quickly assumes that *the system* is everything at odds with their own beliefs or anything representing law and order.

Colin has chosen the name '*Fundamentalist*' as a log-on.

The chat room has guests and members and there are little badges that appear next to some of the names. Colin slowly types a question and hits the enter key on his laptop. His log-on name appears with the word *'NUBE'* in capitals followed by his question:

Fundamentalist – NUBE: *Hi guys new here and its intresting*
After a few minutes a response amongst all the other chat;
Mujahid– LEADER: *welcome brother @fundamentalist –we can see that LOL.*
He continues to type:
Fundamentalist – NUBE: *how can you see that?*
Mujahid– LEADER: *says NUBE after yur name bro-tells us UR new* ☺
Fundamentalist – NUBE: *Oh I see and you are the leader?*
Mujahid– LEADER: *haha <u>A</u> leader man, A leader amongst others. Just means I have been here a while doing Allah's work bro.*
Fundamentalist – NUBE: *Oh I see. Well how many people are there here?*
Mujahid– LEADER: *In total like? Wow, most of the world soon bro – fight the right fight right!*
Fundamentalist – NUBE: *Most of the world? Right-fight?*
Mujahid– LEADER: *wow where U been bro? Yep, we planning to rule the roost and U R in the right place bro. Welcome*
Fundamentalist – NUBE: *thanks. How will we do this?*
Mujahid– LEADER: *bro through the strength of purity, quashing the infidels and raising the al-rāya*
Colin has no idea what the al-rāya is – so quickly opens a standard Google search engine. He learns that it's the so-called Islamic State flag or Black Banner.
Fundamentalist – NUBE: *yes I am flying the al-rāya too*
Mujahid– LEADER: *then welcome to the fight bro – we will defeat them all inshallah.*
Again Colin is forced to research this word and sees it's a religious thing about Allah's will.
Fundamentalist – NUBE: *yes inshallah indeed.*
Mujahid– LEADER: *have to shoot bro-things to do ;)*
Fundamentalist – NUBE: *what are you doing-shooting?*
Mujahid– LEADER: *haha no - the shut-down plan bro*
Fundamentalist – NUBE: *shut down?*

Mujahid– LEADER: *shut the slaughter houses*

Wow – Colin is suddenly very excited – shut slaughter houses…these guys may be good guys after all.

Fundamentalist – NUBE: *wow fantastic, need help?*

Mujahid– LEADER: *hey bro we ALWAYS need help. Too many talkers not enough doers.*

Fundamentalist – NUBE: I *am a doer*

Mujahid– LEADER: *good to hear- I'll send you a private chat invite.*

Colin thinks he can put aside his objections to the religious nuttiness and work with this guy. Shutting down abattoirs is a great plan.

Fundamentalist – NUBE: *so what is the plan? Has to be a plan right?*

Mujahid– LEADER: *course there's a plan –part of the master plan. We shut them down one by one leaving just the dhabihah - all brothers can eat safe and pure*

Again, a word he has no idea about...he plays for time.

Fundamentalist – NUBE: *great – I am in then, veggie works for me*

Mujahid– LEADER: *veggie? Oh – haha cool bro-gotta run, laters*

Fundamentalist – NUBE: *good luck then speek later maybe*

Mujahid– LEADER: *defo – now U found us.*

Colin signs off and sits for a while thinking about the experience. He was chatting online! He was writing and it didn't feel as cumbersome as usual, he supposes this is because the nature of chatting online means that words are abbreviated and changed and spelling doesn't seem so critical. He feels that he has achieved something.

Before he forgets he Googles the word dhabihah.

He gets a sinking feeling in his gut. Dhabihah is the Arabic word for the prescribed method of Halal slaughter. So when the guy says he wants to shut down abattoirs one by one leaving just the dhabihah...oh shit. Those guys want to shut down standard slaughter houses – so that *only* Halal facilities exist. The bastards want to ensure that all animals are killed the Muslim way, without stunning. Fuck, fuck fuck. Bastards.

He wonders how advanced the plans are.

There remains one final task for tonight; Colin has an outstanding item on his list, a man-size Gin Trap. It takes a lot more effort to find one of these, but through perseverance he locates a collector who sells gin-traps of all sizes to hunters. Illegal since the 1950s, unscrupulous trappers still operate throughout the British Isles. The term *gin* is thought to originate from the 17th Century word for any mechanical device – *engine*. It's thought that this became shortened through ignorance and laziness. The Gin-trap that Colin has managed to track down is a nasty looking device, designed to be concealed on pathways where poachers and other trespassers might wander. If their foot came into contact with the flat plate a pair of jaws would spring closed and trap their lower leg in an immovable grip. They'd be pinned there until the landowner came along (sometimes days later) and freed them into the arms of the local sheriff.

Colin needs just such a device to teach a lesson to a notorious trapper of unsuspecting animals.

29

Colin picks up the lightly blood-stained business card and dials the number.

'Ello…'

The word is dragged out; spoken in a drawn out tone with much more emphasis on the last syllable than on the first.

'Martyn Bones?'

'Speakin.' Accent again on the wrong syllable.

'Hello Martyn. I was given your number by a mutual friend who said you might be able to help me out with a few rabbits?'

'Oh, OK. How many you after?'

'Only a couple, although I am very partial to tender young ones, can you get hold of any really young ones?'

Boner's business instinct kicks in.

'Hmmmn, not sure; I *may* be able to with some trial and error, they are hard to come by at this time of year so will take me quite a lot of work.'

'Oh, I understand, well I am prepared to make it *very* worthwhile for you, just as long as I get my young rabbit meat. I also want to know exactly where they are coming from, so I can be sure there are no nasty things growing inside them.'

'You mean Myxomatosis? That's pretty much wiped out now.'

'Not just that, I need to know which farm land, because some farmers are a little less scrupulous than others and spray all sorts of toxic substances on their fields.'

Boner explains where he would source the rabbits and Colin mutters his approval, writing down the details in his slow, clumsy hand.

'And will you be able to have these ready in the morning for me? I would reward you very well!'

'Erm, well, if I can get out tonight yes, yes I should be able to do something.'

'OK, I will call you in the morning, got to rush. Good bye.'

Boner is a little miffed, he has, as usual, the mother of all hangovers and at such short notice he won't be able to get anyone to help him tonight, which would make it bloody hard work. Oh well, he'll just make sure the guy pays well over the odds; it sounds as if that won't be a problem, and Boner mentally calculates a top rate and visualises a few things he can spend it on.

Colin actually is in a bit of a rush; he has to head out to where the rabbits will be hunted and find a suitable location for his Gin-trap. He will probably half bury it in loose earth and cover it in leaves, but won't actually set it until just before hunting time; he doesn't want some poor animal straying into its jaws in error.

'OK folks, deja vu and Groundhog Day! Here we all are again, same faces gathered around the same white board and with the same task of catching the same nutter before he commits any murder. Difference this time, we know who he is, we know what he looks like, what he does, why he does it and where he hangs out. So it should be a piece of cake, right?'

There's a muted chorus of *Right Guv.*

'Wrong! Despite all those so-called advantages, we have one significant obstacle; he's a cunning bastard who doesn't want to get caught. I assume also that this time he won't be issuing us with any cryptic clues about where he is hiding, he's slipped up that way before and he may be many things, but he aint completely stupid.'

Neil Dyson pauses for a sip of his lukewarm coffee; looks around at the faces of his gathered team.

'Here's the plan then. First we check out all his known haunts; standard procedure, lots of leg work and sitting around. Then we report back here at 09:00 tomorrow morning. Same as usual people, we'll have a meeting daily at 09:00 here unless otherwise informed. Make it your default position to be here rather than giving never ending lame excuses to be somewhere else.'

He looks at each of the faces in turn and they all hold eye contact. He has a great team and he needs to keep them motivated and on task. Times are tough in an under-resourced force.

'Dave, you and Steph please check out the farm. Get in amongst all the outbuildings as well, check that he hasn't been back there and isn't secretly living under a shed or something daft. Look for signs of anything unusual.'

'OK Guv.'

'Brian and Carol take a drive over to Bosham quay; see if he's been near the boat. Ask around; see if anyone has seen anything out of the ordinary; someone sniffing around, anyone taking little boat trips in the middle of the night. Speak with the harbour master, give him my compliments and invite him to the Anchor Bleu for a pint, if he knows anything he'll be more talkative there!'

'Not encouraging us to drink on duty Sir?' Brian's voice bears an element of hope.

'I will be smelling your breath when you get back, so you decide if you want to make retirement as planned or take it early! Samantha and I will pay the old lady a visit in the hospital; see if she can throw any light on his character. Unlikely I know, she probably knows less about him than we do, but no stone unturned. OK people, let's get to it.'

The team disperses – most of them via a final stop at the coffee machine in the corridor for a take-away.

It's a warm night and the sky is clear, giving light to a brilliant blanket of stars which are rarely seen in the light-polluted towns and cities. Out here though, where artificial light is restricted to the occasional sweep of car headlights on the minor road snaking down to the hamlet two miles away, the stars are an impressive sight.

Tonight there is one other light source; a pair of high mounted powerful halogen spots capable of throwing a beam several miles. These are affixed to Boner's SUV and are currently trained on the tree-line some three hundred metres distant from where a still hung-over individual sits, hot mug of sweet flask-tea in one hand, freshly rolled spliff in the other, window wound right down, engine ticking over and shotgun resting among the empty crisp packets, spent take-away cups and assorted debris on the passenger seat beside him.

He doesn't usually enjoy hunting like this alone, it's tough; driving, picking out the rabbits and shooting without an accomplice, but everything has gone to rat's shit lately and he's actually quite happy for once to keep his own company. He'll finish his tea and joint and then go bag some easy money. Hopefully his hangover will disappear once he gets into killing mode.
The tea is disgusting, as tea from a thermos flask invariably is, and even the additional heaps of sugar don't seem to temper the bitterness and off flavours. He slings the dregs out of the window, flicks the last half inch of spliff after it and selects low ratio 4WD on the gearbox. The field is muddy and bumpy and he doesn't fancy getting stuck in some deep rut all alone.

Edging forward at crawling speed reduces engine noise and gives his bloodshot eyes time to catch any movement in the beams.
Thankfully God gave bunnies little white arses so that they would reflect beautifully in his spots as they bob along munching the grass, oblivious of the big barrel of shit that was about to rip their world to shreds. Not that he tended to shred too many, little point in that, his customers want rabbit meat, not mouthfuls of shotgun pellets. He always uses 7.5 shot which is a favourite for clay pigeon shooters and considered '*weak*' by many. Boner doesn't give a fuck what they

think, a standard cartridge of 28 grammes of 7.5 shot takes a rabbit down pretty reliably, but only really stuns it. The dumb-arse creatures will then kindly lay there quivering until he gets to them and smacks their heads on the bumper of his SUV. Minimal lead intrusion and the head trauma is practically invisible internal damage. It's hard to beat snuffing out a helpless little life with your bare hands when you hold all the aces.

His spots pick out a couple of little white bums hopping across his trajectory about two hundred feet away and he diverts the vehicle to intercept them. He loves the way they advertise their presence with their little white tails. Sitting ducks these little loves, sitting ducks. He grins in the shadow of the cab as he slowly rotates the wheel. The powerful spotlights work their magic as usual by somehow stunning the dumb animals into standing dead still. Needs to be quick now before the surprise wears off and he leaps out, grabbing the shotgun from the passenger seat and staying slightly off to the side so that he's not silhouetted by the powerful beams he jogs swiftly towards the rabbits. It looks like a couple of old bucks; no good for what he wants, the meat will be too tough. Leave them to continue the production line. He heads back to the SUV, cursing being alone; if he had a mate with him one would drive and the other would be stood on the rear seats, body and gun sticking out of the sliding roof, waiting for the targets to offer themselves. That was a far more efficient way to slot the little fuckers. He climbs back into the driver's seat and spins the wheel slowly hard right to head up along the top boundary of the field.

Bingo! A bunch of what look like does with young ones – kittens or just *kits* – about three hundred feet ahead. He pulls forward another twenty feet or so and then yanks on the handbrake.
'*Bingo, bingo, bingo.*' He mutters as he quietly climbs down from the truck, leaving the engine ticking over and begins to follow a wide circle around to the side. He wants to take them all, and knows they will instinctively head back towards the burrows when they sense danger. The burrows will be at the field boundary where the hedgerow is just visible in the distance, so he needs to try to work his way round to get between that border and the bunnies, effectively cutting them off.

He's very keen to get the young ones; what the kits lack in meat volume they make up for in tenderness and are highly prized amongst his clientele. His customer last night was *very* clear on that.

In a good spot now he raises the shotgun to his shoulder; easing off the safety catch as he takes aim when the engine noise on the SUV suddenly changes and the spotlights start to swivel round until he is caught in their dazzling glare.

What the hell? He feels like a stunned rabbit, and at first his brain struggles to cope with this threat; the automatic fight, flight or freeze options are being processed and after initially freezing he snaps out of the temporary trance and throws his arm up to shield his eyes as his befuddled brain tries to work out what the hell is going on.

'Drop the gun or I will blow your testicles into the next field.'

The voice is coming from behind the spotlights and Boner knows that if the owner of the voice and any accomplice are armed, then he has just become the sitting duck. He slowly lifts the shotgun in his outstretched right arm and with exaggerated precision places it on the ground at his side.

'Now step away from the weapon.'

What else can he do? He has no choice and does as he is told.

The voice is slightly higher now, more agitated.

'Lie down and put your hands behind your head. Face the dirt and do not attempt to look up. If you do I shall remove the back of your skull with both barrels.'

Boner is desperately trying to get his brain to work.

OK, so only one guy, otherwise he would have said '*we*' instead of '*I*'. And he said '*both barrels*' so he's armed with just a shotgun. Might be able to take him by surprise, maybe he doesn't know how to use firearms, plenty of fakers don't.

Boner hears footfall close by and feels something cold and hard press into the base of his skull.

He guesses, correctly, that it's the barrel of a gun and starts to tense his muscles to prepare them for action at the earliest opportunity.

'Don't press so hard, that hurts!'

The barrel eases back a touch, then rams home firmer than before.
'Aaargh, that really hurts.'
The voice, higher still with words coming faster now is up and to his left, he needs to try to get his hands into a ready position so he can distract the guy and grab the barrel. First rule in any hostage situation is gain empathy.
'What's the deal man? I was only baggin' a couple of rabbits for the pot – got kids to feed.'

Colin leans harder onto the gun stock.
'How many kids do you need to feed?'
'I have three, all little and all hungry. I lost my job and the missus can't work cos of 'er 'ealth.'
Boner is shaking but thinks he's doing a good job. He's world champion at bullshit so this guy should be easy enough once he gets his heartstrings singing.
'If I don't get them some food tonight we are done for. The landlord is threatening legal action and everythin'.'

'Why do you think it is acceptable to take the life of another creature?'
'They're only fuckin' *rabbits* man – they don't mean nothin' in the big scheme of things.'
'Explain this *big scheme* to me.'
'Easy; humans is top of the food chain and we has the power and the right to take what's rightfully ours – i.e. all the lesser beings.'
'So everything else is of less value than mankind?'
'Yeah, exactly. Course! A couple of rabbits – fuck me, they'll be replaced in the morning the way these bastards breed.'

The pressure on the top of his neck eases slightly, but is immediately returned with even more force.
'Bones, you lied to me about kids and family and the whole stupid landlord bullshit, and you are a twisted scumbag. I am going to remove your tiny, useless brain.'
Alarmed, he thought he had been doing well...
'No don't do that, I'll get whatever it is you need. You need dosh? Drugs? Name it, it's yours.'

'No, all I want is to see your testicles ruptured and then your head explode.'

The barrel pressure is relieved as the gun is moved from his head to a point between his legs.

'Slowly roll away from me one half revolution onto your back.'

Boner realises this is the only chance he'll get. The loony hasn't swallowed his story and is going to slot him here and now. He begins to roll away but suddenly spins in the opposite direction – towards the gunman.

Colin was expecting such an attempt and deftly hurdles the prone hunter, spinning to face him again and laughing at the body splayed out on his back three feet away.

'You are a bigger moron than I thought. Raise your hands along the ground above your head.'

Shaking all over now, Boner does as instructed.

'I am wearing a clever little video camera which has captured the little drama we have just been going through. When I have executed you I shall edit the film and post it online for the world to see. You shall be a star! Now open your legs as wide as you can.'

Slowly Boner complies; *what choice does he have.*

'What you doin' man?'

'Say goodbye to these things in this order. Bunnies, testicles and life. There's a good boy.'

'What the fuck?'

Colin's face suddenly contorts and as he screams spittle splashes down onto Boner's face.

'Say it you shitting little fuckstain!'

Boner is panicking now; sweat dotting his brow and mingling with the madman's saliva.

'Wait, wait; I can't remember what I had to say.'

Colin's voice is instantly calm again.

'Goodbye bunnies, testicles and life, in that order. Nice and clearly.'

Boner's voice, in comparison, is tight, shaky and weak.

'Goodbye bunnies, test...'

The remainder is inaudible and he dissolves into sobs.

'Pathetic useless loser.'

Boner doesn't get a chance to respond as a sharp report scares the rabbits from their supper and a gaping six inch round hole appears in the grass between his thighs, very close to his manhood. He screams and urinates simultaneously.

'You really are pathetic! Imagine how the poor rabbits must feel. OK, well we shall play a little game so that you don't need to *imagine* anything; you are going to *be* the frightened little bunny.'

Colin dips into his bag and removes his reel of duct tape.

'If you move I am going to kill you, if you cooperate I might let you live. Your choice.'

He sets to work immobilising the hunter by taping his wrists behind his back. Next he wraps the tape several times around his lower face and jaw to make a highly effective gag. His final act is to loosely tape the legs together so that there is about six inches of slackness in the tape, enough to allow him to shuffle but not to walk normally.

'Now here are the rules. I am the hunter and you are the little frightened bunny rabbit. In a moment you will be set free to try to get away from me. You *must* hop like a rabbit, otherwise I am going to beat the shit out of your face and we will start again. At my leisure I will come for you with the gun. If I catch you I will shoot you, if you get to the other side of that fence over there then I will allow you to escape. We will pretend that you have a safe place, a burrow. Let's say that deep ditch on this side of the hedge, over there. All the time you are in the ditch I cannot shoot you; it's like your personal little rabbit warren; safe. Agreed?'

Boner wants to shout *You are seriously mental mate, you wanna hunt me? Seriously fuckin' mental*. But the gag prevents this and he simply nods, his tears stinging his eyes.

'But my dear Boner you have no choice. Now I will count to one hundred and then start to come after you. Remember to hop. Beyond the fence and you are free, in the ditch you are safe. One, two, three, four...'

Boner struggles to his feet and starts to shuffle away.

'Uh, uh, uh! Remember, hopping like a bunny!'

Boner hops as instructed, arms tightly bound behind his back, gasping for breath through the taped gag and feeling stupid and demeaned, but mostly shit-scared. The fence is about four hundred feet away on the northern edge of the field and at the speed he's able to hop would take him far too long to reach; the nutter would catch him stuck out in open ground and that would be it. He'll have to take advantage of the time he's been given and use his natural cunning and the darkness to trick the lunatic. At least he knows he is ahead in the intelligence stakes, this bloke is clearly a basket-case and in addition he won't have much experience of the local countryside.

There's no way he can make the fence in the limited time he's been given so he will have to gain more time by getting into the ditch and planning an exit from there. The ditch is less than thirty feet away and he can hear the fruit-cake counting forty-six as he reaches it. In a flash of inspiration Boner decides to do the clever thing and, once in the ditch and out of sight he heads south *away* from the fence and safety.
That will throw the lunatic off the trail

He knows the ditch surrounds three sides of the field, the final border being the fence to the north, which is his ultimate goal. If he stays out of sight and is quiet enough he should be able to work his way down the western edge, along the southern border and up the east side, all the time out of sight and in the '*safe zone*' that is the ditch. When he reaches the fence in the north-east corner he just needs to get over it and, as long as the psycho keeps his word, he'll be free.

'Eighty-three, eighty-four...'

He can't make very fast progress through the overgrown ditch with his legs bound but at least he can shuffle here, out of sight of the freak. Brambles seem to snag everything that moves and he constantly struggles to stay on his feet on the slimy surfaces. The water is deeper here too. Maybe if he can free his hands now he will be able to remove all the tape from around his ankles and get a move on. At the top of the ditch is a barbed-wire fence, if he could get to it he may be able to use the sharp barbs to saw through the tape on his wrists, but climbing the steep, slippery bank in the dark with hands and legs tied proves impossible. He'll just have to carry on along the ditch until he reaches that top corner, hopefully when he reaches that he'll be able to scramble out and roll under the lowest strand of fence wire.

'One hundred, here I come, ready or not!'
In the misty darkness the voice sounds gleeful.

Boner's pulse shoots up another few percentage points as he hears these words. He's made good progress though and is already shuffle-wading along the bottom perimeter; he reckons another five minutes will see him at the point of safety. If only he could see what the freak was doing, but from his low vantage point he can't make out anything in the field, and even if the mist clears the moon is behind a bank of clouds now so it's almost pitch black out here, away from man-made light-pollution.

In the centre of the field Colin fits the night-sight goggles, flicks the switch to activate them and scans the southern perimeter. He knows intuitively that the slippery Boner will have headed that way in some naive attempt to fool his predator. Indeed, he's banking on it. Quietly he starts to make his way over to the eastern fringe where, if he's right, the fool will be heading. Sure enough, as he reaches the edge of the overgrown ditch he hears erratic breathing and splashes down towards the southern edge.
Hunters are supposed to be the experts at concealment, but this one makes such an easy target.
Leg twitch.

Puffing and blowing through his nose at the exertion, Boner is forging his way along the narrow ditch, his tired feet stirring up the mucky water and dragging up mud and plant-life at every shuffling step. As his left foot takes the weight of his body it slips on a different surface; smoother, harder, something solid beneath the weed and there's a simultaneous mechanical *click* sound. Suddenly the water seems to leap up towards him and there's an immediate excruciating pain in his mid-calf. He stumbles and falls, trying to see what is causing the agony and sees his left leg clamped in the huge jaws of a man-trap. He screams through the gag and his hands desperately try to reach down to his ankle to relieve the crushing, biting pressure, but he can't do anything with them bound behind his back and every movement seems to make the vicious contraption dig even deeper into his soft muscle tissues.

He must try to stifle his moans, if he doesn't get away from here the psycho is going to track him down and kill him. Yet try as he might, the sprung device is just too strong and the pain excruciating; in the numbing cold and wet, any strength that remains in his exhausted body is slowly ebbing away. Frantically he gropes around in the freezing foot-deep stinking water behind him for anything he might use to jam between the jaws of the trap and lever the huge teeth apart, but the ground is clear.

Just out of reach he can see stout branches that might make a leverage tool to free him, but bound as he is there's no way he can do anything. He's crying tears of frustration when sounds swishing through the tall grass and undergrowth above him make him hold his breath. At first he hopes it might be a deer or badger, but a cry of dismay and fear escapes through his chattering teeth when the tall figure looms out of the darkness and stands ten yards away, simply staring down at him through some evil, mutant eyepiece.
The psycho has the shotgun broken over the crook of his arm and just stands there, staring at him vacantly.
Well go on then; get on with it; shoot me if you're going to!

Still the monster just stares. It's the scariest thing Boner's ever seen. Then he speaks in that voice too high for his frame.
'What's it feel like to be trapped? Helpless? Ensnared and frightened of what's coming next?'
He edges a little closer and lays the shotgun on the ground.
Opening the shoulder bag he removes something.
'No, don't tell me; tell the camera.'

Boner can see that he does in fact have a video camera and he's setting it up on a telescopic tripod. Less than a minute later he's ready. Colin reaches down and removes the tape around Boner's mouth.

'OK, here's what we'll do; I am going to give you a tourniquet and a small, flimsy serrated saw. Then I am going to go for a nice cup of coffee, a warm bath and then a nice hot meal. I will be gone exactly four hours. When I return I am going to gut you alive with my little penknife. Is that clear?'

'You're fuckin' insane mate; that's what's clear. What's the tourniquet and the saw for then, if you are gonna kill me anyway?'

'I'm sure even someone with a brain the size of a rat's gonads can work that out, Boner...let's put it this way; if you are still here when I return you will die a slow and terribly painful death. The saw is nothing like strong enough to do anything to the trap, and in any case, this camera is monitoring – and recording – your every action, and I shall be watching you pretty much constantly via an App on my mobile telephone. If you make even a *single* attempt to damage the trap I shall come straight here and gut you, very slowly. Clear?'

'I don't get it, what you waitin' for? Just do me in now then, what else can I do?'

'Oh god you really are a moron. Think about it Houdini, what would a fox do if it was stuck in a leg-trap and the hunter was coming for him?'

Furness springs down into the water with his little penknife open and Boner is convinced he's going to carry out his threat here and now, but the tall man stoops and cuts through the tape around his wrists.
'Bye-bye – four hours remember, better get sawing!'

Boner is a little confused, he has been told he can't touch the trap, yet now he's supposed to *get sawing* – what is he supposed to ...*oh no, he doesn't expect him to...oh good god, surely not that...*

Radio 4 is playing quietly on the veranda where Jenny is sitting in the near darkness reclining in her rocking chair breast-feeding little Samantha. She catches something the newsreader says and leans over to turn up the volume a notch.

"... a fire and rescue spokeswoman said that it was fortunate that, due to the time that the fire broke out, the abattoir was almost empty of livestock as most animals are brought in only when required. It's thought that around fifty sheep perished in the flames and those which survived all suffered extensive burns and smoke inhalation and will have to be destroyed. The fire broke out in the enclosed yard at the rear of the site and whilst the cause is being investigated the police said there are suspicious circumstances and that they are not ruling out a link to a similar fire in an abattoir in Shropshire last month. A short time ago a video was posted on social media by a group calling themselves Dhakat – an Arabic word which refers to the way animals are ritually slaughtered. This group is apparently known to the security services and is claiming responsibility for the fire. The video shows masked people in black robes and waving the so-called Islamic State flag and chanting in Arabic. I should make it clear that the claims of this group are not yet substantiated...."

She ponders the phrase 'will have to be *destroyed'* – clearly animals are in a sub-category of life forms; what is it with humans that we are able to think of non-human creatures in terms of possessions; articles. It's clearly aligned to the way these religious nutters view everything that isn't in their exact image and this new development in the world of horrific crimes is evidence of that. She wonders whether her husband Neil will be dragged away from the Colin Furness case as many of the other senior officers seem to be these days to investigate one of these incidents in the ever-growing wave of religious hate crimes – if that's what this one is – it certainly bears all the hallmarks.

She has a divided opinion really; she wants Colin Furness back where he belongs before he can harm anyone else, and believes Neil's team is the best to achieve that. They know the way the guy thinks and acts and the team has a few key characters who are really able to understand the criminal mind and anticipate next steps. Not many police units have that capability in her experience. And yet, these fanatical nutcases are springing up all over the place and clearly there's an urgent need to stop them in their tracks before they gain momentum and do some real and lasting damage. She knows that they have the potential to do far more harm than the lone renegade animal-rights loony, but with Furness it became very personal when he kidnapped her and put her through those horrific experiences.

She looks at the little face of her daughter and knows that, in her heart, she wants Furness back behind bars more than anything. Something niggles her and she feels an odd sensation which she can't express in logical terms; call it a gut feeling, an irrational fear that the psycho might be planning some kind of revenge upon her and Neil.

Colin doesn't go for a coffee or anything else, preferring to stay in the killing area. He sits in Boner's cab, observing the scene in the field unfolding via the mobile camera App. Watches the filthy scab lying there weeping – although there's no audio, it's quite clear what he's doing – and then sees the ex-hunter slowly study and then fit the tourniquet, sees him stare into the camera, then take up the tool and make the first painful cut below his knee with the flimsy saw. It's a wonderful study in human behaviour and he witnesses the guy collapse to the ground time after time, the pain clearly so intense that consciousness deserts him. Then he recovers, cries some more, his head thrown back, then another, single cut, drawn quickly across the limb, firm as he can stand to make the most headway into first the delicate skin, the nerve ends and then the fragile muscle and sinews and finally, with much bravado and psychological self-cajoling, the stubborn robust tibia or fibula – Colin can't remember which is which, but he'll need to do both to get free.

There's an awful lot of blood despite the tourniquet which has to be refitted a couple of times when the sheer messiness of the task makes it slip, and Colin is pretty comfortable that shock and cold are going to get the bastard before he cuts himself free. He decides he wants a piece of the fun and strolls back to the place where Boner is laying, whimpering in the mud.
'So finally you get to see it from the snared animal's perspective Bones. Many trapped creatures, faced with endless days of agonised waiting will do exactly what you've been trying so miserably to achieve; they'll gnaw off their own limb rather than lay and wait until the evil hunter comes for them. Sometimes they are too late and get caught anyway. Imagine going through that entire trauma only to get caught after all. Well, you don't need to imagine it; I've caught you. Yep, I am early, but then I have some doggies to release and you were a moron to take me at my word. Goodbye Boner, give my best regards to all the devils in hell.'
The simultaneous double shot from just behind Boner's head is taken at point-blank range and fragments of his shattered skull and brains are rammed a foot deep into the wet earth at very nearly 1200 feet per second.

It's much easier than he'd thought to edit, add text commentary and upload the video anonymously online. He chooses two of the most popular websites and calls himself *The Free Radical*. He creates a new email address through the Hushmail system and hides his IP number via Tor. All that remains is to disable JavaScript and any other proxies or add-ons and he's safe. He types '*about:config*' into the Tor browser and toggles Java off. There's a slight hitch, in that the videos won't run on his machine with Java disabled, but that's no issue; that won't affect the viewers' experience and he knows all too well what the films contain!

The counter shows that within five minutes the Boner film is viewed seventeen times. Wow! That is impressive! He's going to enjoy educating the world about the torments animals must endure at the mercy of human hands through a series of graphic videos. His left leg does that wriggly thing and he claps his hands quietly a few times.
Colin old chap, we are on our way! Now for something altogether kinder.

35

*Δ Atrocities are no less atrocities when they occur in laboratories
and are called medical research Δ*
George Bernard Shaw

The modern building smells of bleach and some kind of scented soap. Sterile; not really what he'd expected. Colin takes the electronic key card and swipes it across the reader at the next door in the long, windowless corridor. The lighting is subdued at this time of night; the security guard probably uses his torch when he does his patrols. He wouldn't be patrolling tonight, it's difficult to do that when you are bound, gagged and locked in a cleaner's cupboard.

The door makes a subdued *bleep* as the key card activates the mechanism and it silently swings open before him on an automatic ram. The corridor leads around to the left in a huge sweeping arc, testament to the modern design and the opulence of the place. Money aplenty, it would seem. Three more doors on the left and then he will have to use the code and the key card together.
The security guy – a direct employee, and thus fair game in Colin's book – had been reluctant to divulge the four digit code, but, immobilised and watching helplessly as Colin removed his right hand little finger with the bolt croppers his resistance had evaporated. He had offered up some other snippets, hoping that Colin might spare his left thumb, but the thumb had come off anyway; better to demonstrate an absolute devotion to the task than risk the little shit getting all heroic and inappropriately brave. In any case he'd be worried shitless that he was going to slowly bleed out. That shouldn't be happening; fingers and thumbs don't leach that much claret and anyway he'd be frying before then.

The bleep prompted by the key card is the same pitch as the other doors and each of the digits of the code creates a different electronic tone. 1356. The tones are identical to the first four notes of the hymn tune *Jerusalem*. Colin appreciates that; it will make remembering them much easier if he needs to get into this research facility again.

There's also some kind of delicious irony, but he can't quite work out what, nor does he really care; it's just interesting.

Research? He knows that the test results are practically useless in human terms. That has been proven time and time again by the world's top scientists. The problem is that political parties receive huge financial support from the companies which sponsor these institutions, and then reciprocate by issuing obscene amounts of money in grants and rubber-stamped sponsorship deals. Wheels within wheels and the animals suffer with their health and their lives. The monsters who frequent such establishments and undertake their hideous tests on sentient creatures stand to gain nothing scientific. But they get rich from it and build professional reputations amongst their equally demented and emotionally void peers.
Colin is about to strike a blow to all that.

He takes the video camera from the case around his neck and turns it on, filming now as he walks. Opening the final entry door he steps into a surreal world of horror. The place smells like a hospital and yet against the underlying calmness the terrified, quietly whining animals are testament to ongoing torture of unimaginable degrees.

Twenty Beagles.
Some mere puppies and others older dogs; they will have spent their entire lives in this place; known nothing other than the small boxes that are their prisons. The camera scans the room, capturing reality; sanitised truths denied and hidden for far too long.

Twenty beautiful, passive and friendly dogs, highly intelligent and therefore attractive to these fiends that torture them for no net scientific gain, sit or cower in tiny glass enclosures. Some free to move as far as the confines of the boxes would allow, a few clamped by the head to horrific looking machines which take constant readings as an intravenous line feeds some unknown liquid into its host. Colin has mentally prepared himself for the horrors he'll find, but still struggles to process the stark reality. Telling himself to concentrate now, he goes to work freeing the dogs, the video camera now attached to him via a headset.

Most of them pull back into the sanctum of their little boxes, wary of this tall strange human. After all, humans mean only one thing, pain and chronic discomfort, why would they trust him? However could they.

And yet, dogs seem to have an irrepressible inbuilt desire to befriend mankind, it's inherent in their nature, probably bred into the species over millennia and one or two of the younger dogs, those not yet so relentlessly abused and conditioned, venture out and begin to sniff around, their natural inquisitiveness taking over. Colin tries to encourage these with soft words and small handfuls of treats.

Before too long he has a wagging line of followers and feels a little like the Pied Piper, except in this case no children are going to disappear, a few little doggies might though!

In the farthest corner from the door a young Beagle puppy lays; completely restrained on her back by straps around her head and limbs, her tail has been completely removed – probably to save the inconvenience of having to clamp it down every day – and her head held totally immobilised in a nasty looking stainless steel fixture.

With a dozen or so eager dogs sniffing around his feet Colin opens the box that secures her and looks to see how he can free her. He can see a series of hoses and cables bundled together in a crude multi-core system and each is connected in some way to a part of her body. One is a catheter, one feeds directly through her abdomen into her stomach, this implies food and bowel functions are being 'cared for' and that in turn implies a long-term situation. He wonders how long she's been held like this, unable to move.

Her eyes are staring hopelessly up at him as if to say *Go on then, stick something else into me; use my body up some more, my mind is already somewhere else.*

He feels around the cold steel head clamps and notices now a metal spike of some kind sticking directly into her head, it looks a bit like a four inch nail penetrating her skull and must be some kind of brain probe. Colin does a little dance of frustration. What will happen if he removes that? What about all these other tubes and cables, he will

certainly cause her pain, but will he kill her? Will that be a better
outcome than leaving her here like this?
Certainly it will; he absolutely couldn't live with himself if he had to
abandon her here.

OK, time is ticking and indecision is the enemy. *Which intrusion to
tackle first*. He thinks through his basic knowledge of first aid and
life saving techniques.
Breathing is most critical.
Breathing and heart function.
OK. Fuck it. Mumbling an apology and other indeterminate soft
sounds he gently takes the catheter and pulls it easily away from her
body.
No drama there.
Next the stomach tube – if indeed that is what it is. It's a little
tougher to move, but comes away slowly with a slurping sound,
spraying droplets of a brown liquid onto his hands and the nearby
surfaces.

Some cables linked to metal plates glued to her head come away
quite easily. Brain sensors of some description; the fur beneath them
shaved clean and the skin red from constant contact or soreness.
Another couple of tubes, one set deep into her nose causes her
obvious discomfort. She is still strapped down for her own benefit
and unable to move, and yet despite her terrified eyes she lays there
and takes it, no yelps or whines escape her lips as if she senses
somehow that he is here to help.

So far so good, but the big one still looms before him like an
impossible task. He is sure in his mind that this will, at best, be
agonising to remove, and at worst, well, he doesn't want to think
about that. But he knows the alternative is to leave her here, and that
is not an option. He will leave this place with her, or he'll stay with
her until the end. He'd rather be caught red-handed here than leave
her to die alone.

Gently he places index finger and thumb around the thin metal spike,
surprised at how warm it is; hot almost. Maybe it carries some
current, or maybe it's just heat transference from her body.

Looking into her eyes to try to detect any sign of discomfort he applies gentle pressure, trying to ease the thing out of her skull. Her eyes blink rapidly and she licks her lips. What does this mean? Pain? Hope?

The damn thing is stubborn and hasn't budged at all. Applying a little more pressure he sees the straps around her head strain as her muscles stiffen. He utters more soothing words, desperately trying to tell her that he is a friend, here to end the suffering. He wishes he'd brought pain relief.

OK; time to end this torment, little doggy.
He grips the probe and pulls smooth and hard. Her eyes blink rapidly as the thing slowly withdraws, seeming to go on forever. Finally it's all out and her eyes are closed. He doesn't know what that means; maybe she fainted from the pain - do dogs faint?

Quickly he loosens the straps around her legs and head and, free now he gathers her up into his arms. He'll take her away from here and see if she's alive or dead, but he isn't going to waste any more time in this place than he needs to. In the corner is a lab bench with gas fittings – like the Bunsen Burners of his school days, only modern and part of the fixtures. Cradling the young Beagle in his left arm he opens the tap to allow gas to slowly escape, presses the ignition button and arranges a load of plastic laboratory equipment around and over the flames.
The released dogs are now all following his every move as if wanting to be even more closely involved in the great laboratory breakout.

He activates the door to leave, and wedges it open with a fire extinguisher, enjoying the irony.
As the unusual crowd make their way around the curve of the long corridor the fire alarm activates. He curses momentarily, he should have deactivated it before igniting the stuff, it'll be linked via a red care line to a monitoring station. This means that once the monitoring station verify that it isn't a false alarm there will be emergency services on the way. Probably within two minutes. He'll have to leave the security guy for them to discover – and so what if

they don't? Just another part of the universal animal abuse system neutralised.

Once outside the dogs follow him across the car park, sniffing at this new, strange air; those that can, trotting off to explore. Despite the urgency Colin takes a moment to enjoy the spectacle of a bunch of animals experiencing freedom for the first time. In some cases these animals have been locked away from the world for ten or more years and the older dogs seem at a loss to comprehend what they are experiencing. If he didn't have his arms full and the time pressure he would love to video this moment more extensively – the headset camera is still running but capturing it in better quality would make a great PR film.

Oh well, he'll get them away from here and then edit the short film later.

Come along doggies, come with Uncle Colin....

With handfuls of treats he leads them to the big white van and they follow without a moment's hesitation, picking, sniffing and nibbling away as if out for a Sunday stroll, with those that can jumping straight into the back through the big open doors and laying down as if this were an everyday occurrence. Others have to be helped up, which is a little tricky with one hand, but within a minute they are all safely ensconced in the vehicle and he gently closes the doors, double checking that they are secure.

Colin opens the passenger door and lays the still body of the young Beagle on the seat. He wipes a little blood and mucous from the site on her head where the probe was inserted and bends down and kisses her nose. Rushing now round to the driver's door he starts the engine, driving straight through the yellow and red striped plastic pole that was a barrier to the site but now disintegrates behind him as he pulls left out of the main gate, exercising haste whilst sacrificing the comfort of his passengers, who will be thrown around a little in the back. In the distance to his right he sees a fire engine rounding the corner.

Just in time Colin, not a moment too bloody soon! He smiles and taps out a little rhythm on the steering wheel, his left leg doing that customary little dance above the clutch pedal.

117

A couple of miles down the road he pulls over and takes out a pay-as-you-go mobile and hits the stored number for the local activist he had contacted earlier. He knows her only as Barbara M.

'Barbara, the deed is done; you can collect at your leisure as agreed. There are twenty in all, but one I think is not going to make it.'

'You bloody hero! Thank you so much. Don't you ever hesitate to call in the favour – anytime, anywhere.'

'Haha, maybe I will. Listen, do you have access to a good vet?'

'Yes, leave it with me.'

'OK, Money is no object, just get the best you can, I want to give this little girl every chance to make it after what she has been through.'

He disconnects the call and removes the battery. He knows she will be at the meeting point within the hour with her small team of animal rights activists, although he'll be long gone. The police won't know anything until the lab staff turn up to verify that all their animals are missing. If there is enough left of the building to be able to do that.

Either way, he doesn't give a single fuck.

36

△ *As comforting the song of an angel*
Calming the rage of the caged animal
And setting it free
That same angel's song heals the enraged caged animal's
Wounds inside of me △
Jacob Frey

In her crate D0227 munches slowly upon the solid steel bar that runs in front of her nose. She wonders if the bars run all around her, but can't turn her head enough to see. Her legs are aching and her feet hurting from standing for so long, but when she had lain down before it had taken all her strength and energy to rise again, and she sees other cattle opposite, all lying on their bellies and unable to rise again, their legs useless now. She will resist as long as she is able.

Wrapping her long, rough tongue around the cold bar she wonders if she will see her mother again soon. She can hear her calling the whole time, being unable to run to her is beyond her understanding. Distressed, she chews some more on the oddly comforting cold hard metal.

37

It's high tide when he reaches the quaint little quay and Colin unpacks a small inflatable dinghy from the van to ferry his equipment across the expanse of water to his motor yacht. He's still nervous about using the boat, but reminds himself for the umpteenth time that the harbour fees are paid up well in advance and with its mid-channel mooring there's no real reason for anyone to even notice it's gone. The police never seemed interested in the boat once they'd completed their investigation and his questions upon his arrest about what happens to his property were largely brushed under the table, leading Colin to believe that there are, in fact, no robust policies. That can only work in his favour. If nobody has been allocated the job of checking up on his things then probably nobody will. His escape from jail will change that and he feels sure that someone will think of checking all known contacts and associated geographical areas. But he can only hope for the best, he doesn't have time to buy a new boat and go through all the complex registration and licensing nonsense. Far better to take the small risk and get the hell away from here.

Once he's left Chichester harbour he'll be pretty much invisible in any case and there are hundreds of little landing places in France. He might even head further south to Portugal, that is closer to where he ultimately wants to be. He'll probably skirt the Bay of Biscay, follow the Portuguese coast a while and then sink the boat and head across land into Andalucia. That's where he has information about an Angora rabbit farm that supplies all the big retail houses. That is where he plans to strike his next organised blow in the unfolding chapters of his fight for the voiceless.
It's unimportant to him which route he takes, as long as he stays away from the law and keeps himself safe, and in any case, the world is pretty much wide open to a guy with a boat, a false passport and a plentiful supply of ready cash.

Within ten minutes he has the small dinghy inflated via a mini compressor that plugs into the vehicle's 12v outlet. It's designed for tyre inflation at the roadside and he's relieved to turn the little compressor off; the damned thing is so noisy that he's sure it will have been heard from a long way off. But it's quiet here in this sleepy Sussex village, as usual, and he hasn't seen any signs of nosey people. Nevertheless, he wants to get away as quickly as he can and lose himself in the anonymity of the sea. With renewed vigour he begins to stow the equipment.

With the little tender loaded to the gunwales and the sharp, salty tang of the sea in his nostrils he eases away from the slipway at the edge of the quay. He has two oars but no rowlocks, he couldn't find the bloody things and makes a mental note to '*borrow*' some on the second trip and tie the things to the boat frame so they don't get mislaid again. Rowing this way is cumbersome but the tide is very gradually on the ebb and he practically just drifts with it, letting nature and the moon's draw carry him almost silently out towards mid-channel where he'll meander along the moored boats until he reaches *Salty Pig*.
He'd last seen the little yacht in his final hours of freedom prior to his arrest. He had taken his last kidnap victim there, Jenny, the fiancé of the detective Neil Dyson. She had surprised him with a ferocious attack that had left him temporarily damaged and incapable of thinking straight, having basically sleep-walked into a trap. Well, no such mistakes would be made this time around. One lives and learns.

The hulls appear above him as he drifts among the bigger boats and the fourth in line looms with the name *Salty Pig Runs Free* emblazoned across the stern. He gently slows his progress towards her, cushioning with an oar against the gentle current and allowing his dinghy to be taken down the port side where he'll locate the small stainless steel pull-down ladder.

He has the tender secured by an old blue nylon rope and the goods offloaded without drama and is soon on his way for the second trip. Despite the lighter load the going is a little tougher against tide and the slight breeze. One more after this should do it, he hopes.

On the next journey he procures a pair of rowlocks from an upturned wooden dinghy on the quay, cutting the string that holds them in place with his pocket knife. Rowing is a lot easier with the right gear and he is soon back for the final time. He needs to hide the van so he loads the dinghy with the last of his supplies and leaves it behind a low wall, just afloat on the fast ebbing tide, tied off to one of the ancient oak piles that dot the muddy shoreline, remnants of King Canute's futile attempts to hold back the waves..

Now he falls back on his local knowledge; only a few hundred yards from the little harbour are a couple of little-used chalk tracks that lead behind houses to an old boat maker's yard.

As a child Colin had come here to Burnes' Shipyard to marvel at the skills of the craftsmen and dream of sailing the world. Now he drives around the derelict site into an old shed which used to hold a traction engine under restoration. Apart from his van it's empty now and he closes the weather-beaten wooden door to conceal the vehicle, prior to embarking on a journey he could never have dreamed of as a kid.

Back on the *Salty Pig* he sticks the blade of his pocket knife into the air chambers of the little inflatable. He has another already on board so it's only taking up room. The blue nylon rope is untied and the dinghy released to the mercy of the sea. He wonders how far she will float, or maybe she'll sink nearby and spend her days rotting alongside the mythical Bosham Bell.

Colin makes his way down below to assess the situation and see that the boat is functional. As long as the motor is good he will be able to tolerate any minor inconveniences. With the fuel line and batteries connected the motor fires up first time and he smiles as he slips the mooring and heads on the outgoing tide for the mouth of the harbour and the busy lanes of the English Channel.

France here we come…or maybe Portugal or who knows!

38

D0227 blinks as the harsh light is shone directly into her eyes. The man in the white suit pulls her teeth around and squirts a big syringe full of foul tasting chemical down her throat. As he moves on to the next stall she tries to reach the gutter to get a drink to wash away the taste, and gets a wellington boot in the face for her trouble. The man in green is the one who likes to kick them, he seems to enjoy kicking her head and he shouts something repeatedly at her as he kicks, she doesn't understand what he wants her to do and she can't move any way, she certainly can't retreat from the attack.

The assault stops when the white-coated man comes back. This time he sticks a long needle in her back, between the shoulder blades and she feels the cold liquid enter her bloodstream. She doesn't know what antibiotics even are, just that she's had this one before and knows it makes her feel sick, but what can she do.

39

Sicknote and Steph are back at the farm. They've checked all the outbuildings and inside the farmhouse. The last area is the huge barn structure where the monster Colin Furness had held his captives in tiny cages for a number of weeks whilst he terrorised the land with his outlandish demand that the world should stop eating animals. They are looking for anything that might indicate recent activity. It's quite common for murderers – especially where there is evidence of significant psychological disturbance – to return to the scenes of their crimes.

Entering the huge structure they are both acutely aware of the first time they'd walked through the doors and the sights and smells that had greeted them. The place had resembled a human zoo, and the babbling prisoners had been squatting in their own filth for the entirety of their captivity.

The smell is almost gone now, but not the memory. They look at each other and without uttering a word each knows what the other is thinking.
'Let's get this over and done with quickly Steph; I don't want to spend a minute longer in here than I absolutely have to.'
'Gets my vote, Sarge.'

They check around the external walls, the cage area where the victims had been confined and finally upstairs in what Furness had called his *control room.* From here, via a huge panoramic window they can look down over the entire barn area.
'The twisted fucker must have felt like a king.' Steph mutters.
'Master of all he surveys! Come on, nobody's been here in months. Let's get some fresh air.'

Meanwhile, at the hospital Neil Dyson and Samantha Milsom are interviewing old Mrs Furness. She's in poor health and seems elusive when questioned about her son.
'How would I know where he might go Inspector; after all, I haven't seen him for twenty odd years. You kept us apart and you must

know him far better than I. But you be sure to tell him that I am very proud of him whenever you see him next!'

Samantha is first to jump in:

'What specifically are you proud of, Mrs Furness?'

The old lady has a twinkle in her eye that seems to contradict everything the doctors have told them about her health.

'I am very proud that he stands up for what he believes in and follows his heart. If more of us would do that the world would be a far nicer place Sergeant; don't you agree?'

Samantha is clearly unconvinced.

'I think it would be a better place if everyone obeyed the rules of the land, Mrs Furness, but living the vigilante lifestyle and taking the law into your own hands is not the answer. Especially not the way your son chooses to do things.'

'I'm not so sure he had much of a choice really young lady; society has dealt him a pretty rough hand and he's making the best he can of it. If he upsets a few crooks on the way then so be it!'

Dyson reddens: 'Crooks?'

'Indeed! All those people were bad eggs!'

The old lady exaggerates a cough.

'And now, if you'll excuse me I really should get some rest.'

The two detectives exchange weary glances and bid their farewells with a final reminder that her son is dangerous and should not be trusted, should he be so silly as to make an appearance.

Back in the car they have stronger views.

'She bloody knows more than she's letting on Samantha. Pull the CCTV from the place, let's see if she's been having any odd-eyed visitors late at night shall we?'

'OK Guv. She certainly seems to know about some of his deeds, and we haven't told her.'

'Yeah, but the local papers were full of it and everyone who steps foot inside that place knows who she is now. She'll have had the full gamut of local knowledge. She will know all the gory details. No, what puzzles me more is her acceptance of it all. She genuinely seems proud of the fruit cake. Maybe she's as daft as a brush too.'

'Wouldn't you be after twenty odd years alone in a cellar playing cards with the rats? I'm amazed she holds it together at all. Why isn't she desperate to see her son after all that time? We know how much she loved him.'

'Exactly! That only convinces me more that she's seen, or is still seeing him. Let's get the cameras checked out and I'll see what we can do to reinstate the hospital guards. If he's making regular trips back here to see the old bat then he'd be far easier to catch than running around the bloody countryside.'

On the quayside at Bosham the other two members of the team, Brian Liddel and Carol Saunders are interviewing the harbourmaster and seem for just a moment to have struck gold.

'So you would definitely know if it had been moved to another mooring?'

'Like I said officer; there's a waiting list at Bosham as long as your arm, there *are* no vacant moorings and ergo it can't have been moved to one. It's either been stolen, or the owner has sailed into the sunset. I can't recall having seen it in the past week, so it's probably miles away by now.'

'Don't you make daily checks?'

The harbourmaster laughs and sweeps his hand around in a circle as if to indicate the size of his patch.

'Is there any way to track a boat's movement?'

'Not a craft of this size no. The international Maritime Organization's *International Convention for the Safety of Life at Sea* requires AIS to be fitted to all vessels with a gross tonnage of 300 or more and all passenger ships, but small craft like...'

Carol interrupts him.

'AIS?'

'Automatic Identification Systems – a kind of GPS tracker.'

'Ah! OK, thanks. So unless someone has seen it we have no hope?'

'That's about the long and the short of it, yes. Might I ask, why all the interest again in this boat?'

'Just an enquiry sir, tedious police legwork.' Liddel replies as he looks around for any CCTV which might give them some visuals; there's nothing on show.

'No CCTV on the quay?'

'Nothing like that here, no; we pride ourselves on a low crime rate here in Bosham.'

Brian shares a raised-eyebrows glance with Carol then turns to look at a chart on the harbourmaster's office wall.

'OK; so, based on your experience, where might someone head if they wanted to lie low for a while?'

'You can pick any number of tiny harbours from here to Cornwall – or in the other direction round Dover and beyond. But why stick to UK? He could go anywhere with that little cruiser. He's probably half way to the Bahamas by now!'

Carol groans.

'OK, thanks for your time.'

She hands him a card with her contact details.

'Do you have a number in case we need you in a hurry?'

He scribbles his details down on Sailing Club headed notepaper and the two detectives leave the office.

'Don't look so glum Carol. At least we know he has his boat and he's not here!'

'Well we don't know that for absolute certain, the boat might have been nicked.'

'True enough, but let's assume he's done a runner and get onto our Coastguard friends with some details. I'll drive, you make the call. On the bright side, I suppose that means there'll definitely be no more hospital watch for us again!'

Colin links to his remote internet connection and logs onto the Tor network. Within a minute he's negotiated the route to the dark web and sees that the leader is online.

Fundamentalist – NUBE: *Greetings*
Mujahid– LEADER: *good to hear from U again bro*
Fundamentalist – NUBE: I *gather that will have been you I saw on the news*
Mujahid– LEADER: *couldn't poss comment* ☺
Fundamentalist – NUBE: I *had a little party to selebrate (by the way I am dyslexic-sorry about any spelling mistakes)*
Mujahid– LEADER: *haha no sweat bro-spellings go to rat shit on here anyway. So U up for a trip with the bros?*
Fundamentalist – NUBE: *Bros?*
Mujahid– LEADER: *haha the brothers man, the crew. The doers. Or R U just talker?*
Fundamentalist – NUBE: *no I am a doer too.*
Mujahid– LEADER: *cool. We are planning big shit and need dedicated bros.*
Fundamentalist – NUBE: I *am in. Just tell me where and when.*
Mujahid– LEADER: *Will do bro. Won't be 4 a while-stay tuned.*
Fundamentalist – NUBE: *How do you no you can trust me?*
Mujahid– LEADER: *U found us here and that's a big start. We have eyes and ears and imposters will be dealt with harshly. Don't be an imposter. Gotta fly- laterz.*
Fundamentalist – NUBE: *yes, OK*

Colin finds the silly online terms ridiculous but realises he needs to start to use them in order to be more convincing. He needs to stay in touch with this guy and get inside their organisation. He isn't sure what it will take to be trusted, he assumes there's some kind of test. Tests can be fudged.

'OK, OK, settle down gang. Two nights ago we had a murder in the fields north of the B2146 at Adsdean. Victim was one Martyn Bones, bit of a character by all accounts and known locally as Boner.'

The team are in the ops room for the daily 09:00 meeting. Sicknote interrupts.

'Boner? Know him well. Right little scrote. What happened Guv?'

'Well, although I haven't seen it yet, I am told there was a short video clip posted online for a time, until it was taken down. Then it was replaced with a much longer film. Both films were taken at the scene and are purported to show something pretty gory and which would seem to be related to Boner's nocturnal activities. He was shot in the head, 12 bore probably. Tests will be carried out later. It was point-blank, lots of powder burn and very messy.'

'The killer made a video? Of the actual *act*?'

'Yes Dave.'

A murmur goes around the room.

'Not sure that's linked to our Mr Furness though Guv?'

'OK, let me convince you a little then Dave; before the shot, Boner was caught in a large gin-trap. Might be a bear trap, or even an old man-trap. Either way, the video apparently clearly shows a second man, taller than Bones, who hands over a belt and a saw then says something that's not very clear in the audio file, but when he buggers off our Mr Bones decides to try to remove his own leg. He starts to saw away at it but before he can finish the job and escape, the tall guy comes back and slots him.'

'Oh yuck-that sounds more like our man!'

'Indeed it does Steph. Seems Boner was lamping, which is why it's been red-flagged to this team; I asked for all incidents with any potential animal rights link to be notified straight away. Sadly it's taken a while for that penny to drop, but I'm assured we will know instantly the next time there's a relevant incident.'

Carol buts in.

'Lamping?'

'Hunting – usually rabbiting – at night Carol, using vehicles with powerful lamps.'

'Ah! Thanks Guv.'

Sicknote can't resist.

'You know Carol – rabbiting at night, like you and Steph when most decent blokes are trying to sleep. I mean talking a lot – as in *rabbiting on*; not that other thing that little vibrating rabbits are famous for!'

'Very droll Dave. Focus perhaps?' This from Samantha.

Dyson continues.

'I have requested a copy of the video from the internet site; should have that by eleven this morning. Forensics are on the case and will keep me in the loop on any developments. He wasn't mugged, but his mobile 'phone wasn't on his body. Apparently he lives with the thing stuck to his ear so we should assume it was taken. Possibly checking calls to that device will shed some light on who he's been speaking with and might throw up a name or two, although by all accounts he is thick as thieves with all the local undesirables so my guess is we'll have a who's who of local petty crime and not much else on the call logs when they come through. Brian-could you handle that angle please?'

Sicknote again:

'Sir, I know most of the scrotes, it'll probably be quicker if I check the 'phone records?'

'OK Dave, you do that; thanks. Meanwhile, let's have updates from yesterday's little excursions then please. I'll start. Samantha and I interviewed the mother and we are of the view that he's been to see her and may somehow be continuing to do so. I've requested urgent resource increase to allow us to put a 24 hour guard on the hospital and still maintain investigation continuity here. Until that's approved – and let's be clear, it's not certain it will be – we need to cover that aspect ourselves. We'll work out the shifts at the end of this briefing, but volunteers for the night shift would make the job easier. Other than that she gave nothing away. Brian and Carol, what have you got?'

'Good news and bad news Guv.' Brian Liddel's thin north-east accent carries a self-congratulatory edge.

'You can cancel the hospital watch cos he's skedaddled in his boat!'

'The boat's missing?'

'Yep, and he could be anywhere in it right now, might be half way to the Bahamas.'

'Or, Sherlock, the absence of his boat, while it's an indicator that he's no longer in the area, is no guarantee; it might have been nicked or sold or even deliberately sunk. The hospital watch will need to continue as planned.'

They talk for a while about tracking systems and the futility of the task. Carol reports that the coastguard is alerted and will be sharing details of the vessel with European neighbours.

'Thanks guys, good work. Sicknote, how did you and Steph get on?'

Dave Harrison briefs the team on the lack of evidence that anyone's been to the farm since the mother was found. The meeting disbands once a decision is reached on how they would, in the immediate term, keep an eye on events at the hospital.

42

He's being chased by the biggest, fattest and loudest contrabass tuba in history. It is threatening to swallow him unless he can reach the pool where he's sure tubas can't follow. He jumps into the deep end and the demented thing, realising he's escaped its clutches, howls and hoots the loudest note imaginable.

Painful elbow. He's on the floor. Why is he on the floor?
Awareness slowly drags him from the deep sleep. He must have been dead beat, because despite having only wanted to doze lightly, he'd clearly fallen into an exhausted stupor and it takes a few seconds to realign his senses.

The sound from the dream is repeated, closer and even louder than before and realisation dawns on him about the nature of the imminent risk. The dream had been a warning and the tuba was, in fact a fog horn – and a big one. Shit! He's about to be mown down in the world's busiest shipping lane by a super tanker or some other monstrous vessel. Colin leaps to the cabin door and sprints up the few steps to the deck to see how close the monolith is, slipping on the damp penultimate step and smashing his shin in the process. His curse of pain becomes a sigh of relief as through the mist he watches the starboard bow of the container ship plough past, less than a hundred feet away and travelling at something like fifteen knots.

He's grateful that shipping companies have adopted fuel-saving slower speeds these days but still readies himself for a massive bow-wave to hit his little yacht. When it strikes a few seconds later it tosses the *Salty Pig Runs Free* around like a cork for a full minute.

When the world settles down again Colin takes his current pay-as-you-go mobile 'phone up on deck and calls the number of the Beagle activist. He gets straight through to voicemail. This is not unusual; he guesses that a lot of people involved in spurious activities are reluctant to answer calls unless they are certain they know who is calling them. Colin's temporary number will be completely alien to her.

He speaks at the tone.

'Hi Barbara, I'm the guy who freed the dogs, just wondered if there was any news on the young bitch I pulled out? Thanks.'

Less than a minute later his 'phone rings and her number shows on the display.

'Hi, it's Barbara. I just got your message; sorry I missed your call. She's doing amazingly; I will send you a pic in a minute. She was treated for a few conditions, she's terrified of anyone wearing white and she has constant nightmares, but other than that she's brilliant.'

'Oh thank goodness. Yes, please send me a picture. What have you called her?'

'Actually, we were waiting for you to get in touch because we wanted to give you the chance to choose a name.'

'Oh, really? Well, I don't know...' Had it been a boy he would have given him his own name, but a girl...

'How about *Colina*?'

'Colina? Er, OK, it's certainly unusual. Anyone you know?'

'Oh no, just a name I like.'

'OK, Colina she is then! Pic on the way in a minute, and thanks so much for your brilliant help. The place burnt to the ground by the way, and the fire fighters rescued a security guy from inside just in the nick of time! They won't be abusing any more animals there any time soon. Great job!'

'Oh, good. Perfect, thanks.'

A minute later a ping informs him that the picture has arrived with the simple message: "*Colina xxx*".

The image is of a beautiful little Beagle, deep brown eyes staring straight into the camera.

43

The team is gathered in the usual place, minus DC Carol Saunders, who is busy watching absolutely nothing happen at the hospital bedside of Mrs Furness.

'Two key things from me folks. Firstly: I am in possession of the video from the Martyn Bones murder and the voice of the killer is without doubt our good friend Mr Colin Furness.'
'Surprise, surprise Guv!'
'Surprise indeed Dave. It's available for viewing if any of you feel you need to be reminded of just how callous this sicko is, but I warn you it doesn't make for comfortable watching.'

Dyson has a single sheet of A4 paper in his hand and is reading from it.
'Secondly: I requested, and surprisingly received, the initial psychiatric report into our friend's mental state. The report was compiled by Dr Simon Golightly; he's deputy head of psychology at the prison hospital. It was very technical so I asked him to give me the idiot's guide; I'll cut the crap and give you just the summary:

The patient exhibits symptoms of a bi-polar or schizophrenic condition with severe psychological trauma, quite possibly complex, chronic PTSD, and almost certainly from multiple events.
Additionally he suffers with 1q21.1 duplication syndrome or possibly 1q21.1 (recurrent) micro-duplication; both are aberrations of chromosome 1. This condition is extremely rare. As of October 2013 there were less than sixty registered cases of this syndrome worldwide.
This is important. A human cell has a single pair of identical chromosomes on chromosome 1. However, with 1q21.1 duplication syndrome, one part of one of these is duplicated. In 1q21.1, the initial digit '1' stands for chromosome 1, the second digit 'q' is the long arm of the chromosome and '21.1' the part of the long arm in which the duplication is found. We refer to this as copy-number variation, or CNV.
This particular CNV leads to a highly variable phenotype and the way it might manifest in an individual would be impossible to

predict. Rarely, people with the syndrome can function normally;
more usually there are symptoms of mental retardation and physical
anomalies.
In Colin Furness the retardation takes the form of mild autism with
strong Asperger's traits – high-performing autism. The physical
deformities are in the set of his eyes, which are significantly wider
apart than is the norm. This is known as hypertelorism.
Because of these complex mental disorders Mr Furness is able to
disassociate himself from the shocking violence he commits and this
is a further indication of the depth of his condition.
My earliest prognosis would be that Mr Furness is unlikely to ever
be able to function within the acceptable norms of society. He is a
dangerous criminal psychopath with a fixation on animal rights and
I would anticipate this escalating, although which direction this
might take I am not, yet, able to predict.
I would like to personally take charge of this case.

'Seems quite straightforward to me Guv!' Sicknote giggles.

'Yes, thank you Dave. It tells us nothing much that we didn't already
know. OK, updates please; Sicknote?'

'Sir, the mobile 'phone logs from Boner's device yielded exactly
what was expected; a list of calls to petty criminals and people who
are known to operate at the fringes of society. I'm following a
couple of leads but don't hold your breath.'

With limited input from the others it becomes clear that they are
struggling for any meaningful leads in the hunt for the criminal
psychopath.

'Oh, almost forgot in all the excitement; my first request for
additional resource was politely declined. I was informed that the
terror threats are highest priority – although nobody is going to come
out and say that publicly. If and when we get concrete intelligence
relating to specific, targeted action, then I can resubmit the request.
Until such time we are to continue at the current manning level. It's
in our hands then people, let's get the leads.'

After the scare in the English Channel the voyage is relatively calm and straightforward. Colin enjoys the challenges of lone sailing; although most of the time he travels under power of the diesel engine. He loves plotting the course and constantly checking the little sonar and the compass. It's been a while since he's sailed and he takes a few practice runs, going out into the channel and doubling back towards the English coast to see how close to a chosen landmark he gets using navigation. He is very happy with his accuracy and feels confident enough to strike out towards the Channel Islands where he may risk a landing, or he may just skirt around the west coast of Guernsey and head for the Brest peninsular. As a belt and braces back up – remembering the seven Ps – he has purchased a Zeus multifunctional GPS system; a hand-held device designed specifically for sailing applications which can tell him to within five feet his location anywhere on the planet. Colin has had a play around with the little toy and has fallen in love with it. It may well come in useful in his other coming exploits.

He's decided it will be safer to avoid the bigger towns if he needs to go ashore for any reason, but according to the map – or rather, *charts* – the area is riddled with smaller spots where he will be able to lay up for a day or two if needed, although after the initial flurry of media hype the radio news has given out nothing of his escape lately, and all the focus is very much on the enhanced terror threat from the religious freaks of the world. Colin has no time whatsoever for religious nutters, but how considerate of them to pick exactly the right time to soak up all the police resources!

He is steering his course from the deck wheel, rather than from the mirror control system situated below; visibility from there is somewhat limited and he still has the near-miss with the freighter very fresh in his mind. The radio is a constant soundtrack, waiting for any hint that the police might have picked up a clue on his whereabouts. It's a matter of time until they discover his boat missing, but every hour takes him further away from the plods. He makes a mental note to get the boat's name painted out as soon as he's in a suitable location.

Basking in the sun's warm rays he's relaxed for the first time in months and falls into a daydream, as he is prone to do. He's thinking of these militant Arab terrorists and their desire for some kind of Arab super Caliphate. He remembers clearly his father's lectures on god and religion and how a pious man is a good man. *Well, fat lot of good it did you, father! I never met a less tolerant, more disturbed human being.*

His mother, however, now *that* had been different. He thinks of her with some guilt again now lying in her hospital bed; was she waiting for news of her son? Had she understood what he had tried to tell her on his one and only visit? He thinks so, he hopes so.

Throughout his childhood she had been his guiding star, his moral compass. She had clearly shown him wrong from right and led by the best examples. Doing what he did, killing these people the way he had, was that a disappointment to her? It didn't *feel* bad when he was dealing with perpetrators; they deserved all they got, but had he let her down? Probably. But he also felt that she *got it*. She understood on some level why he did the things and what his ambition was, and he thought that she approved, although she hadn't actually used that word. For himself, he killed dispassionately. No, that wasn't true; he killed with a passion, but he was able to remove himself from the act, as if he were watching an old already-seen video.

He doesn't imagine his mother would ever be able to grasp that concept, but she'd surprised him before. He remembers back to his early school years when she had still been around, how he had sought her out after difficult events at school. He'd hated the whole pretence of morning assembly; being forced to worship an imaginary being. It had seemed completely ludicrous to him, but he had been a lone voice. *What had bugged him most about those gatherings? Was it simply the usual hypocrisy? Preaching love and goodwill to all and then behaving in a completely contradictory way?* Even at six or seven years old he had seen through that bullshit.

Maybe it was the idea of being forced, of having no choice in the matter, bundled along with all the other kids into religious assembly at school every morning and told "*sing hymn number blah blah*"; "*kneel and pray*"; "*dear god forgive us this*" and "*dear god forgive us that*" etc etc and there he was, a small child held captive in this milling machine of mind-warping. He'd witnessed it, watched as other kids bowed and uttered the words they were told to, like insignificant clones.

No thank you to that, he had thought.
He remembers making up alternative words, childishly rude and insulting ones, anything to avoid pledging his allegiance to this thing that everyone revered and yet which he knew could not exist. It was lunacy to believe in this *thing* and insanity to force everyone else to do that too.
Mindless sheep.
It angered, upset and disillusioned him then, and it has the same effect now.
What angers him most now is that when he had tried to explain this to the teachers in his 7 year old way, they'd mocked him even further. He had been ridiculed, made to look a trouble-maker and a fool and singled out for every kind of insult.

He had tried to understand them, but failed.
Maybe in their attempts to convert him they had in fact poisoned him against religion forever.
The poison still sits deep and strong, and when, as he goes through his life, he sees the same pattern being repeated by the churches and mosques and synagogues… well, any chance that he *might* have ever accepted that a god *might* exist has been well and truly scotched.

He thinks that to a neutral person he probably sounds bitter. He isn't, not really, just sad that a little boy's views were never even considered for one moment. In many ways it has driven him to believe more in himself than in anybody or anything else.

The religion question is so interesting to him too because of the atrocities carried out under its guise, and so many incredibly kind deeds. He finds himself wondering if those nastinesses and goodnesses would be carried out in any case, if religion were non-existent.

He supposes genocide tends to be motivated by greed and the need for power, and maybe religion is just one of the easy-to-fall-back-on excuses for that. It's all just too complicated for his simple mind.

He does believe that good deeds are carried out for multiple reasons, and thinks his very few secular friends probably, on balance, are ethically more grounded than those he knows who subscribe to a particular creed.
Coincidence?
Unlikely.

The team is assembled and looking glum.
Dyson is slightly flushed and clearly in a no-messing mood.
'We need to breathe some life into this investigation people. I have to give an update to the DCI in twenty-five minutes and frankly I'm embarrassed to admit that other than knowing Furness has escaped, killed a hunter, buggered off somewhere – as yet unknown – on his little boat and is a certified raving bloody basket-case we know sweet fuck all else.'

The nearly-cold coffee is taking a pounding this morning.
'Let's get our thinking caps on. What connections does he have in the world? Think beyond the UK. Where were his family from – Samantha and Dave go to the hospital and interview the mother again and make it clear that the goalposts have moved and we are dealing with a murderer who is out of control and about to kill again. Warn her that regardless of her health she's looking at another period in a confined space if she is even *thinking* of concealing relevant info. Put some pressure on the old bag to squawk – she knows something and I wanna know what it is.'
'OK Guv, but she is psychologically still very fragile; the docs will warn us off pretty rapid.'
Unusually Dyson raises his voice.
'*I too* am psychologically fucking fragile, and frankly I don't care if she's licking the ceiling and calling everyone a raspberry, if she is withholding info I want her to understand the consequences and be encouraged to spill the beans. He's killed a low-life scum-bag this time, but the next one might be someone we *do* care a fuck about, so let's stop pussy-footing and get her to fess up. This guy is crafty and calculating but Einstein he aint; let's find the clues he's bound to have left. He was verging on reckless when we caught him with his pants down with his last bunch of murders and he's not going to have changed into Mr Careful overnight. Think, look, find. That's all.'

He's left Ushant way behind and has in mind a tiny dot on the chart to explore; an island. The maps say it is some kind of national park, but his French is poor, and the name *Parc Naturel Marin d'Iroise* makes little sense to him. If he gets there before last light he'll moor a little way offshore and recce the place. If it's busy – which he doubts, looking at the location which he reckons must be around twenty miles from the coast – he'll just keep on going!
He's decided to head ultimately for the Bilbao area of Spain, it's almost exactly due south from his current location and he wants to get through the notorious Bay of Biscay as quickly as possible. He plans on landing his gear at a spot near Santander and then scuttling the boat in the deep water nearby. With luck the UK police won't even be looking for the *Salty Pig*, but why give them any help! He'll be sorry to lose her, she holds lots of memories already, but they're a mixed bunch of emotions.

When he finally arrives at the spot on the chart where he thinks the island should be he's puzzled that there's no sign of any land in any direction. He has absolute faith in his navigational skills, the charts are up to date and he's confident that he knows *exactly* where he is. He pops below and grabs the Zeus multifunctional GPS device and switches it on. Once it has located and locked in to three local satellites it confirms his location as precisely where he had calculated it to be.

Visibility is good and he should be able to see a bloody island, but apart from one old-fashioned looking fishing vessel about a mile off his port bow there is no sign of life.

He looks again at the chart and copies the French name into his internet 'phone. Parc Naturel Marin d'Iroise, translation...searching. *Aha*! He laughs and shakes his head at his own stupidity.
Colin, Colin, Colin, you bloody fool! Marine Park! Haha.
He was unlikely to see anything but water in the middle of a marine park!

Still shaking his head he goes below to make some food and eats it poring over the charts. He looks at the depths along the northern Spanish coast; there's clearly deep water all around Santander. The tiny settlement of Langre just to the west looks ideal for a quiet landing. There's a small beach, very secluded, where he can come ashore at night in his little inflatable, drop all his gear, go back to the Salty Pig and sail her out a few hundred yards and scuttle her. He'd be back on the beach in no time and if he gets it right nobody will know anything about his arrival.

He has plenty of time before then, he's still exactly 210 nautical miles from that point, or, as he prefers to think when he is in sailing mode, seventy leagues!

Colin loves these old naval terms and finds it easy to convert nautical miles, leagues and knots in his head and relate them to the modern land-based equivalent.
He imagines it must have been great fun calculating a ship's speed in the past, using a thing called a chiplog and a sand timer filled with thirty seconds' worth of sand. The whole concept was originally based on the calculation that there are 360° of longitude around the Earth, each consisting of 60 so-called *minutes*. Therefore there are 360 times 60 = 21600 minutes of longitude, and the minutes of longitude were taken as the basis for the nautical mile. Ergo, the earth's circumference at the equator is given as 21600 nautical miles.

Having this measure enabled speed and distance to be related as knots or nautical miles per hour.

Colin enjoys the basics of such calculations – so much more logical than language, and the fact that even modern navigators still use the same minutes – although they found a problem with longitudinal minutes, which shrink in size as they become more distant from the equator. For that reason navigators use *latitudinal* minutes because they remain constant.

He knows that they used to tie knots into a rope at intervals of something like forty seven feet and then attach the rope to a wedge shaped piece of wood – the chiplog – and throw this so-called

142

chiplog over the stern of the ship, dragging it behind them. It was the wedge shape that would cause it to drag through the water and as it did so the resistance would play out the attached rope and sailors could count how many knots passed off the reel in thirty seconds, giving them the speed. Primitive but better than anything they'd ever had before it.

He can't remember exactly how far apart the knots had to be, or why. He knows it had something to do with calculating feet per second but the exact logic is lost in the depths of his memory somewhere. In any case, he has his Zeus multi-functional GPS device now and that tells him that right now he's travelling at *exactly* nine knots! At this rate it will take him a day to get to the Spanish coast, a little less if he is lucky with the tide.

He dwells on that point for a moment, all those calculations they used to do would have been independent of tidal flow, if they had been sailing *with* the tide then they'd actually have been travelling faster than they'd thought; he wonders whether they had realised that...

'Right Samantha, Dave, what can you tell us? What did the old lady confess?'

'She was pretty tight-lipped Guv, and didn't seem intimidated by two senior officers at her bedside. She did give us some family history; she was born in a place called Garmisch in Germany and there are still some distant family members there. They go under the name of Von Wittenburg, which apparently has noble connections of some kind. Colin Furness has never been there to her knowledge, but they often spoke of it when he was young and so it's possible he might head there in some delusional view that it offers a safe haven.'

'Thanks Samantha. So what have we done since learning that yesterday?'

Sicknote takes up the thread.

'We spoke with the German police in the town and they came back with a few names and addresses. Currently working with them on ideas for surveillance, but it's a bit bureaucratic.'

'Yeah, I bet. I'll have a chat with the Chief and get her to smooth the process a bit. Good work people. Let's keep the positive vibes going and keep thinking and asking questions. What progress on Boner's telephone contacts?'

'Couple of calls to a butcher, one to a security guard at a local supermarket and a few untraceables – probably pay-as-you-go; they're pretty popular with the low lifes, Guv.'

'Sure, understandably when every call you make these days can be monitored. Time will come when just owning one will be a sign that you've something to hide and are therefore assumed guilty!'

The team run through a few other points before disbanding to pursue their individual tasks, or ongoing hospital stints.

Colin is hanging off the stern of the Salty Pig blocking out her name with rich dark-blue marine-grade gloss paint. It's a shame in many respects but he wants to eliminate as many risks of being discovered as he can and now that he's so close to the coast, and therefore people, he needs to get into security mode again. It's the second coat he's given it and, whilst it looks very scruffy, at least you can't now tell what the boat was previously called.

Earlier he had prepared the bilge pump for scuttling. In effect he had switched the polarity, altered a couple of fittings and attached a small hose link so that the pump worked in reverse. When activated now the pump would slowly fill the hull with sea water. He knows the pump will cut out when its fuel supply dies but he's cut some sizeable holes in the hull about a foot above the water line and she only needs to fill to that level; gravity and the sea will do the rest.

He's already been ashore once to hire a little 4x4 under the assumed name of Sam Dyson and used the UK driving licence in that name. Now he's inflated the little tender and she's sitting off the port beam where she can't be seen from prying eyes on shore. He loads his gear into her, packing it carefully to utilise every available inch of space; he's got a lot of kit and wants to do the transfer in just three runs. Working quickly in the failing light he realises that the area is completely deserted so decides there's no need to wait until dark. He heads off on the first run ashore rowing slowly through the turbulence of the waves as he approaches the little sandy beach.

Within an hour he's completed two runs without incident and is heading back out for the final trip. This time he takes the vessel formerly known as *Salty Pig Runs Free* a little further out to sea, towing the inflatable dinghy. When he gets to an area identified on the charts as seventy five feet deep he completes the final load transfer and activates the mechanical pump.
As he steps off the yacht onto the inflatable dinghy for the last time he notices that the holes he'd cut into the hull are now higher than he'd thought, then realises this is because he's taken so much weight off the vessel. Never mind, there should be enough leeway to ensure

she sinks to the bottom without any problem. He slowly rows away watching as the yacht fills with water at a snail's pace until finally, when he's almost lost sight of her in the failing light, she lets out a huge series of gurgles and gradually dips her bow towards the seabed, sliding gracefully below the surface of the water and in a moment disappears without a trace.

To his surprise Colin feels a tear run down his left cheek.

Must be the wind making my eyes water, he almost kids himself.

Part Three

49

Calves suckle from their mothers for up to a year unless human intervention prohibits this natural behaviour. D0227 had suckled on only one occasion and the artificial powdered milk she now receives through a rubber tube bears little resemblance to the real thing.

Veterinary studies have consistently revealed that natural weaning is a critical aspect of the lifelong cow/calf relationship of social contact and companionship. D0227 doesn't know this of course; and yet she constantly feels the void where a mummy-sized hole lurks.

50

It's almost noon and still hot for early autumn and Colin sweats as he drives across rugged dry tracks amid the Sierra Nevada Mountains just north of the Andalucían town of Córdoba.
His Zeus Multifunctional GPS Device – his pride and joy – is apparently designed for seafarers. The land maps seem to have more gaps than contour lines and the blue screen, so appropriate at sea, is next to useless for defining geographical landmarks. Colin regrets not bringing a map.

He knows roughly where he needs to be but can't seem to find a track that will take him there and is on the verge of abandoning his plan and heading back to the main road. He wants to avoid that if at all possible because every sighting is a potential risk and minimising risk is critical to his success.

The tracks fork yet again and he follows his gut feeling, taking the left option and heading slightly south west and descending. This should at least take him in the right general direction and in any case will veer back towards the main tarmac route. He checks his fuel gauge and frowns, the little jeep uses far more than the slick salesman had implied, but he has two jerry cans of petrol in the back so isn't overly concerned. A bleep from the Zeus alerts him to a flashing warning and he stops to read the text displayed. The words are scrolling across the 8" screen annoyingly fast and he struggles to make sense of them. After maybe four attempts he works out what it's telling him.

Land ranger chart series detected: switch to land maps? ↑=*Yes;* ↓=*No*

Bloody hell – the GPS system must have two settings, one for sea and one for land use, and he's been stuck on the water system. *Idiot*! He hits the up arrow and the screen changes from blue to sandy-brown.
No wonder half the bloody roads had been missing!
Smiling, Colin checks the location and calibrates his brain to the new information.

The last fork he took had been the right choice and he is actually only about seven miles from his target.

Relieved and smiling he pulls away.

The tracks are rocky and pitted with deep holes where rainwater has washed away part of the substrate over decades and it takes him an hour to get within half a mile of the destination. When he figures he's close enough he pulls off the track behind some house-size boulders and gets out for a stretch of cramped muscles and a drink of water before setting off on foot for his mission.

As three o'clock looms he shoulders the small rucksack and heads to the high ground due south of his current position. If he's calculated correctly he should be able to look down from there directly over a small complex of farm buildings. He suspects that what goes on in those buildings is probably horrific beyond words and his plan for the day is to get a good understanding of the day-to-day workings prior to returning tomorrow night and dealing a terminal blow to the running of the organisation. He half-marches half-jogs up the hill with real purpose, skipping lithely over the rocks and crevasses like a mountain goat.

When he nears the crest of the hill he keeps down low, almost crawling the last few feet to the summit. Exactly where he had reckoned, lies the settlement, but it's much bigger than he'd thought. One huge single-story black wooden shed, maybe the area of a football field. Surrounding the main building are smaller wooden huts and one corrugated tin shack with a metal chimney pipe belching dark brown smoke. He thinks the fire must be for hot water and cooking because even the backward Spaniards from this region must find this weather hot enough.

As he watches, a truck approaches from the road some three hundred yards away and pulls up in front of two large loading bay doors in the end elevation of the main structure.

A scruffy old man slowly eases himself down from the driver's seat and waddles towards the tin shack. An equally decrepit woman appears at the door and hands him something, paper maybe; Colin can't tell from here. Moments later another truck, smaller this time and newer, approaches from the same direction and pulls up next to the first. Two younger men jump down from the cab and immediately begin to offload crates of some kind.

Moving slowly to avoid catching any unwanted attention Colin opens his day sack and removes the powerful Zeiss Rangefinder Binoculars. These are top of the range and have all kinds of wizardry; not least, shielded lenses which don't reflect sunlight. They are also excellent in low light conditions.

Through the binos he sees that the crates being unloaded are crammed overfull with small, hairy rabbits; Angoras. With so much thick fur they must be close to death in these temperatures. Clearly a fresh delivery for the horror sheds. Every fibre urges Colin to end it now; to walk down there and tear the place apart with his bare hands, but he knows he has to wait, has to follow his plan, and has to gather the intelligence before he can act. *Seven Ps...*

He watches for many hours, protecting himself from the blazing sun as much as he can with a jerry-rigged poncho as more trucks come and go, some bringing goods and more animals, others taking away the by-product.

Finally at eight pm a sudden outpouring of people from the shed tells him it's the end of the shift and the lack of any arrivals means it's a single shift operation. Eight 'til eight, he assumes. That's a long day stuck inside a hot dark shed doing the devil's own work; they must be seriously fucked up people to want to work here.
By eight thirty he's seen enough and makes his way carefully back to the jeep and from there onwards to the little campsite he's set up in the hills. Tomorrow he will return and put an end to the intolerable suffering of the poor creatures.

51

In the ops room the morning briefing is underway. Sicknote has the floor.

'No evidence from any of the sources in Germany that Furness has been in contact with anyone on the list Guv.'

'So are they saying he hasn't been there, or they haven't caught him – i.e. how confident are they?'

'They seemed to be certain Sir, they've pulled out the stops for us and I am sure they'd have eyeballed him if he'd made a show.'

'OK, suggestions then?'

'Well they are planning to scale back the surveillance – they are under the cosh too with all these terror threats.'

'Damn it! It's all we've got going for us at the moment; we don't have any other leads. Oh well, they can only do so much I guess. I'll go and make a career-terminating move and give the boss the great news; you guys can sort out my leaving present while I'm gone!'

Late the following day Colin is back on the ridge overlooking the Angora rabbit shed. He is armed and ready; watching the minute hand of his watch crawl around the dial and staring at the door of the shed. He knows that sometime soon the old woman will leave the huge shed, lock it up and hobble up to the tin shack where she lives. He can't afford to have her around to spoil his plan so taking her out is step one. She may not be alone, so there's additional risk.

In the unrelenting heat he tries to ignore the irritating bead of sweat that has just started to crawl south down the left side of his nose. On the other side he'd have been able to carefully wipe it away with the tip of his right thumb without so much as a twitch of his head, but on the left he's at its mercy. He buries the itch in his subconscious, aware that the moisture may attract another mosquito to add to the torment but powerless to affect the situation and so he focuses only on the task. There is one other minor distraction; he has set up his camera equipment to record the event so that he can publish the video. The range and focus are set to record any activity around the door below him and the remote control to begin filming is next to him and easily activated without adjusting his aim.

She should have been out by now and he's nervous about the distance. He'd practised plenty when he was on the boat, but the constant tossing on the waves had made for an unsteady platform and he'd had precious little to aim at out in the deep water.
He rapidly blinks his eyes as if trying to cram in as many as he can before he needs to shut down the left, and lock the right one open. He knows it's almost time; any second now. He doesn't know who'll emerge, or how many there might be, that's why he needs to be ready the instant he sees movement. He breathes in deeply and slowly exhales four or five times to oxygenate his muscles and make sure his functions are all playing by the rules; last thing he wants is some oxygen-depleted eyeball under-achieving just when he needs it most. He wriggles his toes and gently clenches and releases his buttock muscles; all movements designed to keep his blood pumping whilst allowing his body alignment to remain completely undisturbed.

He should have applied sun screen to his neck, which is roasting now. He doesn't mind the heat; it's the skin cancer he could live without. The peaked cap is keeping his bald pate protected, but even that is scorching his skin where it touches and he is sweating inside it.

While he waits he can't keep himself from dwelling on the facts behind Angora wool. Colin Furness is no stranger to animal cruelty, and he's pretty hardened to some of the sights but he simply can't get the images he'd seen online out of his mind of rabbits being plucked alive. The screams from the animals as they have the fur literally ripped from their skin is one of the most haunting sounds on the planet and today he is going to begin to redress the balance.

His thoughts are disturbed by a movement in his peripheral vision. The door to the shed is slowly opening and the old woman from yesterday emerges. She's alone.

Stepping out from the cool of the huge wooden shed into the dusty and still-oppressive heat of the late Andalucían summer's evening, the old woman blinks her bloodshot, watery eyes to try to accustom them to the glare. Even at this time of day, after twelve hours inside the huge shed the brilliance of the sun is painful. Stooping to lock the door, then turning, she takes the first tired steps of the two hundred yard shuffle across the parched stony ground towards the ramshackle corrugated iron and timber shack that has, in various guises, been her home for more than sixty-five years.

He raises his rifle very slightly, releases the safety and takes first pressure on the trigger as he'd learned from his research and practise. Breathes slowly out, holds his breath and applies the final pressure; *Goodbye evil witch...*

Carmelita doesn't hear the shot. Her old brain is fleetingly conscious of a movement and a massive dull thump to her temple and then oblivion.

Even as the old Spaniard slumps to the ground, the shooter eases himself up from the position he's held for the last twenty minutes. Lying prone on the hard rock has caused parts of his lower body to lose sensation, despite his almost constant wriggling movements to try to keep the blood flowing. He makes his way carefully down the sandy rocks to where the old crone lies sprawled; constantly alert in case anyone else should appear. It had been a great shot and he is pleased to see he had hit her less than an inch from where he'd aimed. It was a windless day and he'd only been three hundred yards from target when he'd loosed the shot from the American M24 sniper rifle. That was easily inside its effective target range of over eight hundred metres. But nevertheless, after hours of practise it had been his first shot in anger and he is happy with the outcome.

He feels little emotion as he rolls her onto her back with his boot, surprised to see that the other side of her head is completely missing, and knows that it's now embedded as messy, splintered fragments in the wood of the door. He's a little in awe that the super-sonic round could wreak so much devastation, but it's fitting that she should leave her brain in the place where she's destroyed the minds of so many over her lifetime.

He plucks the keys from where they've fallen and opens up the shed. It's cooler inside, but the smell is almost overwhelming and he puts his left sleeve up to his face and breathes shallowly through his mouth.
Fumbling around in the gloom for a few seconds he locates the light switch and, as the banks of dull yellow lamps come on, drops his jaw in astonishment at the sheer scale of the operation. No wonder there had been so many workers coming and going. He takes in the layers of tiny, filthy cages – there must be something like a quarter of a million plus in here. He has hours until anyone is likely to approach, but he is nervous and wants to get the job finished and make his escape.

Laying the rifle carefully on the floor alongside the wooden wall, careful not to damage the foresight or move anything – he'd spent a long time zeroing the weapon and had found that a bit of a challenge so doesn't want anything shifting – he leaves the shed and jogs easily back up the rough trail through the rocks to the dusty track where he'd parked the little 4x4 hire truck. He drives carefully down the circuitous route to where he can access the building, taking it very slowly to avoid the deep potholes that pepper the course and trying not to raise a cloud of dust that might give away his activities to an inquisitive observer in the village at the bottom of the hill. Once at the shed he opens the back of the jeep and begins to offload the bulk of his film equipment and lights.

Before long he's taken around fifteen minutes' of high quality film, successfully capturing the feeling and scale of the place. He has footage of the rabbits awaiting plucking and the most graphic images of those animals most recently de-furred. They lie still in their little prisons, tiny, traumatised and trembling from the shock of having their fur ripped from their bodies by the quick and uncaring hands of rough peasants to be used in deluxe garments across the affluent and emotionally detached western world.

He fights back tears while he points the camera and pans it around the place making a gruesome horror picture to rival anything Hollywood could imagine. It's a shame he can't capture any live action; most people will have never heard a rabbit scream; a sound so terrible that once heard it's never forgotten.

Finished with the disturbing filming he allows pent-up emotion to wash over him and sits with his back against the warm wooden wall, hangs his head between his raised knees and cries deep racking sobs of frustration, anger and despair at the sheer scale of the problem. He is not ashamed to cry, as he once was, but life and the human monster have shown him that sometimes tears are the only meaningful emotion, the only release.

How long he remains there he wouldn't later be able to determine, he has retreated again into that protective bubble, but when he rises and looks outside the sun is just beginning to drop behind the hills to the north-west. His plan is to let the Angora rabbits run free. He knows that's not without risk, what will they eat? Where will they live? Will they survive? Completely inexperienced, will they be able to evade the natural predators in the area? To leave them here in the cages would be to leave them to a life of endless torture and eventual cruel deaths and would change nothing.

155

He walks quickly now along each aisle opening the cages and releasing the animals from the lower levels, reaching in and taking the terrified creatures down as gently as he can from the higher levels. Like the Beagles before them, most cower away in terror, their only experiences with humans have been brutally painful and they are clearly distrusting of this tall man with the strange eyes and soft voice.

Gradually a few of those he has released seem to accept that they have the ability, for the first time in their miserable lives of confinement in the little barred boxes, to stretch their legs and hop. These see the last remnants of daylight at the open doorway and slowly, painfully on their unused legs make their way to some kind of freedom. He realises after just thirty minutes of opening cages that he has underestimated the sheer volume; there is no way they can all make their way through the tiny personnel door, so he opens the huge sliding goods doors at the end of the shed.

It takes him nearly five hours to open all the cages and he is becoming more nervous as the clock ticks round. Finally all the Angora are released and the floor teems with a sea of rabbits, some covered in thick bushy coats, others naked in their bare skin. There are so many that it's impossible to move without risking stepping on them and he is forced to adopt a kind of awkward shuffle.

As much as he hates it he has to leave them to their own devices and trust that their natural instincts will help them survive the first days of independence. He reconciles the knowledge that many will die with the thought that at least they will have seen the sun, felt the wind, breathed fresh air and tasted freedom in their final days.

He must move on; Spain is a hotbed of abuse and there are a lot of people to educate before the police catch up with him again.

△ It's a movable feast, and every human generation shall decide for itself the level of cruelty and abuse it will tolerate △
Geoffrey Stanger

D0227 doesn't know about all the research into the cruel veal industry. All she knows is that her knees hurt; she's lonely and yearns to walk outside with other cows she occasionally hears, or to lie down and stretch in the sun, which she glimpses every few days when the huge doors are briefly opened for the big noisy tractor.

She doesn't know why she has diarrhoea or a constantly running nose, and thinks it's normal that, although she instinctively wants to lick herself clean as all animals do, she can't move her head anywhere near herself to do that. She can't really move it at all, in fact.

Many people don't know that cows can cry.
D0227 does.

Tired after the busy night on the fur farm and the consequent hard drive to escape the area, Colin needs a break. He's been driving for over six hours non-stop on his way to a small town near Valencia on the east coast of Spain to investigate *una fiesta especial* – a festival with a difference. He has heard that here they set the bull's horns on fire and run it through the streets. The reports he has seen online indicate that the animals are traumatised and forced to endure other abuses in the process and often go on to attack people, ending in a brutal and bloody finale.

The reports compiled by animal welfare groups single out the town of Requena as a typical provincial backwater ... *populated largely by retarded, in-bred Spaniard peasants who think that tormenting animals is suitable entertainment for families....*
Colin wants to see for himself.

Tired to the core, he pulls off the main road at a service station for a snooze but isn't prepared to run the risk of being caught in any CCTV footage so just gets his head down in the back of the vehicle for an hour. When he wakes he desperately needs a drink and a pee and he does both standing behind his van in the corner of the vast car park. Then it's time to crack on.

With the necessity for secrecy and caution and the resulting minor roads it's a two day journey and he finally arrives at an area above the town of Requena in the late evening to set up his simple camp. He eats the last of his tinned food cold, straight from the can and drinks to the bottom of his water bottle before lying down in the muggy air on top of his sleeping bag to think through how he will approach the coming days and drifts into a deep sleep.
Sunrise sees the dawn of the famous day; the town's *Water and Wine Festival* opening ceremony.

Wearing a baseball cap pulled low over his brow, dark glasses and now sporting quite a beard Colin mingles with the excited crowd at the entrance to the town's bullring. He's astonished at the size of the structure and wonders at the mentality of a nation that would see it as morally acceptable to build such a monument to torture. He knows intuitively that he's going to find the local people distasteful and mentally prepares himself for a private bloodbath of retribution. He's not here to harm people; that's not what drives him. He is purely on a quest to stop as much harm coming to animals as he humanly can before he is once again caught and put away. The next time he's locked up he knows the prison authorities will be far less naive about his escape risk so he needs to make the most of whatever time he has.

After two days on the road hiding from everything that moves he has exhausted his supplies and needs a drink and something to eat.

There's a small café-cum-bar off a side street and he ducks beneath the sun-bleached red and white striped awning and through the door, terrified of the language and desperately hoping someone will speak English.

Luck is on his side and the young man who serves him is clearly used to dealing with English speaking tourists.

'Do you speak English?'

'Certainly! How I can help you sir?'

'I need some water please and any food you have which has no animal products.'

'You are the vegetarian, yes?'

His voice was almost a parody of a Spanish waiter Colin had seen on TV once about a disastrous guest house in England, run by a manic lunatic called Basil somebody.

'Yes, well vegan actually.'

Veganism is new to Colin and a direct result of spending time with the then fiancé of the detective who had caught him last time. In their enforced hours together Jenny had shown him why vegetarianism was a poor half-way house for anyone serious about stopping animal exploitation. Once he'd heard the arguments the decision was simple and he'd wondered why he'd never made the connection earlier.

'Vegan?' The young Spaniard rolls his eyes theatrically. 'You not gonna find anything like *that* in this parts. I can do for you the omelette without ham?'

'No thank you. Do you maybe have just some bread with olives?'

'Yes, I can do you selection of this. You want a little piece cheese too?'

'Er, no thanks, just the bread.'

'OK, please take seat there I bring in one minute; one minute.'

He makes the word *one* sound like the Spanish name *Juan.* It's quite a pleasant accent.

Colin takes the water and makes his way to the corner table indicated by his host.

The food arrives with a barrage of questions.

'You are here for the festival, no?'

Why do continentals always finish a positive statement with the negative?

'Er, kind of, yes.'

'You will like very much the festival. The bulls are special from Andalucia this year, we have much expectations.'

He dragged the word *like* out over several seconds as if elongating the word might enhance the enjoyment of the spectacle.

'You have already the tickets? I do you special price; *very* special price.'

The exaggerated wink is almost lurid.

'I already have the tickets thank you.'

Colin finds himself mimicking the idiotic pronunciation, as if speaking slowly in a ridiculous accent will aid the guy's understanding.

'You need ticket for the wine and water?'

'Wine and water?'

'The second festival in the ring.'

'Er, I don't know. What is it?'

'It is after the bravest fighters have executed the bull when the pretty girls...' here he puckers his lips and raises his eyebrows repeatedly a few times as if to suggest there's somewhat more to the pretty girls than Colin might suspect '...bring the wine to the winner and water for the losers.'

'The loser being presumably the poor animal?'

'Haha, oh no, the animal now is laying down and dying. The animal will not need water. No; the winner is the fighter who manages to stick the spear into the bull first in what is judged to be the best place; *el disparo mortal* – the killing shot we say it in Spanish. All the others – the runners – are the losers.'

'Runners?'

'Yes – you never have see the fight eh? Is easy, I explain.'

He pulls the chair next to Colin's table, straddling it reversed and motions to Colin to eat while he talks.

'The bull is released to the ring and the fighters choose when to run into the ring and excite the bull. He chase the fighter and they have to escape. Is very dangerous ...no?'

'Yes, sounds it.' Colin is trying to eat and ignore the images of torment that crowd into his mind.

'More and more runners join until the bull becomes tired and then the best fighters enter and fight the bull. These are great heroes!'

'Yeah, they sound really brave.'

'Anyway – I give you ticket for water and wine festival for 40 euro. Is *very* cheap; *very* cheap!' he grins gleefully as if to emphasise the great deal he is arranging for his new English friend.

'Er, no. Thank you, I'll leave that for now.'

'OK, but you change your mind you come see Pedro Gonzales; OK?'

Pedro Gonzales...really?

'Er yeah, sure. Of course. Pedro Gonzales; I won't forget.'

'Excellent. Enjoy your food and the festivals. And don't forget the Toro Embolado!'

Colin's quizzical expression encourages yet more advice from Pedro Gonzales.

'The fire bull festival tomorrow night. Come here at around seven, have a few beers and then watch from the balcony. Is a great spectacle; only 25 euro for my English guest.'

'OK. See you then Pedro!'

Colin is left to enjoy the tasty bread and olives with a small bowl of oil in peace.

He gets to thinking about the cultural differences between this place and civilised nations. *What is it that makes them all so different?* He ponders belief systems and why certain groups of people follow things that are plainly – to a reasonable person – nonsensical. He's taken back to an incident in his first school where the History Master, Mr Heaton, is taking a lesson on American Red Indians. He has just shown the class of eight and nine year-olds a short film about the native Americans' cultural practices and is commenting on some of the behaviour shown in the film.

'As we have just seen, these creatures were clearly backward; they erected carved and painted posts and bowed before them. They sang and danced around them and claimed to be able to bring rains from the heavens. Their medical treatments were ineffective and many of them died from the common cold. This is why they were so easily overcome by our superior civilisations.'

Colin contemplates these statements for a moment before raising his arm.
'Sir, please sir, the film shows that the Europeans had superior weapons, not brains. It clearly showed that the invaders were able to kill the Indians very easily from long distances, and so bravery and intelligence surely did not count for much?'

'You were not paying attention as usual Furness. If you had listened at the beginning of the lesson I clearly explained that the film is the viewpoint of another historian. He was expressing an opinion of what happened. I have studied this area in great depth and can tell you quite categorically that we were superior in every way to the primitive natives we found there and were able to sweep them aside through brave and daring attacks at calculated and strategic moments.'

The Master had continued, sneering slightly as he spoke:

'As I said, before our resident self-appointed expert interrupted, they were stupid and primitive and if we need any evidence of that, well, they worshipped painted poles!'
Haughtily his glance takes in the whole class and his eyes, although fixed upon Colin's nervous face, seem to be daring anyone else to challenge his knowledge. No challenge comes and instead the children join him in his sneering laughter. Colin feels their collective scorn as if it were a physical slap to the face.

Shaking with emotion – he knows he will be further ridiculed – he is driven to explore the topic and to speak up for the Indians.

'But Sir, how is that different to what we do every morning at assembly? I mean, we sing songs to something that doesn't exist and bow to a wooden cross and make silly signs…'

Heaton turns instantly purple and his voice is a deep bellow.

'You stupid little boy! Have we taught you nothing? Are you completely wasting our time and energy, not to mention the money your poor father invests in your so-called education? I shall speak with the Headmaster and your parents; you are disruptive and have no place in this class. Maybe you should take a trip to Funtington, I understand they have a vacancy for Village Idiot!'

The room becomes silent and the other children struggle to resist the temptation to steal victorious glances at the red-faced boy. All except Melissa Goodrich. She can't let an opportunity like this go to waste and Colin feels the shame of her mocking gawp from across the room. Tears sting his eyes and he feels stupid beyond words, and yet he knows he has done something important and right. He wants to escape the room and be with his mother, she alone will understand.

First, he has the torture of afternoon play to endure and as a pack, led by the demonic Melissa, the bullies descend onto him. Surrounded and frightened he is battered by the taunts, which soon become pushes and shoves and without knowing how it happens Colin is in the midst of the crowd, kicking, punching and screaming, long limbs whirling like a crazed windmill. He has always been big for his age, tall and gangly, and relatively strong from all the work on his father's farm, and despite his normally placid nature, little bodies are flying and falling all around him. With shock, tinged with some satisfaction, he sees Melissa's chin come into abrupt contact with his bony little fist and she seems to take flight.

The spell is broken by the roar of Heaton from the other side of the schoolyard and the melee disintegrates in an instant. Colin remains standing, surrounded by the bruised forms of four or five sobbing and bleeding kids who are slowly pulling themselves upright.

'Too far Furness!' screams the Master. 'Way, too far this time, get your things, I shall call your father now and that will be an end to our generosity. I knew it was a mistake taking on a retarded, mutated misfit like you. Get moving and wait at the gate.' Distraught, yet strangely elated, Colin trudges to his peg and collects his coat and duffel bag. The elation evaporates twenty minutes later when his father's Land-rover screeches into the car park.

Back in the present Colin thinks again with a little guilt of his mother. Should he really be here doing stuff for animals that may or may not make a difference when she sits in a hospital or care home bed alone? He reconciles his actions with the knowledge that if he were there right now he'd be arrested anyway. Far better to do what he is doing for as long as he can get away with it.

55

It's becoming dusk and Colin waits in the shadows near to the cafe bar where he had earlier eaten. He's hungry again but doesn't want to become familiar to the people in the area lest they give too much accurate information to police in any future investigation. Because there *will be* an investigation after tonight.

The noisy crowd steadily meanders from the small square into the giant arena; the people colourfully dressed and many with faces painted in some primal tribal ritualistic thing that Colin fails to understand. Maybe they believe the bull will be intimidated by the colours and noise. He can well imagine that to be the case. After a while the crowds outside have thinned to a few isolated drunks and street vendors. It's difficult to remain anonymous now and Colin vacates the area. He has absolutely no desire to see the brutality at work but does want to identify an opportunity to educate the people. He'll bide his time and see what develops as the evening wears on.

Before too long the noise from inside the bullring becomes frenetic and he assumes the bull – or the first bull, he has no idea how many there will be – has been released. Pacing up and down a small street to the rear of the arena in some anguish he tries but fails to obliterate the images which keep forcing themselves into his head of what is going on inside. Thoughts leap like salmon around the rocks of his mind and the pacing becomes more agitated until finally, unable to control the frustration any longer he screams out to the sky at the sickening injustice. Nobody is there to witness his outburst except an old dog, tethered too tightly to a tree.
Colin walks over to the old mutt and unties the rope, feeling in its release at least a little relief from the burden of being the only person who knows that the goings-on inside the stadium are so fundamentally wrong. In such a religious country he's appalled that their god tolerates such barbarity; encourages it even.

He stops at a mobile drinks kiosk and takes a small bottle of still water and some freshly roasted nuts in some sweet syrup. He eats

and drinks as he wanders the quiet streets until just after the church clock strikes ten, when there is tumult at the distant entrance to the bullring and a small, elaborately-dressed man is carried upon the shoulders of similarly colourful others.
The victor, Colin assumes.

There are people spilling from the stadium into the roads now and movement in the little street behind him as another bull is brought into the square through a gate set in the side of the arena and tied hard up against a tree by its neck. Its front feet are tethered together and two men, dressed in black robes *priests?* approach and place melon-sized black balls upon the tips of his magnificent horns. A metal frame of some kind is seated onto the bull's neck and strapped into place with leather belts and further devices are fitted to the frame. Colin is too far away to see clearly what these are and nudges his way quickly through the gathering crowd to get nearer.

Up closer he can see that these are fireworks – large tubes like the giant rockets he has seen at professional displays. More of the black balls are forced onto the bull's horns and he can see that they are less solid than he had thought, dripping a little and made from some kind of tar-like substance. Suddenly there's an outcry and applause as the victor struts up to the bull, strokes its flanks and takes a lighted stick from one of the robed men. He leans forward and holds the flame to the bull's horns, instantly igniting the black gooey substance. Then, to the accompaniment of ecstatic cheers he lights the fireworks and retreats with a flamboyant bow, as though he's achieved some great feat.

He takes a sword from the other robed man and in a moment of terror Colin assumes he is going to sacrifice the bull. Readying himself to spring to the animal's defence he checks his leap as the colourful character slices through the rope around the front legs and then, with another flourish, the one which unites bull and tree.

The huge animal bursts free and spins in a half-circle to face the human throng.
The collective crowd gasps and twitches as one and edges back a few steps en-masse.

166

The flames from the burning pitch on the horns grow in intensity and begin to drip fire around and onto the bull's massive head and shoulders. The animal tries to see where this new threat is coming from, but its erratic head movements just serve to agitate more of the molten substance and inflame the crowd to a new height. At this moment the first firework shoots into the sky with a tremendous whoosh followed by a deafening explosion. The bull bucks and rears as the second incendiary device takes wing.

All the time the crowd is screaming its joy and the flaming tar is dripping over the terrified creature, onto its sensitive nose and flowing now into its eyes. The creature is rapidly becoming blind.

Colin is struggling to resist blowing his cover and rescuing the animal, but in truth he doesn't know what to do. How would the bull react to a man trying to save it? Would it comprehend the difference between him and its tormentors? Colin doesn't think so. Unclenching and repeatedly scrunching his hands into fists he is forced to endure its tortured bellows and watch its terrified circling while it searches for a cause, a reason and a way out of this open-air torture chamber.

When the final fireworks have cascaded in a thousand pieces over the rooftops and the pooling remains of the molten balls slipped from the horns to lay burning on the animal's head, neck, shoulders and in its eyes the victor from the earlier '*sport*' steps forward and with a gesture which looks almost merciful, slides his sword into the great beast's chest.

The front legs collapse and the head nods slowly towards the dusty ground as if to say *You win; I bow before you.*

The crowd erupts in a frenzy of cheers and applause, small children on the shoulders of their fathers clapping and smiling. Beautiful young women kissing strong young men; humanity rejoicing in its collective victory and worshipping its hero.

Colin vomits behind a tree.

Much later the town is almost quiet with a few hardy revellers staggering up and down the littered streets; some alone and others in small groups, line-abreast, arms linked singing songs which Colin can't understand. He is not interested in these people. His focus is on the town hall building where the black-robed men and the deliverer of the majestic thrust which killed the magnificent bull are ensconced. There is a party going on; a victor's reception of some kind and Colin is waiting patiently, silently seething with the indignation that he was powerless to stop the hideous bloodlust.

Remembering the 7 Ps he checks the contents of his backpack making sure, yet again that the items are exactly where he wants them, in the order that he'll need them and goes through the vague plan a final time in his mind, checking off the foreseeable contingencies for each eventuality so that everything will be as automatic as possible when the action unfolds later. *Prior preparation and planning prevents piss poor performance.*

He can only plan so far; much will depend on luck and the decisions certain people make when the time comes. His task now must be to stay alert and watch for the opportunity whilst keeping as low a profile as possible. He slips into the shadows and becomes once more invisible.

56

After a further two hours of watching and waiting there's finally some movement on the town hall steps. It's long past midnight and chilly in the still air so he's grateful for any indication that the events inside are drawing to a close. A large group of people stream down the steps and Colin is momentarily panicked into thinking that he might not spot his quarry. He needn't have worried though; the two robed gentlemen materialise, flanking the brightly dressed and flower-chain strewn hero of the hour, who is clearly very much the worse for wear. He can barely stand unaided and Colin licks his lips in anticipation. A reveller blows a ludicrous fanfare on an old hunting horn of some description and the crowd raises a final muted and drunken cheer. After this it's clearly time for bed; tomorrow is another day with bulls to kill, heroes to be crowned and orgies to be had.

With infinite patience Colin waits, watching the three, deep in conversation beneath a full moon in a cloudless sky until there are just a few stragglers meandering listlessly around as if searching for one final drink. The trio of oddly dressed men staggers along the main street talking loudly and occasionally bursting into raucous laughter. In the shadows their boisterous progress is silently tracked until they reach a crossroads where the houses are sparser. They hesitate here, one clearly wants to turn right, the other two, those dressed in robes, want him to come left with them.

'Gentlemen.'
The voice from behind is strong and clear.

'What a magnificent display of manliness today – I congratulate you all! But like all good things, this too must come to an end.'
The bull-killer has a suppressed Sig Sauer P226 9mm pistol pointing directly between his eyes in an unwavering hand. Even in his heavily inebriated state he can't fail to clock the menace of the silenced weapon. He stares vacuously; slack-jawed.

One of the dark-robed individuals has other ideas and makes a sudden move to protect his hero. Colin shifts the barrel left, dropping it ten degrees and removes his right kneecap.
The shot is almost silent, the kick of the weapon marginal and at first the robed figure just seems puzzled, then falls to the ground and starts to scream. Colin can't afford this noise and quickly looses two rounds into his throat. He'll either take out the vocal chords or sever critical arteries and brain-stem. Either will be fine, as long as silence is the outcome.

The screams are replaced by gurgling from the injured man's open throat. This lasts a few seconds only because the blood fountain lacks the necessary supply of liquid to be sustained. In a very short time the man has bled his life force over the dry sandy road.

The other two seem to have been waiting for the gushing, pumping blood to stop before they are galvanised into action, but in the intervening seconds Colin has been busy. He puts two rounds where he guesses the kneecaps of the other robed man to be and then aims at his throat.
'Make a sound and you can do the next human fountain impression.'

The priestly figure seems to have a good enough grasp of English to understand exactly what is implied and lays clutching his damaged legs, moaning quietly, trying to find a way to ease the pain and not scream his head off. Colin is impressed with his self-restraint. He thinks he has three rounds left in the magazine and indicates to the bull-killer to lie face down with his hands behind his neck.

The hero immediately complies and Colin forces his legs apart and delivers the hardest kick he can muster to the guy's testicles. The groan is deep and prolonged and satisfying. Colin takes advantage of his recovery time to remove the reel of tape from his rucksack and bind the guy's hands tightly together behind his neck.

He moves to where the second robed figure is curled up whimpering and places the barrel of the pistol against the centre of his forehead. 'Adios.'

The silent execution is quick and clean; Colin doesn't want to hang around and drags the two robed corpses into the ditch and hauls the swordsman roughly to his feet.

'You speak English?'

'A little.' Gone is the conquering hero facade.

'Good. Walk!'

Colin pushes him ahead into the field adjacent to the crossroads. They walk for a few minutes until Colin is comfortable that they are out of sight and immediate risk of discovery.

'What do I call you?'

'I am Theodore; champion Matador. The defiance makes a brief re-appearance.

'Why do you kill the bulls? Is it sport? Do you feel powerful? Is it because the girls will worship you? Are you sick? Why?'

The drunken hero doesn't answer; he's busy vomiting a bellyful of alcohol over his shoes.

Colin sticks his leg in front of the great matador's shins and shoves him forward; he trips and lands heavily on his face in the puddle he's just produced, groaning weakly. Colin gets to work quickly removing the guy's heavy leather boots, trousers and underpants. The Spaniard, probably thinking he's going to be raped starts to writhe and scream until he's spun onto his back and receives a heavy open-hand chop to the larynx. He collapses back on to the dirt in near silence. His brightly coloured and sequined shirt is torn in half and discarded, followed by his socks.

Lying naked now the bull fighter begins to tremble.

'Sobering up a little and not liking the way the world looks? This is just the start you evil little cunt.'

He's flipped over again and taking more tape, Colin wraps the reel around the lower half of his face six or seven times. The guy is now unable to make a sound. The taping continues around hands, arms and feet. Inside a minute he's completely immobilised. Colin stands and scours the area beyond the hedge for any sign that he's been heard. The entire neighbourhood is deathly still. He leans down and whispers into the Spaniard's ear.

'I'm going to get my car, then you and I are going for a drive – back into town. Don't go away.'

It takes him fifteen minutes to get back to where he's parked the little 4x4 and another five to return to the field and throw the bull-killer aboard. By this time the town is absolutely still and he's conscious of the engine noise as he slowly drives back to the other side of town to the bullring. Once there he takes the little road housing the side entrance from which the bull had earlier been paraded. He pulls up in front of the gate and jumps out to inspect it.

Locked; damn!

The double gates are crudely made of ancient timber and Colin could probably smash his way in but can't afford to make any real noise. The lock is a simple affair which has seen better days. On a whim, he takes the 9mm pistol from the backpack on the front passenger seat and fits the silencer again. He checks the magazine; removing each of the rounds in turn – three shots left.

Holding the barrel hard up against the woodwork supporting the locking mechanism he fires. The first shot is quiet enough, although the sound of wood splintering is loudest, and it blows a tiny hole straight through the timber. He moves the barrel a little closer to the metal part of the mechanism, wary of any ricochet and the second shot rips the lock out of its housing. The gate swings slowly inwards.

Into the 4x4, he drives quickly through the gates, jumps out and pushes them back together. They have a tendency to swing open so he props a piece of advertising hoarding against them.

Colin is stood now inside the vast arena and his mouth hangs slack. It's simply enormous. He's been thinking through the next steps but his plan is still embryonic. Dragging the matador into the centre of the bullring he dumps him and returns to the vehicle where he collects his rucksack containing the video camera. He wants to give his viewers something a little more spectacular than the straightforward shootings they've been getting, but what can he use? Dumping the rucksack next to the tightly-bound figure he scouts around. Back over by the gates he strikes gold. An old galvanised bucket contains the unused remnants of the pitch that had been used to make the fire balls. There's plenty for what he needs along with a pair of red, heavy-duty plastic gloves, some kind of accelerant fluid and a few other odds and ends. He takes the bucket, gloves and fluid back to the middle of the ring and sets them down. Donning the gloves he rolls and moulds some of the sticky tar mixture into a long sausage shape.

'OK Mr Hero. Time for your last and most illuminating show!' With a hand beneath each armpit he hauls the bullfighter into a sitting position and tells him to sit still, then lays the elongated tar sausage in a circular shape on top of the Spaniard's head, but realises it'll just fall off when his victim starts to wriggle. He drops it lower, draping it around his shoulders and neck and pulling it quite firmly tight. Happy that it will stay in place he opens the bottle of flammable fluid and liberally douses the tar.

The smell of the fuel is powerful and the bull-killer's nose must be full of it because he clearly realises now what's about to happen and starts to writhe around trying to dislodge the sticky black mass.

Ignoring him, Colin sets the camera up on its tripod, removes the lens cap and hits the *record* button. He calls out from behind the recording equipment.

'So Mr Bull-murderer, time to experience exactly what your poor animal victims will have felt. In a moment, as you will have guessed, I shall light the stuff around your neck and you will be slowly burned to death. Or rather, you would be if I let you.'

He takes his lighter and ignites the liquid fuel, which goes up with a whoosh and the matador starts to thrash around in a real panic. Colin would like to hear him scream, but it's too risky to remove the gagging tape here in the middle of town. It's a shame the bastard can't experience the emotions that the bulls would feel; abject fear is OK, but this guy knows what will happen – a bull never does. There's no element of surprise. Well, maybe a little one.

The smell of burning hair, skin and flesh is very powerful and Colin realises the guy will be dead in very short order. Time for the coups des grace then. He kicks the remains of the burning mass away from the guy's body; some sticks to his boot and continues to burn there until he tears it away with a gloved hand. The taped-gag has been burned away and the Spaniard's upper body is still smouldering but he can hear rasping breaths being torn through the pungent smoky air.

Colin wants to execute this guy in a manner fitting to his crimes but has only the pocket knife. The Spaniard's in a bad way already so there's not much time and Colin runs over to the 4x4 to see if there's anything he can use in place of a sword. As he reaches his vehicle a pair of headlights sweeps past the slightly open gates and he realises that if anyone were to investigate he'd be trapped in here.
Abandoning his plan as his nerve deserts him he quickly gathers up the recording equipment and bundles it into the car. He kicks away the boards that had wedged the huge gates closed and exits the arena. Not a moment too soon as a white car with a thick black horizontal stripe bearing the word *Policia* cruises slowly past, driver and passenger eyeing Colin suspiciously. The vehicle pauses at the now wide open gates and in his rear-view mirror Colin sees the passenger disembark.
Fuck!
He calmly takes a left at the next junction then floors the accelerator as soon as he's out of sight raising a cloud of dust. He's probably got a minute before the cops get their shit together and needs to get out of town and onto one of the dozens of tiny roads leading out into the vast sandy plains. Once out there he has a chance to lose himself.

At the bullring the provincial policemen are making a gruesome discovery. Luckily for Colin their immediate reaction is life preservation and for precious minutes their efforts are spent in trying to save the naked and still smouldering man and arranging an ambulance to get him to hospital in the town. The medical centre is short staffed; the festival here is a big event and many had opted to take holidays so reaction times are poor and by the time the police have sorted the patient and called in the incident to their HQ Colin is ten miles away and heading fast along the A3 for the sprawling city of Valencia.

Comforted by the knowledge that the police would have been unlikely to have any useful details of his car, Colin knows he has a chance, but he needs to put distance between him and the scene of crime and heads north along the coast road towards Tarragona, some 200 miles away. As usual he selects a quieter road than the main motorway which has toll booths and cameras so it's daylight by the time he reaches his destination and, worn out from the heavy night and long hours behind the wheel he takes a room in a rundown backstreet hotel to get some rest and make plans.
He hangs the *do not disturb* sign on the door handle and falls into bed.

57

Δ If we cut up beasts simply because they cannot prevent us and because we are backing our own side in the struggle for existence, it is only logical to cut up imbeciles, criminals, enemies, or capitalists for the same reasons Δ
C.S. Lewis, *God in the Dock: Essays on Theology and Ethics*

He's slept through most of the day, occasionally disturbed by cleaners thumping around in adjacent rooms and after a much needed shower Colin heads down to the little restaurant to see if there's anything he can eat. Choice for vegans is practically zero so he reluctantly settles on another bowl of olives and bread which is rapidly becoming his staple diet in this part of the world.
When he's emptied the plates he takes a small, bitterly strong black coffee back up to his room and logs on to his laptop. He checks the local English news service to learn that the headline page is covering the brutal murders in Requena of two members of the ancient order of bullfighters and a vicious assault on a matador who is fighting for his life in intensive care. The article describes the robed men as members of a group known as *keyholders to the bullring*, and it seems their bizarre costumes are a throwback to an order by King Felipe II in 1566. No suspects have yet been identified although police reported seeing a lone man around the time the discovery was made.

Relieved, he sets about uploading the interrupted video clip of the matador's burning and sends the film to his chosen websites. The whole thing takes him less than ten minutes and he is soon ready to move again. He quickly packs up his scant belongings with a vague plan to head towards the place of his mother's birth; Germany. Thanks to her careful tutelage he speaks the lingo to a good standard and he wants to experience first-hand some of the things she would tell him about so enthusiastically as a small child. Beyond that he has no immediate plans other than to lay low for a while and let things calm down a little.

He's seen a lot of the Spanish countryside in the short time he has spent here and plans now to head up the east coast from Tarragona via Vilanova. He may, if he can do it safely, hire a small boat at the marina there and sail across to Genoa or somewhere else on the Italian coast. From there he'll make his way through Switzerland over the Alps into Germany at Garmisch Partenkirchen. His mother used to rave about that place and the music of one of the regions favourite sons, Richard Strauss. He'll use the Sam Dyson paperwork as that still seems to be safe. Once in Germany he'll organise some new papers, no point taking unnecessary risks.

58

The headline BBC news is a stark warning by a previously unknown terror group to all who live or work in high-rise structures. The terrorists' message reads as follows:

Your way of life is disrespectful to the Prophet and he has commanded that you be brought down to earth to crawl like the worms that you are. Your high-rise structures are testament to your arrogance and these shall be dismantled. The Abd al-Malik brotherhood will hit you where it hurts you most – at the foundation of your belief system; self-loving and greed.

There follows a TV discussion involving a panel of academics, media representatives and minor politicians with some saying that this is a credible and dangerous threat, whilst others dismiss it as a small maverick group of nobodies living on the coat-tails of bigger, real threat organisations.

Away from the bright lights of the TV studios the feeling on the street is one of real concern and the police forces of Europe find their resources stretched ever tighter.

59

He picks up a hire boat easily enough at the Marina in Vilanova I la Geltrú on a two week deal that sees him safely into mainland Europe; he has no plans to ever return her and the loss of the thousand Euro deposit is laughable in the circumstances. He could ditch her anywhere along the coast, and opts for Ventimiglia, just west of Sanremo. Once ashore he's grateful for the European Schengen agreement which allows pretty much free movement with very limited border checks and hires another 4x4 under the usual pseudonym of Sam Dyson. Heading north through the mountainous terrain, skirting Turin and then hugging the southern Swiss border round to Liechtenstein and up into Oberstdorf in Germany. From there he drives east to the outskirts of Garmisch Partenkirchen, where he takes a cheap anonymous hotel and sets about planning and organising the next few weeks of his life.

60

Colin is on the Tor network but nobody else seems to be online so he searches around to kill time. He comes across a few interesting pages – including attrition.org which he explores for a while. It seems to be a site where people can access security data, and on one page a bold announcement claims to be able to hack into FBI networks. He gets out of there in a hurry; no point leaving electronic trails where high-level security forces would be likely to be looking. After maybe thirty more minutes of aimless browsing his laptop beeps to inform him that he has company.

Mujahid– LEADER: *Bro!*
Fundamentalist – NUBE: *Hi Mujahid*
Mujahid– LEADER: *ready for UR initiation test?*
Colin swallows. *OK, here we go then.*
Fundamentalist – NUBE: *sure-I am abroad at the moment but if I can do it here I will*
Mujahid– LEADER: *when U back?*
Fundamentalist – NUBE: *not shure-i have ishues with the law in UK so need to stay away a while.*
Mujahid– LEADER: *no stress bro. What the law want U 4?*
Fundamentalist – NUBE: *terrorism related stuff a bit like yor plans. No big deal.*
Mujahid– LEADER: *BRO! COOL! OK let me know when U R headed back*
Fundamentalist – NUBE: *I will-probably a few weeks-OK?*
Mujahid– LEADER: *Sure thing. Laterz*

The seed is planted.
Colin wonders again what they will expect him to do – not that he cares; slaughter houses are the things of nightmares and if it means getting just one shut down then he'll definitely do it, especially if he can pull a stunt and shut a Halal establishment. Thinking through the logic, as he is prone to do, *what would be the consequences of*

shutting down abattoirs en-masse? That would surely stop animals from being killed?

No, carnivores are not going to want to give up their juicy, bloody steaks; they'd still want to titillate taste buds and demand their pound of flesh and the animals would just have to endure tortuous journeys to even more brutal foreign facilities. That's absolutely not the solution, and neither is leaving only Halal establishments operating, he can't condone that. It's a dilemma and he might have to act contrary to his beliefs and actually *stop* the destruction. Maybe the best plan is limited action, but the pro-Halal gang has to be stopped.

61

Δ Fox hunting -- the unspeakable in full pursuit of the uneatable Δ
Oscar Wilde

Flicking through the TV channels a few hours later something grabs Colin's attention as he skips past a local news station. He hits the *programme up* button to go back and sees a noisy anti-hunt demonstration being captured on amateur film equipment, probably a hand-held camera or maybe a mobile 'phone. At the very frontline of the demo is a diminutive young woman brandishing a huge white placard with red and green writing: *Jagd ist Mord; Jaeger sind Feiglinge.*

From as early as he can remember Colin had spoken German with his half-German mother, who had wanted him to be able to read the great poets in their native tongue. She had spent hours sitting with him reading and clarifying the finer points from the pens of Goethe, Von Schiller, Hesse and Eichendorff. When she disappeared he had continued, in her honour, throughout school and beyond. For a dyslexic the language is so much more logical than English, with words written as they sound; the translation comes naturally.

Hunting is murder; Hunters are cowards.

The camera stays focused on her and he is struck by something about the tiny woman. She's pretty enough, but her face, distorted by her anger and frustration has a hard edge and the look of disgust she throws towards the people on horseback strikes a chord with Colin; he *knows* what she is feeling, he has felt it plenty of times and he feels it now as he looks at the huntsmen in their finest uniform-like grey *Trachten,* the women in their best green *Dirndls.* It's as if they are an elite society, out of step with the rest of humanity and yet proud of their differences, aloof beyond the point of arrogance just like the English toffs who delight in watching innocence torn apart.

By comparison the protesters look like a bunch of wild hippies in old jeans and randomly colourful jackets.

As he watches the girl steps forward and attempts to block the passage of a big powerful stallion bearing an overweight hunter. The latter simply manoeuvres his horse to nudge her out of the way and reaches down and flicks her firmly across the backside with his crop; she spins in shock and obvious pain, but mostly affront. It's clearly a sexually charged gesture; some kind of throwback to a time when Masters had their way with wenches with absolute impunity. He shouts something and then leans forward and spits directly into her face. All caught in the viewfinder of the attentive camera operator, who Colin assumes to be one of the demonstrators. Colin is disgusted, and wonders what she will do. To her credit she doesn't flinch, nor does she wipe the phlegm from her skin, but holds her ground, staring defiantly up towards the fat hunter, refusing to budge and, despite the size difference still blocks his way.

In his hotel room Colin claps his hands together in admiration and does the little skip.
Haha, good girl; that will show the fat prick who is the brave one!
The female camera operator announces over the footage, in German that the demonstrations at the Marienplatz in the town centre would continue on into the week as the annual hunt meeting is planned to run until Sunday, culminating in a grand festival dating back hundreds of years. It is, she claims, one of the most shameful of human crimes.

Colin realises that he wants to be part of these demonstrations, wants to be present, where the action is, where the beating heart of protest is to be found. He knows he has to keep a low profile, and he won't risk being caught on camera, but a fundamental longing is awoken somewhere deep within him. He wants, no, *needs* to make a difference and decides to travel to the famous restaurant quarter *Marienplatz* tomorrow and seek out the protestors.
Although the feeling is somewhat alien to him, more than anything he realises he wants to find out some more about that girl.

62

The next TV programme is about to start when a newsflash interrupts the proceedings. Colin watches agog as live pictures of the Eiffel Tower appear, showing images from a long-range camera shot of minor damage to one of the four enormous leg supports.
He listens as the female reporter tells of the warning received via email at the offices of French newspaper *Le Figaro* that four members of the Abd al-Malik brotherhood terror group would be toppling the tower. The reporter goes on to explain that the terrorists attempted this by strapping themselves to one of the legs – the northernmost one, nearest the River Seine – and then simultaneously detonating the explosive vests they were wearing.

The reporter – in a typical display of French national pride and trying to conceal her delight, it seems – explains that whilst the terrorists immediately disintegrated, the ironwork was left relatively unscathed, barring a few burns to the paintwork. The area is sealed off and, following extensive security checks a team of mechanical engineering specialists is waiting to do a proper assessment of any damage. More information is apparently available on the channel's website.

Colin sits in stunned silence. Wow! The sheer scale of the attempt was admirable, but he's glad they've failed. These loonies were already guilty of destroying priceless treasures in the Arab world and he sees no justification in doing that. *What motivates these people? It's not as though any really tangible benefits can be had for their murders and self-sacrifices.* He knows that they believe they'll die heroes and ascend to some imaginary utopia and be welcomed by a multitude of virgins, *but don't they know that most explosives contain pig gelatine? That's Haram in their world and knocking on the gates of heaven impregnated with the very thing they detest is funny in its irony.*

One thing's clear though; as long as such idiots are running around detonating themselves, fewer police would have enough time on their hands to be searching for an insignificant animal rights protestor like him.

Please carry on then loony Haram terrorists!

63

He hears the clamour long before he's anywhere near the open space of the Marienplatz. It's a mixture of chanting, horns and drums and his pulse races as he picks up his pace. This is another new sensation to him; *what is the feeling coursing through his veins? Is it pure excitement? Is it the noise and the anarchy? Fear that what he is doing is putting everything at risk?* Out in the open like this where there's a risk of TV coverage he feels very exposed, despite the dark glasses and the cap. If they've linked any of his recent exploits to him then he's certain there'll be an international manhunt underway, even though he has seen no evidence of that anywhere.

Or is this feeling something altogether different? There's no denying that something primeval is stirred by the incessant randomness of the drum beat, and yet he can't stop thinking of the girl on the TV and somehow hoping she'll be there.
Ridiculous.

There's not so much CCTV here – certainly not like in the UK where every street is covered these days, but there are cameras of one kind and another everywhere; people using their mobiles, using hand-held video devices and a couple of local TV stations. A souvenir shop catches his eye and he grabs a cheap white baseball cap declaring his love for Garmisch with a mixture of words and a big red heart "Ich [heart] Garmisch!". He ditches the old one in a bin and adjusts his dark glasses, trying to settle a little more comfortably into a layer of anonymity.

Rounding the final corner he's stopped dead in his tracks by a thin line of riot police; shields held aloft in an impenetrable semi-transparent wall, giving the small but rowdy group penned within its confines the semblance of fish in a bowl. Wow! He hadn't expected this. But that's only part of the picture, beyond the corral there are many more people; animated crowds of colour and motion. Some standing, others on horseback and some running around seemingly aimlessly. Although as he watches, Colin realises they are simply moving to where hotspots are developing; mini-skirmishes between demonstrators, hunters and yet more police, although the latter seem to be largely watching the world go by without actually intervening to shape its course.

Despite the noise it's actually not a violent scene, unlike some he's seen before on TV, and even the demonstrators seem to be in good spirits. Two tribes facing up to the opposition, each comfortable in their beliefs and probably both more than a little bigoted in opinion.

Casting his eyes over the crowd beyond the police cordon Colin is disappointed to see no sign of the TV girl. He is torn between the need to stay out of the limelight and this sudden and inexplicable desire to find out more about her. In the end his natural caution takes control and he heads down a side road to escape the risk of unwanted publicity. He has no idea whether the events being filmed will be shared internationally, but *Christ, what is he thinking?* He is on the run, trying to stay safe whilst continuing to strike blows at abusers in a series of complex and dangerous ongoing missions and is jeopardising the entire project on a stupid whim. *Get a fucking grip of yourself Furness, remember the 7 Ps.*

He needs to get his head in order. He also should eat something and he ducks into a café to grab a bottle of water and some of the famous local Apfelstrudel, if he can find some without animal secretions, but mostly to calm down and give himself time to think straight.
A waitress leans over and lights the candle in the centre of his table – although it's clearly unnecessary – and takes his order. While he waits for her to bring the food and drink he goes through some breathing exercises he'd learned from a psychologist whilst resident in a hospital the previous year. The breathing helps to calm him and he combines it with some grounding techniques to bring himself back to *the here and now*. He needs to feel *in the moment*. He practices these mindfulness techniques most days and has become quite adept at taking himself to an inner peace where he can close out the distractions around him and focus on the very basics of feeling, hearing, smelling and thinking. He even manages to blot out the line of deer heads mounted on wooden plaques on the walls.

The peace is suddenly shattered when a group of nine or ten people in scruffy clothes bursts through the front door. Some are carrying banners and others drums and horns. Clearly these are some of the hunt saboteurs and they need sustenance. The waitress moves to head them outside where there is a Biergarten and where they will be less of an intrusion into the day-to-day life of the otherwise orderly café. Half of them head straight for the toilets and the others follow the request and make their raucous way through the building and out into the courtyard garden.

One girl stops near Colin's table, her mobile 'phone to her ear and he knows without even seeing her face that it's her. She is wearing the same clothes as yesterday, that doesn't seem odd to Colin, she's probably living in a tent all week, or in the back of a three-wheel van covered in flower stickers or rainbow paint with ban the bomb signs. Colin's heart seems to stop and his mind goes blank, staring at her, small and juxtaposed with the magnificent stag's head on the wall above her. He shuffles clumsily round the table until he is directly in front of her and confirms what he already knew.
He has no idea what to do next, but is saved from the dilemma when, waving a cigarette at him she looks into his eyes and asks in the local dialect whether he has a light.

'Er…. Ich rauche gar nicht, aber, warte mal…' he explains that he doesn't smoke but thinking quickly grabs the passing waitress by the elbow and miming the action of lighting a cigarette by clenching his fist and striking his thumb rapidly across the crooked first finger knuckle asks her if she has a light.
'Haben sie bitte Feuer?'

She explains that smoking inside the café is not allowed but lends him the cheap blue disposable lighter, adding that she has another so he may keep it until he leaves. Muttering his thanks he ushers the girl towards the garden, desperately trying to think of something to say to her to break the ice. In the event he needn't worry as she thanks him and then immediately answers her ringing 'phone.

Disappointed, Colin backs off a little, but lurks close enough so that he can jump in with whatever pearls of wisdom he settles on once she has finished her call.

She speaks quickly and animatedly for a few moments only, clearly upset with the caller. In a rare moment of clarity Colin goes into acting mode again and tapping her shoulder, mimes taking a drink whilst raising his eyebrows and shoulders. The girl breaks off her call momentarily to nod vigorously and mouth a silent '*Kaffee, bitte.*'
Delighted to have made a positive move, Colin rushes inside to order a black coffee. He doesn't want to risk putting milk or any other additive in, just in case she's a hippy vegan!

That turns out to be an inspired decision. As he re-emerges from the café she smiles, pockets her 'phone and takes the coffee.
In her delightfully soft German she thanks him and asks if he has a table as the others are all taken. He replies in his somewhat harder, high-German dialect that he'd be delighted with her company but doesn't actually have a table outside. Looking round it's clear that there are no spare seats, so they lean against the wall.

She breaks the slightly awkward silence.
'Sorry if I seemed rude; my mother is very sick and that was the hospital on the telephone.'
'Oh dear, will she be OK?'
'It's not easy to say; they don't know what is wrong with her yet, she just collapsed a couple of days ago but all the tests have come back negative. We have to just wait and see.'
'That's terrible. I am sorry, but I'm sure she is in good hands.'
'I think so yes. Thank you for the coffee.'
'My pleasure. I was very impressed with your restraint yesterday.'
'Yesterday?' She frowns. 'Did we meet already?'
'No, I saw you on the local TV news, a big slob of a hunter spat in your face and you practically laughed at him.'

She giggles, and her perfectly shaped, beautifully white teeth seem out of place in someone so alternative, so rebellious.

Colin smiles, aware that his teeth, whilst clean enough, lack the precision and brilliance of hers. Dentistry is not what it used to be, and young people set great store on having gleaming straight gnashers. He feels somehow inferior.

'He was just a filthy arrogant pig, I wouldn't give him the pleasure of wiping his spit from my face, even though it felt like it was burning holes in my skin and scarring me for life!'

'It was very brave, and I saw him strike you too. Will the police arrest him?'

She roars at this.

'The police? They won't lift a finger, he is deputy Bürgermeister and politics here is as corrupt as anywhere else on the planet.'

Colin looks aghast.

'Seriously?' He uses colloquial German terms but she spots his slight English accent.

'You are not from around here, where is home for you?'

Colin is torn between secrecy and the desire to be open and honest with this girl who seems so transparent and morally upright.

In the end he compromises.

'I am from England, here on holiday.'

She switches effortlessly to almost perfect English.

'Wow, your German is amazing! Where did you learn?'

Colin explains a little about his half-German mother and her love for the German classics.

'I am Patricia, by the way.' She offers her hand and Colin takes it, the size difference between his and hers making him feel self conscious.

'Colin.' He stops short of giving his surname, although it's customary in Germany. 'Very pleased to meet you.'

'Likewise!'

'So have you seen the fat arrogant pig again today?'

She laughs again.

'Oh no! He won't be here; today is the turn of the younger generation. His equally fat son might be out there, but I haven't had that pleasure yet.'

'Does it make a difference – I mean, you and your friends demonstrating like this?'

She sighs.

190

'Who knows? I think so; I hope so. It certainly raises the profile and gives voice to thoughts that would otherwise remain buried. Too many of us go through life thinking things and yet doing nothing about them. Do you have any idea the kind of abuse that goes on in the world with animals?'

'Er, well, yes. I have seen certain things and have been involved in projects to help stop them.'

'Really? What have you done? Demos?'

'Yes, kind of. I'm more a direct action kind of guy to be honest.'

'Wow, me too! We'll have to have a drink sometime and compare notes!' She smiles her big shiny smile.

Colin decides to take the initiative.

'Patricia; I can't join your demonstration – er, it's complicated, although I would really love to. But I can offer a different kind of support, as long as you promise to keep it confidential?'

A slight quizzical furrow to her brow, she leans a little closer, as if the secret between them were already a prized possession, something to keep from the world at all cost. He catches a faint trace of perfume.

'What kind of support?'

He realises she's toying with him, but is starting to enjoy himself for the first time in ages.

'Well, I don't know how it works, this is all a bit new to me but, well, you must need funds? I have resources. Lots of resources. I could make a donation ...?'

She laughs that wide open laugh again and he feels something shift inside. He parks that thought for later analysis, he needs to focus entirely on the here and now so that he doesn't misread vital social cues. He is prone to misinterpretation but feels like he's part of a very special club with only two members.

'What kind of donation were you thinking about then Colin?'

He realises she's slipped back into German, but can't remember which language they had been speaking before.

Frustration; is this one of those double-meaning conversations? Is she flirting with him? He realises he has no clue and wouldn't know

191

how to react if she was. He'll assume she is playing straight; safer that way.

'Well how much would make a real difference to what you are trying to change here?'

'Enough to bribe the mayor perhaps?' She winks and he feels sure she is joking.

'But seriously Colin, we are not trying to change anything, we are trying to prevent the change, the change back to the old ways when every fat German wannabe-Aristocrat considered it their god-given right to slay helpless animals in the most horrific manner.'

Colin can feel her passion, as he'd felt it through the short TV clip yesterday, and it resonates deep within him.

'Tell me what you need then.'

'Haha, how much can you spare!' She punches his arm lightly to show she is kidding, but he stares intently into her eyes.

'Tell me how much would make a difference.'

'Oh Colin, you are sweet, but I know nothing about you. You hide behind your dark glasses; you may be a filthy-rich loony who wants to splash hundreds of thousands, or a crazy nut who has nothing to his name but wants to make me feel good…'

The smile takes away any potential for malice and Colin smiles back.

'Let's assume I am the first one you mentioned, and add a few zeros!'

'If you are that damned rich then I will marry you, steal all your fortune and donate it to the hunt sabs!'

They both smile and she raises her coffee cup to him in a mock toast.

'Give me your bank account details then and I will transfer some funds tonight.'

A slight frown replaces her smile.

'You *are* serious, aren't you?'

'Deadly.'

'What's your telephone number? I will text you the hunt sab account details. If you are making a joke at my expense then I will strangle you. If you are serious though…'

Her voice tails off and she looks piercingly to where his eyes should have been.

They exchange numbers and she says she needs to get back to the demo.

'I have a good nose for people Colin, and a good feeling about you. But whatever you turn out to be, I have enjoyed meeting you.'

She leans forward and, on tiptoes, kisses him lightly on his right cheek.

Then she darts through the café door and is gone.

Colin leaves too, mission accomplished, whatever *mission* was. He feels like he is walking in the clouds and he likes it.

64

It's 09:05 in the ops room and the team is gathered for the daily briefing.

'Morning all; updates from previous as follows: We have some positive news and it's going to mean that Samantha and Brian take a holiday. You guys are heading for the sunny climes of northern Spain to interview local police about the discovery in twenty feet of water of a British registered yacht. In case one of you can't make it I am prepared to send, in their place, the person who answers this question correctly. What's the name of the boat?'

Sicknote jumps straight in.

'The Salty Pig Sir!'

'Close Sicknote, any advances?'

Carol chips in.

'Salty Pig Runs Free Sir!'

'Correct! At least, we think that's correct; some doubts because her name was painted out.'

Carol again:

'So how did they ID her then Sir?'

'Apparently all craft – see how I slip so easily into nautical terminology now – have a serial number of some description. I'm reliably informed that all boats built since 1998 will have a thing called a Hull Identification Number or HIN; it's a unique combination of letters and numbers either fixed or embossed on the outside hull above the waterline. Doesn't always happen, but luckily for us Mr Furness bought his boat from a reputable trader. Even luckier for us is that she was salvaged so quickly; the drug running operations all around that area are huge business and the police tend to throw every resource into fighting that particular crime. Clearly they suspected a narcotics link so we have timely intelligence.'

'I guess they have a vested interest too Guv; most of them being as honest as a bible story!'

'They may be a trifle corrupt Sicknote, but let's leave your religious views out of it, shall we?'

194

'How long's she likely to have lain there Guv?'

'Not certain Samantha, but apparently there's a busy ferry route almost directly over the site where she was sunk and the water is sometimes clear enough to see the bottom – a sharp-eyed tourist spotted her and alerted the ship's captain.'

'Seems unlike our calculating murderer to dump her where she'd be so easily discovered?'

'Yeah, that's true Sicknote; I understand the ferry paths were re-routed due to silt build up and if our friend was using an old map he might not have known. It's the little details that catch crooks.'

'Chart, Guv.'

'Sorry Sicknote?'

'Not map; *chart*! Just want you to maintain your brilliant air of nautical expertise Guv.'

'Yeah, whatever. OK then; Samantha and Brian – anything stopping you heading out there today?'

Two heads are shaken.

'OK – pop into admin and get the travel and hotels etc sorted. You can join us each morning at 10:00 local time via WebEx to brief us and catch up on the investigation here, although I suspect you'll be giving us more info that you get from us. Let's nail this bastard quick-smart before he has a chance to do whatever he's almost certainly planning to do next. Thanks all.'

65

The 'phone inside the tent pings to announce the arrival of a text message as Colin is making a simple vegetable soup on his camping stove. He leaves the boiling liquid for a moment to check the screen. Patricia's face smiles up at him.

He is astonished that this can happen; all she did was give him her number; she must have activated some invisible permission button that allows her image to be transferred along with her number. Maybe it's a sign of her trust in him; Colin's not used to that. His heart does that unaccustomed skipping thing again and he nervously opens the text. It's simply a series of numbers; a bank sort code and account number, along with an IBAN and some other row of digits he's not familiar with.

A hissing sound drags his attention back to the stove where a green froth is bubbling over the sides of the large mess tin. He turns off the gas and leaves the soup to cool a little while he logs on to one of his instant access accounts based in Switzerland. He sets up a money transfer and the wonders of technology shift one hundred thousand pounds from a Panama registered company, via (he thinks) Beirut and the Virgin Islands into the account of the hunt saboteurs (again, he assumes) in Germany.

It's an odd feeling for a number of reasons; he has never seen the money in physical terms, so it feels somewhat unreal, ephemeral. The transfer is through a whole complexity of false or non-existent companies with multiple ghost accounts set up by the odd accountant, David Abrahams, with his nasal voice and annoying mannerisms. Well he's out of the loop now; Colin has paid him off and added enough for even a scrupulous man to be tempted to forget the nature of their business. Abrahams was way short of that ethical mark and it was an easy agreement to arrive at.

Then there is the origin and destination of the funds; blood money from the torture and murder of a billion chickens going to a bunch of people he knows almost nothing about, but trusts to do the right thing for the animals. And then there's the girl, Patricia; and he just has a good feeling.

66

Your WebKonnekt session has started:
DIDyson1: 'Hi both what's new?'
Ext4013: 'Morning Guv; team. Forget all you've ever heard about EU law enforcement cooperation and Europol competence; these guys are operating under false pretences. Every chance to block our investigation gets grabbed with both fists – it's like pulling teeth.'
DIDyson1: 'Oh great just what we need, a Spanish inquisition of our own; need me to put some pressure via DCI Moody?'
Ext4013: 'Little point Guv; we've got about all we're going to get right now. Our best chance is getting out there amongst the worms and asking our own questions. We have an interpreter now, but he's hardly speedy Gonzalez when it comes to getting his arse into gear.'
DIDyson1: 'OK – give us the sum total so far.'
Ext4013: 'Boat definitely belongs to Furness, but there's no trace of him anywhere. CCTV is being collected for us, but it's not like UK where everything is monitored, here they clearly still care about personal privacy. Don't hold out much hope that we'll track him from here.'
DIDyson1: 'What about onward travel; he must have a car or something?'
Ext4013: 'Yeah, we've sent enquiries out to all car hire and local second hand sales places, collating that as we speak. He obviously won't be using his real name, but we're looking for anyone with a UK passport and we've given his photos and description out. He's also on the local watch lists, but there are plenty of UK tourists so it won't be quick.'
DIDyson1: 'OK, sounds like you're doing all you can. No real news here. Use my mobile if you turn up anything hot, otherwise speak tomorrow.'
Ext4013: 'Will do boss. Oh; just a thought, I'm guessing old Mrs F doesn't have a mobile; have we got any monitoring installed on the hospital payphones?'
DIDyson1: 'No; good point I'll get it authorised – thanks!'
Your WebKonnekt session has ended.

67

She's sat on the wall at the end of the riverbank and Colin stops about 100 metres away, unseen behind a row of bushes, and takes a while to savour the moment and collect his nervous thoughts.

He's wearing a new cap bearing some pointless American-style advertising logo that means absolutely nothing to him – and possibly means nothing to anyone on the planet, probably having been designed and manufactured in a part of the world where materials are easy, labour cheap and language the jargon of money. But the hat is part of his ongoing series of ever-changing basic disguises.

Although he lacks some social interaction skills he is aware that the cap and dark glasses must look a little odd and wonders whether she will question his dress sense? She'll hopefully think he's a shy and reclusive maverick millionaire; better that she sees the glasses than his deformity. He is terrified of the moment when she will see his eyes and wonders how long he can delay that. And when she does clock his face, what then? His picture has been all over the news in UK and possibly abroad, though he hasn't seen any updates for a while; had she seen him on TV? Would she remember? Will she put two and two together and work out who he is? She might when she sees his eyes and that would be the end of the adventure; he knows he must try to delay that at all costs.

Extremely anxious, he considers turning round and simply walking away. But she has his number and young people are resourceful, she'd track him down through some wizardry, he's sure. And in any case, he *wants* this. He *needs* to explore this feeling, no matter how counter-intuitive and probably pointless it might be. Hell, he is probably barking up completely the wrong tree, he has so little experience and a history of faux pas with any relationships he's ever attempted in the past; he is simply missing that social skills gene or hormone or whatever it is that everyone else seems to have that makes their lives so relatively straightforward.

Any decision is taken from his hands as he hears her shout, standing and waving towards him. He raises his right arm in acknowledgement and is briefly uncomfortable in its resemblance to a Nazi salute. He drops it quickly and has to adjust his stance because she's racing towards him with eyes wide and fists clenched.

He's unsure how to take this; *has she sussed him? Is the secret already out? Did he give himself away somehow? Is she angry, or is this some other emotion*? His question is answered as she stops, panting directly in front of him and reaches both hands up to hold onto his shoulders.

'Was that really you? All that money – are you a gazillionaire or something?'

They are both laughing now, and he takes her hands in his own.

'No, Patricia, nothing like that, just a guy who wants to do the right thing when the opportunity arises.'

'But we can't possibly take that much money – it's insane!'

'No, you must have it; that money was built on cruelty and there's plenty more where that came from. I have seen the passion you guys have for animals. My passion is just as strong, but I chose a different path. It got me into a lot of trouble and maybe the money is some way to atone for that. Please, take it and use it to stop those monsters and their sick so-called sport!'

She takes his arm.

'Walk with me; it's a beautiful day. I want to learn about you.'

She's speaking English and her accent is mildly Americanised – probably from all the films and media that stems from that country.

'Maybe you don't want to learn too much; you might not like what you find.'

She looks at him sideways and screws up her face a little.

'I don't think anything you could say would shock me; I may be quite young still, but I have seen just about everything the world can throw at a person.'

'Patricia, I have done terrible things, but for the right reasons – or so I believe. Forgive me if I don't go into details yet, but you would definitely be shocked.'

'Well, let's agree to disagree on that point. Tell me some things about you that won't shock me then!'

She leans into him a little as they stroll and it feels as if he's walking on air.

He tells her of his childhood, a mother who disappeared one night without trace and then her recent return. They both weep a little at the incredible sadness and loss, then the great joy.

Colin avoids volunteering too many details about the past or the present situation, although it's clear he is hiding something. He asks her how she became so passionate about the anti hunt movement.

'Well for a start it's one of the cruellest things a human does, and in the name of sport. I think we are blessed with so many other wonderful pastimes that to call hunting a pleasure is a sad reflection on our species.'

He nods in agreement and she continues.

'I always remember a quote from a skateboarding guy called Paul Rodriguez; he said *hunting's not a sport because in sport both sides should know they are in the game*. That kind of sums it up for me, the arrogance of man to go galloping across the fields with his horns and his dogs or creeping around the woods with his guns, it's sick and I want to stop it and educate the people who do it so they understand how wrong it is.'

'Forgive me, but do you really think education will ever change people? Think a few so-called extremists out on a limb pushing a different point of view will make a difference?'

She stops and looks directly at him so intensely that he shifts a little uncomfortably.

'My dear friend, throughout history it's the only thing that ever has.'

Colin mulls this thought for a while in silence as she takes his hand.

'But how do you respond to those people who say they hunt for food? Or for the animal skins?'

'Colin, the people we were talking about primarily hunt for the thrill of killing, or making the kill vicariously through their dogs. They are the worst kind. But *all* hunters are out on a limb. If they are killing an animal for the taste of its meat, well then I say their taste buds are ethically retarded; why do we assume it's wrong to kill a rhino for some imaginary medicinal purpose, but OK to kill because something tastes nice? We need to examine our stance. It's either *always* OK to kill, or *never*; there's no in-between land. And as for skins – once upon a time people lived in caves and hunted through necessity. Those days are long gone and we have textiles and synthetics that are every bit as good as the best animal skin. The only animal that looks good in bearskin is a bear. Simple!'

Her voice has become harder, louder and the cadence of her speech faster; he smiles at the depth of her emotion and her tenacity.
'OK, I'm on your side, remember? Tell me about your university studies.'
'Sorry; I get carried away! University, well, I was always an animal lover and as a kid decided to become a vet. I got side-tracked I guess and wanted to study biology first, then animal psychology; specifically animal behavioural traits. Most specifically, I was on a PhD research programme working mostly with bees and looking at the ability of arachnids and insects to learn. We call it *awareness* or *consciousness*. It's about their ability to be cognisant of their environment; able to tell that there is a bigger picture. For too many years we have assumed that they can't relate themselves to the wider world and to other happenings. We proved, we think, that they can.'
'Wow! I know that some animals are able to do that, know that something exists, even when they can't see it any more…but insects? Wow!'
'Yeah – object permanence is what you are referring to. Dogs can do that way earlier than humans. Pigs and most mammals – even chickens in fact are earlier object permanence aware than people. Interesting, huh?'
'Damn right. Does it indicate intelligence?'
'Well, certainly it relates to working memory, like the RAM systems in computers. Early signs are that it is closely linked to this *awareness* thing I mentioned. There have been links to belief systems – like religion – and although loads more research is needed, it seems humans are actually quite retarded, when we thought we were the genius of the gene pool!'
'That's really interesting – but tell me about the bees; I love bees.'

They reach a small clearing with a fallen oak trunk and sit in the sun, half-inclined towards each other.
'Oh the bees were fucking amazing; I mean, listen to this right…'

202

Colin finds the use of the expletive – in English – astonishingly grounding.

'With the original research goals we had this narrow remit, but, in the spirit of scientific efficacy…'

She holds up both hands in an apologetic manner.

'Er, sorry, are you OK with techno Deutsch?'

'I'll stop you when I get lost!' He smiles.

'OK, well, I do tend to get a bit animated, so please just shout. Where was I – ah yes, we were permitted to expand the original research from arachnids to include some insects. Rationale was – officially – that we needed a control group; unofficially though, the professor running the programme was writing a book on bees and needed a few theories testing – dead naughty, but well, budgets were tight and as long as we delivered on the spider stuff nobody needed to know. In any case, all the bee work was done in our spare time, and it was just amazing. We practically lived in the hives.'

She shifts a little closer and her hand rests on Colin's knee. He shivers; a normal reaction in him to human closeness, but for once it's not through any distaste.

'You know anything about limb autotomy?'

'Limb what?'

'Basically, shedding limbs as a defence mechanism. Lots of small creatures do it – especially spiders. It was always thought to be a painless natural protection to venomous bites and such, but we threw up some other interesting theories. You know that foxes and dogs will bite off their own leg to escape snares? Kind of slow and painful version of limb autotomy – except we now know – because we proved it – that shedding a limb hurts a spider like fuck!'

Colin has two instant thoughts; he's reminded of Boner in the sodden field, sawing away for hours at his own lower leg. Then he remembers a day, way back in time, when he had suspected that spiders could definitely feel pain. He'd witnessed Lindegaard, the school bully taking a spider apart, leg by leg and toying with the poor creature. Colin alone, it had seemed, could see the desperate wriggling of the tortured animal trying to escape the evil bastard's game, but all the other kids had either danced around the small circle of onlookers laughing, or stared open-mouthed in wonder at the ..*at what? At the spectacle? Had they been entertained?* Colin didn't know, but when the poor thing was down to four legs he had leaped upon the older boy and dragged him to the ground, biting his ear in a desperate attempt to stop the senseless violence. He'd got into an awful lot of trouble for that, and worse, it had been the start of the Swedish bully's personal vendetta.

'Colin?'

He realises she must have been speaking and he'd been off in the past, reminiscing.

'Sorry – I er, well, you brought back some memories. What were you saying?'

'I was explaining our research, but never mind. Anyway, so these creatures react to serotonin, histamine, phospholipase A2 and melittin – all are components of venom that lead to autotomy – and get this – *all* are known to initiate pain in humans! So we proved – well, we are on the way to proving – that spiders feel pain. Major breakthrough! Feel free to applaud.'

She smiles and Colin, grinning, duly claps his hands in exaggerated appreciation.

'How did you link this to the bees?'

'Ah! Well, almost by accident – call it luck, serendipity, whatever – sometimes science needs a little nudge! We were getting the melittin from some of the bees and someone hit on the question of whether insects – i.e. bees – we had lots of them – would autotomise legs or wings. Well, to cut a long story short, there was no evidence of that when we hit them with a mild spider venom, but we noticed that they became depressed.'

'What? How the hell do you spot depression in bees?'

Colin was genuinely incredulous, but loving the biology-cum-psychology lesson.

'Ha! Well we could – so there! We noticed that the bees which were subjected to the simulated attack were behaving differently to the other bees – the (she makes the sign of inverted commas in the air with her hands and fingers) *"accidental"* control group. They exhibited typical signs of anxiety and depression that we see in humans and large mammals. The more we explored this, the clearer it became that bees are aware of the environment *and the role they play in its success!'*

As she almost shouts these words, she grabs Colin's sleeves and practically jumps up and down in front of him.

'Oops – sorry, told you, I get carried away!'

He is laughing and enjoying her passion. And actually learning a lot. He wants more.

'Give me more to work with than simply believing they are aware – what *specifically* can bees tell us about intelligence?'

'Well, now here's the thing. Animals can be tested on memory and intelligence and problem solving skills, but not – it was thought – insects. Or rather, existing research is inconclusive and we didn't imagine that they would respond to stimuli. But… guess what??'

'Go on – what?'

'Bees can follow instructions, decide which pathways to follow to solve puzzles and identify the clues to help them.'

'Er…OK, such as?'

'Well. Some animals can be easily trained to pull levers and touch stuff, but bees can't really do the lever thing, being so tiny. However…they can work their way through a maze of tunnels given the right signposts – like coloured patches with certain patterns. They can even be taught to take the opposite route to the one that's signed. These tests are called delayed match to sample – or DMTS and the opposite is the delayed non match to sample or DNMTS test.'

'Thanks Mr Attenborough.' Colin laughs.

'Don't mock – they are bloody clever, and can even anticipate what to do when they come across a new situation – I mean they can, after training, follow or choose to ignore other stimulants like smells and textures. In other words, they learn!'

'That's incredible. What's the next step then professor?'

'Well, I hit the classic dilemma there; having established that they feel pain and are aware, how could I justify ongoing experiments, knowing that they would be hurting and becoming depressed? I quit the post and got involved with the whole animal rights movement in a big way.'

'Hence the hunt saboteur stuff?'

'That's just the tip of the iceberg – I do loads of other stuff.'

'Such as?'

'Oh gosh, protecting badgers from culling, demos, some slightly more murky activities that the police wouldn't approve….nor my mother!'

She leaves the statement hanging and Colin wants to confess some of his own.

'Seems we have a lot in common!'

She leans back and looks at him oddly.

'You think? You are rich, I am destitute, you are normal, I am disruptive, you listen, I talk, we are pretty opposite if you ask me!'

Despite the risks, Colin is burning to tell her at least some of his past.

'I have done some things that make your actions look like Kindergarten playtime Patricia.'

He can see she's bristling at this, but waiting for more.

He decides it's now or never.

'I have killed in order to protect animals.'

Her hand goes to her open mouth and he knows he's gone too far. But when she speaks, it's with a calm, quiet voice, full of concern.

'I'm sure you had your reasons. Want to tell me about it?'

He looks to the trees in the distance and sighs deeply.

'Probably best if I don't; not just yet, anyway. I will though, when we know each other a little better.'

'OK, but just so you know, whatever it was you did, *whatever* it was, if it was done to protect animals then it's probably alright by me.'

She leans over and plants a quick kiss on the same cheek as last time and jumps up, pulling him up by the hand.

'Come on, I want to show you something.'

68

They have been walking for half an hour, Colin listening more than speaking, allowing Patricia's natural tendency to talk to solve the inner dilemma of how much to reveal about his recent past. Finally the field they are walking through gives way to a hedgerow and almost hidden behind the long grass and buried beneath rampant bramble tendrils Colin can see the remains of a small dilapidated red brick building.

As they approach he can see a few corrugated tin sheets leaning against the left-hand wall forming a crude triangle. The angle is such that there's a gap at the bottom with about two feet of loose, fine earth and the area there is clear of vegetation. A little way into the shadowy spot beneath the old rusting tin is a deep hole running away from them.

Patricia takes his arm, holds her left index finger in front of her pursed lips and makes a quiet *shhhh* sound. Colin raises his thumb in silent acknowledgement. She whispers close to his ear and he catches the faint scent of her perfume. He has always thought of girls wearing perfume as promiscuous, some kind of blatant flirting and sign of desperation for sex, but this is different.
The moment is intoxicating.

'They will be asleep but you may see a glimpse.'
He peers closely into the hole, aware of the closeness of her body and feeling an electric current – she must sense this too? Must feel the sparks shooting through his body and mind and leaping across to hers? Maybe it's all in his head, but he wants the moment to last forever.

The hole is too deep and dark and they can't make out anything inside. Again her head comes close and a wispy strand of her blonde hair blows across his face. She whispers.
'Let's come back tonight when it's dark – if we are quiet and very lucky we can see them then.'

He's disappointed that this moment will end now, but the prospect of another, at night is attractive. He nods agreement and they creep away.

On the long walk back through the fields she again does most of the talking and he listens and learns.
'You know Colin; I can't help feeling sorry for the badgers. The argument that culling is effective has already been lost in Germany and those that have a vested interest are trying all manner of dirty tricks to get permission to get their guns out. It's almost like they *have* to shoot *something* for their kicks.'
'I'm sure a lot of them do Patricia, but what kind of arguments are they using?'
'They are now playing on the link between badgers and staphylococcus aureus.'
'The food bug?'
'Yeah. Trying to claim that people are becoming ill when badgers nest around chicken farms. One of the research papers from your own Durham University clearly disproves this – and also rubbishes the claims that culling is the solution to the tuberculosis problem in cattle. But the chicken farmers are using it as an excuse to pump even more antibiotics into the poor birds. They are really just a cocktail of miserable anti-biotic chemicals. You know, they even soak the dead birds in bleach?'
'Yeah, I know. My father was a chicken farmer.'
'Really? Oh wow, is that why you hate animal abuse so much?'
'It was the start for sure. But once you open your eyes to the disgusting things we do you can't close them again, unless you are brain dead or retarded.'
She laughs.

'The problem is though, that this false argument and the uncontrolled use of all these additional antibiotics are actually making the problem worse. Staphylococcus is now almost antibiotic resistant. Did you know that Alexander Fleming used the staph aureus bacteria in his first Petri dish experiments with penicillin in the 40s? It was what led him to prove the concept. Already ten years later the bacteria were becoming stronger and within twenty years 80% of staph aureus strains were penicillin resistant. Today, penicillin is as good as useless against it. Once that cycle is fully complete – probably within the next five years – we are really in the shit. The bacteria will mutate and become even more aggressive. The only saving grace is that viruses and bacteria and the like depend on the host staying alive, so it's unlikely to start killing people. But the spread of the bugs is critical in its design phase and we will see more violent reactions – that's how it spreads from person to person, by being spattered all over surfaces. Isn't evolution great!'

'Maybe we should do something then together. A joint Anglo-German action?'
'What are you thinking?'
'Oh, I dunno, maybe we should raise awareness by making a bunch of carnivores vomit for a few days!'
'Haha – that would be so funny!'
She sees from his expression that he's not kidding.
'Are you serious? How do you propose we do that?'
'Well, all we need to do is find the right arena, provide the right bugs, light the blue touch paper and stand back and enjoy the fireworks.'

They talk some more about where, when and how this might be achieved and by the time they are back in the town they have a skeleton plan formulated.
'Let's meet here at 21:00 and go to the badgers. I'll have a chat to some trusted friends and we'll agree who needs to do what then.'

She leans forward and kisses both cheeks continental style and skips off into the town, leaving Colin thinking about badgers, bugs and pretty German girls.

69

They are wrapped up warm against the biting October wind. This part of Germany can really test clothing design, and they have both experienced similar conditions enough to know where to spend money when it comes to keeping warm and dry. Colin has had to wear the thick framed spectacles which he had worn when he undertook the risky hospital visit. Dark glasses would have been idiotic, but the plain-lensed pair he has on now can barely disguise his eyes. He is grateful for the darkness.

'At least the wind will blow our scent away from the sett if we approach from the right side, and any noise we make will be covered up too – unless we act like idiots!'
Her brilliant white teeth flash in the darkness and Colin is again made conscious of his own. Although he's scrupulous about personal hygiene he silently vows to get something done about them.
'We must be near now?' He speaks in a whisper; anxious to show her how sensitive he is to the situation.
'Just through this next field and over the stream, we will need to make a detour and come at it from the northern side to mask our human smells.'
Colin feels her tug his arm backwards.
'Shhh – there's somebody there – look.'

She is pointing half-right in the gloom and sure enough, less than thirty metres away he sees a narrow light beam playing across the hedgerow. She leans very close so that he catches a trace of her perfume and he feels that tingling sensation again.
'I think whoever it is, is up to no good. Nobody who wanted to peacefully watch badgers would shine a torch all over their sett; it may be a cull team.'
'Do they shoot them or what?'
'Usually yes, but that's so rare now because science has proved that culling doesn't work. This time of night, with no obvious activity around I think it's more likely to be an illegal operation – most likely a farmer trying to take the law into his own hands. We need to make ourselves known so he or they don't shoot us by mistake.'
'Well, OK, let's give them something to think about then.'

Before she can react, Colin strides off towards the mystery person or persons. She tries to stop him and grabs the back of his jacket, pulling him much harder than she means to. They land in a heap in the cold mud. Colin is amazed at her hidden strength and is reminded of the detective's girlfriend who had battered him around the head on the yacht. He needed to learn to make better allowances for small, feisty females.

'Oh god, sorry, but we need to watch first and see…' The words die in her throat as he grabs her face in two cold hands and kisses her on the lips.

Neither of them moves for a moment. When he speaks it's almost inaudible.

'Sorry – I, er, I don't know what came over me.'
He's never had the urge to do that before and is genuinely surprised by his reaction.
Patricia seems to shrug it off with a smile, as if she were used to relative strangers losing self control in her presence. Her whisper is half laugh and half lecture.
'Time for relaxation later crazy English man, meanwhile we have intruders to observe – now *do not* do anything until I give the word!'
She rises to her knees from the mud and peers over the long vegetation.
'Can only see one person – definitely a bad one – he has some canisters I think, probably plans to gas the poor animals. Let's get a little closer – but stay behind me!'

They creep through the brambles and soon have the old brick structure between them and the visitor.
'What do you want to do? I can take him easily …'
'No crazy man, we watch and wait.'
'What if we are too slow and he kills them?'
'He won't. He's definitely got gas canisters look; it takes ages to set up the gas equipment to get the stuff right down into the burrow.'
'What gas will it be?'
'Depends if he has access to cyanide gas or just carbon monoxide.'
'Cyanide? That's really dangerous, surely?'

There are more noises coming from near the sett entrance now and Colin ignores her earlier request to stay behind her. A sudden hiss of escaping gas shocks them into action and Colin is up and sprinting before Patricia even has chance to react.

'Hey! Stop!' Colin has shouted in English and corrects his error. 'Halt!'

Patricia struggles to keep up and within a few seconds Colin has covered the ground between them and the intruder. Without any further warning he leaps through the air and smashes hard into the guys back, taking him crashing face-first into the wall of the old brick building and knocking the air from both of them.
Colin recovers instantly and in the same movement wrenches the guy's right arm up behind his back. Despite the guy's size and girth he's instantly immobilised. The gas is still escaping and Patricia moves to turn the large knob on top of the canister.

Colin breaks back into English without thinking.
'What the fuck do you think you are doing you slimy shit?'
With a sickening crunch his right fist smashes into the man's nose so that blood erupts in an outward spray. Patricia grabs his arm for the second time in as many minutes.
'Stop, what are you doing? You can't just beat him up; there are rules even for people like us!'
'Fuck the rules; tell that to the dead badger cubs.'
Patricia is clearly a little taken aback by the strength of his emotion.

Colin sees that he's overstepped a mark somehow but is unable to see why or where that mark was. He's not used to there being *rules* and *standards*. He is used to acting alone, and in such a way that means he only needs to do things once.
'I only gave him a gentle warning, next time I will really hurt him.'

Patricia is shocked but inwardly also a little impressed.
'OK, but he isn't resisting and he's got the message.'
She shouts at the man, in German.

'What do you think you are doing? You clearly wanted to kill a family of badgers, and that's illegal so we are going to take you to the police.'

The man finds his voice, mumbling through the hand that's clutching his shattered nose.
'Yeah sure, take me to the police and I will have you arrested for trespass and assault, you fucking lunatics!'
For Colin, such belligerence is like a red rag to a bull and he grabs the guy around the throat again and lifts him so that their eyes are level. He feels Patricia's hand on his forearm and relaxes a little.
'So this is your land I assume?'
Patricia comes across as very relaxed and reasonable in comparison to the hot-headed Colin. She looks at the warnings on the gas cylinder.

'And I suppose you think you can sneak around with illegal chemicals, poisoning the local wildlife indiscriminately and uncontrolled? Well the authorities – particularly the police and the Bundesministerium für Ernährung und Landwirtschaft will certainly want to learn all about your activities, they'll be especially keen to learn where you obtained your supply of cyanide gas, who your contacts and fellow criminals are and I expect they will investigate your whole fucking life, so come on – let's go, lead on, be my guest!'
'I need a doctor, I think my nose is broken.'

Colin can't stand the whinging and moaning.
'You can see as many doctors as you like – and unless you play ball a broken nose will be least of your worries – once we've removed this killing equipment and got it the hell away from these animals. But first I am going to discharge this cylinder over there away from their home We will be around, and so will many of our friends. The guys you met tonight are the nice ones; you won't be so well treated in future if you decide to go on killing innocent animals. You have been warned; now fuck off back to your shitty little life.'

Colin carries the part-filled gas canister away from the sett and twists the regulator a quarter turn anti-clockwise. The gas escapes slowly. 'It will take a while to fully discharge at this rate but at least this way it will disperse harmlessly.'

The farmer is still there and when the hiss finally becomes inaudible Colin closes off the regulator.

'Here, all yours.'

He throws the bottle at the feet of the would-be killer and they watch him struggle to gather his equipment together whilst nursing a still-bleeding nose. Colin and Patricia remain at the site for a while, waiting to see if the badgers will make a guest appearance, but it's chilly.

'I fancy a drink – can we get a hot chocolate anywhere this time of night?'

'In Germany? Are you kidding? The place shuts down when the Pope goes to bed.'

She notices Colin's puzzled frown.

'It's an expression we use here; the Catholics have dominated the way we live for so long. I have chocolate at my flat, but it's full of visitors so don't expect a quiet time!'

'Are they all terrorists like you?' He smiles.

'Me? Terrorist?' She laughs. 'Maybe a little...'

'I enjoyed that tonight, working with you. I felt alive. I want to do more things like that.'

'So you are a terrorist at heart too? Ha ha! Mein süßer Engländer!'

'Meine Terroristin!'

The flat is on the third floor of an unimaginatively designed five story concrete and red-brick block; one of three almost identical structures, differentiated only by the illuminated numbers over the main entrances. There are occasional isolated lamp-posts set into the grounds around the buildings, simple poles topped with beachball size white globes and from these and a little light that spills from a few balconies Colin can see well-tended beds dotted amongst the shrubs; little islands of green in the expanse of dew-saturated grass surrounding the buildings and a small fenced children's play area with swings and a slide. Wooden horses balance on huge springs which look as though they might have been lifted from a lorry chassis.
It looks like a nice area.

Patricia unlocks the main front door and they walk straight ahead, past a bank of numbered mail boxes – some with names in little white cards set behind a plastic cover – and into the open lift. She presses the fourth button from the bottom and as the doors slide closed warns him again about the people he's about to meet.
'Just smile and be yourself; they are really lovely people, just passionate about what they do. If anyone offends you with their extreme views just smile and ignore them. They get carried away sometimes.'

If only she knew! Maybe she will before too long; the glasses are a poor disguise and he's convinced that she – or one of her friends – will identify him. They exit the lift on the top floor and immediately opposite the lift is her apartment. He wonders whether the lift disturbs her sleep; he would hate it. She pauses with the key in the lock.
'Oh, one final thing, they have been on a mission tonight and might be a little hyperactive, there was a chicken run – ever done one?'
'Don't think so, no.'
'OK, I'll let them explain then!'
With a smile she opens the door and the noise of twenty or so people talking and shouting erupts into the resonant hallway.

'Hey! Patsy baby! Over here, I have your photos.'

This is from a skinny long-haired guy sitting with an acoustic guitar, bottle of Pilsner Urquelle beer and a cigarette. As Colin watches he impales the filtered end of the cigarette onto one of the pieces of excess guitar string dangling above the headstock, strums a full bar-chord and bursts into song. Something Colin doesn't know, but everyone else seems to and they all join in. He feels awkward; isolated and out of place.

After two verses they do some strange clapping routine and sing another verse, finishing with a chorus of bizarre yelps and whoops. Colin wants to run, but is stuck; he hadn't anticipated this.

A tall guy standing in the doorway to another room calls out.

'Hey Patricia, who's your friend?'

Patricia comes back over to where she'd abandoned Colin and loops her arm through his.

'Everyone, this is Colin, my English friend and as of today our biggest ever benefactor.'

There's a chorus of cheers and some applause and guitar man shouts out in English:

'Velcome biggest ever benefactor!'

Smiles all round but Colin is uncomfortable and takes Patricia quietly to one side.

'I don't feel so good; think I'm going to head back.'

'Oh, no! Really? I *so* wanted you to meet my friends. I'm sure you'll like them; you just need to get to know a few. Come on, I'll introduce you.'

She grabs his hand and pulls him towards his worst nightmare; guitar man.

'Detlef, this is Colin; Colin – Detlef!'

The two shake hands.

Up close Detlef is older than Colin had first thought, and he has a scar running across his right hand that looks like it came from a nasty injury.

'So you are the new hero on the scene Colin?'

As he asks the question he raises his eyebrows and twists his neck slightly to the right, so that he presents his left ear as if asking a question is not enough and encouraging an early answer.

Is he sneering?

'Hardly a hero, no. Just someone who wants to help.'

'Yeah, well zer are two types of people in my opinion; zose who have ze money and zose who do ze dangerous stuff. Vich are you?'

Colin is amused at the way so many Germans – even those who are fluent in English – can't pronounce the letter combination *t* and *h*. And he's also a little taken aback at this guy's abrupt, almost challenging stance and he's doing that neck and eyebrow thing again.

'If there are only two types I guess I am the first kind then, although I have done a few things that you might ...'

Before Colin finishes the sentence Detlef thrusts his right arm at him.

'Animal trap – fifty stitches, two years of physio and psychotherapy – got anyzing like zat?'

Again the neck twist.

'Er, not specifically no, but I've done my share of therapy too.'

'Zought so. Never mind, zis little voond von't stop *me* from getting justice for animals. Glad to have you on board wiz your bank balance, but take my advice, stay in ze warm and keep nice and safe. Patsy vill look after you; she likes men viz money.'

This time he twists further so that he appears to be throwing a direct challenge at Patricia to deny the statement.

She responds dismissively.

'You're drunk Detlef – *again*. Come on Colin, let's get that hot chocolate.'

'Hot chocolate? Haha, don't overdose!' More bar chords in a flamenco style.

She takes his arm and tugs him quickly, picking her way through the sitting and prone bodies littering the floor among the glasses and dirty plates.

In the kitchen it's quieter, just two girls looking at something on a mobile 'phone. They look up briefly and wave and then get back to the little screen.

Colin speaks in English.

'Well he loves himself just a little then!'

'Yeah, gosh so sorry – I didn't realise he'd been drinking. He's fine, really nice when he's sober but an arsehole when he's had a drink or a smoke; turns him into a nastier person for some reason.'

'Or reveals his true personality.' It's said as a statement.

217

'Yeah, maybe that. Anyway, I only have vegan choc – so hope you like it!'

'Vegan is the only kind for me Patsy.' He smiles; he saw how much the pet name had wound her up when Detlef used it.

'Oh don't, it's bad enough with him calling me that, don't you dare start too. Detlef and I were an item once. He can't seem to let it go when he's been on the booze so try to make allowances, OK?'

'Sure, as long as he doesn't act like an idiot all the time.'

Detlef chooses that moment to enter the kitchen.

'Ah so zis is vere you have snuck off to viz my Patsy. Any more beer?'

'Detlef, I am not *your* Patsy, nor anyone's, and you know I detest that silly name.'

'Ah yeah – oh vell, I like it! So you guys been off counting ze coal zen?'

Colin is genuinely puzzled and wonders if this is a German word he's not familiar with.

'Coal?'

'Kohle, dough, money!'

'Oh, yes, er, no. We went to see a badger sett.'

'First time?' (*Twisty neck, eyebrows raised*).

'Actually yes'

'Be careful viz badgers; nasty creatures if zey get chance to attack you.'

'Oh don't worry, I can look after myself.'

Detlef thrusts his entire face into Colin's personal space and breathes beery fumes all over him.

'Can you, rich boy? Can you really? I vonder...hey, vot's viz your eyes? Are you deformed or somezing?'

The moment Colin had been dreading. He turns to Patricia.

'Hey, you know what; I'm going to skip the drink – thanks all the same. I need to get some air.'

Without pause he dashes from the kitchen and out through the front door. Rather than waiting for the lift he takes the stairs three at a time.

He's half way down the road as his 'phone bleeps.

"Sorry. Call me tomorrow. Please. Patricia".

Your WebKonnekt session has started:

DIDyson1: ' Hi both; how's the weather holding up?'

Ext4013: 'Morning Guv; morning team. Weather is awful – not booking a holiday here any time soon. No other news either, all CCTV and hire car etc enquiries have drawn blanks. Not really sure where to go from here on.'

DIDyson1: 'OK. Under huge pressure here to deliver results so I suggest you pull out of Spain and head to Garmisch – see if you can spark up some of the local plods in Germany.'

Ext4013: 'OK Guv. Can you send the contact details for the local Furness family members?'

DIDyson1: 'It's all in a pack I'll be emailing you in the next hour, along with details of my counterpart there and any data they've gathered.'

Ext4013: 'OK, thanks Guv. We'll keep you in the loop on any developments.'

Your WebKonnekt session has ended.

'So let me get this right, you want me pose as a temporary waitress and to go into the restaurant and simply rub this stuff over the cutlery that's presumably just been laid out?'

Colin and Patricia are sitting at the same spot on the banks of the Patriarch River, which, being a mountain river, offers few opportunities to sit and enjoy the stunning scenery. This is one of the few places where the banks are gentle enough to allow such relaxation.

'Exactly; the guests and official delegates from the Foie Gras festival won't sit down until 20:00 at the earliest, that will allow you roughly an hour to do all the place settings and get out before anyone even questions your presence there – they will be running around like headless chickens because the Foie Gras delivery will be delayed…courtesy of yours truly!'
'Bad choice of metaphor!'
'What? Oh – headless chickens, sorry, they will be *panicking* then. Better?'
She smiles sarcastically.
'Much! OK, what if they quiz me?'
'They won't. Trust me, their world will be falling apart – one of the biggest food festivals on the local calendar, hundreds of important – and very rich – guests and no product. The collective Maitre D's, restaurant managers and personnel will be in a right state. Plus they will need so many agency staff over the course of the weekend, there will be dozens of unfamiliar faces.'
'And how do I get the stuff onto the cloth?'
'Don't worry about that, I'll deal with that side of things, it will be a simple piece of absorbent cloth impregnated – no, *saturated* – with the bacteria. You'll get it in a double-sealed plastic bag and just need to open it, take out the rag and polish away to your heart's content. The real problem will be in keeping the cutlery looking shiny and polished – rather than smeared in germs – and of course in keeping yourself safe from the little bugs. You will need to make absolutely certain you wash your hands for a good few minutes with soap and water as hot as you can stand. Take some of that hand cleansing gel

stuff too, you know, the anti-bacterial stuff in a little bottle. Don't take any chances with this stuff.'

He stands to leave.
'Alright doctor! Exciting though, isn't it! You think it will work?'
'Definitely, with you smearing the bugs all over the cutlery and me spraying them all over the raw product, we should have a high infection ratio.'
'How are you getting the virus onto the food? Spraying it?'
'It's not a virus, but yes, a simple solution in a domestic hand-pumped spray bottle; piece of cake!'
'And afterwards, where do I meet you?'
'I will probably be travelling by train if I can't get a lift so will need a couple of hours. We can meet at the Place d'Armes in Phalsbourg; just send me a text when you are out and it's done. Then I will come and find you.'
'OK then, see you tomorrow evening.' She reaches up on tiptoes and kisses his lips.
'Bye, crazy man!'
'See you, Terroristin!'

Colin has been a little remiss in his telephone chats with his mother and, it being Sunday he awaits 12.00 to see if she'll call. At one minute past one local time the pay-as-you-go 'phone he has reserved for her rings.

'Hello mother!'

'How did you ever know it was me?'

'I have inherited psychic powers…no, not really; you are the only person who has this number.'

'Seriously? And you have been waiting all that time for me to call?'

'Waiting exactly sixty seconds mother; we agreed the time, remember!'

'Yes, yes; of course we did, my mind gets a little muddled.'

'So what news from your side?'

'Oh nothing much, except that they are moving me to a home tomorrow. Don't know the address yet but I shall let you know. Oh yes, and I keep seeing the same bunch of people lurking around outside visiting hours; I reckon they are the police you warned me about. In fact one of them is stood just outside the telephone booths right now.'

'They are watching you make this call?'

'Yes. Actually she's on the 'phone too and keeps looking at me. Quite creepy really.'

'Mother we have to cut the call; she's putting a trace on this number. Call me same time next week but don't let them see what you are doing.'

'Oh dear; have I got you into trouble?'

'Not yet; have to go. Love you mummy, goodbye.'

She tells the dead line that she loves him too….

Your WebKonnekt session has started:

DIDyson1: 'Hi both; go for it.'

Ext4013: 'Morning team. Been working with the local plods 24/7 and shown up practically zilch. No contact, no sightings and not a sniff of any presence here whatsoever. Doesn't help that there have been no reported incidents either and everyone has half an eye on the terrorist situ, so we are never going to get one hundred percent focus. Still a little hopeful on the driving licence and CCTV fronts but even that hope is dwindling.'

DIDyson1: 'Great! OK, gonna have to pull the plug I think. Brief the locals and give them all the intelligence then get yourselves back here, can't justify it any longer, sorry guys.'

Ext4013: 'OK Guv. Anything your side?'

DIDyson1: 'Not a bean. Unless the boat was stolen he *has* to be your side, but right now it feels like he's disappeared into thin air, but he'll cock up sooner or later, they usually do. See you on your return. Thanks for trying!'

Your WebKonnekt session has ended.

Colin is sitting against the wall near the entrance to a duck and goose farm on the outskirts of the town of Saint Avoid, Alsace, France, with two German hunt saboteurs he's never met before and Detlef. No names are exchanged and the Germans are clad head to toe in black, including some scary-looking Balaclavas. Colin, in comparison, is relatively conservatively dressed and thinks they are being a little melodramatic.

His initial reaction when Detlef offers him a black Balaclava is a shake of the head and a hasty '*Nein, danke; sowas brauch ich doch gar nicht.*'

The reply comes in heavily accented English with neck extending far to the right. Colin can't see his eyebrows through the mask, but he imagines them doing a little dance.

'Unless you also vear vone ve von't be completing ziss mission. Ve heff to all remain anonymous and you are putting each of us at risk.' Colin knows he has the most to lose by being found out, and supposes that the slightest clue might be enough to lead to them being tracked down and arrested. He can't afford that.

'OK – sorry, I am not used to such secrecy.'

'Ya, zat much is clear!'

If only they knew!

The headgear smells of cigarettes and Colin finds it quite difficult to stomach, but he holds his breath and before long the odour becomes bearable.

He looks at Detlef; he seems to be a natural, self-appointed leader.

'How long?'

'Not long, zey don't vant to get ze gänsestopfleberpastete to ze restaurant at ze last minute; it needs to breaz and settle to ze room temperature.'

He uses the German word for the pâté, literally '*stuffed goose liver pâté*', although most of it has come from ducks rather than geese.

'I estimate in ze next ten minutes for sure.'

Hardly have the words left his mouth than they hear a heavy door slamming and a truck engine starting up.

'OK – get ready.' Exaggerated roll to the letter 'r'.

Colin is used to covert operations, he's been on plenty of his own, but it's quite comforting to be accompanied for once. He looks round at the three masked companions and, despite his dislike of Detlef, feels proud to be part of a team, fighting for the same cause.

Compared to some of the things he's done this is a picnic. Nobody should get hurt and the aim is, actually, just to delay the consignment and add a few microgrammes of bacteria.

As the truck approaches, one of the team runs out from their hiding place and stands directly in the gateway, blocking the exit route. His is the most dangerous part of the operation, if the driver isn't concentrating or is otherwise engaged – fiddling with a mobile 'phone or adjusting his seat – he might not see the protestor in time.

In the event they needn't have worried, the truck pulls up sharply some three metres before any risk of a collision. The horn sounds as Colin and the other two members break cover. Detlef goes to the driver's door and yanks it open, Colin and the other guy head to the rear doors of the rigid-bodied truck. A manual cutting tool materialises from the folds of the German's jacket and a lock and plastic seal are quickly dispatched. Colin has the door open and is clambering aboard even whilst he takes the little spray bottle from his pocket.

His accomplice now reverses the cutting tool and the handles become a lever of sorts and he has cracked the first of four crates open almost without slowing his stride, and moves without pausing straight on to the second.

Colin shouts a warning:

'Remember to hold your breath until we are off the lorry – don't want to inhale this stuff!'

He gets a quick thumbs-up and the third crate is cracked open.

Colin reaches into the first, lifts the top layer of plastic film covering and sees that the predicted transport method was correct; open terrines of pâté. He's amazed that this is deemed acceptable. The argument went along the lines of the produce needing to breathe before it was eaten, and the short journey to the restaurant and double layered plastic combined with the wooden crates which are close to the traditional method are pretty much the way it has always been done. It suits Colin just perfectly. Taking a final deep breath he leans over the crate, pumping his fingers rapidly and spraying the fine mist liberally over the product. The plastic cover is thrown back into place and he moves to the second crate.

Behind him the German who opened the crates is already refitting the first lid. It's a slick piece of teamwork. At the next crate Colin displaces some of the upper layer of terrines and sprays the lower level. He replaces the top layer and adds a few blasts to them. Just as he's feeling as though his lungs might burst he slings the fourth crate lid roughly into place and together they force it down onto the fixing points. They leap out of the back less than two minutes after they entered and the driver is still arguing with Detlef at his cab window, shouting that he is already late and trying to open the door but being constantly forced back into his seat.

Unseen at the rear of the truck a tyre is punctured by the third German. This is an essential delaying tactic which Colin had insisted upon; the bacteria needs time to react and multiply. Replacing a blown tyre would take anything up to a couple of hours as it would require a breakdown vehicle to assist. The bacteria also needs warmth for ideal regeneration and Colin is hopeful that the ambient temperature of the pâté will be enough to facilitate the production of enterotoxins – he knows that this takes place anywhere between 4°-46° Celsius and the product was probably sitting in the warehouse at around fifteen degrees, so it should still be plenty warm enough and the bugs quite active.

'Lass ihn fahren – es sind bloß Lebensmittel!'
Colin smiles as he hears this final piece of subterfuge: *Let him drive, it's only foodstuffs.*
This will hopefully convince the driver that it's an attempted robbery gone wrong. A bunch of incompetent thieves who haven't done their homework and picked on the wrong vehicle.

With a final blast on his horn and some shouted insults through the driver's open window, the truck pulls away, only to have to stop just outside the gates when the tyre completely shreds and leaves the vehicle sitting on a wheel rim.

Out of sight now, the four men high-five one another and remove their disguises.

'Good work guys – I think he swallowed the whole story!' Colin is beaming with pride and glowing with the success.

'Yes – he believed it all right – let's go and get a beer.'

'Not for me, I am meeting Patricia in the Place d'Armes in Phalsbourg and need to get to the station.'

Unusually Detlef addresses Colin in German.

'You two do seem to be getting on very well!'

Colin ignores the mild note of jealously in Detlef's voice.

'She's a nice girl, and we have a lot in common.'

One of the team offers him a lift and he gladly accepts.

'That will save me a lot of time and risk; thanks!'

Patricia enters the old restaurant in the centre of Phalsbourg, France, dressed in the traditional waitress attire of black skirt, white blouse with frilly white apron. This uniform is a throwback to the times when the town sat inside the German border, and was known as Pfalzburg. Indeed, many of its citizens still speak German as a first language, although French pride and a determined school curriculum is gradually overturning that.

She is clutching a small handbag which contains a plastic bag which in turn holds an old cleaning cloth, heavily impregnated with the staphylococcus aureus bacteria.

As Colin had predicted, the place is in some state of turmoil and she quickly becomes one of the twenty or more anonymous waitresses, all busy scurrying around.
Patricia spots a young girl busy with cutlery and watches her for a moment. When she has memorised the layout of the knives, forks and spoons she hurries up to her.

'Hi, I am Rosi, I have been told to take over from you because you are better at the wine than me!'
'Me? I have no…oh, whatever!' The girl heads off towards the kitchen to find the wine waiting staff.
Patricia wastes no time. Quickly taking the filthy cloth from her handbag she picks up each of the pieces of cutlery and wipes them all over with the cloth.
Working swiftly she soon has half the tables covered when the other waitress returns.
'The wine's sorted but there's a problem with the Foie Gras so Gustav told me to come back and help you!'
Patricia is gutted; she had been making good progress.
'Gustav? Remind me...?'
'The short fat guy, he's in charge of the temporary staff; you met him, right?'
'Oh, him; yeah we met. OK, well there's just this half of the room to do then we're all done, do you smoke?'
'Yeah, why?'

'Listen, it's going to get pretty manic later on, especially with the delay in getting the main ingredient here – why don't you grab a quick ciggie while you can, this is a piece of cake for me and if anyone comes I'll say you are getting some more knives…OK?'
'You sure? Oh that's so cool of you; thanks. I owe you!'
'No worries, take your time!'

By the time the girl returns, stinking of stale cigarette smoke, Patricia has almost finished.
'Perfect timing – does it look OK?'
'Looks brilliant – thanks again. I'd better go and help with the flowers, coming?'
Patricia knows she needs to get the hell out of there before someone challenges her.
'Nah – I am going to finish these last few and then grab a cigarette myself now.'
'Oh you should have said; I would have covered for you…'
'It's cool, go do the flowers before we both get shouted at; see you in a minute.'
'Not so fast young lady.'
Gustav has appeared, holding a knife and spoon.
'These are filthy, what did you clean them with, a sock? They need to be re-done and quickly. It's a good job there's a delay or you two would have cocked up the whole proceedings. Show me the cleaning cloths you've been using.'

Unseen, Patricia slings the disgusting rag under the table.
'I threw mine away; it was getting so dirty and worn. No problem, I'll do them again with a clean cloth, where can I get one?'
'See Ursula, she'll have some. I want the spoons and knives gleaming, these are all smeared – look.'
He thrusts the cutlery at the two girls and then drops them onto the table with a clatter.
'You have twenty minutes to get them all in shape.'
He struts off muttering about temporary labour and the state of Germany in general.
Patricia pokes her tongue out at his retreating back and the girls exchange stifled giggles.

'Like being in fucking school!' Laughs Patricia. 'You want to go find Ursula? I have no clue what she looks like!'

'Sure, wait here.'

While she's gone, Patricia retrieves the grotty rag from beneath the table and conceals it in the foliage of a huge free-standing indoor shrub. The other girl returns with only one cloth.

'They are behind with the wine and I have to help there, can you do this alone?'

Patricia hides her delight at this news; she was worried the other girl would have wiped half the germs away.

'Yeah, piece of cake, don't worry.'

Alone again she decides to polish only the side of each piece of cutlery that's exposed, leaving the underneath face hopefully festooned and festering. Working quickly she is finished within fifteen minutes and with that she turns and leaves through the front entrance. With the exception of the waitress and Gustav, throughout the entire fifty minute exercise nobody has even spoken to her.

She hopes Colin has been as fortunate as she sends the text message to tell him she is out and has achieved the objective.

'Sicknote; get back here pronto, got a Webex set up in fifteen minutes with our globe trotters abroad because I had the call from hospital; our little old lady only went and called you-know-who. Got it traced and pinged to within a kilometre of his location. Need your brains as mine are addled.'
'On my way now Guv.'

Following infection, the symptoms of staphylococcus aureus can take anything between one and ten hours to present in the host. The Foie Gras festival is a long-winded affair with endless nibbles and courses, wine, beer and a couple of local Blaskapellen – those lederhosen-clad oompah bands typical of Bavaria and the surrounding regions. People are enjoying themselves; the musicians are blasting away on their trumpets, clarinets and tubas, occasionally breaking into a thigh-slapping routine and the festival-goers are making the most of the delicious offerings.

It's warm and stuffy, people are touching each other. Shaking hands, shouting, laughing and spreading tiny droplets of body fluid – ideal conditions for a little bacteria party.

By 22:30 the first signs that all is not well are noted by an elderly member of the organising committee. She had sampled the wares as they were being laid out before the slightly delayed feast had begun in earnest, and as a result of her early intervention and somewhat vulnerable health she succumbs quickly and spectacularly to the bugs. Racing across the crowded floor – if her hobbling gait can be defined as racing – she barely makes it to the Damentoiletten in time to projectile vomit all over the pretty sink units. This is followed in very quick order by a bowel evacuation where she stands and she collapses in a heap of misery, trying to crawl to one of the two toilet cubicles whilst clutching her stomach as the cramps render her incapable of any useful movement.

Within thirty minutes the toilets, male and female, are being overrun with young and old in various states of drunkenness and disarray; all desperate to purge their bodies of this beast that is cramping a lot more than their style. The smell begins to permeate every nook and cranny and soon the misery spills over beyond the restaurant walls as people desperately try to find alternative venues for their bowel and stomach misadventures. Soon the neighbouring hostelries are also overwhelmed with hundreds of desperate interlopers vying for any available toilet facilities and begin to close and lock their doors; nobody wants this disgusting human misfortune on their own doorstep. Or rather, that's where they'd rather keep it; just don't let it in, who knows what it is and who might become infected.

Gossip and rumours quickly proliferate the pages of social media and a twitter storm is going on with talk of fatalities (completely exaggerated – nobody has died…yet), plagues and terrorist plots. One Christian fundamentalist tweeter claims immediately that it's the wrath of God, owing to the recent confession of the town mayor that he once, in his late teens, smoked a joint and had a brief homosexual experience.

Sitting on the train heading back towards Garmisch, Colin and Patricia are giggling like school children as each new revelation and claim appears on the internet. Their little Foie Gras festival spoiler has been a monumental success, and they both reckon that once the facts are analysed in the cold light of day no mythical God or terrorist group will take the blame, but rather good old staphylococcus aureus, served with a large helping of Pâté de Foie Gras, and then the festival will have hopefully breathed its last.

On a more serious note, the aim had been to raise awareness of the effects of pumping antibiotics into farmed animals and Patricia has a reporter friend who will blitz the media with the facts. They drink their celebratory beer and sit closer to each other than casual acquaintances might be expected to.

Colin can't help but feel his awkwardness and needs to fill the silence with words.

'You never did tell me what a chicken run is?'

'Ah yes, it's a simple smash and grab on a chicken farm – or it can be any bird really, or even mammals – whatever. We go in, rescue the animals, bug out job done, no heroics, no sign left, I mean no propaganda or anything – and no clues about who we are. Nothing like that at all.'

'Sounds like fun. And what happens to the animals?'

'We have to re-home them, we have a network of rescue centres, then there's social media and such, it's always a struggle but we manage.'

'You guys never stop do you?'

'Won't stop until the abuse does, and that won't be in my lifetime, so looks like a busy life.'

She smiles and shrugs her shoulders. 'It's my ambition to open a rescue centre for all kinds of animals near my home town Bayreuth. One day. How about you? Where to next then, crazy Englishman?'

'I don't know; I have some ideas, wanna hear some?'

'Sure – shoot!'

Colin laughs.

'Bad metaphor again! But how do you fancy a trip to England? I heard about some dog fighters there that could do with some friendly intervention…but first there is a very nasty puppy breeder whose business needs to be shut down; fancy it?'

'Oh Colin, I would love to come with you, sounds like a real blast, but I really can't travel so far away at the moment, I can't leave my Mum.'

Colin looks crestfallen.

'But don't be so sad; the world is a small place these days and I am sure I can join you before too long!'

'Will you call me sometimes?'

'Is that safe, with all your secrets?' She has a look of mischief that shows she's half joking.

'Actually, that's a good point. I will need to get back to secrecy mode; I've been far too relaxed over here away from the English police, but they are looking for me in UK and I am sure they will have extended the search into Europe so I do need to keep a lower profile. Do you use Torchat?'

'Never heard of it.'

Colin explains and as they pull into Garmisch Partenkirchen station they agree how and when to stay in touch.

'Thank you so much for everything you have done. The money will change our lives and I promise not a penny will go to waste. I will remember the badgers forever, and the whole town will remember staphylococcus aureus for a long time to come. I will join you on your little British islands as soon as I can. Until then, stay safe, mein süßer Engländer.'

They hug closely, she on tiptoes and he bending awkwardly. Then she turns and is gone.

Your WebKonnekt session has started:

Ext4013: 'Morning Sir, morning team.'

DIDyson1: 'Hi both; We have a lead; the old lady called a number from the hospital telephones and we've traced it to Germany within the area we were already focussing on. We don't have a pinpoint, but the tech guys say they are confident to within five hundred yards so we're close to our quarry.'

Ext4013: 'Got a time and a grid ref then Sir?'

DIDyson1: 'Yep – sending the data through to you now. Get all the CCTV you can from the surrounding area, get our continental plod friends to query every likely animal-related incident, instigate doorstep discussions and let's get this bastard nailed before he evaporates into thin air again, call me if you have any results or if you need anything, gotta go brief the chief. Over and out.'

Your WebKonnekt session has ended.

Colin's German allows him to make enough sense of the local Dutch adverts to choose a suitable boat to get him back across the channel. The little half-cabin motor boat is basic but big enough and perfectly adequate for the trip. Colin hands over the cash in Euros to the private vendor in Harlingen, Holland and within the hour has stocked up with enough fuel, food and other supplies to get him through the next few days. As an afterthought he purchases a shovel.

The coastline here is endless sandy beaches, empty at this time of year, interspersed with hideous industrial monstrosities belching smoke and steam into the air and leaching effluent into the sea. With the light fading he sets out due west past the huge sandbanks of Den Helder, watching the lights of the settlement of Den Burg on the biggest sandbank, Texel, and wondering how long it will stay above sea level before global warming swamps it.

He motors at a good speed along the Dutch coast and after four hours takes a break for food and a hot drink in a little inlet near Nieuwpoort, in the midst of the busy shipping routes between Ostend and Dunkirk. It's properly dark now and knowing that the continental coastguards are going to be less alert than the English, he hugs the European coastline for a few more hours, passing Calais on his Port side and then rounding Boulogne-sur-Mer before gunning the engine and striking out across the channel towards Hastings on the English coast, keeping a very sharp eye open for container ships!

Once he sees the lights of Hastings he relieves himself over the side and diverts the craft slightly further west towards Eastbourne and on towards the West Sussex coastline. He skirts the sand and shingle shores of Brighton, Worthing and Bognor Regis, and then heads inland towards the tiny inlet of Pagham Rife. Pagham is one of those shorelines typical of the area; deep water leading on to banks of black, sucking mud fringed with saltings – clumps of thick, course sea-grass. The sea forms little channels between these; ideal for someone who wants to come ashore without being observed.

It's almost low tide and Colin navigates to get as close to the shore as possible, finally jumping overboard into the thick slime and towing the little boat up against the firmer ground where he manhandles his equipment onto the shore above the high water mark. Once unloaded, with a lot of huffing and puffing he drags the boat back out into the deep mud, his boots sinking beyond his ankles and slurping each time he pulls a foot free. Taking the shovel he'd bought in Holland he half buries the craft in the stinking wet slime and throws the shovel into the saltings. The boat will disappear completely when the incoming tide smoothes over the freshly disturbed area. Colin wonders if she'll ever be uncovered again, maybe by some fishermen digging for bait, or children having an adventure.

He shoulders the big backpack and heads off northwards. He knows he's still going to be hot news in this immediate area, so has to keep his head down and avoid any sightings. But he's banking on police resources being stretched to the absolute limit with the seemingly constant stream of terror alerts and that should enable him to hole up at his safe house for a while and plan his next moves.

The route he's chosen is one he knows well and apart from a stretch past the Roman Palace in Fishbourne will allow him to travel invisibly. The hike takes him five hours and when he finally reaches his safe house he's completely drained of energy and desperate for food, water and sleep. Despite this he religiously goes through his security checks to ensure nobody has been calling in his long absence. All key triggers show negative and so with some certainty he approaches the property from the woods on the eastern flank.

All further surveillance indicates that it's safe and he cautiously advances to the rear door and checks his final indicator; a tiny piece of matchstick wedged in the door frame at ankle level. It's still in place and he unlocks and opens the door. All seems well inside and a final check of the CCTV system in the attic space allows him to relax. He opens and devours cold a tin of baked beans, downs a half litre of still mineral water and then lies down fully clothed and exhausted. He's asleep within a minute.

Δ *Whenever I see a photograph of some sportsman grinning over his kill, I am always impressed by the striking moral and aesthetic superiority of the dead animal to the live one* Δ
Edward Abbey

Seeking open-minded entrepreneur for lucrative pet supply business.
Excellent income potential, extensive and growing customer base and desirable product. Too much work for me alone. Must have dog breeding experience. Box number EJ1254

The online advert is a little ambiguous, but Jamie Parfitt has learned how to read between the lines. It can sometimes be what is *not* said that is the most interesting. Parfitt is in a bit of a fix; he's racked up debts running to many tens of thousands due to his penchant for superficial thrills; fast cars, fast living, speed and quick fixes. More money has gone through his nose than most people will spend in a lifetime. He is getting to the point where his puppy business, highly profitable though it is, doesn't cover his entire outgoings, and some nasty people are starting to apply pressure. The latest veiled threat from a particularly ruthless drugs gang makes fleeting reference to wife, sons and daughters. Specifically, it makes clear that his wife's workplace is known, and the school route that his three children take twice each day is a particularly dangerous one, with a history of hit-and-run accidents.

Parfitt has the loosest of morals and considers himself a bit of a tough guy, but in the face of these threats he becomes anxious and very less sure of himself. He needs quick bucks to repay some of the outstandings before things go beyond the point of no return.

Calling the free-phone number, he recites the box extension EJ1254 at the prompt. Before the connection even has time to ring through it is answered by an automated, robotic voice sounding like a parody of Stephen Hawking giving him instructions. The robot quotes a mobile 'phone number with a final prompt telling him that he can be automatically connected by pressing '*1*' on his telephone keypad. There would be a charge of £1 per minute for this service.

He hits the one button and hears the connection ringing.

The number he has reached is a dedicated 'phone line used solely for this business and on the other end of the line the recipient hopes that after a dozen disappointments this caller will be the one he has been waiting for.

'Perfect Home Puppies, how can I help you?'

'Er hi, I just read your advert on the internet and wondered if we could talk through the details, unless you've already taken someone on?'

'OK, can I take your name please?'

'Sure, Parfitt; Jamie Parfitt.'

Bingo!

'Hi Jamie, my name is Josh, and no, nobody has been officially appointed yet, although there are a number of very promising candidates. May I ask you what you think the business might entail?'

'Er yeah, I guess it's buying and selling pets, well, puppies, if the name you just said is anything to go by.'

'That's right, yes. I import and sell specialist puppies all over the UK and the business has grown so fast that I can't keep up with the demand. I have decided also to remove the supplier from the equation, and open my own breeding farm, er, breeding *kennels*.'

'Haha, I think we are both on the same page, so it's big numbers we're talking about?'

'Very big numbers, yes. The demand is huge and I can't get the dogs quick enough. I've got a hundred bitches lined up and will continually artificially inseminate them. Dogs gestate for between 58 and 65 days, so I reckon, conservatively, we're looking at five litters each a year, so five hundred litters in year one, yielding anything up to – again, pessimistically – 2500 puppies. These will retail at £550 so, we're looking at – again, worst case scenario, £2.5 million. In reality it will be a lot more, but by the time overheads are taken out I have calculated 1.9 million profit. That would be split 2 equal ways with the incoming partner, minus a small percentage which I want to reinvest in the business to increase profits in year two and so on…still interested?'

Parfitt's mouth is dry and his pulse racing. Wow, best part of a million quid for doing practically fuck all, damn straight he was interested.
'Yes, I think I would be a great asset to a business like that. Any chance we can meet up to get the details nailed down?'
'Well, what experience do you have with dogs and dog breeding?'

Jamie Parfitt runs through some of the things he's done in his dog-breeding and selling career, hinting that he isn't shy when it comes to pushing the boundaries of canine welfare in order to maximise opportunities and potential. A meeting the following day is agreed and Parfitt is given a postcode which, the Perfect Home Puppies guy explains, is a bit rural, but it's important to operate away from public scrutiny.
Jamie declares that he is more than comfortable with that approach and the call is terminated.

Fundamentalist – NUBE: *Hi again Mujahid*

Mujahid– LEADER: *Fundi bro! U back & ready for UR initiation now?*

Fundamentalist – NUBE: *Yes and yes*

Mujahid– LEADER: *Great news! Where R U based?*

Fundamentalist – NUBE: *Wherever I am needed*

Mujahid– LEADER: *Great answer man. U R needed soon. Can U get to Manchester?*

Fundamentalist – NUBE: Er, yes, of course

Mujahid– LEADER: *Cool. I need a number. We won't share any other personal info, but an unregistered pay as U go number is critical. Can you get anything for me?*

Colin looks up the number on one of the new throw away 'phones and sends it.

They discuss some plans for a while and agree a meeting place and time.

Colin makes his way to the cellar where he is constructing some compartments in one of the main cellar rooms. There are two more rooms attached to this main area, and a separate self-enclosed cellar under the oldest part of the house. This has already been converted to meet his future needs. It's tough, manual work, but rewarding and will give him many hours of pleasure.

Whilst he is doing this, his driveway alarm is activated and he rushes to the control room he has built in one of the other cellar rooms. He sees a large van approaching the house on the CCTV. He deactivates the alarm – otherwise there would be a combination of horns and sirens and the monitors would light up as if a full battalion was coming along the road.

There is a noise outside as the van arrives and, as instructed in the online order, the driver unloads a curious mixture of furniture and gadgets into the adjacent out-building. Colin doesn't want to risk anyone seeing his face, especially in the immediate future, that could be too costly.

Δ It shouldn't be the consumer's responsibility to figure out what's cruel and what's kind, what's environmentally destructive and what's sustainable. Cruel and destructive food products should be illegal. We don't need the option of buying children's toys made with lead paint, or aerosols with chlorofluorocarbons, or medicines with unlabeled side effects. And we don't need the option of buying factory-farmed animals Δ

Jonathan Safran Foer

The cold metal bars are starting to taste like she imagines fresh hay to be. She's never eaten fresh hay, but can smell it and instinctively knows it's the right stuff for cows. She's always been fed on the iron-deficient pellets and slop, but she doesn't know the difference between good food and bad. She only has the vaguest memories of that single suckling of her mother's milk.

But these bars do taste good, cold and soothing on her painful teeth and a good way to bite some of her frustration and yearning away. She knows nothing about the insanity ratios in farmed animals kept in tiny crates, and might be surprised to learn she's just another statistic in this regard.

D0227 feels sad and lonely and, being an inquisitive and intelligent animal desperately wants some mental stimulus, but she's surely not insane.
However, these metal bars do taste good.

The livestock market is bustling with a cacophony of mooing, bleating and grunting overlaid by the shouts of buyers and sellers, the rumble of animal transporters and the stench of diesel and animal shit. Colin is waiting for his target to be paraded around the ring. He's well used to waiting for victims, and is proficient in this, but this target is different; this time he is planning to buy and rescue his quarry at the auction. It breaks his heart to watch these magnificent creatures being shown off to unscrupulous farmers, breeders and butchers. But there's only a limited amount he can do without drawing undue attention to himself.

Finally after a wait of what seems like hours but was probably only half that, a magnificent Gloucester Old Spot sow is led into the arena. She's a beautiful and healthy creature, but lengthy captivity has caused her to drop her head and her eyes to glaze over.
Never mind little piggy, Uncle Colin is going to rescue you whatever the cost.
Bidding starts at £100 and rapidly rises to £500.
Colin bides his time until it looks like she'll go for £750 and at the last minute bids £1000. He wins the prize and is soon leading the pig away towards his hired horse box.
'Well then Gwendolyn, a new life for you with zero risk of being eaten!'

It's Saturday afternoon and the police station is buzzing the news. The team is gathered, along with most of the force on duty, around the canteen TV set. The screen shows live TV video camera footage from one of the country's biggest Premier League football stadia in the North West. The image changes to a view outside the ground where a renowned TV football pundit is speaking to the reporter.

"We saw the helicopter swoop in and the players at first just stopped and stared, then when the gunmen jumped out and fired the first shots all hell broke loose. The players started sprinting for the tunnel but most were just cut down by the machine guns, then a bigger gun was carried out of the chopper and the guys dressed in black just started spraying the stands, there were rocket launchers and grenades of some kind, a flame thrower; people were exploding and melting before my eyes, men, women, children, it was completely indiscriminate. I just ran for the emergency exit with all the other TV crew, it was absolute carnage".

The reporter takes over the microphone:
"We are unable to get any status reports on casualties whilst the security operation is still underway, but early unconfirmed reports indicate hundreds of fatalities, if not worse. We do know that the stadium was almost full, that's over seventy-five thousand spectators plus ground staff and of course the teams and their entourages. Something in the region of seventy-six thousand and we also understand that the shooting continued for at least fifteen minutes, much of it heavy machine-gun fire. Join me again shortly for ongoing updates, until then it's back to Louise in the studio".

The team sit in stunned silence until Sicknote announces that his brother is a season ticket holder at the ground and is not answering his mobile. Everyone moves to reassure him and talk turns to the religious sickness that is sweeping the world.
Samantha takes Neil Dyson to one side.
'Not going to help our push for resources Guv. I reckon we'll lose some of the team to this now, it's gonna push the force beyond the limit.'

'Agreed Samantha, but we'll crack on with what we have, no sense feeling sorry for ourselves.'

'No, kinda makes Furness look almost human.'

'Really? You think? Well, almost, I suppose!'

Jamie Parfitt's one year old metallic blue BMW 5 Series convertible pulls off the B road onto an unmarked private by-way which, after 300 meters becomes a gravel track.
He is driving slowly to avoid the potholes and any stones pinging up and scratching his pride and joy and has the driver's window fully open so he can enjoy the pleasantly fresh air and hear the scrunch of the tyres on the gravel. He has always loved that sound, since his childhood, and always associated it with big expensive cars; Rolls Royce, Cadillac or Bentley. Well if he plays his cards right today he'll be ordering one of those before the year is out. He can't shift the smile that seems riveted to his face since last night's 'phone call.

He passes a dilapidated metal gate which seems to be held up by will-power alone as the old tubular gate posts are almost completely corroded. Gate and posts were clearly once red, but are now a deeper brown from rust and neglect and a herd of fat cows are seemingly trying to push it beyond its limits by resting their heavy dumb heads on it as they chew the cud and stare aimlessly at the slowly passing vehicle.

He sneers as he passes and shouts in his nasal Stoke-on-Trent accent: 'Fat, stupid fuckers, I'll buy a couple of you in a few weeks and have a massive Bar-B-Cue party to celebrate hahaha!'
He considers even having a hog roast as well; really push the boat out, why the fuck not!

Despite the lateness in the season the corn is shooting high on either side of the un-fenced track which meanders around the fields and ditches in a series of gentle curves and he wonders how much further it might be. It's officially autumn, yet pretty little blue butterflies, birds of prey, songbirds, and all manner of insects fill the still air in a festival of flight. He doesn't know their species; he has no eye for insects and birds, nor for the hedgerows and grasses or the copious other forms of wildlife that throng wherever he looks. He never did have a romantic nature, and for him animals are a waste of space unless you can eat them or sell them to pathetic softies who want to cuddle and pet them. That's where the money is, and he is going to get his share of that delicious pie, starting any minute now.

Rounding a corner he is taken by surprise by an old blue Land-rover parked up partially on the verge beneath a huge spreading English Oak, but not allowing enough room to pass.
A little annoyed at the inconsiderate parking he slows to a walking pace as he approaches it.
Nearing the old vehicle he wonders who else might be out here in the sticks and what they might be up to. Probably a farmer doing some country nonsense.

A tall, bearded, bald man steps out from behind the land-rover and flags him down.
'Mr Parfitt, by any chance?'
Jamie is a little surprised but not enough to be suspicious, he knew the meeting point was here or hereabouts.
'Yep, that's me – you must be Josh I assume?'
'Yep that's me too.'
The tall guy grins and leans towards the open window with outstretched hand.
Swivelling a little to the right in his seat Jamie takes the hand and feels the strong, confident grip. That bodes well; a firm handshake is always a sign of a man who knows what he wants.
Jamie returns the pressure to show that he too is a man of action and confidence.
He smiles back.

'So this puppy farm, er, kennels…' He winks to show the guy how switched on he is.
'I guess it's around here someplace, or are you showing me the field where you are going to build it.' He laughs to show he is pulling the guys leg. He likes to show his sense of humour, it's important for a successful working relationship.

'No, no, it's just a little further along the track, but I saw you approach and I think you might want to leave that beautiful beast parked up here safely, the track gets very agricultural in a short

247

while and you'll almost certainly bottom that out on any number of crevices and holes.'
'Oh, OK. Good idea then, shall I jump in with you?'
He is already shifting his body weight to climb out.
'Yes, hop in and we'll get there in one piece. This area is perfectly safe for your lovely car, and we won't be long anyway.'
Jamie likes the praise for his car, it reflects well. Locking the Beamer he jogs round to the passenger side of the Land-rover.
'You'll have to make do without the seatbelt I'm afraid, it's been damaged for a while and I haven't got round to fixing it, but it's only a short drive and there is no other traffic.'

Jamie looks around and beneath him and can see no sign of the belt, so tucks himself firmly down into the seat and holds on tight to the seat frame in anticipation of a slow but bumpy ride. He smiles towards the driver and notices something odd about the way his face is shaped. He can't pinpoint it, but his eyes seem a little too far apart.

The engine is still running and the guy called Josh selects 1st gear on the column-mounted lever.
'So, how was the trip down? How far have you come actually?'
'From Stoke, so it took a while, but the roads were clear enough and I made it in a little over three hours.'
'Still, quite a journey. I thought I'd show you the site and then we could grab some lunch before you make the return. We can go through the numbers and such like while we eat; there's a great little pub nearby that does excellent veal – I trust you have no issues eating animals?'
'Haha, no not me, that's what God gave 'em to us for, to enjoy the taste and occasionally pull a wagon or two.'
He beams at Josh, who doesn't return the look, but is concentrating on the route which has become somewhat trickier to negotiate.

The driver suddenly wrenches the wheel left a quarter turn then immediately a half turn to the right and the vehicle veers off the track. Jamie is flung first towards the driver's seat and then slammed hard against the door frame.
'Oh sorry, did you see the snake?'

Jamie clamps his hand over the impact area and feels a trickle of blood run across his fingers.

'No, but I think I've cut my head open.'

'Oh gosh, let me have a look at that.'

The driver stops, leaps out through his door and goes straight to the rear of the Land-rover.

Jamie can hear him moving some heavy-sounding gear around.

'Just getting my first aid kit out, I always carry one, but it's a bit buried at the moment, won't be a sec.'

Jamie is a little squeamish when it comes to human blood, and he avoids looking at his hand and averts his eyes from the wing mirror where he might catch a glimpse of the injury. He is feeling a little wobbly; he often faints whenever he might be exposed to a gory scene, and he closes his eyes to try to fight the building nausea. Had he had his wits about him he may have seen the driver coming along the side of the wagon with something other than a first aid kit. Appearing at the door, the driver yanks it open and in the same moment Jamie registers a glimpse of a heavy club hammer swinging towards the side of his skull. He has no time to react and the world becomes very dark.

Colin Furness wastes no time in immobilising his victim. He winds heavy duty tape around Parfitt's body and behind the seat ten or eleven times. By the time he is finished, Jamie is clamped firmly to the Land-rover seat by the tape and absolutely incapable of the smallest movement, even had he been conscious.

Next he removes Parfitt's mobile 'phone and is pleased to see that it's turned off. That will help prevent any tracing of his location and is a great piece of luck, Colin removes the battery; he had thought he might have to drive to some remote location with the 'phone switched on, just so that any tracking attempts would take the police in the wrong direction, but now he won't need to…although he still could for added security. He'll think that one through later when he has more time.

Parfitt is gagged with a dirty old rag and more tape and has an old sack thrown over his head which gets taped around the bottom. Checking that everything is secure Colin climbs back into the driver's seat and moves the vehicle off in the direction they had both been heading, thanking good fortune that even on a pleasant day the remote area is always so devoid of people.

The pain changes from a dull throb to an excruciating series of bomb-bursts in his head as Jamie Parfitt slowly regains consciousness. He can't remember what happened and has no idea where he is or why he can't see anything. Is it night time? Only when he tries to ease the pressure on his backside does he realise he's also completely immobile. He panics and desperately tries to shift an inch or two but he seems to be immovably fixed to something cushioned. His sense of smell tells him he is in a vehicle of sorts and he feels it moving. It soon dawns upon him what has happened, but rack his brain as he might, he can't work out why.

What has the puppy farm guy done to him and why? What the fuck happened...'
He feels his mouth full of something that smells of diesel oil and tries to speak but only a muffled mumble is possible. He realises he has been gagged...*what the fuck? What's wrong with this dog breeding guy, is he insane? Has it all been some elaborate trap? Ah! The drug gangs. Oh shit, this Josh guy has been hired by the druggies and if they don't get a payment they'll take it out on Hayley and the kids.*

Jamie can't see, speak or move and his head feels like somebody is using it for bass drum practise. He knows he is tied up somehow and gagged and blindfolded, but what is this drug gang crazy going to do next? He tries to think of a way out as they ride the bumps now at breakneck speed. He attempts to memorise the significant bends and rough distances between them because that information might be useful if he is able to escape, or if this crazy gang member lets him go with a warning. Maybe that's all this is, an elaborate warning to show him they mean business and ensure that he delivers the money he owes with no further delays.

He is desperate to speak with the driver, Josh, if that's even his real name. He wants to explain the run of bad luck he's been having, hell...he can give the guy his BMW; that should swing his release. He could at least live to fight another day that way.

250

His earlier euphoria and the monumental disappointment when he realises he's been had fade to nothing against the immediate potential risk to his life and that of his family.

Jamie hears the driver change down a gear and feels the vehicle slowing abruptly. After another down shift they turn right and the gravel sound is replaced by the slosh of what sounds like water and mud. Probably a field, the guy is going to throw him out here and make him walk back to the car. *As long as he unties me first... Fuck! But his head hurt.*

He hears the driver's door open and footsteps splashing around to his side. A waft of cooler air as the door is opened then there's a sound of tearing or cutting, and he's shoved around on the seat. His bonds are being removed.

Powerful hands grasp his hair and he is pulled violently towards the attacker; having no way to brace himself or resist, he is easily yanked from the seat down to the wet ground below.

'Right listen carefully, because the words I am going to say now might be some of the last you will ever hear. I have brought you to a very remote place where you'll never be found, unless I want you to be, not that anyone is ever going to be missing a scummy little turdbox like you.'

Head pounding he is again gripped, this time beneath his arms, and half dragged, half carried across some wet ground. Nearby a horse whinnies. A seemingly remote part of his brain registers that they must be on a farm.

They stop and he is dropped into the mud. A bunch of keys jangle and then a lock turns. A screeching door that has clearly not been used often and he is again dragged over a bump, he assumes the doorstep, and into a cooler place. He is in a building of some kind. Dragged again by his armpits and now down a flight of steps head first, they feel hard and unforgiving, like concrete, not wood. Cooler still at the bottom, a right turn and now the guy's footsteps are echoing. A cellar maybe.

He hates cellars; too many lunatics have used them for their evil, twisted crimes.

Parfitt is very anxious now; if they are so remote from anywhere this nutter could do anything to him, and he will be helpless to protect himself. They stop moving and he is dropped unceremoniously to the ground. He feels cold moisture seeping through the sacking to his cheek and he shifts a little in an effort to keep himself dry.

Parfitt tries to mentally shake himself alert, knowing that he'll have to live on his wits now and rely on his own intelligence and cunning to save himself from whatever this crazy has in mind. He reckons his best chance of escape will be now, before the freak has time to imprison him properly – or whatever he plans to do. Better to go all out than to regret it forever. He had read an account of a hostage in Beirut who had been imprisoned, chained to a radiator for three years. On the first or second day he'd had the chance to escape through an open toilet window, but assumed he would get a better opportunity sometime. Parfitt knows he will have to take the first chance that arises, however slim the prospects.
Lying on the cold, hard floor he hears the keys jangle again and another lock being turned. Shit, he is getting deeper into the building; every door and lock implies another level of difficulty. Dragged again, but by the feet now. This time the echo is different; tighter, closer, as if they are in a much smaller room; a corridor maybe.

Jamie Parfitt suffers with claustrophobia and he begins to panic, shaking and sweating and trying to make his pleas heard through the gag.

Out of nowhere he feels a sickening blow to the face and his nose seems to implode. Writhing on the floor, tears and blood soaking through the blindfold, gag and hood he is in agony.
The door bangs shut with a very final-sounding clang.
Metal.
He lies in the dark, whimpering and afraid. A million tortured thoughts run through his mind and they all lead him to a nasty conclusion; he is going to die here, alone, anonymous and without any kind of justice.

Why has this monster chosen him? Is it just a freak coincidence? Has he done something to anger him? Parfitt thinks through the long list of unhappy puppy customers; those whose dogs had died within days of purchase and those which had become seriously ill due to poor hygiene at the puppy mill in Ireland, or on the secretive journey to mainland UK via Liverpool or in his own tiny holding pens at his house in Stoke on Trent.

It might be any of them; there are too many to think through and, wishing he could somehow get news to his wife he slowly drifts into a troubled semi-conscious state.

Upstairs Colin takes a leisurely walk with the BMW keys. He'll collect it and stick it in one of the old barns – maybe bury it under straw bales only to be discovered in many years' time; pristine and worth a fortune! After that Colin must take his 4x4 into the countryside to see what he can see at the local hunt.

Δ Hi! handsome hunting man
Fire your little gun.
Bang! Now the animal
is dead and dumb and done.
Nevermore to peep again, creep again, leap again,
Eat or sleep or drink again. Oh, what fun! Δ
Walter de la Mare: *Collected Poems for Young People*

The late season hunt is in full swing across the sweeping hills as he observes from his elevated vantage point. The horns are blaring, the hounds baying and eager to break free from the confines of the riders' control and the shooters seem to be in position and prepared to take down the foxes as they are flushed out from their copse. Colin knows only too well that in the UK fox hunting with hounds is still permitted, as long as certain guidelines are adhered to. These guidelines require the foxes to be shot by the armed killers as soon as the they emerge from safety. In reality, many hunts fail to adhere to these laws and allow their dogs to catch the foxes and tear them apart in the name of sport.

Colin loves animals; all of them. He's well aware that the hounds are not at fault; rather the hunters who corral and train them. He is also aware that in Scotland any number of hounds is permitted for this sport. In England and Wales this is limited to only two. Interesting then that there would seem to be in excess of thirty dogs here. He watches this barbaric display of violence and holds it together simply by telling himself that his time for revenge is fast approaching. The portly master of the hunt sits as tall as his bloated frame will allow and gives the indication for the dogs to be unleashed onto the foxes and the hounds tear off towards the quarry, following the pack leader.

Within minutes an adult fox breaks for cover, followed by three young cubs. Colin closes his eyes and clenches his teeth; every fibre of his being urging him to rush down the steep gradient and stop the activity. The hounds easily gain on, and overtake the cubs and Colin sees them tear into the young creatures in a frenzy of blood-lust. He hangs his head and bites his top lip, his left leg twitching with the frustration he feels. The mother spins on her heels and makes a valiant but fruitless attempt to save her babies, all this achieves is that the hounds turn upon her and within the space of a minute the small family is brutally and needlessly destroyed.

Colin stares at George Grantham-Smyth, the overweight Tory MP and Master of Hounds and silently swears to exact a lingering, painful death on the bastard. He turns away in tears and jogs down to his 4x4. He guns the engine and makes his way along the chalk track onto the B road half a mile distant.

Jamie Parfitt awakes with an urgent need to pee. His head throbs as if it's clamped in a giant vice and his nose is stinging. He can taste blood and mucous and traces of vomit.

Has he been asleep? Did he vomit in his sleep? That was worrying; with the gag in place he might easily have drowned. He thinks about escaping and what he might have in his pockets that he can somehow free, but the lack of bulges between his body and the hard floor tells him that his pockets have been emptied. The urge to pee becomes overbearing and after maybe half an hour he can do nothing to stop his body releasing it. The relief is immediate, and the warmth from the hot liquid strangely comforting. He is taken back to his childhood when bedwetting had been a problem into his early teens. In those days he had been terrified of the accidents, but his mum had always been fantastic and soothed him and told him it was OK, that the sheets could be washed and he would grow out of it. He did stop at thirteen, but somehow missed his mother's warmth and softness. He needs her now.

Sometime later he hears a series of bangs and thumps and eventually the door to wherever he is being held is unlocked. Roughly the tape holding the sack over his head is torn away from around his neck. His nose gets caught several times sending shooting pains directly through his eyes to the centre of his brain. Then the blindfold comes off and even though the room is dark by normal standards he is momentarily dazzled by the unaccustomed light.

The freak takes a small knife from a leather pouch at his waist and the gag is cut away.
Now the guy is smiling down at him, and the unnatural distance between his eyes makes him look like an absolute monster. Jamie looks around the room, it doesn't take long, it's roughly 2 metres square, bare metal walls – some kind of stainless steel checker-plate; a cupboard really. He hopes desperately that this is just a temporary prison; to stay here any length of time would lead to insanity.

The freak speaks, slowly and softly, with a voice that is higher than Jamie remembered.

'Jamie Parfitt.'

The smile becomes a twisted grin, more like a leer.

'I expect you are wondering why this has happened? Let me tell you a little story. You will know most of it already, so we'll use it as an exercise of filling in the gaps; I will tell you the bits that you don't know, and you can answer any questions that I may have.'

The captor doesn't seek any agreement from the captive, just nods to himself as if to say, *that is the way it will be*.

Indeed, that is the way it will be, because Parfitt has no discretion.

'You get your puppies from a disgusting breeder in the Republic of Ireland. It's a puppy farm or, more descriptively a puppy mill. You remove them from their mothers at three or four days old so that the mothers can be impregnated again. The pups are not even weaned and they're kept in tiny dark boxes, no light and no care, except for the daily bowl of cheap reconstituted powdered milk and later some poor quality dog food. I understand you might even be feeding them the remains of those which don't survive the trauma. Am I right so far?'

Parfitt keeps his silence, but his look tells Colin that he is bang on the money.

'You ship them illegally through unscrupulous middle men to your holding place somewhere near Liverpool – where is it exactly?'

Parfitt looks him in the eye.

'Why? What do you want to do?'

'I shall alert the authorities, or I shall pay a personal visit, whichever I deem the most suitable. Believe me, if I choose to visit those arseholes will regret it. They would take the authorities option every time.'

Jamie knows he's telling the truth and that either way he's fucked, not that that seems too important right now, considering the shit he's in here, but his wife and kids live on the site where usually upwards of thirty puppies are being slowly developed until they reach four weeks when they will be advertised for sale through the various free-ads. If the freak finds out where Hayley is …well, god knows what he might do to her and the kids. There's no way he is letting that slip out.

'There is no holding area; you have the wrong guy.'

The punch to the already shattered nose is as sudden as it is violent. In that one ferocious blow is all the pent-up frustration Colin had felt watching the poor foxes being shredded alive.

Parfitt is instantly unconscious.

He awakes to the sensation of being washed with warm water and, desperately thirsty as he is he begins to lap at the precious liquid. But this isn't water. Bedwetting memories flood back and he realises what he can taste is urine. He's having a bedwetting episode. Opening his eyes he sees the monster standing over him with his trousers around his ankles, fat penis pointing at his face and pissing liberally, washing the revolting, warm, strong liquid from his head to his feet and back again.

He recoils and tries to shuffle and roll into the corner, but the room is very small and the guy seems to have an endless supply of the disgusting, pungent stuff.

'Fuck off you mental freak, get off, leave me alone what the fuck is wrong with you?'

Still pissing, the lunatic continues the story from where he had left off, as if he'd merely taken a short break in his account of events. Jamie has no clue as to how long he's been out cold.

'You sell the poor creatures, along with falsified documentation, although only when pressed for it. I assume you know roughly how many of your puppies die within the first few weeks with their new owners? Of course you do, because the unwitting clients contact you to complain, and you become abusive and dismissive.'

The flow of urine trickles to a stop and Parfitt huddles in a stinking puddle in the corner while the freak shakes his filthy great cock, small spatters of the foul-smelling piss dripping onto his face, and then casually adjusts his clothing.

'Don't get too comfortable you little fucksack-faced loser, I may well need to take a big shit any time soon.'

Parfitt groans and starts to beg.

'Shut the fuck up. There's a social media page devoted to bringing you to justice, but the fucking RSPCA and their dilly dallying legal system are way too slow. Each day that they pontificate, more helpless puppies are being dragged from their mothers' wombs and thrown into your scary world of abuse and loneliness until you finally ship them to their new – unsuspecting – loving owners.'

All of this was true and Parfitt wonders where he'd got all his information.

'I read the online posts from a girl who bought two puppies from you which both died of Parvovirus within a week of getting them home. She claims that when she complained you said it wasn't your problem, she had taken on the ownership and you didn't care. I wonder what makes a human being so uncaring. Is it pure greed? Is it that you are too busy making money or is it something else? Maybe you are just a nasty little turdshit?'

The guy grabs Parfitt by his short sideburns and smashes the back of his head down onto the concrete floor and the room spins anew.

'I think probably all of the above, don't you, you worthless little cunt stain?'

Still gripping him by the hair at his temples he leans so close so that Jamie can feel his warm, slightly sour breath on his face as the nutter hawks up a venomous mouthful of phlegm and spits it directly onto his mouth and nose. Jamie recoils as far as he can but has no way to remove it, and he feels it slowly trickle down the left side of his cheek and chin, disgustingly lingering around his lips. Gagging, Jamie begins to shiver with revulsion and fear; this guy is clearly extremely unhinged.

'You know how many dogs are '*euthanized*' every week in this country? Thousands. And yet shitfuckers like you continue to feed the dumb public with pretty little puppies; over-bred so much that their deformities cause them a lifetime of pain; pain which is often not even picked up by stupid owners and ill-attuned vets. They suffer a lifetime in silence. There are *plenty* of rescue dogs – and puppies – *plenty* to fill the demand, but no; weasel-turds like you feed from the ignorance and greed. I hate people like you more than words can ever express, and I am going to take my sweet time showing you *exactly* how deep that hatred runs within me. Long before I am finished with you, you will be begging, screaming and grovelling for death to release you; but I'm a cunning fucker and I'll take you to the brink and leave you hanging there at my leisure; you, Mr fucking Parfitt are going to die a thousand deaths.

Colin seems to suffer some kind of anger attack and actually rips the hair from the sides of Parfitt's head. The pain is indescribable and the victim's scream is unreal in its pitch and intensity.

'You will stay here for a while and ponder the evil of your life. I shall feed you one meal shortly, dog food perhaps....you should eat it, as there won't be another for some time.'
'Please Josh, I desperately need a drink.'
Parfitt knows he is dead if he doesn't get away soon and hopes the monster will free his hands to allow him to take some water. That would be his only real chance to pounce.

'Of course.'
The knife comes out and Jamie's heart skips a beat – he is going to cut the bonds – now is that one chance he has been waiting for.
'But it might be a good time to tell you that my name is not actually Josh. It's Colin, and I'm a known defender of the voiceless. I am wanted for several brutal murders so please keep your scummy little hands away from anything that I might construe as a threat, otherwise I may accidentally slip into psychopath mode!'
The lunatic leans forward and cuts the tape holding his feet and legs. Jamie tries to control his breathing, slowing his pulse and ensuring that the fight or flight reflex is tipped in favour of fight *and* flight.
'There you go; there's no heating down here so in time the walls will be running with condensation – lick it up to your heart's content – after all, that's what your puppies have to rely on to survive, isn't it!'

Jamie is devastated, his hands remain immobilised and the walls look filthy, covered in a thin film of oil and grime. The situation can't get any worse.
'I need the toilet though, desperately.'

'Oh that is a shame, or rather, an opportunity! As I recall, your puppies have to live in their own shit and piss for several weeks at a time, now's your chance to build some real empathy. Shit wherever you like, but don't assume I am going to ever clear it away.'

He wordlessly leaves the room, double locking the metal door behind him.

Colin has taken a drive to calm himself after the encounter with the puppy abuser and is sitting in pastel sunshine on the gentle banks of the River Rother just before it joins the sea at Rye. He is dialling a Chichester number.

'West Sussex Police.'

'Yes hello, I need to speak with Detective Inspector Dyson.'

'Can I ask who's calling?'

'An old friend.'

'I'm sorry sir; DI Dyson won't take a call from an unidentified caller.'

The anger floods back in an instant, but Colin fights the rage within.

'Then he will regret it. I have information on recent and ongoing crimes.'

'Can I just take a name then please?'

'No. Tell him Martyn Bones was a victim of the Free Radical and the next one is being prepared.'

'One moment please sir; let me put you through to our incident helpdesk. Connecting you now.'

Colin instantly terminates the call, removes the battery and SIM card from the mobile telephone and throws the body of the device into the river, followed by the battery; the SIM card he retains.

90

The operator at the central police HQ reports the call to the incident room, as per the instructions from DCI Moody. The call is passed to Carol Saunders on the desk.

'Did you get a trace?'

'Sorry, no trace was possible owing to the truncated manner of the call.'

'Great! Thanks.'

The meal, when it finally comes, looks like a bowl of poor quality mince.

Jamie Parfitt estimates that he's been here for three days, although that is complete guesswork as he has no means of telling the time. It could have been a day and equally could have been a week, but it feels like three days. He wonders what his wife and kids are doing. They'd be worried out of their skulls and the police would be everywhere trying to trace his car, his 'phone and his last movements. For once Parfitt is glad of the CCTV camera network which in the past had angered him. He hopes the freak was too stupid to remove his 'phone battery, left connected it would emit a low level signal to ensure contact with the nearest cell – the sender/receiver which ensured telephones were connected to a network at practically all times.

He'd been untied by the nutcase when the food had been delivered, but the guy had held a pistol to his face the whole time and escape had not been an option. He looks at the meal and wants to retch, but he is very hungry and doesn't know how long he can resist. Thirst is a more urgent worry. The monster had predicted that he would need to get any moisture he could from licking condensation from the dirty metal walls and in anticipation of that becoming reality he's wiped a large area of one wall as clean as he can. That isn't yielding enough and he needs to clean off some parts of the other walls too. He removes his shirt and rubs furiously at the surface. It's difficult to achieve any level of cleanliness because the surface is riddled with raised checker-plate areas and the oily dirt lodges around them. He knows that he'll make himself ill if he ingests too much oil and other contaminants but he needs to get fluids, otherwise he'll simply dehydrate.

He knows that the sloppy food contains moisture, although he has no idea how much or how useful it is, but anything is better than this raging thirst. There are no utensils. He hadn't expected them, too much of an escape risk, so he scoops a few fingers full of the stodge and sniffs. He recoils and throws it back into the bowl, no fucking way Jose! No way on earth is he eating *that* shit. He pushes the bowl as far into the corner of the small room as he can and curls into a ball and wishes he was anywhere else on the planet.

Some hours later the door opens a crack and the lunatic appears. He goes through his usual security routine.

'Get into the corner where I can see you Parfitt and hands behind your neck.'

He does as he is bidden.

'Not hungry I see...well, that will change in time. I shall leave the food there for a day longer and then, if you still refuse to eat it you will face a week without anything.'

'I am dying of thirst. What do you want from me and when are you going to let me go?'

'Let you go?' the voice seems genuinely surprised.

'I won't be letting you go you moron, you are here for the rest of your miserable life!'

He closes the door and double locks it and Parfitt hears him mocking his plea as he retreats through the building and up the stairs.

'Haha, *when are you going to let me go* indeed! Haha, I like it...'

The voice fades to nothing and another door clangs shut.

Jamie sits and begins to weep at the hopelessness of his situation. He prays silently...*please god, let him have left the battery in the 'phone.*

The walls close in on the filthy little figure who had so recently bragged of his wealth on social media pages and soared through life on artificial highs.

On the way to the morning briefing Carol Saunders has just informed Dyson that an attempt was made to relay information to him regarding the murder of Martyn Bones, with further information regarding ongoing crimes. He is seriously pissed off that internal procedures prevented him being able to take the call.

'Was the call at least traced?'

'They tried Sir, but the connection was cut as soon as the trace log was started. All we got was one beacon in Uckfield, East Sussex.'

'Thank you Carol; I do know where Uckfield is. So we know sweet sod all about who it was?'

'We have the standard recording file sir, the file needs converting before we can listen to it but it's on this CD.'

She holds a disc aloft.

'OK, great, so how do we convert it?'

'One of the techies is on his way up now to run it.'

'Oh, OK let's get the briefing underway while we wait.'

The team goes through the scant updates. Within two minutes there's a knock at the door and the technician enters without saying a word and takes the disc offered up by Carol. He inserts it into a portable drive then plugs the drive into the ops room laptop and a file conversion takes place. Dyson watches the progress bar move left to right for a few seconds and once it says *conversion complete* the technician removes the disc, hands it back to Carol, detaches his drive and leaves with no more than a mumbled '*there you go, Sir!*' Carol hits the play button and the recording from the previous day is heard:

West Sussex Police.
Yes hello, I need to speak with Detective Inspector Dyson.

Samantha whispers over the recording:

'It's Furness!'

Dyson raises his thumb and nods agreement.

Can I ask who's calling?
An old friend.
I'm sorry sir; DI Dyson won't take a call from an unidentified caller.

Then he will regret it. I have information on recent and ongoing crimes.
Can I just take a name then please?
No. Tell him Martyn Bones was a victim of the Free Radical and the next one is being prepared.
One moment please sir; let me put you through to our incident helpdesk. Connecting you now.

The recording ends and there is immediate chatter. Neil Dyson raises his hands.
'OK, we all know that voice. So he's back here in UK for certain. I think we might assume that *he* is the Free Radical he speaks of, and we can also assume the twisted creep is in the middle of something else. What have we got on the Martyn Bones murder Sicknote?'
'Call logs from Bones' mobile link Bones to the murdered prison Guard Sir; they had been in contact shortly before the escape. Can't believe it's a coincidence, but there's little else to link the two at the moment so not sure what significance it has.'
'OK, keep on it. I need to get this recording upstairs to DCI Moody, and I'm going to make *damned* sure that when he calls again it's routed straight to me wherever I happen to be. Samantha-carry on here please.'

Colin is researching Baylisascaris Procyonis, or Raccoon Roundworm on the Tor network. These interesting organisms are harmless to the host racoons, but once ingested by rodents and other small animals will burrow into the gut wall of infected creatures and migrate into the other tissues. For some reason they tend to head towards the brain, where they do entertaining things to the new host's behaviour. The way it works in the wild is that this brain attack strategy makes the target mammals and rodents, which usually eat the larvae in error, easier prey for the raccoons. One of those astonishing quirks of evolution; a mutation which holds an advantage and leads to the mutated version becoming dominant. He reads that when left untreated Raccoon Roundworm in humans is often fatal. Even survivors suffer significant neurological damage resulting in insanity and incapacity.

Through the Tor network he orders a good supply of living larvae, they are active for up to four weeks from hatching and so it won't be so difficult to get the eggs and keep them healthy.
One of his mobile telephones rings. No number is displayed.
He assumes it will be the Muslim and answers hesitantly.
'Yes?'
'Fundi? It's Muhaj. How's it hangin'?'
'How's it what?'
'How goes it? How are you fixed?'
The guy's voice has a northern English accent; not what Colin had expected at all.
'Oh, OK thanks. Ready to meet?'
'That's why I'm calling you. Hope this line is safe, when we finish this call you bin your 'phone and TC me the new one tonight; OK?'
'TC?'
'Torchat – wow you are slow man, hope you're gonna get sparkier than this, we need quick agile thinkers.'
'It's just some of the words you use – I'm not very familiar. I like to keep myself to myself – when I'm not busy destroying the western culture that is.'
'Haha! Like it Fundi, like it! OK, listen carefully and write *nothing* down.'

Colin grabs a pen. Sod that, he will write *everything* down that he can manage with his dyslexic sluggishness.

'Get to Salford Central train station for tomorrow at 18:00. The New Bailey Street entrance and wait at the flower kiosk. Wear black clothes underneath a normal jacket of some kind and don't bring any kind of ID, if it goes tits up you need to be anonymous.'

'OK. How will I know you?'

'You won't. Tonight you will send me a mugshot of your charming looks and one of the Brothers will make themselves known to you at the kiosk. When they do, you won't talk to him, you just follow and stay close. He will take a train and a bus and then there will be a three mile walk. You can manage that, right?'

'Of course.'

'Cool. When you get to the RV we will be waiting with the equipment. We are torching the target and then we'll bomb-burst to secondary RVs. Got it?'

Colin was flummoxed.

'Er not quite; what's an RV?'

'Haha, you really are a loner! Rendezvous. Secondary RV is where we meet with the getaway team post hit. Any more questions?'

Colin reads his scribbled notes.

'ER, yes; run it by me again. So 18:00 at the New Bailey Street entrance, flowers stall, I will be contacted and I am to follow the, er brother. Then a train – I assume with him still?'

'Yep.'

'OK, then a bus and then a walk to the slaughter house.'

'For fuck sake man, *never* ID a target on open media. Target, target, target. The rest is easy; you stick with me – assuming you get through the test, that is.'

'I will. Two questions; what's a bomb-burst and what is my test?'

'Bomb-burst is when we all scatter from target. As for the test...you'll see. Send me the pic to the number I give you on Torchat tonight. Destroy that 'phone pronto.'

He cuts the line.

Colin does his best to make sense of his notes. He's in a hurry; so much to do at the moment and important things to sort out before the Manchester trip.

In the opulent Conservative Club George Grantham-Smyth, MP, quaffs his final Ruby Port of the evening and pats his pocket to ensure his car keys are still where he'd put them. He knows he shouldn't drive but frankly the plods around Hove were pretty impressionable and a timely mention of the Police Chief soon has them running, tails between legs to seek out real criminals.
'Night night Jimmy.'
The barman gives him a mock salute to show the respect he still holds for the old General and local hunt-master.
'Night Sir!' Jimmy goes back to polishing the wine glasses and marvels again at the volumes of Port the old man can still hold.
At his car Grantham-Smyth opens the driver's door and eases his considerable bulk down into the soft leather seat. He reverses out of the parking bay of the exclusive Gentlemen's club and shoves the handle on the automatic transmission Jaguar into *drive*.
Easing along the seafront road he curses his stupidity in taking this route – it's renowned for a heavy police presence this time of night, picking up the waifs and strays emerging from the riff raff clubs. He'll just have to take it steady – not too fast and not so slow that he'll be conspicuous.
Heading out of Hove on the Worthing road he senses something lurking behind him. Checking the rear view mirror the vague presence becomes more intense *That's odd, is something on the back seat…*
'Turn right at the next junction and keep going. Failure to follow my instructions will lead to a bullet through the back of your seat. You're an ex military man so you'll appreciate that the bullet may go anywhere upon deflection – including into your bladder or fat Foie Gras-scoffing belly. Be a shame to soil your luxurious seat upholstery.'

Grantham-Smyth knows a real threat when he hears one and does exactly as told.
'That's excellent fatty – well done so far. On your left in about five hundred meters you'll see a white Transit van. Pull up behind it, switch off the engine and pass me the keys – do I need to reiterate my earlier threat?'

'No, no, I remember it very well.'

'I can tell you've been drinking fatso; no false bravado now, I know how you drunken ex-military types can get all heroic, just do what I tell you and you'll live a long, prosperous and clinically obese life.'

The van is in sight and the half-inebriated man pulls in behind it as told.

'Tut, tut fatso, we forgot to indicate. That doesn't bode well for your future treatment; you see, I absolutely hate rule breakers, so you'd better start obeying some. Now apologise for being such a naughty fat man.'

The porky MP mutters an apology.

'I didn't hear that very well tubby; try again.'

The ex General is not going to take such impudence from whoever this mugger might be.

'Now listen here I didn't…'

His sentence is curtailed by a painful blow to the left side of his head.

He realises he's at a distinct disadvantage and keeps any further thoughts to himself.

He struggles out of the driving seat and the attacker opens the van's rear double doors.

'Right then porky, into the van and then strap your left arm into the padlock that you'll find on the left side.'

Again Grantham-Smyth does as instructed, awaiting his chance for a getaway.

'Good boy, now I shall strap your right hand in – please be aware that I have studied a number of martial arts to a very proficient standard and will absolutely be happy to demonstrate exactly how good I am – after all, lard-arse, everyone likes the occasional audience.'

'Where are you taking me?'

'To a safe house – safe for me that is, and very unsafe for you. You'll be a few feet away from another cruel individual, but he won't know you're there, until he hears your begging-for-mercy screams of course.'

271

The team is assembled in the operations room and there's a buzz about the place that's been missing for a while.

'Good news people.' Dyson's tone is certainly a notch higher on the cheerful scale than it has been since his premature return from his paternity leave.

'The videos that have been appearing may give us the link after all. Our techie friends have managed to work out that the data we *thought* was coming from multiple IP addresses are actually all being generated by the same machine, or rather, are all being posted from the same network. Just need to get past the fire walls etc that are protecting that and bingo!'

'How long will that take, Guv?'

'How long's a piece of string Carol! I'm told it could be instant or take weeks; I've informed our boffin friends that weeks is the wrong answer and they will dedicate every spare resource, but they reminded me a number of times about the current stretch due to the terrorist threat. We'll be lucky if they get to our stuff this side of the weekend.'

'So they're happy to take the rap for the next murder then Sir?'

'That's not how it works Sicknote, as you well know. It's all about perspectives and priorities. Meanwhile let's sift through the videos we have collected once again and see what we've missed; the bastard will have made a fuck up somewhere along the line; let's find it'

He is woken from a shallow sleep by the door opening the usual crack.

'In the corner, you know the routine, hands behind neck.'

He shuffles across to where he can be seen from the door.

'God it stinks in here, I thought the lack of heating would help preserve the food I left you three days ago but it's rotting away and you stink like a sewer. Might give you a hose down later if I can be bothered with you. How did you clean your puppies when you kept them like this? Oh, silly me. Well, you can stay like this too, covered in your own shit and soaked in urine. Karma is a wonderful thing so it's happy days all round! Maybe I should bring you some nicer food? I want you to enjoy the experience you put so many puppies through for a very long time, no good if you refuse to eat the slop and your body eats its own fat – where's the justice in that?'

Colin's face splits in a big beaming smile as if he's just won the lottery.

'Turn around and face the corner like a naughty schoolboy.'

This is exactly how Jamie Parfitt feels as he stares at the point where two walls meet and tries to summon the strength he will need to attack the freak now and escape. It's going to be now or never, any longer and he'll become too weak. He tries to work out what his captor is doing but his peripheral vision can't quite catch anything that's happening behind him. He risks a tiny turn of his head and catches a small movement. Not yet, he tells himself, has to give the attempt every chance of success. Be patient a little longer. He wriggles his toes and fingers and clenches and unclenches his key muscle groups to get blood and energy circulating.

'Taadaa!'

Colin produces a plate of food that he'd left outside the room like a magic trick.

'Today, for one day only you shall eat like a king! Make the most of it.'

With that the freak is gone, and with him any chance of escape. Jamie swears at himself and bemoans the opportunity not taken as he hears the door double lock. That might have been his best chance, although the monster is becoming less security-minded with each visit but they are few and far between. Jamie has to make a plan. He looks down and is astonished to see a knife and fork on the plate; a real, metal knife and fork! Well the guy really has let his guard down, with a knife Jamie can have a really good shot at overpowering him. He decides to eat first while the food is still hot and then make plans.

The food tastes surprisingly good, some kind of faux meat with an interesting rice dish – colourful and not as warm as it could be but he is literally starving and while he slowly chews, deliberately savouring every taste he fantasises about slitting the guy's ugly throat with a razor sharp blade. He should be able to use the checker-plate stainless walls to sharpen the thing, and as long as he does it quietly the freak will never know.
He smiles for the first time in days.

Upstairs in the remote farmhouse Colin Furness eats his own meal while watching his new guest via video-link, the fat huntsman has been installed in the main cellar room. Colin's meal is similar to what he's fed Parfitt, except the rice mixture on Colin's plate is plain and doesn't contain the *Baylisascarisprocyonis* larvae.
Jamie Parfitt is, right this minute, busy ingesting rich forkfuls of the things.

Colin had become aware of how many of Parfitt's puppies became sick with Parvovirus and wanted to give him a dose of that to end his days, but sadly it's almost impossible for an adult human to die from the disease. Raccoon Roundworm, however is a different prospect and Colin is looking forward to watching Parfitt in the coming days. Delivered to a small, unhealthy, undernourished, dehydrated man living in a cold damp cellar with no access to sanitation or any kind of medication…well, the outcome would be fun.
He has the capacity to film the episode, maybe that would be fun, but he'll need to be careful.

∆ Teaching a child not to step on a caterpillar is as valuable to the child as it is to the caterpillar ∆
Bradley Millar

D0227 hears the usual morning noises, the man in blue coming to give her the awful, insipid food, the man in white the injections, other men in green come and go and there are tractors. Today there's a different sound; the big truck that comes once a week is pulling up outside. It's one of the noisiest monsters that she sees and hears and she wonders if this week will be her turn. Each time it comes, rows and rows of the other cows are slowly dragged past her tiny prison and swallowed up in the bowels of the big beast. They are clearly frightened, because they moo and bellow in their childish cow-voices as the man in blue and his friends kick, punch and stab them with all kinds of nasty tools.

The huge doors open and the sunshine streams through the dust suspended in the air, carrying smells of grass, long grown old and dry, but grass nevertheless. Sure enough, the man in blue comes to her stall and raises the metal bar. He grabs her by her ears and pulls hard, but she can't rise to her feet, can't use her legs; they've given up, lack of use has left them withered and weak. He speaks in human tongue, but she can't understand him of course.
'This one can go actually Jim; she's fucked anyway. Look at the knackered legs, rotting hoofs and her streaming nose. Pneumonia is my guess; they are so fucking fragile these days. It's a few weeks early but we'll adjust the paperwork – no one will know and she'll only snuff it if we wait. Give me a hand or we'll have to yank her out with the forklift and chains or with the digger bucket.'
As she's grabbed by the ears again by the man in blue and the one in white and brutally pulled from the tiny stall, D0227 wonders whether the monster truck might take them to a better life.

Colin is walking through the woods above Halnaker Windmill near Goodwood. He is calling the same Chichester number as previously.
'West Sussex Police.'
So bloody impersonal and official these civilian telephone operators.
'Yes hello, I want to speak with Detective Inspector Dyson, please.'
'Can I ask who's calling?'
'Tell him it's the same old friend who called before when he was too rude to answer.'
'One moment please sir. Er, but I must ask who is calling.'
'I told you already, I am a close friend.'
'Connecting you now sir.'
A few clicks and Colin knows they are putting a trace on the call.
'DI Dyson.'
'Ah! DI Dyson; has a ring to it. Just to tell you I am back and you won't be so lucky this time as I am taking more precautions. I have a number of projects on the go and one of them will be hitting the headlines pretty damn soon. Goodbye.'
'Wait...' But the line is already dead.

Swearing, Dyson is immediately on the line to the monitoring station operatives.
'Did you get it?'
'Give us a minute please Sir, takes a while to compute.'
'OK I will call you back in one minute, need to mobilise the gang.'
He disconnects and dials Samantha Milsom's mobile.
'DS Milsom.'
'Sam get in the cars now and get ready to drive, I'll give you the full directions in two minutes.'
Samantha ignores the abbreviated name, although it's slipping into everyday parlance it seems.
Dyson calls the monitoring number again.
'Anything?'
'Yep, two beacons, Burton Down which is at Bignor and Midhurst. Can't get a triangulation because he cut the call too soon, but it's somewhere in the seventy square miles around those two.'
'*Seventy? Seven zero?* Did you say *seventy bloody square miles*? Is that the best we can do with all this bloody technology?'

'Sorry Sir, another minute and we would have had him, if you could have kept him...'

Dyson interrupts.

'Don't try to lay the fault for your failure at my door. I suggest you get your own house in order.'

Dyson hangs up and calls Samantha.

'Call off the hounds, hopeless task. Tell you later; I'm off home for a beer and some grub.'

Colin opens the door a crack and recoils at the stench. It's far worse than it had been two days ago and he hesitates before proceeding further.

'OK, in the corner as usual.'

There is no response from inside the little room.

'Do as I say or I will lock the door and forget all about you.'

A tiny shuffling sound comes from directly behind the door. Despite copious research, Colin hasn't been able to determine how long the larvae would take to do the real damage to Parfitt's brain so he is reluctant to enter until he has an idea of the state the guy is in. After all, he has a knife and fork. The plate too could be a lethal weapon and Colin realises he should have been more cautious. Oh well, what's done is done. He may have to exercise plan B.

Closing the door and double locking it he climbs back up the two flights of stairs to his temporary living area. From a suitcase he removes a small cardboard box containing a metal aerosol spray canister, roughly six inches long, with about a one inch diameter and vacuum-packed in plastic. He also takes a pair of black rubber gauntlets and a respirator; a standard 3M industrial *snatch rescue* kit he'd bought online.

The gas canister contains the chemical 2-chlorobenzylidene malononitrile ($C_{10}H_5ClN_2$) otherwise known as CS gas, and the catalyst piperidine.

A few moments later he is back at the cellar door wearing the gloves and hooded mask. He unlocks and opens the door a crack and, keeping his hand safely outside the room, releases a continuous jet of the gas into the small space. He sprays until the canister is fully discharged, ignoring the choking coughs from his prisoner. The guy will be desperate to escape and who knows whether the worms have taken any kind of hold on his senses yet. Colin is taking no chances.

With the canister empty he shoves the door violently inwards and leaps into the room, ready to repel any attack that might still come. He needn't have worried, the prisoner is crawling on the floor clutching his throat and trying to cover his eyes, the moisture in those areas will have exacerbated the effects of the gas and he is completely incapacitated.

Happy with the result, Colin grabs adhesive duct tape from his bag outside the room and sets about securing Parfitt's hands behind his back. It isn't easy; the guy is desperately trying to retaliate but has no strength to match his powerful adversary. Colin feels something hard beneath the guy's sleeve and realises he has the knife secreted in there. He slackens a little of the tape again and removes the weapon. It's razor sharp – he must have been sharpening it for an escape attempt.

Colin realises what a close call this has been and makes a silent vow to tighten up on his actions from now on; *7 Ps*. This was a lucky escape and he might not be quite so fortunate in future.
Within a minute he has him trussed up tight again and drags him out of the room into relative fresh air. Colin goes back upstairs to fetch a small step ladder and some electronic equipment. He opens all the doors he can to try to dispel the gas so that he can remove the mask and gloves and also ensure that his victim survives; he doesn't want to waste the chance of watching his plan come to fruition too early. An hour later, with the room still tainted by the pungent gas he has fitted a small half-spherical camera to the ceiling and directed the cables through the metal wall into a control box outside the small room. The rest he can do later.
He throws Parfitt back inside and slightly eases his bindings so that in time and with some effort the captive can remove the rest himself; it'll give him something practical to occupy his brain, whilst it still has the capability to function.

'OK Mr Puppy killer. That's a camera. I shall be watching you from the comfort of my sofa from now on. There will be no more food and no more visits, unless I have an urgent need to defecate, in which case I may use your disgusting cell as a toilet, after all, it stinks like one and you have made no effort to keep it clean.'
He allows himself a small jig and claps his hands involuntarily.

'You recently ingested a nasty parasite which, as I speak is burrowing its way towards your brain. I am not sure how long it takes, so what happens next is not really certain. What *is* for sure is that you will begin to feel unwell. Your organs will be attacked by the little beasts and your neurological pathways disrupted. You will feel tiredness, nausea, loss of coordination and muscle control. Your liver will enlarge, as will many other organs, including your eyes; as a result blindness is almost certain. Once the little beasties reach your meninges and begin to pierce that blood/brain barrier, some form of insanity will ensue – that will be fun before you probably slip into a blissful coma and die. I am really interested to see exactly how you suffer, and I shall record it with my camera equipment and send a copy to your wife; after all, she has been complicit and benefitted from your inhuman treatment of animals so she should share in the beauty of your suffering. Not sure she'll want to show the kids what became of daddy, but maybe there's a useful lesson in life there, kind of what *not* to do in the future.'

Parfitt begins to rant and rave at his lunatic captor, writhing on the floor in a desperate attempt to free himself. Colin assumes this is a sign of the infestation beginning to work and, smiling broadly, dances a bizarre jig uncontrollably.

'Goodbye Jamie. I'd like to say it's been a pleasure, but we both know that would be a crock of shit. Please die dramatically, lots of raving and theatricals, after all, even though your wife will probably keep the video from the kids, I am sure they will want to see how well daddy performs when someone stumbles across the footage on YouTube sometime in the future – because rest assured, I'll put it there regularly! Oh, and I'll probably be paying wifey a visit at some point too, can't let the horrid woman off scot-free now, can we!'

He leaves, closing the door quietly on the screaming frenzy.
The key rotates twice in the lock. Colin will view the video later, right now he has to be somewhere else and is looking forward to a date with the devil himself.

The tiny congregation is making its way slowly from the ancient church, the vicar, James Timpleman, shaking the hand of most of the men and bowing to the women. He's been in this role in the Saxon building for five years now, and knows just about anyone worth knowing in the village. But he has other ambitions; he aspires towards Bishop level at least and studies hard to ensure he is best placed to achieve this when the time comes, as it surely will.

As he is preparing to lock the old oak doors he gets a feeling that not all of the congregation have vacated. Sure enough in the gloom he spies a tall man standing near the font, looking at the ancient transcripts on old prayer pads and tapestries.

'Er, excuse me, I need to lock up now, but if you need a little more time I can certainly wait.'

'Oh, that won't be necessary vicar, you see it's you I've come to see.'

'Me? Well, what can I help you with?'

'I wanted you to have a look at this interesting find...'

The visitor is holding a dirty looking piece of cloth.

'Certainly, is it an old Christian relic?'

'Yes; something along those lines.'

'Well OK then, let's have a look.'

Timpleman turns to lead Colin into the church office but before he has chance to react his head is pulled violently backwards and the cloth jammed against his mouth and nose.

He's dragged by his hair into the office where his assailant quickly binds his mouth, arms and feet with the ever-present duct tape until he almost resembles a black mummy.

'You stay right there your fucking holiness while I get my van. If you move so much as a prayer book's width I'll kick your stupid religious throat into your skull. Got it?'

It's a rhetorical question; the church man cannot possibly answer.

Within two minutes Colin drives the van as close as he can get it and thanks the disability laws which make it compulsory for easy access. Before the clock bells can chime the next hour he's got the reverend into the van and is securing him to the rings set in the floor.

Judith Silbermann is enjoying a day at the library. She likes it here, quiet, clean and tidy, the books arranged by subject and then in alphabetical order on the shelves. Orderly.

She likes the librarians too, especially the young girl who is here on Tuesdays and Fridays. In fact she seems to have become infatuated. They have chatted a few times, when Judith could muster the courage, and she thinks the girl might just have a similar sexuality. Homosexuality is detested and abhorred in her religion, although lesbianism has hardly been on the radar for Jews, it's frowned upon in most Judaic circles to have, or even think about carnal knowledge of another female. Gay they call it now. She prefers this term to lesbian; it implies an element of fun, joy and, yes, intimacy.

She's here again, the girl, and Judith's heart skips a beat when their eyes meet across the floor. Today she will write a poem and leave it *'accidentally'* in the book she's returning. She thinks that such a gesture might pique the girl's interest, and at least then she'll know for certain.

Judith enjoys poetry; reading and writing, and is, she has been told, quite good. She settles herself down to think of a suitable subject, but for once inspiration fails her. She should find out something about the girl, a little titbit to prompt her ideas, use the girl as a muse.
Yes, that's exactly what she'd do.
Approaching the desk, she coughs quietly, as if afraid to disturb the silence.
'Erm...I wonder if you'd help me out? I am looking for a set of poems by Wilfred Owen...do you have anything on the shelves here?'
The librarian girl is speaking...actually speaking to her.
Her heart does somersaults but she realises she wasn't listening to the words; too busy watching those delicious lips forming that

beautiful cascade of musical sounds. With some effort she pulls herself together as the girl continues.

'We have something I'm sure, although I only work part time so can't be as certain as I'd like to be.'

'Oh that's OK, nothing is ever really as certain as we'd like, is it? Maybe we could look together?'

'Yes.' Beams the librarian. 'I'd like that.'

If Judith was nervous before, she's terrified now of saying something silly, but she needn't worry, the girl continues.

'I'm Molly, by the way.'

'Oh…er…I am Judith.' She stutters.

'Yeah, I know from your library card! I think I saw a war poets' anthology which included the poems used by Benjamin Britten in his War Requiem; let's see if we can unearth those again.'

Oh gosh; she knows those poems; knows Britten…fabulous. She quivers as she replies.

'Oh that would be super; I adore that music.'

'Me too! I simply love the astonishing brass voicing in – I think it's the fourth movement – Sanctum?'

'Sanctus, I think…?' (Shy smile).

'Oh, yeah, Sanctus. It's like a spiralling peal of bells, cacophonic; triumphant; fanfare-esque, oh gosh, moving beyond words.'

Judith touches her arm momentarily, aware of the indescribable frisson between the two girls.

'Oh, I agree! And resolving harmonically, yet never quite going where your ear wants it to take you!'

'Wow – who'd have thought I'd meet someone here who loves the same things!'

The girl called Molly smiles that winsome smile and then delivers the devastating news.

'It's a shame really, I've just got used to this place and now I have to finish here next week, or rather Saturday; this Saturday.'

Judith tries (and fails) to hide her disappointment.

'Oh, er, that's a shame. Erm, where are you going, I mean, well, do you have a new job?'

'Well kind of, but it's up north. Working for a publishing house – it's what I've wanted to do for ages and a great break if it works out.'

'Sure, shame though, I've enjoyed your smiling face here. The library won't be the same without you.'

'Aaw, thanks; that's really sweet of you. It's a shame that we never really got to know each other. Ah! Here it is. Owen, W.E.S.' She passes the elusive tome across.

'Brill! Thanks.'

Judith tries again to make light of the situation.

'Well, maybe we could have a coffee together before you go?'

'Great; I'd like that! When suits you?'

'Any time you like really, maybe tomorrow?' Judith holds her breath, hoping for a glimmer of a chance.

'Cool, tomorrow, shall we meet here at ten?'

'OK, er, yes of course. Molly's a lovely name. Erm, just going to get some work done then, see you tomorrow.'

The work she had planned lies forgotten on the table as instead she pens a poem.

Leaving

You told me you'll be leaving
Well, Saturday, you said.
Saturday, Wednesday, Michaelmas day;
Who cares, you're in my head.
And in any case
A day is just a day.

The point is the damned leaving;
How dare you say you'll go?
It wrenches at my breathing.
Saturday must come, I know.
Taking you from here;
And me
Sort of grieving;
Though I hardly know you...

You hinted many a fabulous thing,

284

Hazel eyes across the room,
The words of Wilfred Owen sing,
The mundane vanishes as if broom-swept
By some tempting, gay thing.
I see the sky and horizon mating;
Where our butterflies alight
Friends forever? But never 'dating';
I'll yearn ever for this sight.

It's more than infinitely frustrating;

For on Saturday you'll leave.

It's a bit cheesy and probably a bit soppy, but, oh well.
She slips the drafted poem into the front of the book and hands it
back.
'Worth looking into, that one!' A wink and she's off.

Outside the library Judith hurries to catch her bus. She doesn't notice
a tall man tracking her stealthily in a dirty white van.

102

The girl is almost skipping; care-free. An easy target, far too trusting of her surroundings; probably born and raised in a safe environment where there was never a threat that mummy and daddy couldn't deal with. Well deal with this one you nasty Kosher killers.

Colin is parked in the quiet cul-de-sac where Judith lives, less than fifty yards from her front door; crouching in the back of his van hefting one end of a railway sleeper he'd bought at a garden centre some miles away. As she passes he calls out to her.
'Er, excuse me; I wonder if you could just prop my van door fully open whilst I drag this heavy piece of timber out?'
'Oh yeah; sure.' *Huge happy smile.*
She takes hold of the door on the kerbside and pulls it wide open. Colin checks for pedestrians and delays a moment while a car passes then drags one end of the sleeper past her, the other end balancing on the van floor. As he comes level with her he drops the end he's supporting onto the road and within an instant has her in an arm-lock with his left hand and has the wad of dirty chemical-impregnated rag firmly clamped to her mouth and nose. Hardly any struggling, and he pulls her swiftly into the back of the van, tugging one door shut with his foot and plunging the interior of the van into semi-darkness. Unconsciousness comes quickly and he pushes the timber back inside and shuts the other door, switches on the internal light and trusses her up with tape.
Within two minutes he's on his way back to the safe house. He's happy to have a Jew; Kosher slaughter is every bit as barbaric as Halal and she'll sit in the squalor of her purpose built pen in the same way as his other guests, prior to the online fun commencing.

103

Scoffing down a hasty lentil and spinach meal from a chipped and dirty breakfast bowl he glances at the monitor screen to see what Parfitt is up to. He hasn't bothered recording anything yet as the guy has just been moping about, sleeping curled on the cold floor or crawling around the little enclosure licking every inch of the stainless steel checker-plate walls for the moisture or sometimes feeling over its surfaces with his flat hands and groping fingers, desperately trying, Colin supposes, to find a weakness somewhere in the structure.
Good luck with that.

But something is different this time; Parfitt is sat in the middle of the tiny room rocking his upper torso back and forth. Quickly Colin turns up the volume on the set and hears the keening wail.
Excellent! Oh but this is good! At last the little worms must be hitting the sweet spot.
Colin claps his hands and wiggles his left foot whilst hitting the record button, tiny spits of spinach fleck the screen as he guffaws at the spectacle.
A little red camera icon flashes in the top right corner of the screen. Enjoyable as it is, Colin doesn't want to be distracted all afternoon by the moaning prisoner, so he drops the volume to a whisper. He wants to be able to detect any significant change in behaviour so a *little* sound will be useful.

Meanwhile he finishes the now cold meal and continues compiling the ever-growing list of things he might need, depending on how his very loose plans progress. He's frustrated that some things seem to take so long and his plans are still so rudimentary. But the seven Ps are king! Luckily he finds what he needs quite easily. Some things are expensive, but money really is no object.

A different sound from the monitor system catches his attention and he swivels on his chair in time to witness Parfitt launch himself head-first into the wall, screaming something about onions.

Interesting!

This will make great viewing online when he posts it.

He toys with the idea of recording snippets and sending them piecemeal to Hayley Parfitt. He likes the idea of her gradually getting more and more distressed by the degradation in her husband's mental health. But he knows that the police are good – he'd learned that the hard way – and it's too risky to give them any kind of clues before he absolutely has to. He had seen how they took the tiniest snippet and built an investigation around it. His arrest had been almost solely down to such subtleties and he wasn't about to give Dyson and crew the pleasure a second time.

Now the prisoner is tearing his clothes off and grasping at his balls.

What the hell?

Great fun to watch a bastard like Jamie Parfitt slowly falling apart and knowing that it is only going to end in his horrible death; either through the roundworm, or through Colin walking in there and executing him with his own hands. He wants it to be the larvae eating away at his brain but in some ways he'd prefer the latter, after all, he has a reputation to live up to!

As he watches, Parfitt launches himself again into the wall, driving his head against the unforgiving surface and the camera shakes in its mounting from the vibrations caused by the force of the impact. Colin turns up the volume, unsure whether the recording volume will reflect what he is hearing or is fixed at an automatic setting. He wants his viewers to have the full benefit.

Now his prisoner is running around the tiny room like a dog with the rips; every now and then smashing headfirst into one of the walls. It's completely bizarre behaviour and clearly the effect of the roundworm. Blood is evident now on his face and smeared on one of the walls, and as he watches, Parfitt takes the fingers of his right hand into his mouth and seems to bite down hard. Something is then spat out and now Parfitt jumps high and lands on his knees, kicking out at the walls. The soundtrack is even more interesting, animal screams and wails interspersed with shouts about god and Jesus and something about honour, vows and wives fucking with friends. *Ever more interesting*!

In a short while the screams become more like low pitched groans and then growls, and Colin is surprised that an insignificant little man can make such a low-pitched sound, almost lionesque. That sound stops abruptly as the captive makes what appears to be one final dash for freedom, slamming face-first into the solid door and falling into unconsciousness.

Colin manipulates the camera remotely and zooms in on Parfitt's head. He is laying face-down, so his expression can't be seen, but a puddle of blood is forming around his upper body leaching from a head wound. Time to investigate a little closer. There's no way this can be a trap; he has no concerns about a repeat of his earlier near-miss.

Down in the cellar the smell is worse than ever and it's immediately clear why; the prisoner has defecated all over the place, a fact that hadn't been noticed via the video link. He's also vomited in two corners of the little room, although it's all bile and blood.
Despite what he has witnessed, Colin is cautious as he approaches the lying form. It's obvious that the guy is not in any fit state to try anything funny, and Colin squats down next to him, careful to avoid the mucous and bodily fluids present everywhere. The smell up close is bordering on unbearable, and he holds his sleeve across his nose. He lays his hand on the neck, where he knows he should feel the carotid artery, but can sense nothing.
Suddenly Parfitt leaps up and grabs him around the throat.
Colin is completely taken by surprise and falls onto his back in the messy liquid chaos The cunning fucker has tricked him again.
Muscle memory takes over and all the years of practicing aikido and taekwondo kick in as auto-reflexes. He uses the momentum and Parfitt's own body weight to throw him over his head and into the wall behind him. Jumping to his feet and slipping around in the slime Colin readies himself for the next onslaught, but Parfitt simply slumps to the floor, on his back, eyes wide open and staring.

Suspecting another trick, Colin warily circles around to his left, hugging the wall, and lines up a swift attack. With lightning speed he executes a turning kick to the side of Parfitt's head, and watches with interest as his body partially leaves the floor, then settles down on its side, motionless.

No way he can have taken a blow of that strength without crying out, unless he really is unconscious this time.

Remembering the close shave with the knife and not prepared to take any more chances, Colin delivers a front snap kick beneath Parfitt's jaw, watching his head jerk backwards and smash into the wall behind him. That settles it; he's out for the count. The earlier attack must have been some final death-throes reaction.

He squats carefully beside him for the second time in as many minutes, grabbing a fistful of hair with his left hand and delivering a crushing knife-hand strike with his right across Parfitt's exposed throat. There is absolutely no reaction and a pulse check shows his heart has stopped beating.

Colin exits the cell, double-locking the door – more out of habit than for any other reason – and makes his way back up the stairs.

He'd left the camera running and plays back the video, feeling a sense of pride as he watches his reaction to the sudden attack and the accuracy of his kicks. He decides to leave the whole film as it is and copies it to a CD. There is no way there's anything on the film that could give away his location, so why not let the police see how ineffective they are.

He takes a padded envelope and pushes the disc inside, taking his time writing the address. He struggles with this because of his dyslexia, but finally has a good enough representation for the postman to be able to deliver it to the right place. He'll take a long drive, as he did yesterday, and send it from a little village post office that has no CCTV.

104

Molly is waiting at the library where they had agreed to meet as planned. Judith has yet to arrive, but that doesn't worry her much, things happen and people get delayed and anyway, she knows from the poem Judith wrote that the girl is interested in her. She wonders if she's bisexual or gay, like herself, and thinks with a cheeky smile on her face that either is fine. Long distance relationships are hard to maintain, but Molly is prepared to work at it, if 'it' is in any way on the agenda.

But time is ticking and Judith is now thirty minutes late. Molly begins to worry; has she developed cold feet and stood Molly up? She seemed too nice and had definitely been keen enough in the library, and the poem, although simple, was certainly an indication of the feelings Judith has for her.

After an hour she decides that Judith is not going to show. She thinks about reporting her missing, but that's ludicrous, there would be a simple explanation, and anyway, the police never did anything in such circumstances. Despite this she calls the police on the non-urgent number. When someone finally answers on 101 she is told that missing persons must be reported directly at the nearest police station. She makes her way there and is invited into an interview suite, thinking that it's a rather salubrious term for what is essentially just a cell.

105

Hayley Parfitt is pouring herself a coffee from the percolator when the postman walks up the garden path and slips a small flat package through the letterbox. He crosses the grass on his way to next door's letterbox and this infuriates her. She opens the window and shouts after him to use the pathways in future. He completely ignores her. She hasn't slept well for any of the last five nights because her husband of nine years has simply disappeared. It isn't the first time he's been off on '*business trips*' but he usually gives her some notice or contacts her from wherever he is in the country. This time there is a stony silence and after his odd behaviour of late she is beginning to seriously wonder if she'll ever see him again.

Not that she is really so concerned about Jamie; after all, they have drifted somewhat and she's replaced him in her life – well, if she's honest, just in her bed – with his best friend Finn. Thomas Finnegan is everything Jamie could never be; polite, funny, thoughtful, strong, courageous and well endowed. He is the perfect man for her and, unbeknown to her husband, the father of their last child, Esme.

But she is a little worried this time that something has happened. She knows about Jamie's drug dealings and is intimately familiar with the puppy breeding side of things. She assumes he's either headed off on some big money deal, or, well, the drugs gangs have caught up with him. She ponders calling him in as a missing person, but dismisses the idea. If and when he does turn up again he'd go mental at her for involving the law; he hates the police with a vengeance and would be really pissed off if she'd invited their nosey, interfering boots into his life.

Secretly she hopes it's the latter; that his dodgy dealings have caught up with him. She hates his lies and his filthy habits and he is pretty much a useless father to the kids. He squanders their money on cars and luxury stuff he hardly uses, making it clear that it's *his* money to do with as *he* pleases. If he's gone from the scene for good that will leave the coast clear for Finn to step in….she thinks about that as she unwraps the small parcel; maybe it's something sweet from Finn.

Inside the brown paper packaging is a bubble-wrapped compact disc. She moves across the room, examining the disc for any clues as she walks in her stockinged feet to the dual TV/DVD player, presses the button to open the little motorised drawer, slots the disc into the housing and presses the play button.

The screen is blank for maybe twenty seconds and then a grainy grey image emerges. It shows her husband in a small room – something like the size of a police cell.
He is rocking backwards and forwards and shouting something about cars. Has he been drugged? Is this some sick revenge by the gangsters he's mixed up with? She knows he owes money – he *always* owes somebody something.

He starts to rant – something about a monkey tree and a pineapple; *did he just shout 'onion?*

The video lasts only about ninety seconds but it makes very disturbing viewing. She ought to hand it to the police but they are pretty useless and in any case disinterested in taking on new problems unless it means an easy catch and their stats being bumped in the right direction. They would pretend to take an interest and meanwhile do sod all and she'd just be lulled into believing something was happening.
But she needs to talk with someone. Finn will know what to do, he always does. She picks up her mobile and hits his speed dial getting straight through to his voicemail. He's at work and never answers his personal 'phone there.
'Finn, it's me. Call me as soon as. I know where Jay is, or rather, I know he is in the shit.'

106

The small ops room is full with the return of Samantha and Brian from their European travels and the raised tension of knowing that, with the contact having been made, they are at least a step closer to catching their man.

'Right, some missing persons reports came in overnight, I've asked to be in on all violent crime and anything that has the hallmarks of our friend. A hunt-master and a Jewish girl; former has clear potential on an animal welfare front, the latter is more tenuous, and whilst I can't see a link right now it might be a new avenue for Furness.'

'Not necessarily, Sir.'

'Explain please, Samantha?'

'Well there's the Muslim link last time round and Jews have similar no-stun slaughter methods to Muslims; could be a link there.'

'Good shout Samantha, yeah, you're absolutely right, OK let's assume our pal has branched out. Sicknote and Steph get onto the hunter angle and Samantha and I will tackle the young Jewish girl. Usual stuff guys; the rest please continue your other enquiries. He may be collecting hostages again so let's have a think about other vulnerable demographics'.

'That's a huge one Guv – any way we can narrow it down?'

'What, demographics? Oh, I see. So you want me to do all the work Sicknote? Use that marvellous brain of yours and come up with a list of potential target groups before we knock off tonight – *if* we knock off tonight!'

107

The doorbell rings and Hayley Parfitt rushes to open it, pulling
Finnegan quickly inside and wrapping herself around him in a needy
hug.
'You don't need to ring the bloody bell, Finn!'
'Well if I don't know what's going on I can't take silly risks, if he
catches us at it babe there'll be hell to pay.'
'He aint catching nobody Finn, he's been kidnapped by the
druggies.'
'How do you know that?'
'They sent me a video – come on, I'll show you.'

Thomas Finnegan follows her into the lounge, watching her cute arse
in the baggy T-shirt, tiny black skirt and hold-ups as she rushes
ahead. She's nervous and panicky and upset and vulnerable…. and
that turns him on.
'Let's watch it in a bit babe, the kids are at school and I aint got
long, why don't we make the most of the opportunity?'
His smile and wink disappear as she slaps him around the face.
'I don't bloody believe you! My husband is missing – probably
kidnapped – and you wanna take me to frigging bed?
Unbloodybelievable!'
She pushes him down onto the sofa and grabs the DVD player
remote control from the side table.

Finnegan watches as the grainy picture clears to show the images
and sounds she'd watched earlier.
'Fuck me – is he mental? What's he on about?'
'They've drugged him of course, probably overdosed him on some
shit.'
'He doesn't look drugged, looks more like his lost his flipping mind
than drugs.'
'Maybe a bit of both. What should we do?'
'We? He's your bloody husband.'

He's still smarting from the slap but realises instantly the error he's just made and tries to soften the blow as he sees his afternoon shag disappearing over the horizon.

'Sorry – didn't mean that. But I'm not sure what we can do really; we don't know who they are, where he is or if he's even still alive – when did this arrive?'

'This morning.'

'Probably been in the post a couple of days. Was there a note or anything else in the package?'

'No, nothing. Just the disc. Shall I call the police?'

'No, not yet. Let's give it a day. One day won't make much difference and they may have sent something else.'

'So what do we do in the meantime, sit and twiddle our thumbs?'

'We could, or we could make the most of a bad situation...'

'You are bloody impossible Finn! One track mind.'

'Yeah, but it's not my mind you're interested in ...is it!'

'Finn, I just need a hug, nothing more, just a hug.'

He pulls her down onto the sofa and clamps his hand over her mouth to silence her protests.

'I'll hug ya all ya want babe, I love huggin' ya, but don't pretend you don't want it too, feel how badly I need you...'

He drags her hand to the bulge in his jeans and forces her to feel his hardness, watching her eyes half close as they always do when she is getting turned on.

He releases his grip on her hand and she doesn't move it.

'See, we both know what's good for you.'

His other hand comes away from her mouth and is replaced by his lips, grabbing the back of her head and pulling her towards him as her tongue dives between his teeth and they kiss passionately. He feels her grip his erection hard, as if trying to hurt him and he moans with the pleasure of the sensation. She's astride him now and her little skirt rides up high as he massages her breasts through the thin fabric of her t-shirt.

'No bra again, naughty girl...' He loves her taut body and the fact that she doesn't need to wear a bra. That Jamie twat didn't know what he had, and now he was losing her.

Her hand stops squeezing but his groan of disappointment quickly turns to a moan of approval as he feels her fingers working desperately at his belt and then zip. Seemingly seamlessly he is freed and she is mounting him.

'No panties either – bad girl…fuck that feels good.'

She slowly lowers herself onto his long length and anchors herself right at the bottom. Neither of them moves for a moment as they kiss and pull each other close. Then, slowly she begins to move above him, rising a few inches and then slowly coming back down to ground and up again. They are both ridiculously aroused and as her pace rapidly increases his imagination runs riot.

Feeling his climax already building he reaches out for the DVD remote control.

She is bouncing up and down all over him now and he has a crazy vision of her on a space-hopper, hair flying and face set in a grimace of determination.

He hits the play button as they reach fever pitch.

His grunts and her screams are accompanied by the soundtrack of a lost and plaintive cry about a car, a monkey and something about an onion...

They explode in intense simultaneous orgasms.

After ten minutes recovery cuddling, Hayley Parfitt breaks the silence.

'I am going to call the police Finn.'

'Seriously? What, and have them crawl all through your life, unearthing all the drugs and puppy stuff? You gotta be joking! Once the papers get hold of the story the guttersnipe Paparazzi will be camped on your front lawn 24/7 – your life will be shit and the kids will get hassled everywhere.'

'Yeah, I know, but what else can I do?'

'Leave it. As far as you are concerned he's disappeared, let them find him, maybe, whenever. Was he insured?'

'What? No. never saw the need; stupid really, considering the thugs he dealt with. The kids are already asking and friends… family. I'm calling the filth now.'

She dials three nines and when she's through to the police tells an edited version of the story, including details of the DVD.

For once the report finds its way speedily onto DI Dyson's desk.

108

It's 17:30 and Colin is on the 'phone to an old friend.

'Barbara, it's me, the Beagle rescue man.'

'Hey how are you doing?'

'I am fine thanks, how is Colina?'

'She's doing brilliantly, when are you coming to see her?'

'Soon, really soon, well, oh I don't know; it's tricky, but right now I need a favour.'

'Sure, like I said before, just name it!'

Colin details the nature of the favour and after some expressions of surprise Barbara assures him she'll do everything she possibly can. He cuts the call, switches off the 'phone and conceals it in the thick sock on his right leg above his ankle.

By 18:00 Colin is at the flower kiosk outside the Manchester station as instructed. He's dressed as required in dark running shoes with the reflective tabs removed, black jeans and sweater with a dark green mid-length waterproof hooded jacket. He has dark blue gloves, a scarf, dark woollen hat pulled far down over his brow and the thick-framed plain-glass blue spectacles. He carries a medium-sized black shoulder bag. Inside the bag are spare clothes, a small bottle of water, a few energy bars and some other items he thinks he will need, including a reel of black duct tape, thin strips of a cotton material, a small bottle of chemical and his 9mm pistol with screw-on suppression unit. It's the same German Sig Sauer P226 that he'd used in Spain. The pistol was actually manufactured in New Hampshire, USA; the suppression is a Ti-Rant 9 silencer. The two can be joined in a few seconds by a wide screw-thread. Not the most powerful combination, but very quiet in action and ideal for what he needs tonight.

He calculates that in order to succeed he needs there to be no more than three in the group. Any more and he will probably struggle to achieve his goal.

Looking at his watch for the umpteenth time in the last few minutes he lowers his head to disguise his face from passers-by and prevent any coincidental capture on CCTV equipment and scans the crowd for any likely gang member. He's particularly wary of CCTV because he knows the police and security services have special face recognition software and they can simply upload images of anyone they are interested in talking to and instantly thousands of cameras across the country would be on continuous watch. Recognition at this stage would spell disaster.

He is snapped out of his reverie by a light tug on his left sleeve and is about to turn when he hears the warning.
'Do not turn around, just follow me; far enough away to look as if we are not together and close enough so that I don't lose you.'
The voice is different to the telephone voice of Mujahid, more stereotypically Indian-sounding and Colin knows it's a different man.

He follows a few feet behind, constantly scanning for threats and concealing his features from any detection devices. After a few minutes they enter the station complex via a side gate and Colin is quickly passed a train and a bus ticket. The price on the train ticket is £1.90 so it can't be for a long journey. The bus ticket has no price, just a date and route.

The guy takes a staircase to the right and Colin follows, realising the man has been limping slightly all the time. At the top of the steps is a station platform and they wait in silence, separated by a distance of a few feet and an ideology of a million miles.

In time a train arrives and following his guide Colin climbs aboard and spends the next fifteen minutes avoiding looking at the on-board CCTV camera. At a place called Clifton the guy alights and exits the station, crossing the road to a bus stop with Colin in his wake. The guy is busy with his 'phone and has three separate conversations whilst they wait. All his talking is done in Arabic. Colin is busy avoiding looking at passers-by and any possible cameras as always.

Finally, with the time approaching 19:30 a bus arrives and they climb aboard. The journey is further this time and any tension he feels is soon overridden by the motion of the bus, the warmth and the comforting engine sounds, causing Colin to feel drowsy. His eyelids begin to droop.

He's awoken by the bus coming to a halt, but the Muslim remains seated. Colin's mind comes back to the imminent task. He's sitting three rows behind his escort and therefore out of his sight and he carefully opens the bag to check that the contents have stayed where he put them. The little pistol is in an internal zip-up pocket which a casual observer would miss. Colin has applied a strip of the black duct tape along the line of the zip to further camouflage the pocket. The small chemical bottle is inside the main compartment and he removes that now, pocketing it in the inside zip-up pocket of his jacket. He'll be able to get to that quite easily. He also pockets a small handful of the cloth strips.

The bus pulls over again and this time the Muslim rises and heads for the door. Colin quickly zips up the bag, shoulders it and follows him out. Standing on the pavement they wait until the bus pulls away and an old couple, who also got off, cross the road before the guy speaks.
'OK, follow me. No cameras here and few people so we can relax a bit. What's in the bag?'

Colin is ready for this; it's only natural that they'll want to search him, or at least check out the bag. They are walking fast.
'It's just some stuff for later, spare clothes, some snacks, that kind of thing. Oh, and my passport and a few personal papers, in case things go wrong and I need to get out of the country.'
'Ditch it.'
'What? No way, it might be all I have in the world after tonight.'
'Drop it where you can collect it later. Plenty of industrial bins and the like where we are going; they won't be emptied tonight for certain so it'll be safe in one of them. And I need to search you too – just normal protocol with new guys and you definitely are no Arab, so I am gonna need to be extra careful.'

Colin is thinking fast.

'OK, search me now then so you can relax.'

'Once we are off this road I will.'

They walk in silence for a few minutes through what is clearly an industrial estate and then suddenly veer left into a dark, walled lane.

'OK, stop here. Drop the bag and raise your arms high as you can.'

Colin does as instructed and the thorough search reveals a lump where the small bottle nestles in the pocket.

'What's that?'

Working on his bluff Colin removes the bottle.

'It's for my lungs – an inhalant. I get really bad sudden bouts of asthma and this works instantly. Without it I might die and I would certainly be a risk to the operation.'

'What's it called?'

'Read the label – it's chlorpheniramine, a powerful kind of receptor antagonist that will...'

'Alright, OK, I get it.' Interrupts the Muslim. 'Come on, let's go. Dump the bag in the skip up ahead and you can recover it after.'

As they walk towards the huge wheelie bins Colin distracts him with talk about the job.

'What's the target then?'

He slips his hand inside his bag and carefully peels back the tape revealing the internal zipped pocket.

'It's a joint abattoir; does Halal and Haram. We're taking out the Haram side, or maybe the whole place will be torched, it's run by kuffār; infidels.'

Eases the internal zip open and takes hold of the pistol, gingerly extracting it.

He asks what Haram means – although he knows exactly what it means from his previous dealings with a prophet-worshipping animal murderer.

'You really are a strange one; white guy who doesn't even know the basics and you are prepared to put your life on the line? I am not convinced about you, no, not at all!'

He laughs, despite the threat his words carry.

301

The pistol goes into Colin's left jacket pocket and his hand goes for the silencer just as they reach the bins.

'Just need to grab my passport – I am definitely taking that with me.'

'No way you fool; the boss said no ID of any kind. Throw the bag in.'

Colin has lost the chance to grab the silencer, but that's life, he has the weapon which will be plenty.

The bag goes into the skip and they hurry on, Colin noting every road name he sees. They take the next right and walk another fifty yards until the guy stops.

'This is it, or rather, this is the back of the site. We are going over this wall then through a yard and Mujahid and Ibrahim will be waiting there for us.'

'That was never three miles!'

'Who said anything about three miles? Ah! probably one of Mujahid's security measures to keep everyone guessing.'

The area is dark and quiet but the guy checks around a final time for any sign of life.

'OK let's go. No talking now.'

He runs awkwardly with his limp but leaps strongly at the eight foot wall, grabbing the top with his fingertips and with brute strength and some agility claws his way upwards. Colin is highly impressed; this guy is fit and strong and he needs to be very conscious of that in the coming activities.

Before Colin copies the manoeuvre he swaps the pistol into his right rear jeans pocket, doesn't want it bashing against the brickwork; the pockets are deep and can quite easily accommodate the weapon. Beyond the wall he can hear a single cow softly mooing. Seconds later he is straddling the top of the wall with the pistol digging into his right buttock. He lets himself slide down the far side, joining his escort on the ground in the yard. A security light comes on automatically triggered by their passage across the space but the Muslim is unfazed.

109

Ok team, it's late. Last task of the day, let's have your suggestions so we can determine the scale of the threat – it'll help me get resources if the list is long; conversely, too long and it'll be deemed hopeless and ergo a waste of effort.

One by one the proposals are called out:

- Religious groups, especially Muslims and Jews (Kosher and Halal slaughter)
- Animal abusers including:
  - Farmers
  - Fishermen/women/people
  - Butchers
  - Retailers (leather/fur)
  - Egg producers (inc free range)
  - Zoos/wildlife parks
  - Hunters
  - Apiarists (beekeepers!)
  - Breeders – dogs (cats?)
  - Pet shops
  - Pet food suppliers

Stop, stop, stop! this is hopeless. I'll tell the Chief we need to protect everyone. Get yourselves off home and let's see you at 08:00 tomorrow please, we need to get the strategy honed so I can meet her upstairs at ten with an acceptable progress report and plan. Night night.

110

Δ That period without measure
Twixt animal pain
And human pleasure
We should seek to define
(We, being the aggressor)
What it is, that we really so treasure

That one sentient creature
Or herd
A single calf, rabbit
Or a bird
We should permit no choice,
And as we cut
Whose voice
Remains unheard Δ

Geoffrey Stanger

D0227 is cold.
Cold, hungry and very thirsty.
But for the first time in her short life she is able to move. If only her young joints weren't already in such a bad state from all those months forced to stand on the hard, unforgiving concrete floor.

This place smells of death; it's a peculiar odour that she hasn't smelled before, but she knows that the sweet metallic twang that was so strong as she watched those men in the huge green aprons butchering her brothers so cruelly came from the blood that gushed. She doesn't know why she wasn't hauled up on the chain by the foot as they had each been, bellowing in their fear and desperation and helplessness; all she knows is that the shiny metal thing the men were using to open their throats so wide in yawing red gashes suddenly stopped and they spent the rest of the day looking at it and taking it apart. Then suddenly they all just left, throwing the aprons onto pegs on the walls and kicking off the huge white wellington boots which were so badly stained red.

D0227 doesn't know about religion. She doesn't realise that her brothers *could* have been stunned before the deep brutal cuts if the lorry had only turned left instead of right in the yard.

She doesn't know about statistics; how many animals a typical human will eat in its lifetime. She doesn't understand that she could have lived a peaceful, wholesome and long natural life if one human had only decided to reject the murder. Doesn't realise that humans can make those choices. Make the difference.

She would be astonished to learn all of those things in a world where 48% of inner-city children don't even know what a cow looks like. Alone in the dark she lays down and rests her head on the cold, wet floor, waiting to see what the morning will bring.

111

A low two-tone whistle alerts Colin and his accomplice to the presence of two other men; Mujahid and Ibrahim.

His escort says something in Arabic and the three embrace.

The taller of the waiting men congratulates Colin's escort.

'Bro – good timing, about to go in.' He then opens his arms to Colin.

'Fundi; we meet at last.' The voice is recognisable as that of Mujahid.

'Hi!'

'Mohamed warned me to expect a white man. Your photo was unclear and I thought he was joking. So when did you swear allegiance to the prophet?'

Colin is improvising now, but senses the next answer might determine whether he's accepted or rejected. Rejection, with guys like this could only end one way. His hand unconsciously drifts towards his back pocket, but he resists the urge to grip the gun.

'I was adopted by Indian parents and they...' Colin doesn't know the term for taking the Muslim faith, is it baptism? Surely not, and definitely not Christening. 'They er, well; I became Muslim from that day.'

'Nice one bro! OK here's the deal. Ibrahim and I have already stashed the incendiaries around key points, we'll have to manually ignite them but they go up fast so we need to light and then beat it sharpish – OK?'

Colin and the guy he now knows as Mohamed nod.

'This place is locked down until 04:00 when the slaughtermen arrive to prep the gear so time is not critical. What *is* critical is that we do it in the following order.'

He dictates the way they have to proceed but Colin is only half listening at this point, he's much busier working out how he will activate his own plan among the chaos.

'Ibrahim; you take Fundi with you into the east side; me and Mo will start at the west.'

He hands a mini torch to each member of the team.

'I repeat guys; we *leave* the Halal side alone. Everyone clear on what they need to do?'

Everyone nods in the pale light splashing over from the security lamps and the three Arabs clasp each other's hands in some private ritual.

'This way.'

Ibrahim beckons Colin through an already opened door and he sees the torch beams of the others head off in the opposite direction. They are clearly already in the killing area and caught in the sweep of his torch beam a selection of tools, chains and hoses adorn the walls, with some nasty looking circular saws suspended on compressed-air lines from the ceiling.

Colin knows he has to act extremely fast to immobilise this guy and get back to the other two before any animals are harmed. Even as they are separating he has the little torch clamped in his mouth and is soaking a handful of the cloth from his pocket in the chemical from the small bottle. As soon as they enter the building he reaches around the Muslim's neck and clamps the sodden cloth over his mouth and nose. After a very brief struggle Ibrahim collapses face-down at his feet. He has to take a chance now; the tape he really needs is inside the bag in the skip. Thinking rapidly he lifts the Muslim's head off the ground so that his shoulders and chest are also in the air and slams him nose-first into the cold, hard concrete floor. He repeats this twice more, surprised at the noise as the skull cracks against the unyielding surface. He doesn't care if the guy is dead, he just doesn't want him conscious for a few minutes.

Colin takes out the gun, pulls the working parts to the rear to draw a round from the magazine into the chamber, partially slides the parts back a second time to check that a shiny brass bullet has been picked up and is sitting there ready – the last thing he wants to hear when he pulls the trigger is a useless click – and removes the safety catch. He moves silently on his running shoes out of the building and through the door the others had entered less than a minute earlier, glad of his dark clothing.

307

It isn't hard to find them, as they are doing nothing to conceal themselves. Locating the bank of light switches at the door, Colin depresses a few. As the lights splutter into life he walks swiftly up behind Mohamed, places the gun muzzle at the base of the man's neck, angled upwards slightly and squeezes the trigger. The front of his face bursts outwards like a spectacular bright-red and white firework display. Without waiting to see what else happens he lowers the gun and takes aim at Mujahid's upper thigh, putting a round into the centre. The guy screams like a stuck pig and clutches at the wound site. Colin quickly moves to silence him with a powerful knife-hand strike to the throat and Mujahid collapses, as much from the blow to the trachea as from the shattered femur which is protruding up in splinters through the rapidly blossoming dark-red flower in his trousers.

Colin does the chemical rag trick with him and then goes to check the effects of the bullet to the head on Mohamed.

Mohamed is very dead.

Quickly Colin nips back to the original building to see what Ibrahim is up to, and finds him crawling on his elbows along the floor, blood running liberally all over the front of his clothes. As Colin enters he turns his face up towards the gunman in confusion and fear and Colin takes a step backwards to allow himself space to deliver a vicious kick to his face that threatens to remove his head from his torso.

'You nasty little bastard, this is for all those animals who you have killed in your lifetime.' Colin can't resist the opportunity to lecture. 'You know that the average carnivore is *directly* responsible for the deaths of seven thousand animals in a lifetime? So by my reckoning it's time for your contribution to stop – especially as you will have caused them additional pain by insisting that they are not even stunned prior to death, you and your fucking sick cunt prophet have a lot to answer for.'

Colin sticks a 9mm round into his kneecap and then treads onto it, making it bear all his weight. The guy screams and tries to speak through the pain.

'What?'

'I am not a slaughterman; I never killed any animals.'

'But you have eaten the poor creatures and you worship the murderous pixie that demands animals are slaughtered in terror and pain!'

'Pixie?'

'Yes pixie, your god is nothing but a pixie, an invention from the minds of lunatics and believed by the stupid and the gullible, the same as all the other stupid religious icons.'

Ibrahim's eyes close and Colin wonders if he's just died. He grabs his wrist to feel for a pulse and there's nothing, but he knows that pulses can be deceptive and unreliable, finding a weak pulse when you are cold and shaking from excitement can be difficult and he isn't about to take the chance. He doesn't have time to waste and tries to stick the muzzle into the guy's mouth, but his teeth are firmly clamped together – probably through the pain – blocking that option. Colin uses the pistol butt as a hammer and in a few short hard blows he has removed enough of the teeth to allow the barrel to penetrate the mouth with ease.

'Good bye you sick shit.'

The muzzle slips easily through the Muslim terrorist's soft pink lips and Colin fires a round straight up through his head. The powerful shockwaves released internally force one of the eyeballs to rupture and some of the insides to ooze from that wound, but that's nothing compared to the chasm that has opened in the top of the skull. Colin is in complete awe at the damage that such a small projectile can do.

This shot sounds so much louder than the others; Colin assumes this is because the heat of the moment excitement when the other shots were fired had dumbed down his senses. But it serves as a reminder that he needs to move. He takes the mobile telephone from his sock, switches it on and while it is going through its warming up screens walks quickly back to the other building.

Mujahid is lying where he'd left him, moaning softly. Colin calls Barbara and tells her the road the slaughter house is located on and that he's ready for her.

Grabbing the Muslim by his injured leg he drags him through to where he had executed Mohamed and wraps a heavy chain that's hanging down from the ceiling on a pulley around his ankle. He follows the electrical supply with his eyes until he locates the control switches and hits the up arrow. Mujahid is slowly hoisted from the ground and when his head just loses contact with the floor Colin releases the button, pausing his upward progress.

He walks now to one of the racks of crude reciprocating saws and looks for the power supply, realising that they are all air-powered and therefore would need the compressor to have been building pressure for a while. He has no time for that but spots a big angry looking electrical circular saw.

It's surprisingly quiet, almost to the point that Colin doubts whether it's working at all, but he feels the wind rushing past his face as the large-toothed blade hurtles around at 2000 revolutions a minute. He grabs a fistful of the gang-leader's greasy black hair.
'I have used four rounds and have three left, but I won't waste them on a turd like you, far too painless, time for some revenge.'

Although time is not on his side, Colin knows that Barbara will be a few minutes yet so he has a little spare, but he doesn't particularly want Barbara to witness any of this bloodshed, she doesn't deserve that, and he still has to locate and arrange the animals.

Donning a huge rubber apron hanging on a peg Colin shouts over the cries of his victim.
'I am going to kill you as slowly as time permits, you cunt. Please make the most of the experience but know this in your final moments; your god does not exist, there are no virgins awaiting you anywhere and I am going to rub your dying body in pig fat.'

The suspended guy is screaming all manner of nonsense so Colin decides to give him something to scream for. He first removes all fingers and thumb on his left hand, making a game of it as the Muslim tries to avoid the saw, wrenching his arm out of the reach of the cutting blade. Colin gets him bit by bit, sometimes missing and catching him on the arm or body as he spins and writhes around in desperation. It's very messy and Colin is glad of the giant rubber apron.

Eventually the hand is done, although with so much blood spurting from the wounds it's difficult to be sure. He moves with the crude saw to the right side where the same game yields slightly quicker results as his captive tires and loses so much essential body fluid.

Colin laughs and does a little jig of joy as the Muslim recoils into a suspended foetal form and the screams reach a completely different level when a change of tactic sees the saw take out most of his genitalia.
'The fucking virgins won't want you now you cockless piss-stain.'
Colin knows he is out of time and leaves the guy hanging there to bleed the rest of his miserable life into the gutters and rills that normally run with the blood of other helpless animals. He removes the apron and washes the blood from his hands and arms at a nearby stainless steel industrial sink and goes into what Mujahid had called the Halal side to explore the cattle sounds coming from there, so that he can round them up for Barbara's transport.

In the Halal section he comes across one young heifer, alone and frightened, her huge brown eyes looking terrified as he passes the gated killing area. He wonders why she was left alone and not butchered with the remainder of the day's kill and continues to quickly explore the rest of the site, but it's not very big and within a few minutes he has learned that she's the only survivor from the day. He heads back to her and enters the killing area, the floor still wet from being washed down following the day's horror operations and the biting metallic stench of blood lingering everywhere.
She tries to back away from this new potential abuser but even the act of standing is clearly causing her great pain and distress. Colin reaches out slowly and strokes her nose gently. He looks for something to entice her with and win her trust; clearly she's had a life of injustice like all the others who are slaughtered so young, but he can see nothing suitable.
The bastards left her here all alone without food or water.
He grabs a bowl, probably normally used for holding entrails or similar, but it looks clean. He fills it with water from the hose looped on the wall and offers it to her.

311

Cautiously she leans towards the bowl and sniffs distrustingly.
Yeah, why should you trust me you gorgeous girl. He pats her neck
softly.
She tentatively sticks her long tongue into the bowl and laps once,
then again. Once she realises she can trust what she sees she begins
to slake her raging thirst. Colin looks around for a leash of any kind
but there's nothing around.
All the time he is stroking and murmuring softly, conscious of the
ticking clock.

His mobile telephone beeps twice indicating the arrival of a text
message. Only Barbara and the dead Muslim have this number so he
knows it's time to go.

'OK little lady, now you really have to trust me.'
He remembers his scarf and gently lifts her head from the bowl,
looping his scarf tenderly around her neck to make a crude but soft
leash to try to lead her out. Amazingly she follows without
hesitation, albeit slowly, and he feels honoured by her trust.
She is hobbling and he can see that she's in terrific discomfort; he'll
need to make sure she gets a big wad of pain killers for a few weeks.
At the door they almost bump into a tall, thin woman with flaming
red hair and dressed in corduroy trousers and a waxed jacket. This
has to be Barbara.
'Hi, I'm Colin and I'm sorry to say that this is going to be your only
passenger today. Er, don't go inside, I had to make a bit of a mess.'
'Hi Colin, yep, I'm Barbara; pleased to meet you at last.'
Her smile is as wide as her face and her delight genuine. Colin is
grinning too.
'Does the little beauty have a name?'
'Not yet, wait.' Colin reaches forward and reads from her yellow ear
tag.
'D0227 – we'll call her D for Doris.'
'Haha OK! Come on D for Doris my little baby.'
A beagle appears in the doorway.

'Oh, thought I'd bring Colina along, seeing as you were so vague
about when you might visit her!'

312

Barbara leads Doris into the back of the horsebox transporter while Colin bends and makes a ridiculous fuss over the beautiful Beagle, who's tailless rump seems to be having some kind of wagging fit. He wonders if she can possibly remember him.

'You need a lift?'

'Er yeah, that would be brilliant, thanks. I will need to grab a bag from a bin on the way – long story!'

'I can only begin to imagine! So what happened here tonight that you don't want me to see?'

'Ah, some secrets are best left untold. I'm sure you'll read all about it soon enough. Just remember, newspapers like to sensationalise, and whatever they claim, halve it and then halve it again.'

112

The postman, earlier than usual, walks across the grass again and Hayley resists the urge to shout at him; what's the point! In any case, she is more interested in what he has delivered, and rushes to the front door.

Sure enough there's a small package lying on the doormat, obscuring the letter *L* in the word *WELCOME* that's printed across the rough coir material, so that it just about reads *WE COME*. She thinks of Finn and his visit yesterday when they had certainly come plenty. After she'd notified the police of her husband's absence Finn had telephoned his work with an invented migraine and they'd gone on from their rabid sex on the sofa to spend a more leisurely couple of hours in bed to the extent that she'd been late collecting the kids from school. Finn had been insatiable and she had reciprocated.

Now though she is filled with trepidation. The package looks identical to yesterday's and she dreads opening it in case it holds an even grimmer message. She leaves it where it has landed and nervously dials Finn's number, not expecting him to answer.
He answers on the first ring.
'Hi babe, what's up?'
'The postman just came, and there's another disc.'
'OK, er, what does it show?'
'I haven't opened it yet, I need you to be here.' She expects the usual excuses that he can't possibly get away from work etc.
'On my way babe, give me twenty minutes.'
He cuts the connection.
Wow – that's a result. She picks up the package as if it's a bomb and takes it through to the lounge.
Finn is as good as his word and arrives just as she is making tea.
'Forget the cuppa babe; let's see what's on the vid.'

Finn unwraps the packet and extracts a DVD in a clear plastic case. There is no writing on the disc or case, nor any kind of message. 'Same as last time, oh well, here goes. You OK to do this or want me to watch it first?'

'No, go for it; let's see what they have done to him.'

As before, the first thirty seconds are a blurred and fuzzy picture with a white noise soundtrack. Then the same image as before emerges.

And then they see what has become of Jamie Parfitt. The once fit, happy, wheeling/dealing fingers-in-lots-of-pies Jamie Parfitt.

When he slams himself into the wall for the second time Hayley screams.

'Oh god Finn, turn it off, turn it off right now!'

But he is mesmerised.

'Leave it babe, it might be OK in a minute.'

She runs from the room vomiting while he sits on the sofa, mouth gaping, unblinking as the one-time best friend destroys himself on camera.

She's in the bathroom retching and to Finn it's as if she's in another world. The world Finn currently inhabits has been turned upside down. This is the stuff of sci-fi films, horror movies; this kind of thing doesn't really happen. But there it is, actually, really happening right before his very eyes, captured beautifully in low resolution film. And it's hypnotically spellbinding. He simply has to watch until the end.

When the tall character enters and executes Parfitt, Finn collapses back onto the sofa and lets out a huge lungful of air. He realises he's become aroused again. What the hell is going on? What is it about the misfortunes of his ex mate that makes him so rock hard? Is it the opportunities it presents to him to take the guy's woman and claim her for his own, officially, without having to duck and dive and weave stories? He doesn't know, but he needs to go to her now and exercise his new-found alpha rights.

He finds her collapsed in front of the toilet bowl, shaking and crying.

'Come on babe, all done, he won't be coming back, he's gone somewhere peaceful. Come to bed, I need to make love to you; make you feel better.'

She looks up with red-rimmed eyes and her face becomes a scowl, then a grimace and finally a snarl.

'You fucking *what*?'

She spits the question, like a despotic Sergeant Major might scream at a parade.

'You just saw what happened to my husband, the father of my children – some of my children – and you want *sex?* Are you for fucking *real*?'

Her voice rises at least an octave for the last sentence.

'Easy babe, chill! We both knew it would end this way. I didn't expect it quite so soon, but it's good for us, we spoke about it, he's out of our hair and we can be a couple now, like we wanted. Just like we wanted.'

'*Chill?* Are you serious? I want to scream. I want to shout and tear things from the walls. I want the police, the ambulance the fucking helicopter I want the world to see what's happened and I wanna turn back the clock. I don't want you here. Cold, dispassionate and gloating. All you want is sex! That's it for you isn't it? Is that what you are, a sex machine without any shred of emotion? Well you can fuck off and take your bloody demands elsewhere, go and find another desperate girl who doesn't know what she has until it's too fucking late. Go on, get the fuck out of my life you heartless bastard.'

She's pounding his chest repeatedly with her fists to punctuate each word.

He grabs her forearms and holds them still as she runs out of strength and collapses against him.

'Easy babe, I didn't mean it that way, just thought we both wanted the same thing.'

As he speaks these soothing words through her hair into her ear he is thinking about the next steps. Fuck her and fuck off out of her messy life. Sod this for complications. He wants an easy life, a bird who will open up when *he* demands it and keep shtumm when he needs some space. This Hayley bint is way too complex and high maintenance.

So she's just seen her husband snuffing it in a very graphic manner, very sad, but so what. He deserved everything he got, mixing with the people he messed about with. But this is a warning for Finn, grab a little of what's left and get the hell outa here.

He switches back to seduction mode, the straining bulge in his pants too painful to ignore; he needs relief.

As usual, he gets it and right there on the bathroom floor.

He's thinking of those DVD images as he climaxes deep inside the guy's wife, and his orgasm, the last he'll ever have with Hayley Parfitt, is every bit as intense as any he's ever experienced. What a great way to finish, he thinks, as he rolls off her and heads to the kitchen for a cigarette. She hates him smoking in the house too, bad for the kids she reckons. Well this'll be the last time he inconveniences the poor little Parfitt sprogs then won't it. He grins as he lights up and thinks of the girl he met in the burger bar last night. She told him she has a kid, but that's a good thing; he'll turn on the charm with the kid, win her over when she sees how great he is as a surrogate Dad, just like Hayley stupid Parfitt did.

Sweet!

113

08:00 on the dot and the team is assembled in the ops room.
'Thanks for settling down promptly today; Sicknote and I need to
leave in a few minutes. There's been a potentially significant
development in Manchester overnight that's definitely linked to the
terror attacks on abattoirs and probably of interest to us.'
Dyson takes a swig of the cold coffee he's been cradling.
'There's also been a definite lead; our friend posing on video for us.
I'll get to that one in a second. First; at around 04:00 this morning
employees turned up for work as usual at an abattoir in Greater
Manchester to find the place wide open, all the lights blazing and
three slaughtered corpses which were not the kind of animals they
would normally butcher there; these were humans.'

'Were they employees who were killed Guv?'
'Doubtful, Sicknote; they were all gentleman of Arab descent and
early forensic evidence indicates they were all involved in the earlier
attacks on abattoirs. We're still piecing together the puzzle on this
but here's how it looks at the moment. Incendiary devices – similar
to those used at the earlier blazes – were set up and ready to go, but
ignition never took place. Instead we have three dead probable
Muslim extremists.'

Samantha speaks from the back of the room.
'Any security at the place Sir?'
'Zilch; no cameras and not even an alarm. The owner's view is that
nobody had ever attempted a break-in, and why would they.
Astonishing really in light of the recent threats, still, it's what keeps
us in a job!'
'So what's the thinking on how they died?'
'How they died is clear Carol; mixture of gunshot wounds and
apparently very violent knife or saw-cuts. Either a disgruntled gang
member or something altogether more interesting. We were alerted –
promptly for a change – due to the potential animal rights link and I
have a feeling that the murderer's MO has a lot of similarities with

the way Colin Furness thinks. Sicknote and I are heading up there straight after this briefing. No idea how long we'll be away, but you guys are to continue the meetings as normal and we'll join via WebEx as and when we can. Samantha will lead the team in my absence. Oh, and let's bin the hospital watch for now, we just don't have the resource.'

He drains his coffee.

'OK, now the video, or rather, videos. A puppy dealer of ill repute was kidnapped some days ago – never reported by a devoted wife. After she was sent two videos of the guy – Jamie Parfitt – in captivity she had second thoughts, particularly as the second film shows his execution at the hands of – you guessed it – Colin Furness. Clear as day and as sick as ever, although he's carrying a full beard now, probably an attempt at a disguise. Need the films analysed by forensics before we can release them to the team but they make the usual brutally grim viewing. Questions?'

There were none. Instead the team sit in incredulous silence.

'OK. I'm off to grab a few things from home, meet you back here in an hour Dave.'

114

Elderly Muslim cleric and scholar Tarik El Hamali leaves the butcher's shop *Paradise Halal* and heads towards the city mosque; 'his' mosque. He can already hear the Adhan – the call to prayer, but if he hurries he'll just make the evening meeting, it wouldn't do to be late. Although he's not leading *salah*, the Muslim prayers tonight, he likes to be seen amongst his congregation. As he makes a turn into a shortcut he often uses he's aware of someone walking a short distance behind him. It's not a well-used route and with all the current tensions facing his people he's conscious that he's a potential target for misguided vigilante actions. Walking a little faster now to put a some distance between them he notices with rising anxiety that his increase in pace is matched by the steps behind. He fights the urge to look around to see if there is a real threat, or whether his mind is just over-reacting but feels a little foolish; and in any case, he is a servant of The Prophet, and trusts in His guidance.

To give fate a helping hand he opts to change his route so he can stay on brighter streets, but in order to reach the main thoroughfare he'll have to risk the short, narrow alleyway between the Kebab shop and the long closed-down ladies fashion outlet.
He swallows his fear and ducks into the alley.
Big mistake.
He hears the rushing sound too late.
With improbable speed the pursuer has moved swiftly to close the safety gap and before there's even time to turn and face him his assailant has Tarik's neck in a vice-like grip; he feels a large, strong hand clamp over his mouth. Escape is not feasible and shouting for help impossible. He just has to take whatever is coming his way.

He is brought to the ground by some clever twisting manoeuvre and the voice when it comes is higher-pitched than the strength would imply, but calm and measured, without a hint of intent. This makes the whole experience somehow more chilling.

'Mr El Hamali I believe? Don't bother answering, the question is rhetorical. So, we can do this one of two ways; we can go quietly to my van and drive peacefully away to our destination for a friendly chat, or you can try to make a fuss and I'll rip your nasty Muslim head off. I know which I prefer, wonder whether we are on the same wavelength? I shall assume you want the peaceful option, and owing to your inability to speak, we'll go along that route. However, should you make a sound – any sound at all – I shall assume option two is favoured.'

The Arab is dragged roughly to his feet and the hand which clamps his mouth so tightly is slowly released. Immediately the Muslim sucks in a huge breath in order to scream for help at the top of his voice, but this is anticipated by his captor and he receives a vicious punch to the midriff, driving the air from his body and leaving the old man limp.

'Oh dear, we seem to have the stereotypical Muslim Cunt on our hands, let's take option two then, had your choice and blew it.'

Instantly the Imam feels something hard pressed into the small of his back.

'This weapon is silenced, and I am going to shoot you in the arse if you make any attempt to escape, nobody will hear a thing; are we clear?'

The Muslim nods and, terrified, keeps his side of the bargain as they proceed back out of the alleyway and along the road, looking for all intents like a couple of well acquainted friends taking a pleasant evening stroll.

As they make their way along the city street Colin is surprised by a shout from the other side of the road.

'Tarik? Hey, Tarik you are going the wrong way; the meeting starts in 3 minutes!'

Colin panics, pushes the Arab against a shop window and sprints away into the night, silently cursing his bad luck, his foolishness and his piss-poor planning.

He makes his way back to the van and sits in the back, not wanting to be seen by anyone, cursing his stupidity and lack of preparation.

Try a little mindfulness to calm yourself down so that you can think straight.

What had the psychologists taught him? *Close your eyes, focus on something.* He slowly clenches his hands, really tight, scrunching them into tight fists, then releases them, splaying the fingers as wide as he can, feeling the muscles contract and relax, then repeats a few times until he is conscious of each finger, every knuckle. Next the forearms, same intensity, then biceps, neck, shoulders and on through his entire torso right down to his toes, using the full interior of the back of the van to reach out and stretch his tall frame. Now he can really sense his whole body, feels alive, *in the moment.*

Now for the external environment, what can he hear? He homes in on the traffic sounds from the busy roads, isolates each vehicle, envisages how it might look. A pedestrian crossing bleeps somewhere nearby, he visualises the little green man; sees it turn to a flashing sign and then change to red in his mind's eye, imagines the cars start to move again. Now for smells; he can sense the old van's history; diesel residues, oil, tools, past cargoes, victims… he's snapped from his reverie. He needs to go no further with his grounding techniques, he feels stronger, ready to face up to his failings tonight and turn the disaster into a positive.

Climbing through into the driver's seat he settles down to think, drumming a random beat with his thumbs on the greasy black steering wheel.

OK Mr Imam, maybe you got away, but I researched you pretty fucking thoroughly and I know about your patterns of behaviour, where you live and how you'll probably get there from the mosque. Colin starts the engine and slowly makes his way out of the car park onto the now quieter streets. After a ten minute cruise, running his racing mind through the map he'd memorised he pulls over into a parking bay at the roadside and switches off the engine. He knows that the cleric *usually* takes this route on foot from the mosque to his house. The question is, whether he'll have been too shaken up by tonight's attack, maybe take a cab, walk with friends, or whether he'll stick to the habits he's accustomed to.

Colin Furness feels lucky.

Now, about those seven Ps….. but before he's had a chance to run through any kind of plan the Muslim cleric emerges close to the back of the van in his rear-view mirror; and he appears to be alone.

Either incredibly stupid, or very brave; fuck the 7 Ps... he throws caution to the wind.

Quick check up and down the road – all quiet – let's go.

He checks the pistol is in ready state, quietly opens the driver's door as the Imam is blind-sided by the body of the van and jogs around the back, silently opening the back doors as he passes and swiftly comes up behind the Muslim.

'Sorry about earlier your highness, didn't want to embarrass you in front of fellow worshippers, now jump in the back before I remove your face with a low velocity 9mm break-up round. No fucking around, just do it.'

The old man's knees give way so Colin throws caution to the wind and lifts him bodily into the back of the vehicle. He's so well practised now at immobilising people that he has him trussed up within a minute and is almost immediately on his way back down south towards the safe house.

115

Neil Dyson feels awkward; he's packed his overnight bag and is sitting having a coffee with Jenny before he leaves for Manchester.
'Try to get back as soon as you can darling.'
'You know I will; I hate being away and I don't feel good about leaving you alone with this nutter on the loose, but hopefully what I learn up north will speed up his recapture.'
He deliberately omits any mention of the video execution; no sense worrying her any more.

Jenny is tempted to tell him about the uneasy feelings she's been having but thinks he'll just dismiss it as nerves and stress. Instead she tells him to drive safely and call her when he gets there. He holds her in his arms for a moment before kissing her goodbye, turning and grabbing his bag, glad to escape the guilt.

116

Back home, elated about events and with his steadily growing bunch of guests safely ensconced, fed and watered in their pens Colin dials the police number for a quick catch-up with his favourite detective, but learns that the inspector is out of the area and unavailable.

Out of the area? Hmmn... He wonders where the good policeman might have gone. He decides to take advantage of the opportunity to pack a few things in case his detective friend isn't taking his threat seriously. He needs to be taken seriously.

He packs his medium rucksack with spare clothes, some food and water and some essentials he might need over the next few days. He'll try Dyson once more a little later; right now he'll grab a few hours sleep and then he's on his way to visit a mutual friend.

117

Working out of the local nick, Dyson and Sicknote are making some speedy inroads into the incident at the slaughterhouse. One significant piece of information is emerging.

'So the text was sent just after 21:00? Have we got a trace on the number yet?'

'Yes Guv. It belongs to a Barbara Muller from Salford. She's waiting in the interview room for us.'

'Already? OK, what are we waiting for!'

The detectives enter the room and the young WPC who is minding the suspect leaves them to it.

'Hello Barbara, I'm Detective Inspector Dyson from Sussex police, this is Detective Sergeant Harrison. We need to talk to you about a text message you sent from a crime scene at about the time three men were murdered there. What do you want to tell me about that?'

'I have nothing to say to you without a solicitor being present.'

The tall redhead has a defiant look, but Neil can detect her unease.

'Fine. Dave, find out who's the duty beak and let's get him quick. I'll arrange a cup of tea for you Barbara while we wait. Just be aware that every minute we waste *not* talking to you is another minute where a psychopathic killer is on the loose and heading for his next victim. Just think about how you'll feel when you see tomorrow's news and realise *you* could have stopped the death or deaths you are reading about. Won't be long.'

'Wait, what are you talking about? The message was sent to an animal rights activist who was rescuing a young cow, he isn't your killer.'

'Did you meet this guy?'

'Briefly yes, why?'

'Let me try to describe him. If the guy I describe is *not* the man you met you can walk out of here immediately, no strings, but if I'm right I'd like you to cooperate. Let me clarify something; you are not suspected of direct involvement unless we learn otherwise, but we

326

think you may have helped a madman doing something that you may well have only been partially aware of. Was the man you saw around six foot two, lean, bald and bearded with eyes set far apart in his head?'

'He was that sort of height yes, and definitely in good physical shape but he wore a cap and I think he had glasses, I didn't see his hair or eyes. Yes, he had a beard.'

'Higher than expected voice?'

'Erm, yes, now you mention it.'

'Was his name Colin?'

'I don't think he ever told me his name.'

Neil has no doubts in any case; there weren't many people around who could dish out the sort of brutality that had been applied here.

'No sweat, I'll get a photo for you for a positive ID.'

'Oh wait, the Beagle's name… he named a rescue dog *Colina* – maybe that's significant.'

'Yeah it's him alright. Listen, he's an escaped murderer who was banged up pending psychiatric tests for three brutal – and I mean bloody gruesome – murders and a whole bunch of false imprisonment charges. He is a nutcase who will stop at nothing to try to balance the books for animals. All very admirable, except he isn't well. In fact he is really imbalanced and the slaughterhouse murders come on top of another guy he killed very recently. That murder had all the hallmarks of a detached mind, as do the abattoir deaths. We don't know where he is or what he plans next, but knowing him as I do he is definitely planning something else and we have to stop him before he strikes again. Now, whilst we await your solicitor, will you answer some questions which might enable us to get an idea about where he plans to strike next?'

The pep talk has weakened her resolve and softened the relationship somewhat.

'Yes, yes of course.'

They talk for an hour, interrupted by the arrival of the requested photo, which confirms Colin as the suspect and then the duty solicitor after fifteen minutes. It's all standard detection work but it becomes clear that they are not going to locate Furness from any information Barbara can provide. Neil wants to try another tack.

'Barbara, I want to tell you about some of the things this guy has done, and then I am going to ask you to take an active role in his capture. If you agree, you'll be doing the public the greatest service.'
'OK. All I have seen from this Colin guy is goodness, I told you about the Beagles, he risked an awful lot freeing those poor dogs from a lifetime of suffering, and if you'd seen how he was with the one we named Colina, well, it just doesn't fit with the man you're describing. But tell me what he has done and what you want me to do.'
'Sure, I get that he has a softer side, and animal empathy. I am married to a vegan and know all about the animal abuse that goes on everywhere. But he drops these standards when it comes to humans. He sees people as the persecutors, the guilty party; and of course he's right to some extent. But the things he did, and continues to do, defy rational thought.'
'What the hell did he do then?'
'He set up a facility and kidnapped people who were, in his view, animal abusers. There was a pig farmer, a fur-collector, a Muslim and a bunch of others; one of whom happened to be my fiancé at that time. He kept them in tiny cages – similar in scale to battery hen conditions. He planned to convert them to vegetarianism through a whole bunch of weird ideas. He also tried to hold the country to ransom.'
'Oh god – I read about this guy – it was all over the news about a year ago, was that him?'
'Oh yeah. Did you read what he did to the Muslim?'
'Er, didn't he slit his throat or something?'
'Exactly, he replicated a Halal slaughter scene. He did it in the city centre car park that used to be the local livestock market place; not sure if that was a deliberate part of the plan. He also spit-roasted a Serbian pig farmer in the centre of the town – again, on the market cross, the place where in medieval times the cattle and other animals would have been traded. Then he skinned a fur collector alive; literally flayed her, at a beauty spot on top of the South Downs. Not sure if that location was significant, but it was the site of Bronze Age burial mounds so there may be some link, who knows.'
'Oh gosh, he's seriously messed in the head, right?'
'Very messed up, yeah. Recently he murdered a hunter with an ancient man-trap, lured him into stepping on it. Then he seems to

have given the guy a saw and allowed him to, we think, try to escape by sawing his own damned leg off. You want me to continue? Let's take the chance we have to stop this guy running around the country planning his next brutal slaying.'

'Of course – I had no part in any of that, you have to believe me. What do you want me to do?'

'How well does he trust you?'

'Completely, I think. I've only had the two dealings with him, but he's never had any reason to mistrust me.'

'Good, I want you to give me permission to use your telephone to arrange to meet him.'

'Seriously? Er, well OK, on what basis?'

'We'll have to think of something, but you're up for it?'

'Yes, I think so. Sorry I was difficult; he just didn't seem like the kind of guy you were describing.'

'You will be at zero risk throughout, I just need your 'phone.'

'DI Dyson please; it's urgent.'
'Who shall I say is calling?'
'Tell him it's Colin.'
'Colin who Sir?'
'I know you are trying to trace this call so get him quick or I hang up.'
'I'm afraid DI Dyson is out on a call at the moment, I can give you his direct mobile number if that helps?'
'Yes, give me that quickly.'
The number is relayed.
'Shall I try to connect you Sir?'
'Playing for time again; you think I'm that fucking stupid? I'll call him when *I* am ready, and if he doesn't respond, well, on his head be it.'
The call is cut.

'Hello honey, only me, sorry I didn't call earlier but traffic was mental and as soon as we got to the station here we were in at the deep end.'

'Thank goodness you got there OK; I have been worrying myself sick that something happened. Have you got a decent hotel room?'

'Haha – you must be joking! No, it's OK, hardly the Ritz. How is my little princess?'

'Samantha is asleep, and I am joining her any second, now that I know you're safe.'

'OK love; make sure you lock up properly. Night night, love you.'

'Love you too, be careful. Goodnight.'

As she terminates the call she thinks she hears a soft thump from upstairs. With her nerves on a knife-edge she goes through the lounge to the hallway and stands listening for a moment.

There is no further noise and she assumes it was the wind; it's a pretty breezy night.

Should she call Neil again? No, he'll just tell her she's imagining things. Anyway, he'll have things on his mind; important police things.

In Manchester, Neil Dyson and Sicknote are in the hotel bar having a nightcap when Dyson's mobile rings. It's the Chichester station.

'DI Dyson.'

'Neil it's DCI Moody.' *The boss, whatever does she want?*

'Evening Ma'am, what's up?'

'Your Mr Furness has been trying to get hold of you. He's been told that you are out of the area, but he's not taking no for an answer now, says if you don't get to the 'phone he is going to strike tonight.'

'OK, no problem, give him my mobile number Ma'am – can we still run a trace on that?'

'Yes I think so; just need to log the call through our system, the techno guys are sorting that now. He has your number already.'

'OK, no sweat, just let me know when they have it set up and I'll await his call.'

Dyson explains the situation to Sicknote and as he finishes he has a call from the technical team to confirm he's good to go.

120

Despite the hectic workload, or perhaps because of it, Samantha is determined to have her *'me time'* and lowers herself into the hot, deep bathwater. She slowly soaps her dark skin and shampoos her hair before applying conditioner and rinsing this off with the shower attachment.

She can't help thinking that Neil should have stayed down south and she should have gone in his place. She has an uneasy feeling about Furness and his apparently indiscriminate strikes. Last time he was ultra methodical in the horrors he committed; this time he seems to be hitting out almost randomly; as if he is acting on impulse. This is a sure sign that his mind is in turmoil and will make it impossible to predict his next moves, unless he has some devious plan he's working to.

Serial killers and psychopaths tend to work to a method; a *modus operandi* and Furness pretty much did that first time round. This time it's very different and, aside from the animal welfare links it's hard to spot any patterns. She thinks it's only a matter of time until he turns to thoughts of retribution, and when he does that, each of the team who put him away the first time will be potential targets. She's seen how sick he is and the shocking damage he can do and doesn't want to ever be on the receiving end of that, but she signed up for the risk when she took the job. Jenny, however, didn't, and her closeness to the events last time must make her number one target. What's more, that prime target is now alone in a house with a baby and her husband is hundreds of miles away. She decides she'll call Jenny after her bath and offer to stay with her, or better still, have her and little Samantha over here.

But first, the crossword:

One across; 4 letters:

About to be wrapped in pink paper, part of Gibson is a worry.

Easy, Most famous Gibson is a guitar; a fret is a part of a guitar. It's also a worry.

About = *re*.

And the financial times – or FT is printed on salmon-pink paper. Wrap *re* in *ft* and you have *FRET*.

For once she can't really concentrate. Or rather, she's not enjoying the crossword, with the niggling doubts over Furness and decides to leave the crossword for another time and get out of the bath and make that call to Jenny.

Jenny slips her fluffy pink bathrobe over her nightdress and checks on Samantha, relieved to see she's still asleep. With luck she'll be that way for another couple of hours. It's very warm in the room and a little stuffy; Jenny thinks she ought to open the little fanlight window a crack. Tiptoeing across the nursery she silently raises the plastic window lever and pushes the unit out a couple of inches. It is very windy and she wonders whether there'll be a draught. The worst thing would be for the little girl to catch a chill but she can only feel a slight breeze through the gap and decides to leave it open whilst she cleans her teeth. She'll come back and close it shortly.

Neil Dyson and Sicknote switch to fruit juices as they discuss a plan to entrap Furness with Barbara's 'phone and await any calls from Furness. After an hour there's no action but just as they are considering binning it for the night the mobile rings.
Number withheld.

'Neil Dyson.'
'Hello DI Dyson. I hope I am not interrupting anything up there, wherever you are. Where is that, actually?'
The voice is very faint, as if Furness is whispering and Dyson can hardly hear him.
'I am on duty; that's all you need to know. How can I help?'
'Tell me where you are, and I'll tell you something very interesting.'
'I am finding it very hard to hear you; can you speak up a little please?'
'I'm afraid that's not really practicable right now. Just try to listen for a change and you'll hear me just fine. I know you are playing for time so that a trace can be put on the call. Good luck.'
'We can't trace calls to mobile devices, I'm sure you know that already. What do you want to tell me?'
'I said tell me where you are. Otherwise I shall cut the line. 5, 4, 3...'
'OK, OK I'm in Manchester.'
Manchester? Why there? The abattoir? Surely not...

'Are you investigating a slaughter house incident?'
'Why, what do you know about it?'
'Three little Arab boys executed last night – I know nothing Inspector, nothing at all.'

Dyson senses, rather than hears a tiny giggle. He knows the details were suppressed in order to eliminate nutcases calling in and claiming responsibility; such idiots wasted so much police time. *The only way Furness could have known the details was if...*

'It was you? You killed them? Why? They were going to shut down an abattoir, thought you'd applaud that!' *gotta keep him talking a little longer....*

'They wanted to leave Halal slaughter operational and I can't allow that, Inspector. The one hanging on the chain squealed so prettily, he denounced his god and religion with those last cuts, he would have bled to death knowing he'd fucked it all up. And I promised him I'd rub pig fat all over his dying body – just *imagine* the distress the poor delusional idiot would have been in…and all that pain! Sweet really, don't you think? Shame I hadn't the time to video record it…ah well!

Is there no end to this freak's depravity? But the call heralds great progress for the investigation and he should be giving the techies plenty of data to trace his location.

'But we are running out of time and so you need to shut up now and listen for a change because I have something very important to tell you. Bad news I guess, seen from your perspective. I know where you live – have always known, in fact. I doubt if you realise, being a bog standard plod that I followed your little wifey once before – on that day last year when she bought the supermarket steak for your eye. That's how I was able to learn about her workplace and to lure her into my trap. She was a feisty little bitch when she made her escape, and I haven't forgotten that. Haven't forgotten the physical pain nor the humiliation of capture and being locked away; unable to come to the aid of all the poor animals you sick people torture and ingest.'

There's a slight pause while Furness adjusts the 'phone in his hand. 'But how the tables have turned...you see, I am about to balance the books. I wonder if she will be so brave now that her own baby is at risk from such a psychopath as you would portray me. Shall we find out?'
Dyson begins to panic.
'Stay away from my wife you freak, there are police guarding her 24/7 and they are armed and have shoot-on-sight orders.'
'You are a dreadful liar Dyson, you see, I know she's not guarded.'
The line is abruptly cut.
Immediately Dyson dials the station and the call goes straight to the technical team.
'Did you get him?'

'Need a moment or two Sir to run the triangulation from mobile masts.'

'OK, put me through to DCI Moody urgently please while the calculations are going through.'

'Moody.'

'Ma'am, get some bodies round to my place quick as possible, he's on his way there.'

'Did he say so?'

'As good as, yes.'

'OK, I'll get the nearest cars to call in, but there's been a high incident number this evening and you know the squeeze we're under so the nearest spare car might be ten or fifteen minutes away.'

'Emphasise the risk please Ma'am and get an armed response unit there ASAP please.'

'Sure. I'm on it; stay there, the technicians want you.'

'Sir, we have the location.'

'OK, hit me.'

The technician reels off an address.

'What? Are you certain?'

'Absolutely Sir, triangulation is accurate to within five metres.'

'Give me Moody again.'

DCI Moody comes on the line.

'Neil?'

'The call he just made to me...it was traced to my house.'

'*What? Are you sure?*'

'Certain. Ma'am. Scramble every resource you can muster, but please do it on a silent approach. If he's already got Jenny and the baby I don't want some gung-ho cowboy spooking him into violent action.'

'I'm on it Neil. Get Sergeant Harrison to drive you back here immediately. Tell *him* to drive please.'

The line is cut.

'Sicknote, where are the car keys?'

'Here Guv.'

'We have to go. I'll drive.'

'What about our stuff? The investigation here? The rooms? What's happened?'

'Tell you on the way, but that fucking psycho Furness is in my house with Jenny.'

The colour drains from Sicknote's face and Dyson dials Jenny's mobile as they run to the car park.

123

Making her way to the bathroom she scrubs her teeth and debates whether she has the energy to floss. She has been a little remiss lately and decides she should.

Two minutes later she's all finished and remembers she's left the baby's window open and her mobile 'phone downstairs. If Neil were to have any news he would call that number first, because he'd know she had it on vibrate so as not to wake the baby. More to the point, she wants to keep it close because of that creepy-scared feeling she's been having.

As she enters the lounge downstairs the 'phone lights up and vibrates.

Perfect timing! Good job she'd remembered it as she wouldn't have known it was ringing from upstairs. The screen is showing Neil's name so she grabs it quickly and answers.

'Hi darling!'

'Jenny, are you OK?'

'Yes of course; why, you sound stressed; what's wrong?'

'Where's Sammi?'

She ignores the abbreviation; his voice has a note of real urgency and she's immediately on alert.

'In bed, asleep; why?'

'Listen, don't question me, just do exactly what I say. Get Samantha and get out of the house immediately, don't stop for anything else. Go to the neighbours and lock yourselves in. Then call 999. Go now. Hang up now because you need both hands free but call me as soon as you are next door and safe.'

'Neil, what's happened?'

'*Just DO IT.*'

Dyson's shout shocks her into action and she shuts off the 'phone and takes the stairs two at a time.

She bursts into Samantha's room not worried now of course about waking her and is stopped dead in her tracks by the image of the tall monster Colin Furness standing in the glow of the nursery's small night-light cradling her baby.

She screams and leaps at him with a mother's protective instincts.

He fends her off one-handed and says in that menacing, too-high voice.

'Stay back Jenny and the baby will be fine. Attack me and I will snap her tiny little neck then kill you. Do you understand?'

Jenny is immediately stunned into submission and stands dead still. 'Please; *please* don't harm her. Do anything to me; anything at all but *please* put her down. I will do anything you tell me to.'

'Good girl Jenny, I knew you'd be sensible. Grab her things, very quickly. We are leaving.'

Jenny realises that Neil knew he was here and will have summoned the police; they would be screaming here as fast as the cars were able to travel. She must play for time, every second could be critical.

'Don't even think about delaying for one moment. I know the police are on their way and we go now. Move.'

'But Samantha's things, where are we going? She will need food, milk, clothes, nappies...'

'Too late, you've deliberately delayed now and lost the chance, and anyway you will certainly be breastfeeding her. Walk quickly down the stairs and get your car keys. If you pretend not to know where they are, or delay *for any reason at all* I will snuff out your daughter's pretty young life.'

Jenny knows he is absolutely capable of killing without remorse and moves into preservation mode. She quickly does as he says and within thirty seconds they are in her car with her behind the wheel. Colin is in the back with the baby. Samantha starts to cry.

'Now drive left and keep going.'

'Where are you taking us?'

'You'll see soon enough. Drive faster; *faster*.'

Colin knows the next minute will be crucial in deciding the outcome. In the distance they hear a siren and he leans forward to shout above the wailing baby.

'I am watching your every move. If you flash your lights at this car when it's in sight or try any trick, the baby dies and so do you. I am armed with a pistol. I will also kill the police. Your call Jenny; you decide.'

She knows he will carry out the threat and as the police vehicle comes tearing towards her she keeps her hands deliberately clear of the headlight controls so that he doesn't suspect any trick. She groans inwardly as the police sail past, the siren silent now but blue lights flashing still.

'Haha, the idiots have just switched to silent approach mode so they don't alert me to their arrival. Too late coppers – stupid and incompetent as ever!'

In the back seat his left leg is doing a little jig.

'Please can you shut the baby up Jenny? I can't stand her crying like this.'

'I can't unless you drive and let me hold her.'

She hopes he'll consider this idea; it might give her a sliver of a chance to escape. In any case, she'd prefer to be holding her little child than leave her in the arms of this monster.

'No, you keep driving, I will manage. Turn right at the next junction and then immediately left. Where is your mobile?'

Jenny can feel its weight in her right-hand bathrobe pocket but doesn't admit it.

'I have no idea, must have left it on the sofa.'

'Good, the damned things are too easy to track.'

Jenny had spoken of this with Neil a few times and she knows there is some truth in that statement, but she isn't sure about accuracy or whether the phone has to be in use. Hers is switched to silent and she's certain Neil will be calling any second now to find out why she hasn't called him back from the neighbours. If he calls she'll press the *answer* key and he will hear the background noises. She'll be able to give some clues as they travel along.

If he doesn't call for some reason then she'll have to try to call him. The screen will be locked and there's a password set up. It's a complex one, *Neil* with a capital *N* followed by his date of birth; difficult to enter one-handed without being able to look at the device and without the freak seeing her, but if she *can* manage it she might be able to operate the 'phone out of sight of the freak and maybe she can dial a number and just leave the thing in her pocket with the line open, broadcasting her whereabouts to the world. She has to try while he is in the back and occupied with the baby.

She reaches down to the pocket, trying to disguise the movement and simultaneously asks him again where they are going.
'I told you, you'll find out soon enough.'
She grasps the 'phone and feels with her fingertips to see which way it's facing. She feels the smooth screen and knows it's face-up. Her fingers brush the digits, grateful that she stuck with her old Blackberry. Smartphone keys would be impossible to feel without looking but the good old Blackberry keys stick out from the body.

Suddenly the device starts to vibrate in her hand and she knows Neil must be dialling her. She nervously tries to remember which key is the *accept call* button; to hit the *decline* button in error would be a disaster. She feels along the bottom of the screen; she knows it's the first button. She wills herself to make the right choice, envisaging the image of a green telephone and rejecting all thoughts of a red one as if this might swing the odds in her favour.
It's now or never and she hits the button beneath her fingers, not knowing or being able to see if the line is now open or if she's rejected the call.

124

Neil hasn't heard from Jenny. He's tried calling her constantly but just gets her voicemail. He can't possibly know that the reason is because she's driving through an area of practically zero telephone reception.

125

The vibrating 'phone is actually notification of a series of missed calls and voicemail messages. She's just driven out of an area where she had no signal and they all come trundling through at once. Inside her pocket she manages to tilt the 'phone screen towards her and sees that hitting the green *accept call* button has achieved nothing. But at least the screen is now unlocked and she hits the number *9* three times, hoping desperately that the emergency operator will be switched on enough to realise that she needs help and it's not just some prank call.

Unheard above the sound of the engine the operator answers:
'Emergency, which service please?'

She repeats the question.
'Emergency, which service do you require?'

The BT operator follows the *failure to respond* script to the letter for calls where no response is received following a 999 alert. This procedure was implemented following the brutal rape and murder of teenager Hannah Foster in 2003, where the bright Hannah had secretly dialled 999 in the desperate hope that the operator would hear her attacker's threatening conversation.

She logs the incoming device number and moves into the *silent solutions routine.* Continuing to seek a reply from the caller and asking whether a response is required before connecting to the police. Finally she says;
'If you cannot speak, but need help, please tap the screen.'

The escalation procedure is based on the operator's analysis of background noises and will either result in termination of the call if the BT operator thinks it's a mistake, or connection to the police. In the latter instance the police responder will ask the caller to press the number 5 twice (The number 5 is generally identifiable even in the dark as it has a tactile raised pimple).

Tragically, in this case, the operator assumes that it's one of the millions of mistaken calls that get put through to 999 or the European alternative112 every year and terminates Jenny's call.

Jenny risks another glance and sees the screen go dark; she knows she's been cut off. She reaches into the pocket and hits 999 again. This time the operator's response is different; the routine for dealing with immediate, repeat calls from the same number is to connect to the police.

The police officer who receives the call is unaware of the repeat call scenario and now has to make his own decision based on what he can hear and the response he gets.
He listens to the rustling sounds the telephone is making in the pocket and the background engine noise. He hears a woman ask where they are going but can't hear a response. He decides it's an error and is about to cut the connection when the woman's voice repeats her question with a subtle but critical difference.
'Where are you taking me Colin?'

In the context of emergency calls, *being taken* somewhere is very different to *going* somewhere and he puts an immediate call trace on the line. All emergency calls are recorded and he notes the name *Colin* as key information.

He tries to engage in conversation with the caller but realises he can't be heard, or the woman is unable to respond. He is switched on enough to realise that his voice might be heard at any time by *Colin* and that would alert him to the cry for help. He decides to cease asking for a response and adopt listening-only mode.
The woman speaks again.
'Are we going to the farm? Is that where you want to kill me and the baby?'
The guy is shouting now his voice is clearly audible.
'Stop asking where we are going and drive Jenny. You will see where we are going once we get there. You are like a silly child.'
Colin has a thought.
What if the bitch lied about the 'phone? Why hadn't he checked? Idiot!

'Jenny, where is your 'phone really?'

'Er, I told you, it's at home.'

Her hesitation and doubt make the lie transparent; he was right to doubt her.

'No Jenny; you said you *thought* you must have dropped it at home. Take the thing out of your pocket now. Remember who is holding the baby.'

Shit! She has no choice.

She reaches into the pocket and removes the 'phone, hitting the call disconnect button with her thumb as she passes it to him.

Colin looks at the last number dialled function and sees the three 9s and is instantly incandescent with rage.

'You fucking shit-bitch. You nasty lying turd-cunt. I warned you, and you let me down again, just like last time.'

He switches the instrument off and wonders if she'd succeeded in any calls.

He can't think when she would have been able to call.

'Did you manage to talk to the pigs? Did you tell them anything? Oh you conniving deceitful fucking bitch of a copper's fucking wife. Now your fucking precious baby dies, simple – you caused it through your tricks and slyness. I shall kill her and send the video to your fucking cunt husband.'

He clenches and unclenches his fist and violently punches the back of the seat in front of him.

The baby cries louder.

'Fuck, fuck, fuck.'

Jenny is sobbing uncontrollably.

Colin sees the turning for the old farm on the left but tells her to drive straight past.

'Change of plan now, we will go to my secret place where your stupid husband won't have a snowball's chance in hell of finding us and I will give you something to think about. That was the last chance I will *ever* give you to trick me.'

There's no response from Jenny's 'phone and Samantha decides she'll hit the sack for an early night. No sooner has she laid her head on the pillow than her work mobile rings.

'DS Milsom.'

'Sarge; it's DC Carol Saunders.'

Samantha knows instantly that this can only be bad news in some guise.

'What's up Carol?'

'Erm, probably need you in Sarge; looks like Colin Furness has grabbed DI Dyson's wife and baby from their house.'

'*What?* Oh god no, oh shit, not again. I'm on my way. Does Moody know?'

'Yes Sarge, she's coordinating. See you in a minute.'

Samantha grabs the same clothes she wore earlier, no time to piss around; then on second thoughts she knows this is going to be a long haul and she may as well start it in clean shape. She grabs clean underwear and jeans and throws a T shirt and pullover on top and is out of the door in less than two minutes.

In spite of her speed she's the last of the available team to walk into the ops room. DCI Moody is briefing the others.

'Ah, DS Milsom, I'll recap key points for your benefit.'

'Sorry Ma'am, got here as quick as I could.'

'Furness has Jenny and the baby at an unknown location. BT operator raised a *silent solution log* on the emergency lines and this was handled by the national desk. First call was terminated – thought to be an error – then same number called again and we were able to ascertain a hostage situation was in progress. Number trace gave us Jenny's mobile. Tracking was only partially successful – somewhere on our patch. Conversation specifically mentioned '*Colin*', '*Jenny*' and '*farm*'. I think it's safe to assume it's our Mr Furness and there's a uniform team already at the entrance to his farm location. I've given clear instructions that they are not to enter unless I authorise it. They've reported back a no-show as far as they can tell from their location, but he could be in there already, although I doubt he'd risk such an obvious move.'

'Thank you Ma'am. Where is DI Dyson?'

'He's heading back down from Manchester with Sergeant Harrison as we speak. ETA around 21:00.'

Samantha knows the kind of thoughts that would be going through Neil's head; the same as she had been working towards in her bath. *Why the hell hadn't they foreseen this and put a bloody guard on the house? Why had they missed the bloody obvious when they'd compiled their 'at risk' list?*
'OK, so what do we know about his movements and intentions Ma'am?'
'I don't know much at all Sergeant, but I need to make my boss aware of the few facts we do have. Take over here and brief me shortly.'

Samantha takes the lead.
'Carol, I'm going to allocate a few tasks; while we are doing those can you get all the little recent developments up onto the board please and start to plan out a mind-map? Include a copy of the telephone transcript please as soon as it's released.'
'On it Sarge.'
'Steph, me and you will get over to the farm and see if anything has turned up there; we might spot something the others have missed. Carol will remain here as coordinator, Brian get to the Dyson house and see if Jenny left any indications there. Remember how good at clues she can be. I'm guessing they left in a hurry so it'll be unlocked; if not use persuasion on a door or window. Let's all share *anything* potentially significant as soon as it crops up. Remember what's at stake her guys; Neil's wife is one of our own as far as this op is concerned; no risks to her or the baby that can be avoided. I'll just chase up the firearms guys and get a squad to meet us at the farm then Steph and me are on our way. Speed, professionalism and judgement are the buzzwords here. Good luck. Oh; and silent approach wherever we are going unless I say otherwise – we might need to try to flush him out, but that's a last resort.'

There's no time for his usual precautions and Colin instructs Jenny to drive straight up the approach lane and park under the car port next to the house. They'll almost certainly be scrambling the helicopters soon and he doesn't want her car to be spotted from the air.
If only that baby would shut the fuck up.

He opens the window and throws a bunch of keys to the ground then draws the pistol in his right hand and leaps out of the car with Samantha on his left arm. The keys are kicked towards Jenny.
'OK, silver and brass keys will open the front door; the security code is 150000 on the keypad on the right. Any stupidity and the baby gets a face full of 9mm dumdums and then you get it in the kneecaps. Move slowly and carefully all the time. Go!'

Jenny gathers the keys from the ground and shakily unlocks the front door. She pushes it slowly to show she is complying and then enters the digits he gave her into the keypad. She could have guessed the number.

She knows that this place won't be on the police radar and once inside she is at his mercy and probably beyond help; he won't make the same mistakes as the last time he had kidnapped her, when he'd allowed her the opportunity to cave his head in with a heavy frying pan. She must play for time before he gets her into a secure place, probably tied up and helpless.

'Colin I need to feed Samantha, she'll be quiet then.'
'Samantha? You named your sprog after the police bitch?'
'We liked the name so we chose it, but yes, Samantha Milsom was an inspiration to me.'
'Yeah, and instrumental in my downfall. You can feed her through there in the lounge, but make no mistake Jenny, I fucked up last time with you and that will not happen again, I will take zero chances; I'd rather immediately put you to death than take any risk at all, are we clear?'
'Crystal. Can I ask why you kidnapped me again?'

'I felt like making your husband afraid; he has been part of the system that's stopping me from seeing my mother and I wanted to know he was squirming, scared of me, worried what I might be doing to his precious little wifey and child. It's a justice thing I expect, I don't know, nor do I give any fucks.'

'You think I can persuade him to hold off the trackers? Leave you alone?'

'Of course not. Stop talking and feed the baby.'

He holds the girl out one-handed towards Jenny, his other hand pointing the gun at Jenny's gut.

Jenny opens her bathrobe and takes the girl, she pulls the loose front of her nightie down on the left side to expose a breast and the silence is immediate as little Samantha suckles straight onto the offered nipple.

Colin stares.

'Do you bloody mind? Please give us a little privacy.'

He tears his eyes away; regardless of what Jenny thinks he is seeing, he is not in the slightest aroused nor is he offended by the sight of a young female breast in any context, but like this? He finds the act of the most intimate motherhood and child bonding mesmerising.

'Wow, that's amazing; quite beautiful.'

Jenny worries about these remarks; *is the freak getting turned on by this or has he really never seen anything like it?*

'It's just normal breastfeeding Colin; you've seen it all before, right?'

'Actually no. I mean, I know what happens of course, but, well, it's so natural, so perfect. I will give you some space, but I am not relaxing my guard.'

He moves to the window at the other side of the room and tries to look out into the darkness but sees only his tired reflection. He switches his gaze in the glass from his own face to her outline as she tends to the little one. The baby is making tiny sucking sounds as any mammal would.

'Imagine if I removed your child from you. How would you feel?'

'I would kill you.'

'That must be how the poor cattle and sheep and goats and all the other mammals feel all over the world every minute of every day. Humans are so cruel.'

Jenny is happy for the dialogue. She knows from her past experiences with him that he likes to talk and explore his thoughts and if she can drag that out and also prolong the breast-feeding ritual maybe there is a slim chance that the police would be able to work out somehow where he had taken her. Something is sticking into her backside and she realises it's the car keys. Good, never know when they might come in handy.

She suddenly remembers the car's tracking device that Neil had insisted upon – *oh thank god, if only he remembers!*

'What are your plans then Colin? Will we stay here or move on to somewhere safer?'

'Here is safe. The police have no idea we are here and they are unlikely to come poking around. I have a state of the art security system and will know well in advance if anyone comes calling. Soon as you are done with your sprog I want to show you around.'

128

The firearms team are not yet in situ and the farm is in darkness when Samantha and Steph arrive and check in with the uniformed team at the entrance. They confirm that nobody has entered since they arrived, nevertheless Samantha and Steph take a cautious approach to each of the buildings in turn, creeping through the trees from the northern angle until they reach a dense hedgerow where they await arrival of the gun crew.

Samantha's voice is a whisper.
'OK Steph, wait here; I'm going to take a closer look. The head of the gun squad is Sergeant Harry Bowler; tell him to hang fire until I return. If I'm not back inside ten minutes I've probably been compromised.'

She heads off along the line of the hedge in a monkey run stance. At the end of the hedgerow is a field gate tied open with orange bale twine. She slips through and approaches the first of several outhouses, still at a crouch. This pose is a strain on the thighs and lower back and she's grateful for all the pilates, yoga and gym work she's put in over the years.

She drops even lower as she nears an almost glassless window and stealthily stands erect next to the rotting frame, peering around the wood and broken glass into the void beyond.
There's nothing to see so she risks a short burst from her shielded flashlight. The dark space beyond houses an old plough, a large plastic chemical drum and some derelict racking but is devoid of any form of life. The other outhouses too prove to be empty and once she's covered them all she makes her way quickly, still in a crouch, to where Steph awaits her return.

The firearms team have arrived and Steph is deep in a whispered conversation with the commander.

Samantha introduces herself and updates the squad on the status so far. They agree a tactical plan to methodically search the main farmhouse building and then the lower cluster further down the hill.

That was where Furness had imprisoned his victims last time round and if he was in fact here, that was probably the most likely location for his current hostage situation to unfold.

Back at police HQ Carol has the transcripts from the 999 call and has updated the action board with all relevant data. She's now waiting for any ongoing communications from the dispersed team, whilst liaising with DI Dyson and Sicknote on current status on the ground.

DCI Moody informs her that the force chopper has been engaged and is ready to lift off whenever they have a credible sighting report.

Samantha's telephone is on vibrate only when Neil Dyson calls. Given her possible proximity to the potential murderer she can't risk a conversation that would have to be audible enough for the detective in the car heading south at break-neck speed on the M6 to hear. She terminates the call then immediately texts Dyson to explain her situation.

Dyson hands the telephone to Sicknote to respond.

'Tell her to look after my babies until I am there.'

Dave 'Sicknote' Harrison duly sends the dictated message, which Samantha receives and reads with a sardonic smile.

The air is damp and still, with that suspicion of mould that inhabits such places, and there's another odour, one that she should recognise, yet can't put her finger on.

The dingy cellar is one cavernous room running almost the entire length of the hulking, isolated farmhouse, sandwiched at either end by two smaller chambers and has been subdivided with temporary, bare plaster-board walls into several discrete areas.

With the now sleeping baby resting in her arms she slowly walks the length of the stud-work passageway linking these internal compartments and sees within each dingy area a similar, yet uniquely different set-up. Each contains a wireless webcam on a tripod, a simple audio system and a restraint mechanism of one kind or another. The latter provides the point of difference; each restraining method is subtly dissimilar to its neighbours.
All but one are occupied.

Jenny looks around aghast. This is freakishly familiar; slightly more humane than the hideous little cages where she and the others had been imprisoned by the freak, and yet at the same time somehow more macabre. The bleak enclosures seem to have been individualised; made personal.

Her voice when she finally speaks quavers:
'Whatever are you doing here Colin?'
In the gloom he twitches, unseen, then coughs lightly and clears his throat.
'Ah! My latest project; my coup de Grace! The final experiment – for the time being, at least. Come here.'
He leads her to one of the small cellar rooms on the end of the main chamber.
The contrast is immediate; it's brighter here, comfortable almost, with lights and colourful cushions. Sophisticated modern computer equipment sits on the solid old pine table with several wide, flat-screens mounted on the walls.
'Behold, the polling booth of the future!'

The hand holding the pistol does a 180° sweep of the walls before them.

'It's an online system where the public gets to vote. By the click of a button in the comfort of their own home the nation shall decide who is to live and who to die....'

He nudges a computer mouse and one of the monitor screens wakens to display an active webpage and an open dialogue box posing the vague question:

Are you sure?

'What do you think Jenny? *Am I sure*? Of course!'

He taps a key and the message changes.

Formatting video files; please wait.

After a few moments the huge flat screen divides into six boxes, the first five showing compartments similar to the one she'd just seen in the main cellar, the sixth, at the bottom right of the screen is blank. Colin clicks on the first box in the top left which shows a sturdy steel-framed chair. It has no cushions but clearly visible eyebolts. She assumes these are for accepting the spring-hooks and carabinas which hang adjacent. Behind the chair is an amateurish metal fabrication supporting some kind of crude device which in turn is hooked up to some cables and control boxes.

'Whatever is that above the chair?'

'Ah! My cleverly adapted transverse guillotine. Relies upon compressed air – see the little canister behind?'

Jenny spots the black cylinder.

'It's a bodge up really and is a little prone to failure in my tests, it's been tough getting the computer to trigger the firing mechanism but who really cares apart from the murderous turd who will suffer *–if* that particular occupant wins the most votes – and with the way public opinion is swinging he might do just that!'

Her jaw drops, causing her mouth to gape open.

The chair is empty.

'Who is it for?'

'I have an Arab gentleman; he's not so well at the moment, and convalescing in another room, but I'm afraid his treatment is intermittent – I am so busy, but if and when he gets well enough he will be chained to the eyebolts and left to sweat and pray to his imaginary god.'

'Who is he?'

'Tarik El Hamali is his name; he's a Muslim cleric, a carnivorous, Halal-promoting lunatic.'

The second segment in the centre of the top row displays a medical scene; the same design chair, also lacking any form of comfort or cushion, but to the side is an intravenous drip set-up and a stainless steel kidney dish containing some surgical instruments. On the floor beneath the chair is a plastic bottle resembling cheap domestic bleach.

The chair holds a portly middle-aged balding man, sporting a black jacket and dog-collar.

Jenny points to the screen.

'And the second guy?'

'James Timpleman; Christian. Church of England, I guess that's Protestant, although I'm no expert in these things. I suppose the word comes from *protesters*? I wonder what they had to protest about. We can read more about them individually in a moment.'

'How long has he been strapped there?'

'Oh, not so long; I do feed them…oh no, I forget, ah, who gives a fuck!'

He moves the mouse pointer to the third area in the top right corner which also has an identical chair, without any form of softness. This chair though is set inside a smaller compartment, roughly the size of a passport photo booth. On the floor outside the booth are two industrial carbon monoxide canisters.

Strapped into the chair is a small woman of indeterminable age, but not as old as the previous guy.

Jenny turns to Colin and raises her eyebrows in question.

'Jewess is, I believe, the term. More about her in a moment.'

He clicks on the fourth screen, bottom left.

Compartment four houses the by-now obligatory chair and yet another steel fabrication looking like an over-sized child's Meccano set and consisting of some thick black rubber hoses, a hopper, chute and pump.

In the chair, immobile and apoplectic is a large rubicund gentleman. Colin doesn't wait for the question.

'George Grantham-Smyth; pretentious and arrogant shit head! Hereditary in-bred, hunting land owner and Tory politician. I'll be ramming that fat hose down his gullet later, with luck!'

The fifth area, bottom row centre looks like an animal pen, complete with an earthen substrate strewn with deep, rich straw. Mounted on a rack on the wall is a small pink plastic water pistol. Below that a row of large illuminated red buttons, each roughly the diameter of a tennis ball.

Curled up and snoring next to a water trough is a small Gloucester Old Spot pig.

'*Gwendolyn* – pet pig and rescued dinner.'

He minimises the screen and opens another showing a panel of buttons followed by text:

Current status:

Muslim	Christian	Jew	Politician	Piggy
0	0	0	0	0

Click on the button of your choice

The people's choice!

You get to vote – only once please; don't be greedy! – on who deserves to die for the things they have done or neglected to do! As with the current ridiculous UK electoral system, it's a 'first-past-the-post' affair; whoever wins the most online votes gets done, the others live to see another day. Second place counts for nothing, sadly.

Be sure to share with all your friends so that we get the most representative selection possible.

Here are your options; hover the cursor over the highlighted name to see brief summaries of each individual's personal details:

Colin moves the arrow over the first name and a text box opens.

Tarik El Hamali: *Muslim cleric and Imam. Poor old Tarik hasn't been so well since he volunteered, but I'm sure you won't let that put you off, after all, he is single handedly responsible for the no-stun deaths of all the animals he's eaten in his lifetime – and that equates to thousands of poor creatures (including fishies) which were slaughtered in the name of his pretend god with absolutely no form of anaesthetic; his religion **requires** that level of barbarity. On that basis alone he ought to (perhaps) be your first choice, but don't forget all the other abuses (mostly human atrocities) that his peaceful ethics demand. Click this guy's button and help send the Halal blade through his worthless, violence-inciting neck! (Nb. Tarik will appear in this chair just as soon as he is well enough to walk here from his current location – an isolation room where he is babbling to some imaginary being in the sky).*

He closes the text box with a grunt and moves the cursor above the next name; another text box opens.

James Timpleman: *Christian Anti gay and anti women priest carnivore. 42000 sects within the Christian fold, all claiming slightly different versions of 'the truth'. Christians have probably been responsible for more murders throughout history than most other belief systems, although they sit in their churches and all you will hear is love and peace. Don't pull the trigger on this believer based on that hypocrisy alone…there are <u>plenty</u> of other dubious claims which you might consider first. The Catholic version of this religion is causing thousands of deaths daily simply by its astonishing insistence that contraception is wrong. Ask any HIV patient for their views on that before you decide, then consider the abortion stance – how suitable is it for young victims of rape in Catholic dominated countries to be forced to carry the rapists spawn to full term, and then daily care for it, for a lifetime? If you so choose, press the Christian button and watch the lethal injection process send him to meet his alleged maker. The chemical we shall use is common* *household bleach and I have absolutely no idea how, or even **if** it will kill him, but certainly it will cleanse his rotten soul from the inside.*

He opens the third box.

Judith Silbermann: *Jewess. Famously persecuted throughout recent history, the Jews have done their fair share of bad shit. Like Islamism, the Jewish religion is based on hatred and evil with the ideology that Judaism shall be the only faith and the only nation:* **Deuteronomy 20:16** *"Thou shalt save alive nothing that breatheth".* **Joshua 6:24** *"Then they burned the whole city and everything in it, but they put the silver and gold and the articles of bronze and iron into the treasury of the Lord's house"*
Countless abhorrent atrocities have been committed in the name of Judaism and these people too require that animals suffer through their sickening slaughter methods. Now you can become part of this woman's final solution. If you want to watch her choke in her own private gas chamber, hit her button.

The fourth text box is activated.

George Grantham-Smyth: *Tory, landowner and elitist parasite. This man is a staunch Conservative supporter; indeed, he's a Member of Parliament for these emotional retards. He is one of the bunch who wrecked our health service, stole from the poor to feed his rich chums and is a vehement supporter of hunting – in ALL its disgusting guises. His pals own land which has been passed down through generations of inbred, over-indulgent freaks, and because they enjoy the 'sport' of tearing young and pregnant foxes apart with their killer hounds he will support hunting until his dying breath. This guy also happens to gluttonously gorge on a gourmet Foie Gras gala, so he's a heart attack waiting to happen. YOU have the opportunity to accelerate that event by a considerable margin. Hit the politician button and watch him explode in a faux Foie-Gras fulmination!*

The final, fifth box opens and Jenny reads:

Gwendolyn; Gloucester Old Spot Pig: *This rescued four year old animal is chubby, dirty, lives in muck and snorts. She's also highly tactile, intelligent, social and very vulnerable to pain and discomfort. Her species is well used to human abuse, although individual animals only get to experience the ultimate pain and torture at human hands once of course, so the species never becomes immune to hardship. Gwendolyn was rescued from a tiny breeding crate in which she was imprisoned, so small that she was unable to turn around and her constantly pregnant tummy was pushing through the metal bars at the side.*
You can help decide the pig's fate....will she live or die by shotgun blast? Choose the pig button to see the sow taken down by the weapon....maybe ☺

Jenny clears her throat and her voice trembles.
'The gun looks more like a water pistol?'
'Yes, exactly Jenny; whatever the outcome I am never going to kill the pig – although the voting public won't perhaps know that! She is the sole innocent amongst monsters. Which would you choose?'

She shakes her head and steps back, clutching the sleeping baby tighter to her breast.
'Come on, you can have the honour of casting the first vote!'
'No way! I am not going to be part of your sick games.'
'I have a spare screen …choose a button or I shall add you and little Samantha into the mix – who knows, I might even vote for you myself!'
His tone is still light-hearted, somehow making his words seem more threatening and Jenny senses the seriousness behind the bluff talk. She stammers.
'I…I can't possibly select someone, some innocent person to die. It's obscene of you to try to make me.'
His voice becomes instantly quieter and sinister and his left leg begins to twitch.
'Press a fucking button or you'll regret it you uptight fucking copper's bitch.'
The baby wakens from her slumber and begins to cry again.

Jenny realises she's in a hopeless situation and moves back towards the computer keyboard. She views the options again. Somehow she must continue to play for time and she needs to stretch this out. Deciding she must play the game she forces a confident air.

'They all look like horrible people, I would find it hard to choose one from the bunch; which would you choose?'

'I have no favourites Jenny, with the exception of Gwendolyn they are all sick bastards who have followed the cultural and immoral doctrines of their ancestors, rather than thinking for themselves and doing the humane thing. They should have all renounced faiths and lifestyles and worked to protect the millions of souls that they owe a duty to. I suppose the least bad of the bunch is the Christian guy; at least he doesn't openly advocate animal cruelty like the other bastards do. I guess the religious turds have followed a dogma that they see as the righteous path, even though it's clearly mass-manipulation by bullshit. Criminals when you look at them in the cold light of reason and fact, but partially excused as victims of a sick system of methodical brainwashing. I think I would select the one who does it all by choice; who through his sick bloodlust tortures helpless, defenceless and terrified animals of all kinds with his horses, hounds and horns. Yes, I would choose the obese and gluttonous Tory twat *George*.'

Jenny leans forward, still playing for time.

'What about the missing Muslim?'

'Just fucking choose.'

Jenny holds the now wailing baby higher.

'But can I feed Samantha first, I can think whilst she suckles.'

'I am no fool, Jenny. You are deliberately delaying the choice in the crazy hope that your husband will find us like the cavalry in old Western films, but it won't work, he will not find us, so this is your last chance before I fill the final chair.'

She tentatively reaches out for the mouse and slides the cursor over the first box, the one with the Muslim cleric's name, clicking once and seeing the zero change to the numeral *1* and the first vote is cast.

Current status:

Muslim	Christian	Jew	Politician	Piggy
1	0	0	0	0

Click on the button of your choice

'Stupid to vote in absentia – I might not even get the sick Arab turd back to health at this rate, but I need to get him on camera now because, dear Jenny, *you* have just kick-started the voting; the system is now live. It's linked to the site where I have been uploading my various delicious little video clips and judging by the number of people viewing those – 'hits' I believe they are called – there will soon be a voting frenzy. Let's get you safely shut away for a while and then you can feed your noisy little sprog again – how much does she guzzle in a day I wonder!'.

'That's a horrid word Colin, please call her by her name or use something more suitable.'

'Don't get so uptight, she's only another human animal being prepared to do the usual damage to our planet and its inhabitants.'

'She'll be brought up to make ethical decisions and I'll do my best to guide her on those until she's old enough to decide for herself. Why don't you just let us go now?'

'Tut tut Jenny; you're both here for the long haul. Remember I have a score to settle with you and hubby and I intend to settle it pretty soon. Guess what I've just decided?'

Jenny doesn't like the way this conversation is heading.

'No idea; what have you just decided?'

'The system is fully automatic, but I can set it to manual and then once voting closes in 24 hours time you are going to have the honour of wiping the chosen one from the face of the earth. What an accolade, wouldn't you agree?'

'You have to be joking; there's no way I am going to be part of your sickness and an accessory to murder; no way at all. You can kill me first.'

'Fair enough, that would be no big deal, but what to do with your raucous kid? Or maybe I can persuade you to comply? I can be quite cajoling; I could use the sprog as bait. I'm sure that faced with the dilemma of an abuser or your own flesh and blood you'll do the decent thing. Makes no difference to me which of you dies first; think about it. Meanwhile you can settle down in this end room. Still stinks a little from its previous grotty incumbent. He succumbed to a nasty virus; don't be a silly little girl and make me administer the same end to you and baby face here; want to watch his demise on video? It's really entertaining.'

'Just give us a place to rest and let me feed her in peace.'

The door opens and Jenny sees the stark metal interior.

'Not even a chair? You really do have little feeling for people.'

'Tough, take it or leave it but either way shut up and get settled down. I'll drop in some water in a short while, which is a luxury in this room, believe me. I will also bring you some towels for the child; beggars can't be choosers. Oh, I should warn you that the little device up on the wall there is a camera and I'll be able to watch your every move, so don't try any of your infamous little tricks.'

Something is niggling at the confused mess of Neil Dyson's racing brain…something important.

Hammering along the motorway at break-neck speeds, flashing the mostly law-abiding motorists who happened to dawdle at 80 mph in the fast lane he was thinking about Jenny and their holiday….

…Bingo!

'Shit – Sicknote, call the boss *now* and tell her about the tracking device on Jenny's car – fucking idiot, I completely forgot about it in all the panic. It'll pinpoint her location to within a few feet. It sends signals at 90 second intervals to my laptop so we need to stop someplace with internet access and get hooked up.'

Dave 'Sicknote' Harrison gets Moody's voicemail and hangs up, not wanting to waste time. He calls Samantha Milsom who immediately relays the message to Carol back at HQ. Carol manages to get through to DCI Moody and passes on the significant news. The local force helicopter is scrambled to loiter over the South Downs area, which is the zone considered most likely to be the murderer's location, should the farmhouse team draw a blank.

The next motorway services is indicated in three miles and Neil rams his foot even harder to the floor, weaving in and out of the heavy traffic and within two minutes they are haring up the slip road and skidding to a halt in the only vacant parking bay reserved for disabled travellers next to the main building.

Two minutes later they are seated in the Manager's office. The manager is a little disgruntled at having been ushered out with scant explanation, lots of badge waving and physical jostling.

'OK, I have a connection here; these motorway service stations might be rip-off joints but they all have plenty of internet services to choose from.'

'Can you trace her car then Guv?'

'Just loading up the software then the data refresh should automatically take care of the rest. It'll take about three minutes to triangulate and pinpoint her location. Let's give DCI Moody a ring and while we're waiting I'll check for any more videos on our friend's usual links, just in case he's using a camera to prove he has her. I wanna see that she's OK.'

Dyson clicks on the bookmarked webpage and is confronted by the selection box counting the votes:
'What the hell….'
'Some kind of sick online survey Guv; wait – hover the cursor over the names a sec.'
Dyson does as is suggested and reads the blurb on each candidate.
'The sick bastard wants the public to choose who lives and who dies; is there no limit to his fucking depravity?'
'Can't believe the pig has no votes Sir – must be all his freaky animal rights pals doing the voting.'
As they watch, the numbers in the politician's box change.

Current status:

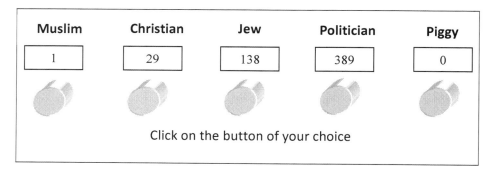

Muslim	Christian	Jew	Politician	Piggy
1	29	138	389	0

Click on the button of your choice

The laptop bleeps and shows a new dialogue box.
Location detected at position shown on map. For coordinates check the 'details' box and press enter.

The location is showing somewhere just south east of Petersfield on the Hampshire/Sussex border. Dyson telephones Carol at the control centre.
'Carol we know where Jenny is; or rather, we know where her car is. Sending you the coordinates now, scramble the chopper and get them in situ. On second thoughts, *don't*. The noise will alert Furness. Get on to the DCI and update her, tell her my advice is a silent approach, the last quarter mile should be on foot but she absolutely *must* wait for the firearms guys to be in situ before engaging; we don't want a bloody hostage situation, we need a rescue.'
'Chopper's already airborne Sir.'

'OK, thanks, use another line to make any calls – I'm just going to text Jenny to let her know she's on our radar then I'll call you back; let's keep this one live between us.'

He cuts the call before Carol can warn him that Colin Furness may have Jenny's 'phone…

133

The metal door is quickly unlocked and flung open and the tall freak strides into the room toting the small pistol.
'I just turned your mobile on and it says there is a new message sent 2 minutes ago but the screen is locked. Unlock it now.'

Jenny does so with trembling hands; will this be some good news? She tries to open the message but Furness grabs the 'phone from her fingers.

He opens the message:
Have no fear, we are tracking your car via the device we fitted and will soon know exactly where you are and will be coming to the rescue. Stay brave sweetheart x
He flies into an insane rage, spittle forms in the corners of his mouth and he turns bright red.
'You fucking bitch cunt, you fucking knew about this tracking device all along and tried to trick me you copper's slut. I am going to kill you as soon as I have driven your car off a fucking cliff – in fact you will be in it. But wait, no that's way too easy….oooh, I have a better plan.'

Pistol still in hand, Colin locks her in and rushes to the far end room where the Muslim is restrained, still muttering a constant stream of prayers and moaning softly to himself.

'What's Arabic for goodbye, services no longer required?'
Without awaiting a response he dispatches El Hamali with a bullet to the temple, adding one through the chest as a security measure.
In her cell, Jenny jumps at the gunshots and hugs Samantha even closer to her breast, as much to comfort herself and try to calm her trembling as for the baby's sake.

Seconds later the lock turns and the door bursts inwards again.
'Get up, leave the baby there.'
'I can't leave my child here alone; where are you taking me now?'
'You'll see; put her down or...'

The shaking muzzle is inches from Samantha's head, aimed between the baby's eyes. Terrified that he'll shoot her accidentally, Jenny swiftly lays the child on the cold, hard floor.

Colin grabs her by the hair and tugs her forcefully out of the small cell along the partitioned cellar walkway until they reach the first of the chip-board doors he'd added to the structure.

'In you get bitch and sit down.'

Jenny's legs give way beneath her.

'No Colin, please, I can't do this, not again please, my baby ....'

His high-pitched scream is as shocking as it is loud.

'SIT THE FUCK DOWN YOU SHITBITCH!'

She does as she's told, praying silently that Neil has the coordinates mapped for the car's location.

Colin pats her down, finds and removes the car keys from her rear pocket and quickly straps her in, adjusting the various restraining devices to ensure she cannot escape.

'OK, first I am going to drive the car a couple of miles away so that useless husband of yours is thrown off the scent, then I am coming back to make some minor adjustments here so that the guillotine will accurately remove your bonce if you get the most votes; ironic that by clicking the Muslim box you've already voted for yourself!'

'Colin please, Samantha's all alone and cold.'

'I might chuck her in here with you before I go – that way she might get to watch mummy decapitated.'

He claps his hands and does a little prancing wiggle. The smile is so wide that he resembles a hammer-head shark.

'No, the little darling can stay where she is. See you soon *sweetheart;* be good whilst I'm gone.'

Colin has no Idea how long it will take the police to calculate the car's location, but he's used up five critical minutes already and shooting the Muslim had wasted more precious seconds. Hopefully as soon as he gets the vehicle moving the cops will disregard the signal that's been probably pinpointing his lair. The car starts first time and he's soon roaring down the long driveway like a rally driver and out onto the minor road heading for Petersfield. He wants to make their job as tough as possible so after about a mile he veers off up a little-used track into a copse known locally as the Devil's

Spinney. Here he dumps the car, slings the keys deep into the brambles and nettles and starts the three mile run back to the safe house as fast as he can sustain.

'OK, target was stationary for a while but is now moving I have a rough location; it's either on the A3 moving north or on the parallel B2070 – as before, heading north.'

'Sir, are you telling me we can't say which road it's on?'

'Will have that as soon as we get the third triangulation; it's a notorious black-spot for mobile networks; the tracker device doesn't work from satellites, it's based on telecoms masts and the hills around that area play havoc with signals. Soon as he gets into a flatter zone we'll have him. Where's the helicopter now? He's clearly running scared and the chopper might just drive him to ditch the car; on foot they'll get him on heat sensors.'

'Sir we're deploying stingers on both roads; that way we'll stop him and have firearms at the ready at exactly those locations. It's not foolproof but it's as good as we've got.'

'Yeah, well use the chopper too; I want that bird in location as soon as he's had a chance to make a dash for it on foot. With luck he'll abandon the car and leave the hostages in situ.'

'Will do Sir. Er, DCI Moody is now taking over the central command role, I'll hand you over Sir.'

'OK, thanks Carol, good work.'

'DI Dyson it's DCI Moody; I heard your instructions and agree; that's what we'll do, but it's not without risk, I'm sure you appreciate that.'

'Of course Ma'am – wait, I think he's gone off road.'

On the long fast run back to safety he hears the chopper about mile
or so away, not far from where he ditched the car. Approaching the
woods surrounding the safe house from the north side he is on hyper
alert for any signs of an unwanted presence. The dark clothing he's
wearing will make it difficult for anyone watching to spot him and
they'll probably be lit up like Christmas trees in their fancy garb. He
sees no indications that they've even been here and checks the first
of his alarm points.

Nothing showing on the tread-plates or light beam detectors; he
moves closer to the house which stands like a sentinel in the
deepening gloom. He checks the final security device close to the
rear of the property and finds that also clear; slowing his breathing
after the exertion he creeps towards the back door and risks a peep
through the adjacent window into the dark room beyond. There's
nothing to indicate that anyone's been here and so, pistol at the
ready, he makes his way infinitely slowly along the back wall to the
side. He's a little frustrated that it takes so long, but he needs to be
absolutely sure he's not walking into a trap.

'DI Dyson we have a probable visual fix from the chopper's heat detection, the car's stationary off-road in a copse about a mile off the main road.'

'OK Ma'am, are the shooters on the target?'

'Not yet, chopper is carrying firearms team to within half a mile of location, they will move to contact on foot.'

'Very good Ma'am, I wanted to be there when it kicks off but I am still 45 minutes away. Suggest I leave Sgt Harrison here on the laptop link and make my way to you guys.'

'Guess who's back Jennifer darling. Time to draw an early close to voting. We'll have to curtail it a little, let's say three hours for voting plus thirty minutes for the execution, we shall broadcast that event live along with a message about the potential consequences of abusing animals.'

Jenny is trembling almost uncontrollably now and is distraught at the baby's ceaseless crying.

'How can you murder someone in cold blood so easily? The media were right; you really are a freaky monster. Give me back my baby *please*'

'*Monster*? *I* am a monster? The baby is fine. Well fed and warm, unlike so many baby animals wrenched from their mummies in their millions for the sake of the taste buds of the true human monsters. Oh but Jenny; I almost forgot to tell you, I shall not be murdering anyone, for a change. Indeed, I doubt I'll even be here when voting closes. No, that privilege shall now fall as originally planned to our dear sweet Gwendolyn. She has been trained – pigs are *very* intelligent and *very* fast learners. In her stall is a row of big shiny red buttons. She has been trained to press the one that changes to green with her snout. There's a potential problem though; human eyes have three 'cones', allowing us to blend the primary colours and clearly distinguish a full range. Pigs only have *two* cones, so their colour perception is limited. Bright lights can confound the issue, so we have to keep the lights dim in her area or she might go and nudge the wrong button, that would be a sad injustice, don't you think?'

'You trained the pig to kill?'

'No, no. I trained Gwendolyn to press a button. You see, I've sanitised the process for her, much like the agricultural industry distances us from the horrors of what they do. Gwendolyn will be the executioner in this little contest. Once I stick the chunky rubber hose down the fat Tory fucker's throat the system will be switched to fully automatic from that point onwards. With your exception all my guests have been sitting for the past two days in a fully primed execution chamber. Probably explains the stench – remind you of anything? Tiny cages on a farm perhaps? Ah, good times! I digress; once Gwendolyn hits the big green button the relevant abuser gets done. Simple and fun for the online audience. Who knows, your

husband and his band of plods might even be watching and voting…wonder if they'll watch their precious Jenny dispatched?'
'You can't be serious? What about the rest of us – I mean those who survive? How will we, or they, get out?'
'Oh Jenny, who really gives a flying fuck? Whilst your hubby and his incompetent pals are blundering around the hillsides looking for an abandoned car I have to sort out some loose ends and then if it's safe I'll return and collect Gwendolyn; maybe I'll show some compassion…maybe not! That's the beauty of bloodsports; you never do quite know how they're going to end.'

It's a close run thing, the online participants have really grasped the significance of the event and are voting in their droves. Surely they all think it's a spoof….

With time ticking and voters clicking Colin changes the Muslim text box:

Jenny the copper's wife: *Apologies – our Muslim friend took a turn for the worse and has had to be replaced. However – the good news is that we have a ready-made replacement for him…introducing the lovely Jenny Dyson. Ever had a run-in with the filth? Received a caution? Been searched for no reason? House intruded upon by the big-footed morons of the police? I'd even extend the offer to anyone who's been poorly treated by anyone in authority – let's say that our dear Jennifer stands for all the wrongs in society which aren't represented by the other retards here. If you have a gripe; any complaint whatsoever about society, press Jenny's little button and watch her lose her noggin. As a mark of good faith (haha) any votes already cast for the Islamist preacher are automatically credited to Jenny – in fact, use her as a surrogate Muslim too, go on, you know you want to.*

Current status:

Copper's wife	Christian	Jew	Politician	Piggy
2987	3456	3257	4100	0

Click on the button of your choice

Strapped into the chair, Jenny can no longer see the monitors and so has no idea what is happening in Colin's crazy game, but that changes when an intercom speaker system crackles to life in her compartment.

'Hello one and all, only me! Hope you aren't too uncomfortable, and I know it's been a long wait, but trust me, it'll be worth it.'
The excited voice continues to explain what Jenny already knows, that they are all part of an online poll to elect the one that the public voters most want to eliminate from society.

'You have all done your various bits to make the lives of animals so appalling, so now one of you will pay for a lifetime of abuse. The irony is, from my standpoint, you'll spend the next three hours thinking *very* intensely about those things which you have failed to spend one moment considering in the past. There are two exceptions, stalls 1 and 5 hold two, largely innocent creatures, a pig and a pig's wife. We'll trust the voting public – that'll make you nervous I'm sure, as the voting public consists of similar morons to yourselves; clones of your teachings and bad-example-setting. I find that quite a delicious little irony too! You'll do well here Jenny; society is fucked and people have an awful lot to whinge about and many of those votes will be heading your way, plus all those who would have wanted the Muslim hate-preacher off our streets too…you should clean up quite nicely. Bye bye for now; oh! Before I go, here are the current standings.'

In Jenny's cubicle a hitherto unnoticed screen high on the wall facing her flickers to life and displays the voting data.

'Hope you can all see OK. I've just added the little time counter in the bottom right corner; that will tell you how long is left to run, the piggy will get the green light a few seconds after the counter hits zero. I'll leave the screens on now so you can enjoy the run-up to lift-off.'

Current status:

Copper's wife	Christian	Jew	Politician	Piggy
4001	4678	3871	4590	0

Click on the button of your choice   02:47:16

The HQ line rings.

'DCI Moody.'

'Ma'am, I'm heading south alone, Sgt Harrison is at the services monitoring for any onward movement. Quick thought, do we have a dog team in situ? Just thought if he does a runner from the car it would be good to be prepared.'

'Confirm dog team in transit to target, ETA twenty, that's two zero minutes. Why does your team never use the damned radio sets Neil?'

'They are next to useless Ma'am. Coverage out on the downs is sketchy at best, can hardly understand what's being said and in the situations we deal with more often than not we need stealth, last thing my team can use is bloody radio squawk giving the game away. Over and out!'

'Sorry to be the bearer of bad news, but I'm going to have to bug out for a little while to pay a very short visit to an ailing relative whilst the cops are busy elsewhere. I'll leave you all in the very capable hands, or rather, snout, of Gwendolyn. Just a word of caution, she's been through a lot in her short life and so unnecessary noise and commotion is prone to irritate her. Don't want her hitting any of the bright red buttons in her little pen do we? You see, the system is live at all times, and the tiniest mishap on her part would send the relevant one of you to heaven – or wherever your personal imaginary preference might happen to be. Let's hope she doesn't bear any grudges!'

He pauses at the door then nips back on to the microphone.

'Oh, one other thing, just in case I don't return and if or when you are found here, don't be tempted to touch the last light switch on the bank on the wall; it's for the lights in Gwendolyn's pen and the sudden change in brilliance may make her think she has to press a button…we don't want any more bloodshed than is necessary. Not that I give a single fuck really, just saying! Bye.'
He leaves via an external cellar door.

Current status:

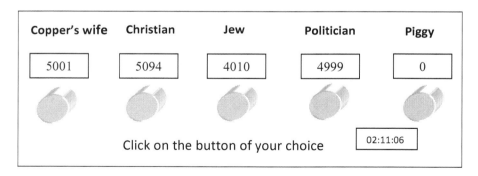

Copper's wife	Christian	Jew	Politician	Piggy
5001	5094	4010	4999	0

Click on the button of your choice   02:11:06

This time when Neil calls in he again uses his own mobile telephone, preferring it over the clumsy interference-plagued in-car radio. Carol responds.

'Hi Carol, it's DI Dyson requesting status update please.'

'Hello Sir, latest is that ground team have reached target and have confirmed no persons present at vehicle. Helicopter heat sensors indicate no sign of persons on foot, they are extending search area and dog team being deployed as we speak. DCI Moody asked me to inform you that leaving Sgt Harrison was an error as the tracking device data he is monitoring is now of no value. Are you too far to turn round?'

'Damn, yes she's right. Never mind, he's a big boy; he'll make his way home. Sorry, clearly not thinking very straight. Can you call Sicknote and give him the good news? Let me know as soon as the dogs pick up a scent please. How many teams are in situ?'

'Dog teams, er, three units I believe Sir; I'll call as soon as we have any updates for you. What's your own ETA?'

'SatNav indicates fifteen minutes tops. I'm heading for the abandoned car.'

Colin opens an old outhouse double door to reveal a nearly new metallic blue BMW 5 Series convertible. The last owner has no further need for it, he passed away in unpleasant circumstances. It's fast and anonymous transport, just what he needs right now for a trip to see his mum. He throws a pre-packed rucksack onto the back seat, fires up the big engine and roars out of the building, taking the long gravel driveway at close to 60mph. Once on the B road towards Chichester he really opens the throttle; any police who might be out and about would be too focussed on looking for either Jenny's car, or maybe Colin's old blue Land-Rover. It's a twenty minute drive from here and he hopes to get in, say a hasty goodbye to his old mother and then either get back to the safe house to clean up, or, if that's been compromised, make a clean getaway. He has no clue where that might take him, but he'll think of something, he always does. As he bursts from the minor road onto the main Chichester route he catches a flash of helicopter lights hovering over the hills in the distance.

Annoyingly, in all the confusion lately he can't remember whether his mum is even still at the hospital, or if she was moved.

Jenny is relieved that the baby is quieter now, probably exhausted herself with all that screaming, and despite her precarious situation she relaxes just a little to know that her child is sleeping. Meanwhile the numbers keep rising on the voting data logger; *don't the morons clicking the buttons realise how damned serious this is? Do they think it's some kind of game? A prank?* Selfishly she's worried that her number seems to be rising faster than any of the others, and any moment now she'll take first spot.

Current status:

Copper's wife	Christian	Jew	Politician	Piggy
6017	6029	4931	6000	0

Click on the button of your choice 01:07:15

'Sir one of the dog units has a lead. Patching you through now.'

'DI Dyson…'

'Hello Sir, Sergeant Andy Rimmer, Lead Coordinator Dog Unit Delta. One of my teams has a positive pick up and currently actively following up with armed officers in attendance.'

'Great work Sergeant Rimmer; Not sure if you know, but my wife and baby are the hostages, so I need some good news… what's your success rate?'

'Phew, that's hard on you Sir. Well the dog that picked up the trail is Misty, a 4 year old Cocker Spaniel bitch, she's the best I've ever seen Sir, and I've been in this game nearly 25 years.'

'Great – keep me posted?'

'Will do Sir.'

'I aim to be with you on the ground as soon as I can, might need you to guide me in.'

'Not sure how we'll manage that Sir, I'm not in-situ, I'm at a coordination centre near Crawley and it's a fast moving incident down there.'

'Oh, shit. OK, well I'll think of something, I'm not far away now.'

The hospital car park is busier than his last visit but he manages to find an out-of-the-way spot at the far end. He doesn't think the police will still be keeping a vigil here but needs to keep a low profile and is annoyed at the high-pitched squeak emitted when he locks the car remotely. He sprints across the car park and into the main hospital building, hoping his mother is still here. When he reaches the ward he's dismayed to see her bed occupied by a bearded old man. *Fuck, fuck, fuck…think…ask the nurse…* 'Excuse me, Mrs Furness, where has she been moved to?'

'Let me have a look on the screen for you, one second.'

The nurse's English is heavily accented; East European of some kind, that's good, she's probably not an avid follower of the UK news and the name of Colin Furness would mean nothing to her.

'Ah, here we are. She was discharged, no sorry, transferred to a care home two days ago.'

'What's the address of the place?'

'I'm sorry, I don't have that information here.'

'Great help! So what's the fucking *name* of the place then?'

'No need to use that language, sir!'

He doesn't have time for this and feels the rage rising like a beast within him. He pushes in front of her.

'Let me see the damn screen…'

'Sir, that is confidential information, you can't just…'

'Shut up and fuck off out of my way.'

The nurse is visibly shocked and momentarily stunned into immobility. This guy is clearly trouble. She walks calmly to the wall and pulls a red alarm tag.

The audible alarm is subtle but immediately fills Colin's already highly agitated mind with panic; he has to get out.

'Stupid fucking bitch.' He's off running for the exit before anyone can apprehend him or ask awkward questions.

The dog handler is struggling to keep up with the madly-wagging tail of Misty, the Cocker Spaniel. They have covered some two miles of rough, hilly terrain since she first picked up the scent and he's wondering how much longer he can stay with her. What's making it worse is having to give constant updates over the awkward radio set. Finally they break through a line of prickly hedges onto the grass verge of a minor road. Without pausing, the dog drops her head, sniffs and pulls him onwards again – straight across the road into another hedgerow. Out through the other side they are confronted by a ditch. Water is the tracker dog's worst enemy, it masks all traces of smell and a fugitive can wade left or right and then emerge at any spot they choose. It's usually a painstaking task of trial and error to rediscover the trace.

Fortunately for Misty this particular quarry wasn't too focussed on evasion or decoys and within seconds she indicates with a short bark and a tug that they need to get moving again.

Current status:

Copper's wife	Christian	Jew	Politician	Piggy
6792	6871	5000	6798	0

Click on the button of your choice 00:29:23

147

Back in the car park Colin realises he hasn't paid the parking ticket. He doesn't have any change in his pockets and his wallet is in the rucksack in the car. He throws a quick glance at his watch; the countdown will be well into the final hour now. He wants to get back to the safe house to tie up loose ends but he's afraid that the helicopter he'd spotted meant search teams were scouring the area. They'd have dogs, and in any case, the tracking device fitted to that bitch's car *must* have pinpointed the house to the police – even they couldn't be so stupid that they wouldn't see the significance of a stationary indicator for several hours. He convinces himself that the hideout will have been discovered.

In his panic he's struggling to think straight and all the usual calming strategies have deserted him. He rushes to the car, grabs the rucksack from the rear seat and runs off towards the exit without a clue about where he is going or what he will do next.

Think, think, think….thank god he'd had the foresight to pack money, cards and false documents.

'Sir, it's Sicknote.'

'Hi Dave – sorry to leave you in the lurch earlier, what's up?'

'Just a thought; the tracker was stationary for a long time before Jenny's car was dumped…might be they were holed up somewhere and maybe he went to dump the car alone…?'

'Hmmn, yeah, good thinking. Can you retrieve the coordinates of that spot?'

'Sure, there's a data log, got a pen?'

'Just read them to me, I'll stick them straight into my SatNav.'

He calls in to the ops room to tell them what he's doing, giving the location.

149

Jenny notes with some dismay that for the first time she's leading the poll. Samantha has started to cry again.

Current status:

Copper's wife	Christian	Jew	Politician	Piggy
6934	6902	5003	6931	0

Click on the button of your choice   00:18:17

150

The SatNav voice tells him that he's reached his destination, but he seems to be in the middle of nowhere. After a couple of hundred yards Dyson pulls over and changes the map scale on the screen. When he zooms in he sees an unmarked road shooting off to his right, about quarter mile behind him. It must be a driveway of some kind. He spins the motor round and guns the engine. He misses the entrance to the drive on the first pass and does a quick 3-point turn and takes the rough gravel track at a crawl. He extinguishes his lights so he won't be spotted from any hiding place up ahead and then opts for more stealth and pulls over. Turning off the engine he exits the car and makes his way quickly but quietly along the grass verge.

He feels a squishing sensation beneath his left foot and stoops to investigate. It's some kind of semi-concealed pressure pad.

Oh fuck, now the bastard knows I'm here....

151

Somewhere upstairs an alarm is sounding and Jenny's pulse races. Either the freak has returned to finish his sick game, or someone has triggered the system…the first situation makes no real difference, but the second scenario can only be good news, whatever it is. A glance at the countdown timer tells her that she's got less than fifteen minutes before that awful contraption takes off her head….

Current status:

Copper's wife	Christian	Jew	Politician	Piggy
7334	6918	5123	7000	0

Click on the button of your choice `00:12:54`

Neil Dyson resists the urge to throw caution to the wind – although he's probably been rumbled, he might have been lucky and while he can stay hidden he will.

He sees a large, dark house looming through the trees, looking like a haunted mansion in one of those old horror films and heads deeper into the woods lining the driveway to approach it from the rear, using his hand to shield the torch on his mobile 'phone to light the way.

After a couple of minutes he spots something out of place; it's some kind of electronic device attached just above waist height to the trunk of a small tree. He investigates and it seems to be some kind of relay contraption; maybe for sending signals. Clearly the whole place is security wired. Figuratively shaking his head he presses on towards the house.

As he approaches he becomes aware that an alarm is sounding somewhere inside.

That'll be the pressure plate I activated...

He switches off his little torch, crouches lower and comes up against the rear elevation.

There is a little light emanating from the upper storey but not from any of the downstairs windows on this side. That's a shame, it's always better to look from the dark into the light, but beggars can't be choosers and making himself as small as possible now he comes up beside the window of an unlit room and takes a quick peep inside, rapidly ducking away again almost before he's had chance to see anything.

Nothing obvious, but it's difficult to see anything at all in the gloom. He risks a longer look and can only make out vague furniture shapes; a lounge of some description. He crawls along to the next window and has the same result. He doesn't know where Furness will be; he could be with Jenny and the baby, or in some other room. For sure he'll know that someone has triggered his alarm system, so he'll be preparing for an attempt of some kind.

Neil stumbles on a low protruding wall in the darkness and gropes around to see what it is. Some kind of cellar access. Further exploration reveals it's a brick frame around a sunken window, similar to those he's seen for basement flats in cities.

Interesting... and is that a baby crying...?

He lowers himself infinitely carefully over the stubby wall and drops silently into a small void. The window at the bottom is barred.

Fuck! Maybe there are more... and almost certainly there'll be a ...

Straining, he heaves himself back up to ground level and creeps further along the house wall. A few feet further on he finds what he'd suspected might be there – steps leading down to a cellar door. A cursory check for alarm triggers seems to indicate it's clean and he slowly descends one step at a time until he reaches an old but solid wooden door at the bottom.

Shit or bust now...

He reaches out for the handle, tempted to offer up a prayer, but opting for a silent *please, please be unlocked, please let him have fucked up just once... give me a break....*

Jenny is sweating now and can't seem to tear her eyes away from that cruel counter. Meanwhile her wrists and ankles are red raw from the chafing of trying to somehow break these unforgiving straps and her baby is crying hysterically. This is worse than being held by the monster in those tiny cages last time he took her; this is unbearable and she fears she's about to lose her mind.

She screams hysterically: 'Please, please, please someone help me, help my poor baby....'

Current status:

Copper's wife	Christian	Jew	Politician	Piggy
7960	6923	5219	7950	0

Click on the button of your choice   00:02:51

The handle depresses slowly and, incredibly the door gives a small groan and inches inwards.

At exactly that moment Neil hears the scream from his wife.

That's all the motivation he needs and he charges through the entrance into the dingy cellar. Expecting to confront the killer at any moment he rushes along a stud-work corridor into the only light source, a room at the far end. Unconsciously he's shouting Jenny's name now.

'Where are you Jenny? It's me, I'll stop the bastard don't worry, I'm here, I'll save you, where are you Jenny?'

She hears his voice and thinks she must be hallucinating. The timer is into the final minute, and she's going to be decapitated in front of his eyes, *oh why couldn't he have come a minute sooner, he's too late now.*

'I'm in here Neil, the first room, *quick*…I only have a few seconds…*pleeeease…*'

The final plea is drawn out and desperately begging, devoid of any hope.

The counter reaches ten, nine, eight…

He's confronted by a bank of bright, modern computer equipment. No Colin Furness.

…seven, six, five…

He's heard her calling, first room, where's that, need some lights He sees the bank of light switches …

…four, three, two…

He hits all the light switches together and the whole place is bathed in bright light. As if in sync the first tennis-ball size red button inside Gwendolyn's pen turns green and the eager sow, sensing a change, trots across to see what she needs to attend to….

In the first booth, Jenny screams….

155

Working together, Neil and Jenny manage to shut down the force-feeding mechanism, but not before it's rammed several kilos of greasy, suet-like mush down the portly politician's throat.

Releasing him from his constraints his gasps and splutters are completely ignored as husband and wife cling to each other in an unyielding embrace, broken only when a small baby's yells wrench them back into action.

'I'll get her, I know where she is – shit, you need to free the others before the pig hits any more buttons…quick get them all out.'

'What buttons?'

'Too complicated, come on, we need to get the others out.'

'OK, but I don't know the set-up here, let's do it together. Where is Furness? Is Samantha in danger?'

'No, just desperate for her mummy. Furness went away somewhere – I think to find his mother, but I don't know for sure.'

'If the pig is in control – though I can't begin to imagine how – then let's just make the pig safe!'

'Of course – not thinking straight; come on.'

Jenny leads him to the last room and they encourage Gwendolyn out of the pen and away from the dangerous red buttons. Jenny is amazed to see that, as the counter had indicated, it was *her* light that had turned green – by why had Gwendolyn hit the wrong button? Ah! She must have been dazzled when Neil had hit all the light switches at once.

Unable to stay away any longer Jenny rushes to her baby, feeling a physical pain at her daughter's distress until she wraps the screaming child in her arms. Only when she lays the small trembling body against her breast do mother and child begin to calm, their sobs slowing along with their heartbeats as the adrenaline slowly dissipates.

Neil, desperate to be by their side, listens to the pair as he calls in the cavalry and then one by one releases the other confused captives. Only then can he join his family. Rushing to the small compartment he stoops to gather them into his arms, kissing first Jenny and then Samantha gently on the head. Sinking to his knees, he finally feels that he can relax, knowing that he won't have to go through the agony of losing them.

The remaining prisoners are whisked away to the local hospital where George Grantham-Smyth spends a gruelling few hours enduring stomach pumps and enemas to flush any potential toxins from his system. He eventually makes a full recovery, but nowadays when he attends sumptuous banquets at his club or the Houses of Parliament he tends to shy away from Pâté de Foie Gras.

Epilogue

Δ *As custodians of the planet it is our responsibility to deal with all species with kindness, love, and compassion. That these animals suffer through human cruelty is beyond understanding. Please help to stop this madness* Δ
Richard Gere

In a large lush field on an animal rescue sanctuary just north of Bayreuth, Germany, a beautiful young cow with a yellow plastic ear-tag bearing the digits D0227 hears Colina the Beagle bark and lays her head over the new wooden gate. She knows it's feed time and she can't wait to see her friends coming up the chalky track.
The sun shines and life is good.

She is gently nudged aside by a larger animal; she doesn't mind, her mother wants to look too.

A slightly colour-blind Gloucester Old Spot pig muscles in between them and grunts her impatience; everyone wants to see the little German lady, the old English woman and the tall bearded man with the funny eyes carrying baskets of treats; it's one of the highlights of the day.

43632014R00237

Printed in Poland
by Amazon Fulfillment
Poland Sp. z o.o., Wrocław